The Book of Ravens

Volume One

Published by Fitzsimmons Road, 2024.

This book is a work of fiction. Names, characters, places, and incidents either are products of the author's imagination or are used fictitiously. Any resemblance to actual events or locales or persons, living or dead, is entirely coincidental.

Copyright © 2024 Andrew McDonald

Hardcover Edition, License Notes
All rights reserved. No part of this book may be reproduced in any form or by any electronic or mechanical means—except in the case of brief quotations embodied in articles or reviews—without written permission from its publisher.

Introduction & Acknowledgments

Believe it or not, the Book of Ravens (not even the original title) has been nearly 30 years in the making.

Like any story, it began with an intriguing idea, that originated somewhere around 1995, but it wasn't until my Dad gifted me his aging laptop some years later that the story actually started to take shape. The laptop itself was a heavy, clunky piece of shit, capable of nothing BUT creating documents and spreadsheets, but to me- it was everything I needed.

I don't know if I ever thanked my Dad enough for that (who, as of this writing is sadly no longer with us), but one might say he was the one responsible for giving me my start.

And then? Having only written a few chapters, life happened. And for many years, I barely wrote a thing. Every now and then I would dabble with a chapter here and there, but life, or rather my excuses, kept rudely interrupting. That being said, I wasn't completely idle. Because as time went on, while nothing appeared on paper, the story itself continued to grow, if only in my mind.

Fast forward nearly 20 years later, I finally just decided to do it. I'm not sure what exactly motivated me, or where the sudden inspiration came from, but I just felt like the story was finally ready. I was ready. But instead of starting the story from the very beginning, I wrote significant parts of the ending first.

But it's not uncommon among writers I think, to start one's story from the end and then begin to work backwards. Because most authors already have an idea of what the ending is going to be. And so, the real challenge, at least from what I found, was figuring out how to get there. And personally, the "getting there" is what made me truly fall in love with writing in the first place.

Because it's not really about the ending, no matter how memorable we try to make it. Without everything that comes before it, the ending has no real meaning. So what it's really about, at least for me, is the journey. The captivating journey to finally arrive at your destination, anticipated or not.

Think about the last time you went on a vacation. That feeling when you board a plane, or even the night before packing. There's so much excitement in those moments, the anticipation, the expectations which I think we all blow out of proportion.

"This will be the greatest vacation ever!" We think. And we fantasize about everything going just perfectly from having booked the ideal room to eating a fancy dinner at the finest supposed "place to be."

But then something happens. The flight is delayed. It rains on what was supposed to be your day at the beach. You misplace your wallet. All sorts of twists and turns that you never anticipated.

Writing a story isn't so different. Because when we first start writing? We don't have everything figured out. Not even close.

We have our drafts, our ideas, possibly even crucial moments planned at certain times. But these things alone aren't enough to fill a book. The real challenge is what happens in between those moments. Coming up with that shit.

Personally, that was a large part of what made the process so exciting. Because just like someone reading this for the first time, I too had no idea what was going to happen next.

Because as time goes on, characters start to live and breathe on their own. They say things you never intended. Do things you never thought they would do. And then? Something truly magical happens: the book literally starts writing itself.

It's almost kind of eerie. And before I knew it, after 5 months of writing almost daily, I finally had a rough draft on my hands.

However, the editing process took a lot longer, spanning the course of several years until I finally felt somewhat satisfied with the finished product. Then I was fortunate enough to have the book "polished" to its final shine by my own Aunt Chris, who worked with me night and day over another 5-months.

Nearly two years later, due to life's inconvenient interruptions, I finally had the book professionally formatted for print only to discover a concerning problem: the book was incredibly long in its present state and would barely meet the necessary printing requirements.

I then made the difficult decision to split the book into two volumes. Mind you, I did not write The Book of Ravens with any intention of dividing it into two parts. It is intended to be one book and meant to be read thus.

Volume Two is not a sequel. It is simply the second half of the original intended story.

Some efforts were made of course, to end Volume One at a reasonable place, but I do feel the need to explicitly explain that it was not written to have an intended ending, much less an ending at all. It's as if someone pressed pause in the middle of a movie.

If you happen to be reading via ebook or the massive complete hardcover version? You are in luck, as these versions contain the novel in its entirety. It was important to me to preserve at least a few options for this, so as to present the novel as originally intended. With this disclaimer now out of the way, and provided you view the two volumes as one entry, all will be well! (And well worth the read!)

So here we are, nearly 30 years later. Better late than never, right?

Without further ado, please spare me just a few more minutes of your time to thank the following people. For without them, I wouldn't be here today.

First and foremost, I have to thank my wonderful parents. To my Dad who provided me with the initial tools and kept prodding me to just write the damn thing, and to my Mom, who has always been my biggest fan. From day one, you both supported my dream, and that will always mean the world to me.

Mom- There are not enough thank you's for all that you have done, for those things are too numerous to count. You never stopped believing in me and I love you both so much!

To my editor, my awesome, incredibly talented Aunt Chris, both you and Uncle Eric were instrumental in making this happen. From late-night phone calls, to dozens of emails, and even some much-needed Texas hospitality when I desperately needed a vacation, I thank you so much for your tireless efforts.

I can only guess at how much time you put into this, and can't thank you enough for the countless hours you poured into this project. Go Team Ravens!

To my Uncle Paul- I can't thank you enough for all of your legal advice, your unwavering support, and for helping me launch Fitzsimmons Road LLC. (and for also being part of my inspiration for "Henry.")

To Terrell Harper- once my best friend, now lost to me in time. It pains me that we somehow lost touch, but I'll never forget who helped fuel my creativity. You mirrored my enthusiasm every step of the way. To this day, you are the only one who truly understood my vision, and because of you, I was finally able put this on paper. You were my advisor, my confidant and the only person who could keep up with my imagination without even trying.

To the rest of my family all around Wisconsin, Indiana, Florida, and Washington state, and especially to my loving sister Megan, who always saw my shine, I thank you for your support.

To Corbid McDowell, Leif Gabrielson, Tyler Schmidt, Bryson Ferguson, Marco McDaniels and Fred Diggins. I'll never forget the golden years we shared together, nor the inspiration you all gave me. Thank you. 17th and O, HLC, Quest, Young Gunz, Anomalous, Temple of Doom 4 life!

To Erin Tillman- Thank you for your nearly 30 years of friendship. We don't talk very often, but you've always been there for me anytime I've needed you to be. It's amazing how you and I can still catch up in literally 5 minutes.

To Ed Fontaine- When we weren't setting the night on fire, you were always incredibly supportive, even though you always laughed at how utterly ridiculous I could be with my wild ideas, but I know deep down you always thought they were pretty cool. Ha! Thank you for being the friend you've always been, both to me and to our family.

To Olivia (@olivaprodesign) for designing such awesome covers and banners, Dora Ella for your endless patience in building the Fitzsimmons Road/The Book of Ravens website, and to Belinda LaPage for your insight, advice, and for formatting such a large manuscript. Thank you all so much!

To the person who shall remain anonymous by request, you know who you are. But what I think you don't realize is how hard you actually pushed me. Inspired me. Impacted my life. There was never a single conversation or opinion you dared to sugarcoat. With you, it was always brutal honesty. Even at the cost of my own feelings.

Words alone will never be enough, you know that better than anyone, but you lit the fire when I needed it most to push myself over the finish line. Because of you, I was able to discover what I was truly capable of.

You gave me the drive. And that's no small thing, nor something I fail to recognize or take for granted. Because had you not done these things, I'm not entirely sure I would be where I am today. And though I know you would never seek to take credit, I lastly need to thank you for coming up with the original concept for the Fitzsimmons Road logo design.

On a side note- I meant every word I ever said...and to this day, nothing has changed. You know it, GK. Thank you for everything.

And last, but certainly not least- to my son- Mason Ezekiel McDonald, whose bright smile, contagious laughter, endless imagination and bottomless energy has transformed some of my worst days into memories I'll cherish forever. You inspire me far more than you will ever know and give me strength when I need it the most.

When you are finally old enough to read this? I hope you come to know how much love and joy you've given me and how, as a father, I couldn't be prouder of the incredible person you already are. Always be yourself, Mr. Amazing. Daddy loves you tons.

People always ask writers where they get their ideas, but all you really need to do is to take a moment to look around and indulge your imagination. Right, Mason?

Believe me when I say there's a lot more to come…and that this is only the beginning. My final thanks go to you, the reader, for the gift of your time and interest.

Let's go.

-Andrew Kenneth McDonald

Contents

THE BOOK OF RAVENS (volume one) 1
Prologue 2
PART ONE The Book of Amparo 10
Chapter One 11
Chapter Two 19
Chapter Three 27
Chapter Four 34
Chapter Five 41
Chapter Six 45
Chapter Seven 47
PART TWO The Book of Ravens 52
Chapter Eight 53
Chapter Nine 60
Chapter Ten 64
Chapter Eleven 69
Chapter Twelve 78
Chapter Thirteen 89
Chapter Fourteen 98
Chapter Fifteen 109
Chapter Sixteen 114
Chapter Seventeen 127
Chapter Eighteen 135
Chapter Nineteen 142
Chapter Twenty 147
Chapter Twenty-One 154
Chapter Twenty-Two 174
Chapter Twenty-Three 183
Chapter Twenty-Four 189
Chapter Twenty-Five 192
Chapter Twenty-Six 198
PART THREE The Book of Zekiel 202
Chapter Twenty-Seven 203
Chapter Twenty-Eight 206
Chapter Twenty-Nine 209
Chapter Thirty 214
Chapter Thirty-One 225

Chapter Thirty-Two 236
Chapter Thirty-Three 244
Chapter Thirty-Four 257
Chapter Thirty-Five 260
Chapter Thirty-Six 265
Chapter Thirty-Seven 271
Chapter Thirty-Eight 274
Chapter Thirty-Nine 281
Chapter Forty 285
Chapter Forty-One 289
Chapter Forty-Two 299

PART FOUR The Second Book of Ravens 306

Chapter Forty-Three... 307
Chapter Forty-Four 310
Chapter Forty-Five 318
Chapter Forty-Six 323
Chapter Forty-Seven 329
Chapter Forty-Eight 332
Chapter Forty-Nine 340
INTERLUDE 343
Chapter Fifty 348
Chapter Fifty-One 353
Chapter Fifty-Two 360
Chapter Fifty-Three 362
Chapter Fifty-Four 368
Chapter Fifty-Five 376
Chapter Fifty-Six 378
Chapter Fifty-Seven 382
Chapter Fifty-Eight 385
Chapter Fifty-Nine 390
Chapter Sixty 404
Chapter Sixty-One 410
Chapter Sixty-Two 418

PART FIVE The Book of Val 422

Chapter Sixty-Three 423
Chapter Sixty-Four 428
Chapter Sixty-Five 431
Chapter Sixty-Six 434
Chapter Sixty-Seven 437
Chapter Sixty-Eight 439

Chapter Sixty-Nine..446
Chapter Seventy 453
Chapter Seventy-One..465
Chapter Seventy-Two.. 471
Chapter Seventy-Three...478
Chapter Seventy-Four..484
Chapter Seventy-Five... 488
Chapter Seventy-Six.. 491
Chapter Seventy-Seven...504
Chapter Seventy-Eight...507

For Mason Ezekiel,
Mom and Dad,
And for the Sunshine I cannot live without....
Even though *we* do.

The Book of Ravens

(Volume One)

Written By
Andrew McDonald

Prologue

Azuul stood back to examine his work, seeking the slightest imperfections but could find none. Nothing that his vampiric vision could see.

He hesitantly reached for one of the twin daggers with his tongs, very much wanting a closer look, but the blades had not yet cooled. Even now, they still hissed from being bathed in his vampiric blood and not just his blood alone. He reluctantly drew his hand away and replaced the tongs on the small table nearby.

"Patience," he murmured to himself. "Patience." Yet he could not deny his rising excitement. Not after so many months of labor. The blades, even though they were completely submerged, looked absolutely perfect, their craftmanship exquisite...and he knew that his Master would most certainly be pleased.

He paced the small dimly lit chamber, the many minutes feeling like hours, and again reminded himself not to rush the process for such a thing had never been attempted before. For never in all of his immortal life had weapons been crafted such as these. Of that, he was absolutely certain. Thus, with nothing to do but wait, allowing the blades to soak in the dark and thick crimson fluid, he continued to pace back and forth, constantly inspecting the basin for any visible changes.

Alas, some many hours later, and knowing the sun to be rising, even though safely underground in the dark chamber, Azuul was forced to abandon his work.

"Damn our curse!" he muttered to himself. "Damn the rising sun!"

With much regret, he knew at once that his work would not be completed this night. Still, much had been accomplished despite what he considered a minor respite, for Azuul despised interruptions, even for rest, and he still felt very pleased with his work. What was one more day after all in a vampire's world of centuries?

Lingering as long as he dared, not wanting to abandon his all-important work and refusing to sleep in his richly appointed bedroom chamber far above, Azuul slowly slipped into the narrow wooden box that had served as his temporary resting place during all of these laborious nights.

How long had it been since he had even been in his own room? A year? Possibly more? But Azuul quickly reminded himself that such inconveniences were minor. All that mattered was that he complete this work of utmost importance, the very pinnacle of his studies having come to fruition. From the ancient texts he had pored over, to his experiments in dark blood magic and sorcery, to mastering the tedious art of blacksmithing...all had been done to reach this point.

"Patience," he muttered again, a word that had become his mantra. "Patience."

And besides, he reminded himself, as far as his own private chambers were concerned, those located far above, he actually felt far more comfortable in the elaborately constructed forge. For this was his Church, his domain, his place of sanctuary.

As he stretched and lowered himself into place, securing and locking the lid above him within the crude sarcophagus, Azuul whispered one last time.

"Patience."

But for the excited Azuul, tomorrow night could not come soon enough...

As soon as the sun had barely dipped below the horizon the following evening, Azuul's eyes instantly snapped open, even in the underground chamber. Like all vampires he awakened at dusk, and Azuul silently gave thanks to Cain for being an earlier riser than most.

Most vampires would not awaken until the sun had completely died away but Azuul could rise while remnants of pale light still remained. He literally sprang from the coffin, overriding his instinctual thirst to immediately seek out mortal blood.

Azuul still had much work to be done.

With much trepidation and nervous excitement, he forced himself to slowly approach the basin. It seemed to take many minutes but he was simply overly anxious. Once there, he peered over the edge of the tub, his hands clenched in anticipation only to discover that the blood he had emptied into it, his blood, Cain's blood...was completely gone.

"How?" he breathed. "How is this possible?" he asked himself out loud.

The daggers were still there, of course, his newly forged daggers, but not a single drop of blood remained. None. Not so much as a trace.

"Treachery?" he wondered, openly speaking his questions. But no, no one had come. He was sure of it. No one could have entered these chambers without his knowing. No one but Cain himself.

No, he reasoned, Cain had not come. He knew that implicitly. He would have felt him; every vampire could *sense* him whenever the ancient vampire was near.

"Then how?" he demanded. "How?"

Cautiously, no longer able to restrain himself, he reached to slowly curl his hand around one of the two hilts and lifted one of the daggers to inspect it more closely.

Immediately, he knew that the balance was perfect, without flaw, but still scrutinized the dagger from every possible angle. The dagger had as fine an edge as any weapon he had ever made. Finer, even. Indeed, this weapon had been crafted from the very pinnacle of his skill. He then slowly reached for the other.

Once both daggers were securely in his hands, a sudden shock passed through his entire body causing the startled vampire to nearly drop the weapons. But even more shocking was that Azuul, at that exact moment, distinctly heard a voice. A voice seemingly coming from the daggers themselves.

Ask.

The voice he heard had been neither male nor female, sounding otherworldly, neutral. But even more confusing was that Azuul felt quite certain that it had not spoken aloud. In fact, he was confident that this voice had originated from inside his head. Such as when Cain would seek to communicate with him from afar.

Was his mind playing tricks on him? Was he so starved for human blood that he was starting to become delirious? Delirious from his countless nights in the dark forge?

Ask. The daggers distinctly asked again, startling the vampire once more and this time Azuul did, in fact, drop both blades. They clattered to the ground, the metallic noise echoing loudly throughout the chamber.

He stood still for many moments, not daring to move, simply staring at the mysterious, and now conveniently silent blades with deep contemplation.

How? He asked himself, quite certain now that the blades had indeed spoken. How?

Naturally, it had been his goal to create a heavily enchanted weapon. That much he had anticipated, having used his own dark magic and secrets long thought forgotten. He had even purposely attempted to create a weapon without peer.

But what had Azuul *actually* done? Was it even possible to create something...sentient? If indeed that was what they were?

He had created enchanted weapons before, even experimenting on two separate occasions using vampiric blood to quench those blades, similar to what a blacksmith would do with water to quickly cool the hot metal. But on both those occasions, he had used very little, and mostly his own, never wanting to drain himself or Cain without good reason.

But on this occasion, having found moderate success with his past two creations, Azuul had taken it further. A large step further, by draining nearly half of his own vampiric blood and half that of Cain's, and using nearly all of it just to fill the deep basin. But Azuul had not stopped there.

With the little remaining blood of what was left, Azuul had actually used the precious liquid during the tempering process, letting that blood hiss and coat the blades, all while shaping the daggers with every meticulous stroke of his hammer.

Once formed and heated to the precise temperature, each step being handled with the greatest care, the idea had been to fully quench the weapons in blood, something Azuul had never attempted before. He couldn't quite recall how he came by such an idea, though few rarely do for such experiments. And yet, despite having been successful on those past two occasions, having produced weapons endowed with powerful enchantments of their own merit, Cain had not been pleased when Azuul had approached him with such a bold request.

Only after much prodding and promises of even greater power, had Cain reluctantly agreed, which came at no small cost. For Cain's blood was precious beyond measure, he being the oldest vampire in existence, as well as the very firstborn of the highly secretive race.

Cain's blood was older than nearly time itself, and thus asking for his blood, along with the power contained *within* that ancient blood was equivalent to a fortune without measure. And Azuul had not asked for a small amount. No minor thing. Thus failure, as Cain often reminded him, was something Azuul could ill afford. And standing here now, uncertain of what he had actually *created*, Azuul swallowed hard.

An hour went by, then another, before Azuul would find the will again to move.

Taking a breath to steady himself, he slowly reached to pick up one of the daggers, his hands already trembling, reluctant to handle both. His hand closed around it tentatively, cautiously, only this time he heard no voice and immediately wondered, seeking to unravel the mystery, if it might be required to hold both at the same time. For wasn't that when he had heard the voice before? When he had held both? Together?

Partially relieved, for Azuul's pragmatic mind was above all else patient, he again scrutinized the single blade he held, welcoming the silence.

Again he felt that perfect balance, could feel and see the sharp and fine edge. But only upon closer examination did Azuul notice that the blade had a distinctive rose red tint to it, yet likely imperceptible to mortal eyes. Stained from the blood, he wondered?

He carefully set the first dagger down on the table nearby, again refusing to hold both at the same time, and picked up the other.

Unlike the first dagger, this one, if he wasn't mistaken, had a soft pale blue tint to it, adding to these growing mysteries.

Why? Azuul wondered. Why the discoloration? Why did one appear distinctly blue and the other red to his discerning eyes? Both were truly far more silver in color, similar to the unique and various ores that had been used in their creation, but then why would each have its own unique tint? Again, Azuul silently asked himself, why? They had been crafted at the same time with the exact same materials. They had even both been quenched as a pair, so how? How was this possible? A defect perhaps? Some imperfection he had yet to discover? His blood having been mixed with that of Cain's? None of it seemed to make any reasonable sense.

No longer able to contain himself, Azuul's free hand at last reached for the other blade, needing at that moment to hold them both, seeking the answers to these mysteries.

Again, he heard the voice. Almost immediately he heard that soft sentient voice.

Ask. The blades said a third time and Azuul, far more prepared this time, was now certain of their origin. The voice had indeed come from the daggers, and yet from within his mind. For he was also certain that the voice had not spoken out loud.

But what did this mean? Could he communicate with them? Was that even possible? And what did they mean: ask? Ask what?

Azuul visibly trembled, not knowing at all what to say.

Ask. The blades repeated a fourth time and Azuul finally summoned the courage to speak.

"I...I, the vampire...the vampire Azuul...created you," he began, forming his words slowly, feeling far more comfortable speaking his thoughts out loud. Admittedly, he felt rather foolish for speaking to his creation but there could be no mistaking that the daggers indeed had a voice of their own. But did they possess intelligence as well? Would they respond now in turn?

But the daggers had gone silent. Instead, they seemed to softly pulse in his hands, a feeling unlike any other he had ever experienced and Azuul once again nearly dropped the blades to the ground. He forced his hands to remain firm and gripped the weapons tighter.

The pulse in his hands was warm, welcoming, and no doubt brimming with some kind as of yet unknown power.

But what had he created? What had he done?

After another long pause, he decided to speak once more, desperately needing more answers.

"As...as I said," he started again slowly. "I...I am your Master. I...I am your creator. Can...can you acknowledge as much?" he tentatively asked.

Ask. The blades repeated, and Azuul began to wonder if they were the only words that the blades could say.

"Ask *what*?" Azuul dared to respond, needing something. Anything. Some clue as to what this meant. Thinking the blades were merely going to repeat the word "ask" once more, Azuul was indeed surprised when the blades said something else.

Desire. They intoned. And almost immediately repeated the word again: *Desire*. Azuul struggled to make sense of it. To decipher their cryptic meaning.

Desire. But what did that mean? Were the blades asking him…what he desired? Did that even make any sense? Was that even possible? And how would mere daggers achieve such a thing?

Azuul attempted another question. "Can…can you understand me? Are you able to read my thoughts?"

Yes. Came the almost immediate response and Azuul, completely overwhelmed by these revelations, dropped the blades to the ground once more.

Part One

The Book of Amparo

Chapter One

CAIRO, EGYPT 571

The vampire Amparo stared intently at the mystical weapon, knowing them to be Cain's most prized possession...

Save for Amparo herself.

She took a deep breath to both steady and remind herself that at this moment, she was completely alone. Alone now with this weapon, this most valuable but deadly weapon. Or rather, weapons...for the sight that now drew her complete attention were the two nearly identical daggers; the only noticeable difference between them a slight variance in color, surely imperceptible to the human eye. But while one was distinctly tinted blue, the other red, Amparo was keenly aware that this was hardly their only differences. And though the daggers were impressive in their own rights, rumored to be the sharpest blades in existence, piercing flesh was hardly the beginning of what the formidable blades were capable of.

Amparo knew the history of the blades well and now drew all of that information from her memory.

The creation of the daggers, "Quest" and "Armageddon" by name, as Cain had often told her, had been forged during Cain's first years as a vampire. Shortly after he had sired the vampire Azuul. The legend, or story, as Amparo knew, was in truth more about Azuul himself, despite Cain's attempts to claim otherwise, for it was Azuul alone who had actually forged the blades.

He had used dark magic, ancient magic...along with a large amount of his blood. Vampiric blood. And not just Azuul's blood alone.

This is where the legend, or as Cain would have her know, would go on to explain that he was equally responsible for the blade's creation, taking far more of the credit for himself, for much of his powerful blood had been used. More than Azuul had given himself. And as Cain had dramatically told Amparo time and time again, it was from *him* that the blades had gained their incredible power.

But regardless, no matter which version of the story was actually true, for the clans told their own tales, what a power they were to behold indeed.

For the blades could grant any fate. The blades could guide one to any destiny, to one's deepest desires...and that had only been the beginning.

The blades could guide one to riches, to power, to glory, to all that could be desired. And that was precisely what Cain had done, increasing the size of his already vast empire along with wealth untold. But for all they *could* accomplish, for all the paths in which they could lead, the price for such knowledge and desire came at a terrible, terrible cost...and for that reason alone, they were not presently being used. Even Cain recognized as much.

"Quest", distinguishable only by a slight tint of blue, would supposedly lead one to whatever it was that the wielder sought; a person or an object, while "Armageddon", the far more dangerous of the two, would see a given task done, such as if the request called for more than simply finding something specific. Such as changing one's destiny...whatever the cost.

The two daggers were typically used in tandem, Quest seeking the path to the objective while Armageddon devised a way to complete it. Together, the blades could guide one to great fortune and could seemingly grant the impossible, but the blades could also lead one to unspeakable doom, even to one's own demise.

Amparo recalled that singular event now.

Long ago, in her own first years, the daggers had once been stolen by one of Cain's trusted servants, a vampire by the name of Remiir. Remiir had seized the daggers, and with their help had fled far away, to seek his own fame and fortune...but ultimately, the daggers had betrayed him, and instead led him to his own death.

For Remiir had unwisely and impulsively asked the blades for riches, for a power greater than that of Cain and the blades had responded by guiding Remiir back to Cain himself; for it was the only place where such a thing could be found...and where Cain had been waiting for him. In truth, and to be fair, the blades *had* done exactly as they had been instructed by guiding Remiir to the only place and person to where such riches and power could be *found*.

His greatest mistake had been his lack of patience and sheer carelessness, for he had asked the wrong questions, had failed to be specific. Had he asked the blades to guide him to riches and power other than what *belonged* to Cain, it would have then been possible that the blades could have, in time, fulfilled his request. He also could have wished for Cain's death, and Amparo mused that this should have been his utmost priority. For Remiir, perhaps blinded by his own ambitions, had failed to protect himself. Had failed to ask the blades for such protection, failed to navigate their cryptic instructions safely. Thus it was upon Remiir's death, beheaded by Cain himself, that the blades and their many mysteries were supposedly understood.

Amparo knew better. And she knew from her years of observation that both blades could be used separately, by using one without invoking the other, but both had to be held at the same time for either to function. Neither could truly operate alone.

Quest would guide her to any object, this she had ascertained through many years of painstaking research. But the danger, as Amparo very well knew, was that asking Quest to lead her to an object often coincided with "objective." One blade could rarely accomplish a given task without triggering the other, for object and objective were typically, and more often times than not, interpreted by the blades as the same thing. There wasn't a large enough distinction between the two and "objective" was often times when Armageddon came into deadly play.

Armageddon was primarily used to grant the seemingly impossible, to facilitate the requested task, but also rumored to do so with no regard at all as to the safety of the wielder, often choosing the most dangerous method possible.

For Armageddon's task was simple: accomplish the goal by whatever means necessary and Quest, working alongside it, sought the most direct route possible. And once on that path, Armageddon would see the objective done, whatever the cost, whatever was required. Even if completing the objective required the wielder's own life. Thus, rarely could one blade be used without invoking the other. It was a conflict of interest, such as was ultimately and fatally proven by Remiir himself. Only with careful planning, exacting scrutiny, and precise wording (and much caution there, Amparo knew) could one successfully navigate themselves to their final goal with relative safety. When requests were made to the blades in haste or even with complete disregard for the consequences they might bring, disaster usually followed.

For in the beginning, their powers were poorly understood and open to wide speculation, but Amparo had the advantage of years in which to contemplate countless outcomes and study the failure of Remiir himself...as well as what Cain had successfully achieved.

She also knew that Cain had made all of his requests with a complete disregard for his own safety, in sheer arrogance, confident that none would dare oppose him, much less challenge his rule. And for a time, at least in the beginning, Cain was likely quite unaware of any disaster or misfortune the blades could bring. But poor Remiir, drunk on visions of the grandeur and ease that came with the possession of such almighty weapons, ignored every warning and instead wondered why none before him hadn't sought to take that power for themselves, to claim the blades as their own. Remiir had thought them all to be fools. Cowards.

The truth was, as Amparo had come to know, is that others *had* entertained such thoughts. But in those days, Cain was seldom found without them. And much like Remiir himself, all waited. All waited for that perfect opportunity. But as fate would have it, it was Remiir who had come across such an opportunity first. After all, he had been one of Cain's most trusted servants and was ever by his side.

However, shortly after Remiir's untimely demise, few, if any, still harbored dreams or delusions, be it fame, power, or fortune...and Cain knew it. All had seen the fate which had befallen Remiir and it was assumed that this lesson, directed to those who would seek to strip Cain of his power, had been a lesson well learned. It was simply a risk none now dared to take...save one, one with nothing left to lose, and that vampire now stood before them.

Amparo was certain she could wield them, and wield them successfully, but even now as she stood directly before them, she couldn't help but second guess her own carefully thought-out plan. She took another glance around the enormous chamber, again making quite sure that she was completely alone, though this gesture was simply a natural human reaction and hardly necessary. For Amparo, like any vampire, would have detected even the slightest presence in such close proximity.

The room itself was a vast collection of Cain's most valuable artifacts but also in need of no guard. For Cain lived here himself, albeit in another grand chamber on a completely different floor in the massive complex and could sense any presence, as well as that person's location with an almost uncanny precision, including that of Amparo herself. It was almost as though Cain left the room unguarded to encourage temptation, and to demonstrate in no uncertain terms the dominion he held above all, for none would dare such treachery.

But Cain did *not* know, not on this particular occasion, nor on this particular night that she was there, for Amparo had seen to that all-important detail herself.

"At least the worst is over," she whispered, recalling with a grimace the unspeakable things she had done to come here. And here, in Cain's treasure room, she silently vowed to never subject herself to such degradation again. With a small growl escaping her lips, she once again turned her focus to the most important task at hand.

The daggers rested on a tall circular pedestal of polished black onyx at the end of the long room, practically daring someone to touch them. To just simply reach out and take them...and that was precisely what she intended to do.

Amparo tentatively reached for one hilt, the dagger known as Quest, and then slowly but determinedly, curled her slender fingers around the other. Almost immediately she felt the sentient presence, the intelligence of the blades, acknowledging her almost at once.

Ask. They suddenly imparted to her telepathically.

But Amparo knew it would be thus. The blades were asking her, asking her much like any other, what it was that she desired. But curiously, and much to Amparo's surprise, it almost felt as if the daggers desired and even welcomed her as their new owner. She wasn't sure how this message was imparted, or if this was a reflection of their dangerous design, but the message was unmistakable.

Ask. The daggers repeated after her ensuing silence, but Amparo knew that this was neither the time nor place to make any such request.

Instead, she made ready to leave, silently as she had come, securing the daggers in two identical sheaths she wore on her hips (sheaths she had carefully crafted herself), only to draw a second and completely different pair of daggers worn behind her back (her first and *other* dangerous theft of the night), and called upon their innate power to completely and quite visibly, disappear.

Within minutes, having carefully and stealthily exited the massive complex, she was already running, moving at full speed, her body becoming nothing more than a blur in motion, leaving Cain's vast fortress far, far behind. Her only thought now was to escape at that moment, and so Amparo pushed herself even harder, pumping her powerful legs and seeking to gain as much distance as possible. She was certain Cain would learn of her betrayal soon enough, perhaps even before the dawn, and the pursuit was guaranteed to be swift...for he would not be happy to learn that *three* of his most coveted treasures had suddenly and quite inexplicably vanished from his grasp.

A full hour later, after covering many hundreds of miles, Amparo finally slowed to a stop and found herself surrounded by nothing but a vast, dry desert. She breathed neither hard nor felt at all labored, benefits of her very nature, which had only been made stronger from yet another heist that evening: Cain's own blood.

She stood completely calm; felt no diminishing at all of her power, for while Amparo had been created strong, as well as carried the advantage of having been the fourth born vampire in existence, she had also fed that very evening on none other than the eldest vampire himself. No small accomplishment in itself, for rarely did Cain allow any of his offspring to drink from him a second time. She lamented the horrors she had subjected herself to in order to acquire such a gift, but while Cain's blood was potent beyond measure, with a taste she had savored with every mouthful, knowing it had come from *him* still made her want to retch. And yet despite it all, having come this far, she knew it had all been worth it. Worth her deception, betrayal, her very dignity, and having that now behind her, it was time for the second part of her carefully thought-out plan to be put in motion.

She was visible now, having ended the enchantment of invisibility by replacing those daggers behind her back, and now drew out the far more deadly daggers that she had most recently taken.

She had no more than a half-hour to spare, for her plan had to be timed perfectly, and she silently congratulated herself for the pain and considerable risks she had taken to get this far. As such, it was time to examine her reward, to fully inspect these blades, these blades that could in time, change her entire destiny.

She had one other appointment yet to make on this night but that had been carefully planned as well, and she could ill afford to be late. Especially considering that in a mere few hours, no more than two, she knew the sun would rise. And by that time, she was to be buried safely, ten feet or more below the ground.

Chapter Two

Silas gave the slightest lift to the reins. The horse obediently broke gallop, falling into a slow trot before whirling half-circle, coming to rest at a complete stop. The dark horse breathed mighty gusts of air, its nostrils flaring in the desert night.

Surrounding both rider and mount was nothing more than endless hills of rolling sand. In every direction, they seemed to go on, as though nothing else existed beyond.

Silas looked over this barren environment, searching carefully in every direction. The horse moved as if mirroring his thoughts, circling this way and that, in every direction he wanted to gaze. Finally, to his satisfaction, Silas leaped off the animal gracefully and effortlessly, landing face to face with his steed. The animal, obviously accustomed to this type of behavior seemed spooked not at all by the swift and sudden motion and merely gave him a passing glance as if to await further instructions. What followed instead were soft kisses on his warm muzzle and whispers of praise. The horse nickered in response to the welcomed affection, even adding a few taps of approval with a single hoof.

"Thank you," he whispered. "You have done well. Now rest, for I shall have need of you again, and soon." His voice was soft, almost inaudible. The horse snorted in contentment and gave him a slight nod.

Turning away from the horse, Silas stood to examine his surroundings once more. He looked in all directions and again saw nothing. Nothing but desert. And then-

"Silas," a figure behind him said quietly. Not the least bit surprised, Silas slowly turned around to regard a woman garbed in similar attire; simple garments of white linen, light and nearly translucent, as if to survive the desert sun. She was unmistakably beautiful with long wavy blond hair, deep blue eyes and an impressive figure to match. His own face was no less impressive, handsome and perhaps a bit rugged, which only added to his charm, with distinctly Roman etched features. His brow was strong, as well as the stare from his black eyes, with dark hair cut short and clean. His body was rather well proportioned and somewhat muscular, standing far taller than she, as her head barely reached his chest.

"Were you seen?" he asked in a quiet but firm tone.

"No," she returned. She slowly extended her hand and he immediately grasped it with both of his, kissing it repeatedly, gently. He smiled at her then, breathed a sigh of relief and suddenly wrapped her in his arms.

"Amparo. Every time I see you, you only become more beautiful," he said with perfect grace.

"I thank you for your words, but consider them foolish. Simply because I never change, no different than you." She smiled back flirtatiously.

"Are you sure no one saw you? Has followed you?" he asked, quickly changing the subject. "I sense nothing...but remain wary. If but one eye has seen you..." he warned.

"No," she interrupted. "No eye has seen me. Most importantly, not...*his*."

"For surely, his eyes matter most," he added, fully understanding the great risk she was taking, that they were both were taking, meeting as they were in secret. "Were you able to secure the daggers?" he asked, a subject of no small importance. Amparo smiled.

"You did!" Silas exclaimed, matching her smile. "You did! Didn't you?"

"More than that," she responded, her smile growing even wider. Silas wore a confused expression, quite unsure of her meaning.

"Quest and Armageddon belong to me now," she clarified, and from under her garments, she suddenly drew forth Cain's prized blades.

Silas's eyes grew wide. "And you are certain? Certain that he does not yet know?" he asked, more than a little concerned.

Amparo replaced the daggers and immediately closed her eyes, concentrating for only a moment. "No," she confirmed. "Not yet. But I plan to be away from here, far away before he learns of my treachery."

Silas nodded. "Where will you go? Where are we to meet?"

"You...you will not leave with me now?" she asked incredulously.

"I...I cannot," he responded with sincere regret. "I...I have other matters," he continued hesitantly. "Other matters that require my attention."

"Speak!" she demanded, suddenly growing very angry.

"I hate so dearly to rush, sweet Amparo," he began again, carefully choosing his words. "But I fear we do not have much time. Cain will not at all be pleased to learn that one of his lieutenants has gone missing...along with *that* which he values above all else."

Amparo surely did not miss the reference while also noting that Silas's voice had become far more urgent. Far more serious in nature.

"Are you just now having second thoughts?" she was forced to ask. "Tonight of all nights? And speaking of time...what time do we not have? If not what is needed to be away from this place? Is that not the one thing we do have? Time? All of eternity no less?"

"Amparo, please. Please listen. I beg," he pleaded. "I know what risks we both take by meeting here in secret and I know what further danger I have placed myself in...by altering our well-laid plans."

Amparo now stared at him incredulously but continued to listen intently.

"Know that I would never do anything to put either of our lives at stake, unless it was truly necessary, and for this, those very reasons, I very much seek your council." He paused only to take in a breath and slowly guided Amparo to sit with him upon the now cooled sand.

She rested upon her knees, taking both his hands into her own and directly faced him. She knew from his expression that he was about to reveal something very private, even personal perhaps. His mind remained closed to her, but more importantly, she knew better than to read it without his consent, although she easily could have done so. She would wait for him to explain.

"I...I have found one suitable to receive this curse. To join us in our cause," he finally said after a long moment of silence as Amparo's blue eyes grew wide in shock. They glimmered in spite of no visible light, save for the millions of stars scattered across the desert sky.

"This mortal comes of his own free will," Silas continued. "He knows what we are. He knows what it is that I ask of him..."

"How dare you speak so...so foolishly?" her voice said trembling. "So casually?! After all that we have done. What *I* have done!" she roared now, rising to her feet. He tried to follow immediately, attempting to stand himself only to be struck down hard. He had scarcely seen her hand move, the movement impossibly fast.

"No mortal can comprehend what we are!" she continued. "How dare you even suggest such a thing? And you tell me this only now? Now of all times?"

"Amparo..." he began again patiently, ignoring his lip which had been split open. "This mortal has seen me feed. Has seen me kill," he tried to explain. "Several times."

Amparo's face now showed signs of curiosity. She said nothing yet in response to this newest bit of information, but her gaze remained deeply disturbed.

"Mind you, this changes nothing. Our plan remains," he resumed, seeking to calm her. "But I will not leave Kadar behind. And I will do this Amparo. I will. Kadar will come."

"Kadar?" Amparo asked in a questionable tone.

"Yes. He is the mortal I choose," Silas responded. "He is special, this one. Truly my blood would be a gift to him."

"Our blood is a curse," she spat.

"Mind my words, Amparo. I am not asking for your permission. I am merely telling you what I intend to do."

"And I thought you wanted my council," Amparo responded bitterly. "You claim you do not need my permission and yet..."

"You would stop me?" he asked, challenging her unspoken threat out loud.

For several moments awkward silence passed, neither of them speaking a word. After several minutes however, Amparo was unable to contain herself.

"Do you love him?" she asked in all sincerity.

"I do," he confessed. "Much like I love you. I am fascinated with this one, with the gleam in his eyes. There is a fire in this one, I tell you. A certain...determination. Not at all unlike yourself."

Amparo laughed. "You speak of love as if giving it is such an easy thing. Ever are we enchanted by mortals. Of those different from us. Of what we once were."

"And what of the love I feel for you?" he countered. "Are you to tell me that what we share was so easily exchanged?"

"Do not speak to me in riddles, Master Silas," she mocked. "With clever words nor with what you think I long to hear."

"I only speak the truth."

"Indeed."

"Long have we planned this," he started again. "But Amparo, we also cannot do this alone."

"Never have I disagreed. But in *time*, Silas. Everything in time..." she argued.

"My Dearest Amparo, why delay what *can* be done now? Are we to turn away those who would help us? Wasn't that always the plan? To start over? With those we would share this unique life with?" he questioned. "Why wait? Are you not tired of the Master's hand? The way he treats you? Have you not suffered enough?"

"You know nothing!" she screamed, and for a moment, Silas thought that she was going to strike him again. "You and I..." she went on, her full fury spilling forth. "You and I were to leave this place! This very night! Together!"

"And we *will* be together," he promised, desperately trying to reassure her with his voice. "Consider this a minor delay. Nothing more."

"I cannot go back," she growled.

"Nor do I expect you to."

"Nor can I wait." Amparo turned away then, having made the decision to leave.

"Amparo..." Silas begged, rising to his feet. "Please...please try to understand."

"No," she replied flatly, turning ever so slightly to look upon him over her shoulder. "Understand *me* and hear me well, Silas. I trusted you. I trusted your words. But it has become painfully obvious that your love for this mortal has clearly impaired your judgment. Going back? To do this thing? Is suicide. And mind you, Silas, I do not have the luxury of time to argue with a fool."

"Amparo."

"And if this is to be your wish," she cautioned. "If you seek to place both of our lives at even greater risk, I will not be a part of it."

She suddenly drew forth a second pair of daggers, concealed under her dress, and Silas thought for a moment that she meant to slay him right then and there. But instead, almost faster than he could see, she flung the daggers behind her, nearly striking his feet but instead plunging harmlessly into the sand.

"Take them...for they have already served my purpose. Though I believe you are making a terrible mistake, I will not have you foolishly risk your life without any aid."

"Those...those daggers!" he stammered in disbelief. "Those are not the same daggers that you showed me only a moment before!"

"No," she answered. "Quest and Armageddon are to come with me. But recognize these others and know them well. Know their power."

"The blades...the Blades of Shadow!" he said in awe, recognizing them at once.

"Yes," she responded, her earlier riddle becoming clear.

"Amparo..." Silas began again, but Amparo cut him short.

"Consider this a gift. A parting gift of our friendship. I will not forget all that you done for me but I will lament what could have been. And to that end I say farewell, Silas. You have made your choice...as I too, have made mine. I can only pray that one day we shall meet again." And without another word, without any warning, she simply turned and vanished.

Silas did not bother to look around for her and simply stood staring blankly in silence at where she had just been. She hadn't really disappeared though, he knew, it was simply her incredible speed, although moments before she certainly could have, using the very daggers left behind.

Had he made the right choice? Was the mortal Kadar really worth putting his entire future and life with Amparo at risk? He took a deep breath and gazed in the opposite direction as far as his eyes could see. Tears began to well in his eyes but he wiped them away quickly, resolving to move forward with what he had chosen to do.

In the next moment he gathered himself and slowly bent down to retrieve the wondrous blades. And as soon as his hands closed around them, and knowing full well their enchantment, he was somehow able to watch himself, along with the daggers, disappear before his very eyes. He silently gave thanks to Amparo for so great a gift. Not only could the daggers render one invisible but they also cloaked the wielder's presence from other vampires as well. Indeed, he would need them, likely this very night, for he still had much to do.

He tucked the daggers safely away then, hiding them beneath his loose garments, thus ending the enchantment and instantly regaining visibility, his sorrowful encounter with Amparo having reached its tenuous conclusion.

With a deep sigh, and reflecting again on the enormous risk he was undertaking, Silas slowly returned to his patient horse, who now came to full attention as he approached.

"Well, old boy..." he said sadly to the animal. "It's time to go home."

Chapter Three

THE VAMPIRE STARED intensely at Kadar. His physique was small and short, his frame thin and bony. Still, the body was strong, shoulders slightly wide, his arms and stomach somewhat muscular. His skin was nearly black in the desert night, with a sienna like undertone that almost glowed beneath the rising moon. His face was sly, even a bit mischievous, yet possessed with a certain seriousness. Silas was now admiring all these physical qualities endowed upon this unusual mortal, who exuded a similarly unique personality.

Kadar wore a somewhat toothy grin but as Silas maintained his silent posture for several long moments, Kadar suddenly erased his smile. Was Silas going to back out? Kadar wondered. Why then was he staring at him so? No, Kadar reassured himself. If Silas was willing…

"I am willing, Kadar," Silas answered out loud, startling Kadar in the process. He was more than just a little surprised, still unaccustomed to having his thoughts read without consent.

"Are you so quick to forget that reading the minds of mortals is such an easy task when dealing with my kind?" Silas added with a wide smile.

"If only but for a moment, Master Silas. You are quick to remind me," Kadar ventured awkwardly, as though he required permission to speak.

"As I have already said, I am willing," Silas resumed. "To teach it all to you. All of it, Kadar. All of our gifts. Our secrets. It is simply that..." Here Silas paused as if to consider his next thought carefully. "I only wonder what...repercussions await me for performing this...evil. This evil, evil deed," Silas said with concern. "And mind you, Kadar, we are evil. *I*...am evil."

Whether or not Silas had intended to place such emphasis on those very last words, Kadar couldn't help but feel a chill run up his spine.

"If not so much in heart," the vampire went on. "We do what we must to survive. I *kill* your kind, Kadar, for even now your blood calls out to me," he finished in a whisper, his smile having disappeared. Instead, his face now wore a look of malice, replacing the beautiful expression of moments before.

Kadar stood frozen before his Master's eyes, whose body posture continued to shift until Kadar felt a sudden and unbridled fear, unlike anything he had felt before. Silas seemed to grow taller, his eyes becoming like those of a wild animal, his vampiric fangs now clearly showing...and then just as suddenly, as suddenly as the change had begun, Silas regained control, abruptly resuming his previous thoughtful demeanor.

He took a few breaths, to fully compose himself, then spoke to Kadar once more. "Kadar, you must understand that what you will become...it *may* leave you...grotesque. Sometimes, and this will be beyond my control, but at times a vampire is born...*unnatural*. I have seen more than one transformation go horribly wrong and you must bear in mind that I have never...."

"Master?"

"I have never done this before," Silas finished.

"Master?" Kadar asked again after a long pause.

"Yes?"

"Might I ask how you came to be...?" And here Kadar paused to find the proper wording. "I mean...how you became...?"

"A vampire?"

Kadar nodded.

"I see," Silas said thoughtfully. "But it is a tale too long in the telling...and one I would prefer to tell in full. When we are not so pressed for time. Far more important than that though, Kadar, is not *how* I became this way, but *what* I have become."

"Master?"

"As I said, Kadar...even as you yourself have seen, I kill your kind. Yes, to survive but also at times, very much against my own will. And not against my will as though beyond my control, but rather what I am *ordered* to do. Many otherwise good men have died, Kadar. Have died by my hands. My very nature, rather."

"But why?" Kadar found himself pressing. "Why would you do this?"

"Why else?" Silas responded sadly, as if the answer were obvious. "I do no more than what you are told to do, just as would any slave. Because I am ordered to do so."

"This...this other Master you serve. You have mentioned him before."

"Cain," Silas spat. "His name is Cain. The very first of our accursed kind."

"Cain," Kadar repeated, committing the name to memory.

"Think your own Master's evil?" Silas asked. "Their cruelty with a whip?"

"If the marks on my own back aren't proof enough of this..." Kadar started.

"You speak to me of mere physical scars, Kadar. Marks of torture I do not question...nor what you have suffered at their hands. But I pose these questions to convince you, to make perfectly *clear* to you, that you have yet to know the infinite definition of suffering. We are both slaves, Kadar...that much we share in common. But tell me this. What becomes of you, or anyone for that matter, once they are too old to work?"

"If not death for disobedience? Then most will live with their families, as we have always done, depending upon those who still work."

"And then?" Silas asked.

"Why old age, of course," Kadar answered.

"But what if one *could not* die? What if you were forced to serve without end, ever forced to do...*terrible* things. Destined to live out an existence conceivably worse than the most dire fate presumably awaiting humans after death. What would you do then?" Silas whispered.

"I would run away. Far away," Kadar answered without hesitation.

"You make it sound so simple. And what if you could not run? What if there were no refuge in this world from Cain? What then?"

"I would find a way."

"And those who would seek to oppose you? What of them? How far would you be willing to go?"

"You are asking me if I would kill," Kadar said flatly.

"Among other things? Yes. Yes, I am."

"I...I don't know," Kadar answered honestly.

"Forgive me," Silas interrupted. "I am not being fair. Suppose too, I should add, that those who seek to oppose you are men undeserving of death. For would a good man stop another good man from a better life?" he asked rhetorically.

"Are you asking me if I would kill an honest man?"

"And what if I was? And what if that choice was taken from you in order to ensure your own survival? Imagine then, Kadar," Silas went on with all seriousness. "Imagine, if only for a moment the unspeakable crimes I have committed in the name of such a Master. A person as evil as to surpass the very definition itself."

"Then you make my answer all the more easier," Kadar replied. "For I would either escape this Master of yours..."

"Or?"

"Or kill him," Kadar said without hesitation.

"Oh? Is that so? How far are you truly willing to go, Kadar?" Silas pushed, shifting his tone. "You see before you a vampire. A creature with gifts too wondrous to count. You see beauty, you see strength. And yes, immortality. Oh, how your kind covets *that*. To never grow old. To never get sick. Imagine that if you can, Kadar. Simply imagine. But what of that which you do not see? Consider how much I suffer. How much our entire race...suffers. And I speak not of days or weeks. Or even years. Think of all we have had to endure over centuries, forever oppressed by the one we call Cain."

"Master..." Kadar offered. "Whatever weight you carry, whatever sacrifices are required...we would find a way. I know that we would. Together."

Silas turned away then, his present emotions overwhelming. The future he ultimately sought, as well as the decision he was now struggling to make, staggered him and he visibly struggled to retain his focus. He took a short moment to steady himself and cautiously continued.

"There is...there is also a chance that...you might not even survive the process. I cannot stress this enough. I have seen it done, only a few times before...and there's...there is still much I need to think upon," he warned, placing a hand underneath his chin in a pensive manner.

"If I may Master, I am willing to take that chance. Any chance. Accept any danger just to be with you," Kadar interrupted, taking Silas by surprise. But his response had been too quick, too eager.

"How could you possibly conceive of it, Kadar?" Silas suddenly roared. "Do you not understand, mortal? Your life! Your very life you wager! And then what?" he went on. "You become *like me*! This *creature*! This *slave to evil* itself. Can you even *conceive* of the things I have done, the horrors, the atrocities which have haunted me every night since I have come to become this...this *thing*? Can you?" he growled. "Women, Kadar. Children. Innocents. Killed for his pleasure. Murdered. Families ripped apart. And that says nothing, *is nothing* compared to Cains's own unspeakable acts. He may as well be the Devil, come amongst us to amuse himself."

"But Master Silas...surely there's a way to..."

"Even now. Being here with you..." Silas went on, ignoring him. "A mortal. Sharing what we are...telling you what we are...these things alone are more than enough for Cain to skin me alive."

Silas took a deep breath.

"See me as I am Kadar. See me for *what* I am. Never again will you walk in the light of day. Never again will you see the sun. Never again would you be free to live among the living. We live *only* in secret. And if these things were not enough, we will become outcasts among my kind. Relentlessly pursued...and I fear we will have to depart this place, never to return, perhaps this very night. *Do you understand*?" Silas paused, exhausted from having attempted to share everything that weighed so heavily on his mind. He knew then a final decision was needed, and soon, as time was quickly running short, a mere hour now remaining until sunrise. Even if all went as planned, he still needed whatever precious time remained if he were to have any chance at rejoining Amparo, who was surely far away by now. Already his Master might have realized he was gone, away from his appointed tasks. And if Cain already knew...

"Will you forgive me, Kadar? Could you?" Silas pleaded, knowing the long anticipated moment was now upon him. "For you may come to loathe me, perhaps even despise me after this. Could you honestly forgive me, even in death, if that is to be your fate?" Silas genuinely asked.

Kadar was unsure as to how to respond, not knowing at all what to say. And so when Silas, after a long moment motioned with his hand for an answer, Kadar felt compelled to take another deep breath, in hopes of finding the appropriate words.

"Master," Kadar slowly ventured. "I know I cannot possibly see all that awaits me. And I know that the things you say I could and would only fully understand if I become as you are...but again, I am more than willing to take the risk. Any risk...and only ask that you allow me to determine that of my own fate. I am thankful for all you have told me, all that you have given me...but most of all, I am grateful for your friendship...and the companion you have been. You know already that I love you, no matter what I become, no matter the outcome. If this is to be the day I die, then so be it, for I come of my own free will, aware of what I, myself have asked for. I want to be with you, Silas. We can be free! I tell you we will find a way. To live as we were meant to live, Master. To see the World, a different World. One we could create together."

Silas realized then what he had always known. And why he loved Kadar as much as he did. Because he was full of spirit...and unquenchable hope.

"No life have I here, or anywhere else...but with you," Kadar continued, pausing to wipe the tears from his eyes only to notice Silas's fighting tears of his own. "If I end up hating you..." he gravely continued. "Should the worst occur, other than my death, please forgive me now, for I apologize, while my mind is clear...and know that I understand and accept the risk I take."

Silas smiled once more, having heard all that he could ever have hoped to hear.

"You choose your words wisely Kadar and it pleases me to know that you come of your own free will." Silas paused only a moment. "Come to me then my dear, Kadar. Come to me. Come now for what you seek. Come be with me in this darkness...and together we shall share its heavy burden."

Chapter Four

KADAR HESITATED. His body frozen, unmoving, while Silas continued to meet his blank gaze, once again holding the same patient smile, arms open wide. Swallowing hard, Kadar forced his feet into motion and felt himself slowly approaching the vampire almost against his will. As he drew closer, Silas's features again began to change, once again assuming that menacing look akin to that of a wild animal. Yet Kadar never slowed, not once, until he found himself face to face with his Master. And then...

Silas suddenly vanished. Right before Kadar's very eyes. Wearing a look of utter confusion and fearing that his Master had unexpectedly decided to abandon him, he looked all around, in every possible direcion, turning this way and that...but Silas was gone. As if he had never been there at all. For several long excruciating moments of doubt, and not knowing what to do next, he suddenly heard an unmistakable growl emanating from behind him. What followed next was a sound that Kadar would never forget. The sound of his own screams.

Silas was suddenly upon him, attacking, clawing, and Kadar found himself forced to the ground, in a primal battle for survival. It hardly mattered, for the vampire had him pinned tight, the strength of ten men in his arms. Nevertheless, Kadar continued to thrash about until he came to the realization that his struggle was useless and that Silas would not let go, his grip, simply too powerful. Kadar willingly allowed himself to go limp, only to feel his neck being brutally punctured by two sharp fangs, forcing a moan to escape his lips. And before long, Kadar's moans were soon joined with that of his Masters, who heaved harder with each passing second, devouring Kadar's blood by the mouthful. Louder and louder the two of them cried out until Silas began to fight the overwhelming urge to kill, his instincts threatening to possess him, wanting to drain Kadar completely.

"*Enough!*" Silas hissed, recoiling from Kadar's dying body, and forcing his powerful urges into submission. Kadar was wheezing quietly, his head dizzy, his body weightless, as if any and all strength he ever had, was gone. At that moment, he simply wanted to die. To tumble into oblivion, to simply be allowed to sleep.

"Now Kadar…" Silas whispered. "It is now your turn to drink. Come now, my child. You must remain conscious."

Kadar nodded ever so slowly, only vaguely hearing the words, his life force threatening to flee.

"Drink, Kadar. You must drink from me," Silas instructed.

His voice was beautiful, Kadar thought. Each word so elegantly pronounced. His familiar voice so very comforting, soothing. He vaguely saw Silas smile, and then an arm had appeared before his bleary eyes, the wrist already gashed, dripping with blood. Using his free hand, Silas gently cradled Kadar's head, pressing his mouth to the wound.

"Yes…yes. Drink, Kadar. Drink. Drink deeply."

His tongue lashed out, quite on its own accord to collect every last drop of the precious liquid. He drank and he drank and time ceased to exist. There was only this moment, this eternal nearly unbearable thirst; and he knew he never wanted it to end.

"Yes, Kadar…take more. You must take even more of me…" Silas breathed into his ear, but Kadar no longer required any encouragement, much less had any intention of stopping.

Silas continued to breathe softly, fully absorbed in the moment, until his breath began to quicken, only to belatedly realize that he had allowed the dangerous exchange to go on for far too long. Silas began to feel real pain then, horrific pain unlike anything else since he had become an immortal, and knew full well that Kadar was now fatally draining him, killing his own Master, pushing him beyond his limits.

"Let go," Silas pleaded. "I ask now that you let go. *Release me!*" He shouted. But Kadar failed to register his words, already beyond his reach. Growing desperate, he struggled to separate the crushing grip Kadar had forced upon his wrist. "Let go!" Silas commanded. "Stop..." He begged. "Kadar, please!"

On the verge of losing consciousness, Silas fought with every bit of his remaining strength, knowing that if the exchange continued...

"Let go, damn you! *LET ME GO!*" he roared, and somehow, at last managed to free himself, literally drained but managing to somehow throw Kadar clear, his strength now all but spent.

Kadar landed with a solid thud a full 10 feet away but was already getting up slowly, swiftly shaking off the impact, looking no worse for wear. In fact, Kadar actually appeared as if nothing had happened, looking far more concerned for his Master, and quickly came to his side.

"My Master! Are you...?"

"Concern not for me, young one," Silas managed. "I...I shall be all right. But as for you..."

Suddenly, Kadar collapsed. "Ugh," Kadar muttered, curling himself into a fetal position, his hands grasping for his stomach. "The...the pain!" he cried out. "The pain..."

"Yes. You are feeling...the *changes* Kadar," Silas whispered. "Try now to relax. Do not fight that which torments you."

Silas managed to stand then and only wished he could spare his friend this agony, watching Kadar suffer a series of intense convulsions.

"So it was for me, Kadar, but in moments you shall feel no more pain. And then...you shall be as I am...and will be so forevermore."

Kadar remained in a state of shock and was vomiting repeatedly, soiling his clothes, his entire body caked in sweat.

"S-such p-pain...*it hurts so much...*" Kadar moaned again.

"Soon Kadar, there shall be no more pain. No more pain for you...no more."

And although Silas was still standing, he remained in dire straits himself, still weak and struggling to formulate thoughts much less words. His body still shook with minor convulsions of their own, but otherwise, he would be fine, in time, he knew, though at great personal cost. His greatest concern instead rested with Kadar, who had by now nearly completed the change and in but moments, would be changed for all time.

Silas smiled. Kadar endured minor seizures for a few more minutes before lying completely still. He had uncurled himself and was now reclining on his back. The moaning had also stopped and his breathing had returned to normal. His eyes then opened.

"Am...Am I still alive?" Kadar questioned aloud. Though in all truth, he had never felt more alive in his life, but was he alive? He wondered.

"You are very much alive," Silas answered, responding to Kadar's unspoken thoughts. "Just not in the human sense."

Kadar continued to lie still, eyes full of wonder, but after a moment, Silas broke the silence.

"Stand up, Kadar," Silas suggested, extending a hand to help bring Kadar to his feet. "How do you feel? I can still easily read your thoughts, you know...though I am merely choosing not to. I would hear your own voice, the new voice I have given you. So now tell me, Kadar. How do you feel? Do you hate me? Do you..." Here Silas paused for just a moment, realizing he was overly anxious. "I am...I am sorry," he resumed. "By all means, take your time. I mean not to rush you. I am simply excited."

Silas stopped talking. He felt as if he was rambling and even felt slightly embarrassed. But Kadar took no notice and merely smiled back at his Master, no doubt feeling the profound changes coursing throughout his entire body. After another uncomfortable pause, Silas found himself once again becoming impatient.

"Please, I beg. How do you feel? I must know," he pleaded.

"I feel..." Kadar began. "I...I feel..."

But before he could finish his thought, a disturbed look came over his face. He suddenly felt a paralyzing fear and a deeper dread than he'd ever experienced, and worse yet, noticed that Silas's face now mirrored his own.

"M...Master..." Kadar whispered. "*Who*?"

"*He* has found us, Kadar!" Silas whispered in a hushed panic. "Oh my God, he has found us! He *knows*!" he cried.

They had both sensed it. Could verily feel a heaviness in the air. The swelling of some foreign power around them.

Kadar was unsure what to make of it, this feeling of absolute dread, but Silas knew that presence all too well, this evil entity, drawing closer by the second. Another of their own kind, The Master himself. The cruel and unforgiving Master of them all.

He was still at least 10, possibly as much as 15 miles away, but Silas knew just how swiftly Cain could cross that distance. Even more terrifying than that was the malice Cain surely wore on his face and his reputation for commanding absolute carnage when enraged...and that scarred Silas to death.

But *how*? Silas pleaded to himself. *How could he have possibly known*? It then occurred to Silas that Cain was not alone. No. Silas was sensing several more forms nearby, no doubt Cain's personal guard for he rarely traveled alone, and he felt the shift as he grew to understand that he and Kadar were being surrounded from all sides.

Silas stood stock still, undecided as to what to do, his body and mind equally frozen. Kadar shook him roughly, begging for his attention in hopes of awakening him from his trance.

"Master!" Kadar cried still shaking his body. "Master! What are we to do? Do we fight? Do we..."

"Run," Silas whispered, his face full of panic. "We run," he urgently repeated. "RUN!" he roared. "RUN!!!"

Kadar awkwardly lurched forward, unaccustomed to his new body but soon easily outdistanced his Master. He broke into a flat run, racing at a speed he couldn't have previously imagined. Silas, he noticed, was struggling to keep up with him, appearing both labored and drained.

His Master was weak, Kadar realized, completely spent from the exchange. And as if to actuate the point, Silas suddenly collapsed. He had been running full-out when his feet tangled, no doubt brought on from exhaustion, and had gone down hard. Kadar slowed an instant later, turning quickly to assess the damage.

"Master!" Kadar cried out.

"It is useless," Silas hopelessly replied as Kadar helped him to his feet. "We cannot outrun them. They are even now all around us," He panted.

"Can we not fight them?" Kadar protested, though his own face betrayed his fear.

"Kadar, you do not understand. Those that now surround us are many. And even if we were by some miracle able to prevail, My Master *alone* could kill us both and more than likely, this he will do...though both of us need not die tonight."

Kadar felt his blood go cold, dreading what Silas was then about to suggest, what he in so few words was already attempting to say.

Silas was saying goodbye.

"One of us still has a chance to escape," Silas quickly continued. "And I tell you now, it will not be me. For if we remain together, the two of us will surely die. No. I will not needlessly sacrifice your life to pay for my own mistakes. Both of us need not perish."

"No, Master!" Kadar pleaded.

"I should have been more careful! More cautious!" Silas scolded himself. "Cain bides his time now...if only to consider our next move...but wait long, he will not."

Silas closed his eyes, his tears forming quickly and Kadar felt his own eyes brimming as well. Silence seemed to suddenly surround them and Kadar found himself longing to believe that no such threat existed. That all of this was part of some horrific dream. Or that at any moment, Silas would laugh and say it was all just a test.

"I would like to believe that too, child," Silas said, responding to his thoughts. "But you must mind your thoughts now, for even those are no longer safe. You must guard them closely, Kadar. Now. You must forget the danger around us and focus *only* on my voice. I will not have him discover our plans." Silas paused briefly, his face now completely serious. "You must leave me, Kadar. You will leave Cain to me. Both of us cannot escape and I no longer have the strength to go with you. You will mind what I taught you. Mind what you have *seen* and remember all that you have learned. You know already so much about us and need only time to discover all else you need know."

"Master..." Kadar interrupted.

"No, Kadar. *You listen*. You listen like you've never listened before. We have but moments..."

Chapter Five

"Amparo," Silas said. "It would be wise for you to remember this name, for I have never mentioned it before. Whatever else you may forget, do not forget this name, Kadar. You will need to find her one day, or better still; she will need to find you. Your own name, she knows..."

"Amparo? Who is this woman?" Kadar asked. "Why do you mention her now?"

"She and I have served the same Master, the same Master who sired us both. Yes, Kadar, it is Cain himself who now seeks us...but Amparo will know what to do. She shares my same hatred for him, even more so perhaps, for she too shares our curse. She will help you." Silas paused only briefly to concentrate on Cain's location and to gauge how much time they had remaining.

"He draws near, Kadar. The time now is almost upon us."

Kadar sadly nodded, not daring to interrupt.

"Is there anywhere you can hide? Some place nearby? I fear I will not be able to give you much time. I am weak as you know..."

And then it hit him. The daggers. Kadar could use the daggers! Without question, or giving it another thought, Silas quickly pulled them forth, becoming invisible in the process.

"Master?" Kadar whispered in a sudden panic, thinking Silas had somehow abandoned him.

"Be at ease, Kadar..." The voice of his invisible Master remained directly before him. "I am yet still here with you."

Silas became visible again an instant later, having placed the daggers on the ground as Kadar's eyes grew wide in wonder.

"Master? What...what magic is this?"

"Listen to me, Kadar. There is no time to explain. Only know that when they are in your hands, you will not and cannot be seen. I'm not even certain that my own Master can sense your presence if they are securely in your hands, their enchantment be that strong. But mind them, Kadar, for if you strike with them, should you seek to strike back at our foes, any attack that draws blood or contact will end their enchantment. That is the extent of their power and know their limits well. They could very well save your now-immortal life. Still...we must take no chances and I ask you again. Is there any place, anywhere at all you can hide? You will need to escape the dawn as well."

"Giza, Master Silas. And few know those dark passageways better than I. I need only but a few moments to get inside..."

"Good. Good. That is where you must go."

"But what of you? What shall become of you?" Kadar asked, expressing his concern.

"It...it is my time to die," Silas pronounced gravely. "Say nothing more, Kadar. I give you back the life I took from you, by providing you now the chance to live as I would have liked to live. Only...I hope you will be able to live yours in peace. But survive you must, Kadar. You must. Do not let my death be in vain. For once the Master places his hands upon me..."

Silas then paused and quickly rose to his feet, Kadar a second behind.

"Master...I beg..." Kadar quickly urged. "I beg you to reconsider. Flee with me now. Together we can escape. Together we could..."

"I have told you, child," Silas said, clasping Kadar on the shoulder. "Together, it is a surety that both of us would die. This is the only way, Kadar. *The only way.* You will not look behind as you flee, nor will you attempt to help me...I will have your word on that. Now run, Kadar. You run. Trust now your new senses. Trust in your body's strength. Your gifts. You have already responded most favorably in this regard and I tell you now that I am most proud of you." Silas paused to give Kadar that patient smile. That smile which Kadar would never forget. The smile Kadar would never see again.

"I will give you all the time I possibly can, but make haste. They will come quickly for you, Kadar. At the very least, they will detect your scent so you will have to be swift, *ever on guard*, quiet. Silent as a shadow. They will find you if you let them...even with the daggers. And they will come, Kadar, they will."

Kadar nodded, trying to fight back his tears.

"You will have a slight advantage in that the sun will be rising in little less than an hour. They will not have much time to search for you if you are able to get a sizeable lead..."

"They will not catch me, Master. And if they do, I will fight them to the death," Kadar promised.

"So brave..." Silas whispered. "Now listen. If you are to survive, you must remain hidden until the following evening. Upon rising you will need to feed quickly, as you will be weak when night falls again...and you will need all of your strength. Set about gathering whatever resources you need in order to leave Egypt. You are no longer safe here..."

Silas felt rushed then, wanting to say so much more and yet he knew they were out of time, this precious bonding with his newly born fledgling at its end.

"Forgive me, Kadar for this evil I have unleashed upon you. I never meant for this to happen. I only wanted us to be together always...for you have been as almost like a son to me in the time that I have come to know you. Please, I beg, forgive me." Silas could hold back his tears no longer and Kadar now held him close.

"Do not cry, Master Silas. If I die tonight, I shall join you...and we will be together in death. But if I live, I will stop at nothing at finding a way to slay the one that will take you from me. And when I am strong enough...*he* will run from *me*," Kadar promised.

Cain's contingent was nearly upon them and Silas reacted immediately.

"The time has come, Kadar. Go now. Run as hard as you possibly can and I will do all that I can to deter them. Mind your thoughts, Kadar. Always mind your thoughts. Lest those very thoughts betray you..." Silas then took his hand. "I love you, Kadar. And be safe, my son."

In that final moment, Silas said as much as he could with his eyes, unspoken words of love, protection, and even hope. For once Kadar left his side, Silas would cease all communication, for it would be far too dangerous, and thus his fledgling was now on his own.

"Now go," Silas begged him. "GO!"

"I'm gone," Kadar replied with a choked voice. The space about him blurred and he vanished even before Silas's keen eyes, having used the daggers at once.

Silas genuinely smiled one final time, a smile Kadar could no longer see, but intended for him nonetheless. Kadar had shown real courage, Silas thought to himself. Real strength.

"And that same courage I shall have in being delivered my own death," Silas vowed.

They were the last words he would ever say.

Chapter Six

HUNDREDS OF MILES away to the East, Amparo still heard the screams. Like most vampires, she had the ability to hear others of her kind from afar when pain, or some other momentous event that could cause the vampire in question to remove his or her mental barriers. It wasn't always discernable who the vampire in question was, but on this particular occasion, she had no doubt at all of the one who had cried out.

Silas.

The vampire who had cried out had been Silas.

And then, just as suddenly as she had heard his screams, those screams were suddenly silenced.

Silenced forever.

Silas was gone, of that, there could be no doubt, and Amparo, having been in mid-run, involuntarily collapsed to the ground, tumbling a good way before finally coming to a stop.

Torn with grief from inside, and nearly blinded by a flood of tears, she knew exactly what had happened.

Silas had proceeded with his plan, his foolish, dangerous plan to convert Kadar to their cause and through Kadar's creation, Cain had been alerted. Somehow, through an ability that Amparo had never understood, Cain could always sense when another of their race had been born. Brought over to the darkness.

Amparo wept and then wept some more. And when she no longer had any tears remaining, she screamed out in rage, cursing the one who had once again taken someone from her. Someone she had held dear. Someone she could never hope to replace.

"Why?" she demanded out loud to no ears but her own. "Why didn't you listen to me? Why did you not leave with me when we had the chance? Why did you risk it all? Why did you risk everything for a single, stupid mortal? Why!!!" she wailed, screaming into the night.

She went silent then for some minutes, pondering all that had transpired. All the events that had led to this...*existence*.

Anger replaced sadness. Hate replaced despair. And in her eyes now burned a vow of revenge.

Amparo clenched her fists, wishing that the old vampire was here now. Wishing more than anything to end Cain's vile existence. To savagely rip out his throat. To destroy the bastard once and for all.

Suddenly, she drew forth Quest and Armageddon.

Ask. They immediately demanded, once settled in her cold hands.

"Hear me and hear me well. Both of you," she said addressing the blades.

They went abruptly silent, acceding to her command and Amparo found herself breathing hard, hands trembling, but still managed to hold out the blades before her.

"Quest..." she began, staring intently at the pale blue blade in her left hand. "You will lead me to the one who will in time have the power to destroy Cain."

Immediately, the dagger began to weakly pulse.

"And you..." she continued, turning her attention now to Armageddon.

"You will see it done. You will see Cain dead."

Chapter Seven

Amparo waited in desperate silence. Waited for any sign. What if it could not be done? She wondered. What if the blades refused her request? What if there were no such person, no such vampire in existence?

Yet both blades were now pulsating, throbbing warmly in her hands, a sign that the blades were becoming active.

Not only that, but the blades were now plotting, were even now attempting to guide her, confirming to her at once that this task could be completed.

And thus, it would be done.

Whatever the cost.

That much was now certain, for once Armageddon became active, there was no stopping the newly created destiny, or avoiding the path she had chosen. Quest and Armageddon together would lead her, perhaps to even her own death, but such a person or creature would be found before she met her own potential demise.

She took comfort in that fact, and assurance in the dagger's promise to keep her safe until such a person could be found.

Her request had been made in haste, in anger even, but she remained confident that there had been no mistakes in her wording. And because she had asked the daggers to guide her personally, she was awarded the promise that they would keep her safe until the task could be completed. Because they were even now attempting to guide her, to make clear her direction, which also confirmed her answer.

As if that line of reasoning were not enough, the daggers themselves abruptly spoke, startling Amparo in the process.

Follow. They urged, speaking as one, their words unmistakably clear.

"Follow?" Amparo asked a moment later, desperately trying to regain her composure. "Follow what...?" she started to ask but her left arm suddenly moved. Moved on its own, quite against her will, pulled by the dagger itself.

Follow. They repeated as one voice and immediately she understood. Even now, Quest was attempting to guide her. To guide her in the appropriate direction.

"What...what about Cain?" she asked them before committing to their instructions. "You will need to keep me safe," she implored them.

Follow. They repeated a third time and when Amparo refused to move, having never used the daggers before, the blades spoke once again.

Safe.

Follow.

Again, they relentlessly attempted to point out her course and Amparo hesitated only a moment longer.

"So be it." she whispered, understanding both their meaning and intent. "Lead on."

And so they did.

Quest and Armageddon led her swiftly, far into the night and Amparo never slowed once, never letting up, following their guidance precisely.

And when dawn was at last approaching, after she had covered many hundreds of miles, they instructed her further.

Stop. Dig. They implored.

Dig.

Sleep.

Amparo did not question these instructions, throwing herself upon the ground and immediately began digging a hole. A hole large enough in which she could comfortably rest. And when she had constructed one suitable and deep enough, she burrowed her way in, covering herself with mounds of dirt in the process.

She had done this before, many times, and just when she thought her task complete, the daggers spoke once again.

Deeper.

And so she began her labor again, digging a hole deeper than she had ever had dug before.

In times of stress or when a vampire could not find shelter, burying oneself safely beneath the ground was a perfectly acceptable alternative. She preferred a coffin or a long narrow box as most vampires did, simply because it was practical, but she was not at all unfamiliar with resting in the earth.

But in the few times she had sought refuge in such a way, those holes had always been shallow. Deep enough to conceal and protect her form, but not so deep as to allow any inconvenience. But the hole she dug now, the hole she continued to dig, was becoming deep indeed. At least forty feet, she gathered. When she finally began to tire, having delved even further, and now sensing the rising sun, she began to wonder how deep the blades would insist she go.

Enough. She heard suddenly, the now familiar voice sounding in her ears. And to Amparo's continued amazement, she realized at that moment that she wasn't even holding them. Quest and Armageddon had spoken of their own accord.

While she had been digging.

Amparo had been so preoccupied, so intent on following their continued instructions, her mind consumed with her need for revenge, that she only then started to grasp what they had done.

They had spoken without being held!

She climbed out of her hole then, lacking the ability to leap so high, and retrieved the daggers quickly, sheathing them safely in the process.

They would guide her again if needed, she knew.

It was somewhat difficult to burrow back into the hole she had constructed, what with bringing any remaining dirt down into the deep pit with her, but with stern determination, Amparo saw it done…and just in time.

The sun was beginning to rise but even this deep underground, she could feel herself nearing the paralysis that all vampires faced each dawn, regardless of where they were. No matter how dark a given place.

Her eyes started to close then and she silently said farewell to Silas. Farewell to the life and the vampire she had left far behind.

Sleep. The daggers said, speaking a final time.

Sleep.

The vampire Amparo knew no more…

Part Two

The Book of Ravens

Chapter Eight

SCARBOROUGH, ENGLAND 1066

The day I met her, that's when everything changed. That's where my tale begins.

I had never seen her before in my village, though visitors and travelers did pass through every so often.

I was in the surrounding forest, but a mere mile from my home taking a brisk walk, as it happened to be a beautiful night. It was early September, the weather slightly cool, and the sun had set only about an hour ago. My dark cloak was wrapped around me and I thought not at all of the lingering cold, but of the difficult decision I was still in the process of making.

After some time, having pondered enough thoughts for one night, I made ready to turn for home when I was startled to hear what sounded like a girl crying nearby...no. A woman.

Unable to see much farther ahead, I decided to follow these cries without question, thinking someone might be in danger. Possibly even lost. Thinking she must be close by, and moving with a sense of urgency, it took but moments to reach their source, for in the very next glade, I saw her.

She appeared to be a young woman, if my eyes were to be trusted in the dim light, and she was simply weeping, down on her knees...alone. She raised her eyes immediately, noting my approach.

"Stay away from me!" she hissed and I halted abruptly, surely having startled her. I certainly meant no harm, but from her vulnerable perspective, and being quite alone, that also wasn't a given. As for myself, I couldn't help but find the encounter peculiar. It wasn't just the fact that no woman had cause to be out this late, much less alone. But especially one I didn't recognize? Knowing my village to be the only one nearby? Equally strange had been the tone of her voice. For it had sounded strange. Foreign. With an accent I didn't recognize. Certainly, I could forgive her defensive nature, considering the late time of day and isolated location, but I had also felt a strong pull to her words. Naturally, as well as respectfully, I was inclined to heed her command but...that wasn't it. For I would not have been able to walk forward a single step had I the desire to do so. Almost as if I felt...compelled? Given that I intended to honor her words regardless of the strange sensation I felt, I simply stood there, saying nothing, not daring to take a step closer. I then noticed her regarding me closely.

By doing nothing was I unintentionally causing her more distress?

I waited in place for a seemingly long while, as she slowly and cautiously collected herself, her features still hard to make out. She stood up then, boldly moved closer, and even from that distance, I could not help but notice what appeared to be dark stains covering her garments. Over the dress she wore, rather. Blood, I wondered?

I feared at once that she was seriously injured, perhaps recently attacked, but she, along with the dress she wore, were still so very difficult to see clearly in the dark save but for a bit of moonlight, desperately clawing at the surrounding trees. And while I probably could have made it home nearly blindfolded, had I the desire to do so, my eyes were of very little use here. Even so, I strained and begged of them to locate some sort of wound, possibly find some visible clue but my eyes could discern nothing. Odd, all of this was.

Who was she? Why was she here? And why alone? I struggled to make sense of all of this.

"Why are you still here?" she irritably questioned, breaking the ensuing silence.

"I...I heard you crying," I stuttered, feeling forced to make a response. "I thought maybe you were in need of some assistance..."

"And how could you possibly assist me?" she interrupted. "Like most men I have known, you all think you are the answer to a woman's problems. Foolish," she finished.

"My lady," I started, offering a slight bow. "I mean no harm, nor proffer to gain anything from this encounter. I meant only to offer my kindness," I returned in all honesty.

"Mmmm..." she mumbled back. "Step...closer."

Strangely, much like the pull I had felt only a moment ago, and through no will of my own, I found myself approaching her without meaning to. My feet seeming to move of their own accord.

But that is when I saw her clearly.

From a distance, and with many shadows playing against the trees, nightfall had done much to obscure her face and that of her small frame. It was only now, standing directly in front of her, did I realize she was unmistakably beautiful, fairer than any woman I had ever laid eyes upon. Her face was almost elvish, if such a thing could be said, with deep blue eyes and golden hair containing many subtle shades I had never seen before. Stranger still in this darkness, for it verily shimmered even in the dark of night.

She was quite small, standing much shorter than I, despite not being very tall myself compared to most men. I also could not help but notice that her petite body was more than well-endowed and likely, I had stared far longer than intended and what would have been appropriate.

She suddenly smiled. "You find me attractive," she said as if reading my very thoughts.

"You're hurt, or appear to be," I returned, finding no other response. "If I may..." I began, in a futile attempt to regain my manners.

"If you may what?" she asked with a certain mischief.

"May I...at least inquire whether or not you are in need of a physician? A bandage perhaps?"

"Bandage? Oh. You mean the blood," she said, catching on.

"Yes. If you are hurt, in need of aid, my village is nearby. I would help you..."

"You would help me?" she asked, raising a brow. "Asking nothing in return?" she finished, with the same mischief in her voice.

"Of course. I was taught and raised to help others in need. Simon always said that if..."

"Simon?" she interrupted.

"Forgive me. Simon... he's the one that raised me...who is also our village priest. I live with him. In Scarborough." I paused, pointing in the appropriate direction. "Simon taught me that I should always help those who are in need, if I'm able to, of course. And I am certain that Simon would have no objections if you were to come with me. So, if you are hurt, I would ask that you permit me to help you. I promise no harm will come to you. I am unarmed."

"And do you think I cannot take care of myself?" she questioned with a certain ire.

"No, my lady. I meant no offense," I wanted to clarify. "I merely wanted to make clear *my* intentions." Christ, this woman was asking a lot of questions.

"Do you think I ask a lot of questions?" she asked, surprising me and catching me quite off guard.

"Well, yes..." I said plainly, finding no reason to lie. "Especially for someone who might be hurt." I finished, looking once again at the blood-stained dress she wore.

"You need not concern yourself with tha—" She paused suddenly, looking quickly to her left, her eyes narrowing as if...looking for something? Someone? She motioned with her hand that I dare not move and instinctively I obeyed.

"What is it?" I whispered, going along with this strangely developing situation.

"Shhh," she said looking directly in my eyes, while placing a finger over her lips, adding emphasis to her caution.

She hunched down low then and beckoned for me to do likewise and I did so, crouching close to the ground. She paused a moment longer, listening again, her head strangely cocked upright. Was she straining to hear something? And if so, what was she listening to? What was she trying to hear?

I could hear nothing at all, nothing but the natural sounds of a forest, but her look was unmistakably serious, and I took it as a clear warning. But for what?

"Did someone hurt you?" I whispered. "Is someone looking for you?"

"This is not your problem," she confessed. "Concern not for me."

"Concern not for you? Your dress is covered in *blood*. It is blood, is it not?" I boldly asked. The truth was, she was showing no signs of having been injured. And if she was, she was certainly showing no signs of pain. But if that was the case, then whose blood was it if not hers? I only wanted to know...

"The truth?" she inquired.

"*Who are you*?" I asked, more than curious, both of us continuing to whisper.

Suddenly, taking us both by surprise, a strange and unknown light appeared, moving slowly across the sky. It appeared to be as far away as the stars themselves, but this light; this odd light appeared to be one of them. A star itself. Not a shooting star, but something else. Something I had never witnessed before. It moved painfully slow and I stood there transfixed just to be certain it in fact, moved. But after a long pause, I was sure of it, made more noticeable by leaving what appeared to be a trail of...fire behind?

"What is *that*?" I asked, forgetting my previous question. "This star that appears to have a tail?" She stared at the sky a moment longer before returning her attention to me. Her gaze once again intense.

"A sign. A sign that I have been here far too long," she responded, slowly rising to her feet. No doubt she remained cautious about something, something else, something I did not understand. "For better or worse..." she resumed. "A sign."

"But what is it? Who are you? Who is followi—" I said, leveling all my questions upon her at once.

"I must leave you now," she interrupted sadly, crossing the remaining distance between us to place both of her hands on my face. Her touch was cold, like that of snow, and my arms hung loosely at my side. I again felt unable to move. "Farewell, my chosen. Pray that we shall not meet here again..."

"Chosen? What are you...?"

Without warning she kissed me, catching me quite off guard, fiercely, with passion, pressing her lips hard against my own. But her lips...her lips were so cold, so much like her hands, but after a moment I could have cared less, for I suddenly felt enraptured by this woman, this woman I did not even know. Instincts guiding me, I kissed her in return, but having never kissed a woman before, certainly never before like this, I stood completely still, my arms hanging limp at their sides, no doubt looking very much the unexperienced fool. She then guided my hands to rest upon her hips but even as I then felt allowed to draw her closer, finding myself starting to become lost in her, the moment was already fading for she started to pull away.

"I must now go," she said with a bit of sadness, even then starting to turn away.

"But why? Why so sudden? Will I...can I see you again?" I pleaded, unable to accept this, not wanting this encounter to end.

"I don't know," she replied carefully, turning to address me. "Nothing at this time is certain. I can say no more."

"What is your name? Can you at least tell me your name? The name of your village perhaps?"

"So handsome, you are. So serious..." she responded, completely ignoring my questions. "He would have liked you."

"He?"

"Farewell, Zekiel," she said with a fleeting smile.

And then she disappeared.

Chapter Nine

"But *why*?" Simon protested. "Why must you do this?"

"I am sorry," I said, attempting to say as little as possible.

"But why? Why now? Why so sudden, like this?" his wrinkled mouth said. "And at this hour of night? This is madness!" he cried.

"I am sorry," I said again, having no other response.

"How long have you planned this?" he questioned. "How long?" he demanded.

I did not answer. All I could think about was that woman. How could she have vanished like that? Right before my very eyes?

"How long have you been planning this, this journey of yours?" Simon asked again. He was growing impatient, as he often did at times with me, his anger and disappointment beginning to show.

"Simon," I said, drawing him outside with me. "Please. Please try to understand…"

"Understand what? This insanity? You're up to something, and I demand to know what."

"I'm taking Merlin with me," I said, ignoring his question and approaching our donkey who was tethered to a post directly outside of our home.

"You're acting so strangely. Impulsively!" he cried, tears now forming in his eyes, his temper having been only temporary. I knew then he was only concerned. Confused.

"Simon," I said calmly. "The truth is, I *have* been planning this for some time. I just didn't know it."

"Or maybe…you didn't know how to tell *me*."

"Would it have made a difference if I had? I'm telling you now."

"This is different," he pleaded. "Because there is no cause to simply just leave in the middle of the night. Come to think of it, this entire night has been most peculiar for that matter. Why, it's a miracle the whole village hasn't gone mad. What with that strange sign in the sky, some say we are doomed. And now this?"

"We are *not* doomed," I reassured him, loading the animal with but a few supplies. "Everything is going to be fine, Simon. You'll see. No one will even remember in a week's time."

"But what of you? Where do you plan to go? *What* will you do? The Church needs you, Zekiel…"

"Someone else needs me more," I snapped, immediately regretting my words.

"*Who* needs you?" he demanded, and I knew this exchange was wearing on him.

"Something *else* is calling me," I clarified, attempting to cover the slip. It hurt me to lie to him like this but I knew he wouldn't understand. He continued to stare at me, his old face sad and torn with grief.

"Look, Simon," I began again, having to respond to that face. "Maybe, God is calling me to a different path, maybe something else. I honestly don't know. But whatever it is, whatever life I am to have, I…I know that it is not to be found here. I've been here too long, Simon. Far too long. Please try to understand."

Simon cast his head down then and I knew he wasn't going to try and stop me.

"At least let me give you some provisions," he finally said. "If you insist on leaving me, and leaving the Church, then I won't have you go off completely unprepared."

"Then you are fine if I go?" I asked him.

"Do I have a choice in this? No. I'm simply very much aware that I cannot stop you. I...I long feared this day would come," he admitted, new tears forming in his eyes. "Long did I want to believe that your place was here with me. Here with the Church, to follow in my footsteps. But your eyes. The look in your eyes always said otherwise."

"My eyes?"

"Come, Zekiel. Come with me," he bade, ignoring the question.

Simon re-entered our small home which was connected to the much larger church, and I followed on his heels. He was moving very fast, fast for Simon anyway, and he was taking bits of this, and that from our stores. Mostly food he gathered, even some of his freshly made famous stew. Blankets he collected also, along with his sharpest knife. He was practically giving me a small fortune.

Finally, he raised a finger, as if some wonderous idea had struck him and quickly ran to his bedchamber where he retrieved a small leather pouch.

"This is from the collection plate," he admitted, hefting the small pouch and shaking the contents.

I knew it was filled with coins...what few coins we had.

"This will be our little secret..." he continued. "But is it not the Church's place to help those in need? Even my own adopted son?"

"Simon..."

"Listen to me, Zekiel. I have always known that there was something very special about you. Something very special indeed. You've been a wonder to me all these years and a blessing...and I have never, not once, been ungrateful. You've been a good son to me. The son I could never have..."

I silenced him with a long-lasting embrace and he gently sobbed into my shoulder. Indeed, I would miss him. I would miss him very much.

After a moment we separated, and I inspected my gear one final time.

Merlin was ready...and so was I.

Chapter Ten

By the following few evenings, Merlin and I were well beyond the village of Scarborough and on our way to York. We had at least a full week's travel ahead of us, perhaps more, before we would reach those borders, at least according to Simon's estimation.

The night was cool, much as it had been of late, and I turned my gaze to the sky. Again, I bore witness to that same mysterious star, moving as it had before, slowly, silently, streaking across a backdrop of stars. I felt a chill from the slight breeze that moved over me and drew my cloak in tighter, turning my thoughts once more to the mysterious woman I had met only the night before.

How had she known my name? I wondered. I couldn't recall having mentioned it, nor had I introduced myself. Of that I was certain. Would even swear to God by it. And yet *she knew*, somehow she knew...unless I was by some chance mistaken. But even then, several days removed from our encounter, I felt as if I could remember every last possible detail. And the mention of my name was only the start of things I could not explain away rationally.

Who was she? And how did she simply vanish? Such a thing was impossible! And yet, I know what I had seen. And what about this strange omen which continued to appear in the sky? Had this anything to do with her disappearance? Did it have any significance? Was there any connection?

I quickly banished this last question as I realized such thinking was beyond foolish. Still, she *had* disappeared and she had known my name. Of this, there could be no doubt. But how could such a thing be possible?

I consulted my memory for all I could remember, but nothing that I was able to recall could explain how such a trick had been done. I hadn't so much as even blinked when she had inexplicably vanished. Not even the slightest sound of a person running away.

"Damn!" I swore, unintentionally startling my donkey. He made a noise that sounded like disapproval and found myself laughing until doing so made me think of Simon. He had always been so fond of Merlin.

I sobered almost immediately, recalling again how I had left him so abruptly. It truly pained me to have done so, but I knew he would not have understood. Even I didn't fully understand these rash actions…and now I had left my home.

The impact of my decision suddenly dawned on me then and inside I couldn't help but feel torn. For even I couldn't believe I had left my life behind. Simon abandoned. Just like that. Alone. And for what? A woman, no less. A woman, whose name I did not even know…along with my own selfishness and senseless pursuits.

The oaths that I had taken, the vows I had sworn to uphold should have forbidden any such action. Leaving my post like this. And all at once I felt as though I had betrayed myself, my studies, those teachings, and perhaps even God himself.

Simon. But it was Simon whom I had betrayed most of all…not to mention an entire village, which no doubt was starting to look upon me as his eventual successor.

Yet in all my confusion, this moment of self-pity and now countless sins, I know I longed for her. I longed in my heart to *know* her.

I confess that in all of my 23 years, I have never *known* a woman. Never in the biblical sense. And while her face remained firmly etched in my mind, her body, her voice, her lips...her cold, cold lips; I knew in my heart, beyond what I desired physically, I desired more than anything to know who this woman *was*. To know the truth. To answer these maddening riddles.

It was then I noticed Merlin was gradually tiring.

"Can you not move any faster, Merlin?" I teased, removing myself from these thoughts. "Maybe we should stop here for tonight," I considered, speaking out loud while surveying our current surroundings. "This is as good of a place as any and by Simon's reckoning, and if we keep to our pace, we should arrive in York no fewer than five days." Merlin, of course, said nothing and merely maintained his slow pace. "And besides," I added. "I am fairly certain that you are rightfully as hungry and as tired as I am."

I brought Merlin to a welcome halt but the truth after I had thought about it, was that I wasn't nearly as hungry as I supposed. Still, my feet were tired, as were Merlin's no doubt, and a solid rest would certainly do us both some good.

I unloaded Merlin's heavy pack at once, tethering him to the closest tree and set about preparing a small camp.

The ground was flat, thick with worn grass as I had deliberately avoided entering the forest which remained directly to the East, but would still, in fact, serve as the border to my camp. As long as I kept to the road, what road I could make out (another good reason to stop for the night), I intended to stay well clear of those dangers. Naturally, I felt quite safe within the forest near my own home but out on the open road, with dangers untold, I had no plans of entering the wood unless I had no other course. Especially at night when wolves were known to be about.

Merlin was soon cropping at the lush grass, tired as he was and like Simon, old age was beginning to show. And yet, he remained as strong of a donkey as ever and had always been my friend.

"Ha, ha, ha." I laughed out loud. "My only friend, the donkey." I said moving over to him. He paid me no attention, of course, far too busy eating and I gave him a friendly pat on his neck.

Not much later, I finished my own supper. Just a bit of stew that Simon had prepared for me, but it had been thick, and the meat was good, making for an excellent meal.

The small fire I had made was then starting to die down, and I took that as a sign that it would be wise to take heed and do the same. After all, it had been a tiring two days.

As I laid down upon the soft turf, wrapped in heavy blankets, my thoughts once again drifted to the peculiar events that had occurred only a few nights before. With her image still fresh on my mind and my memory clear, I tried to remember that entire conversation, lingering on every strange detail.

Something then dawned upon me.

Witchcraft? Maybe this woman had been a witch. Such tales were commonly told but I had never met anyone who claimed to have had an actual encounter with one. *Could* she have been a witch? Did she somehow fool me into thinking she had actually disappeared when it could have been nothing more than a clever trick?

My teachings through the Church had made it perfectly clear that those suspected of practicing dark arts were evil. Simon himself had said such people were evil, for such individuals did not worship God. But as far as our small village was concerned, Simon *was* the Church. And by extension, *I* was the Church, and knew firsthand that any person bearing any resemblance to these things could only be the work of the Devil, and as such, should be avoided at all costs. And yet, here I was, potentially seeking out such a person, on the trail to God knows where.

A sudden rustling nearby, brought these thoughts to a halt. This noise coming directly from the forest's edge.

I jumped to my feet immediately and shot a glance over to Merlin. He remained silent but had his ears perked; and while he was not yet alarmed, I knew he had heard something as well.

An animal perhaps?

I reached for my staff, which was a little more than a stout walking stick, but if it was an aggressive animal, it was the only weapon I had. I did have the small knife of course, the one Simon had given me for cutting simple things, but it would hardly prove useful against a pack of wolves.

The rustling sound rapidly drew closer, and I to it, moving low now against the ground. I had purposely chosen to camp on open land, hoping to steer clear of dangerous animals, but I had also chosen to do so in order to see clearly any and all who would approach. I realized now how foolish this was, as it was equally easy to see me and yet I now had no choice but to wait for the intruder. But if I could see this creature first, whatever it may be, I may yet still retain the element of surprise.

I gripped my staff tightly, my fear quickening, and I think my body started to tremble, thoughts of wolves invading my mind. How easily they could take me, rip at my flesh...

No. The sound indicated a single entity. A single person? Maybe a lone wolf? Whatever it was, it was covering ground fast. Making directly for my camp. Merlin snorted nervously and pulled at his tether, starting to grow uneasy. I was increasingly anxious too. I draped the hood of my cloak over my head, my long blonde bangs streaking out like razors.

With little warning, the source was suddenly upon us. Not an animal, but a person dashing out into the open. I sprinted to my left, unseen, moving as quickly as I could while the person pushed past, only to skid to a sudden stop, no doubt alarmed by the sight of my donkey along with that of my camp. He knew then he was not alone.

I sprang from the ground, eyeing no weapon, and prayed that this person was unarmed. Regardless, I was not about to gamble away this chance. He whirled on me quickly, sensing my movement, only to be blocked by my staff.

I closed my eyes, the rightful coward I actually was, and made to strike...

Chapter Eleven

Val saw the staff too late. It swept under her legs, throwing her off balance and she met the ground roughly, landing flat on her back. The staff that pursued her shifted and settled below her chin and told her in no uncertain terms that she was trapped.

"Please..." she cried, quite out of breath, her own face hidden by the hood of her cape. The staff moved slightly away. "Please...do not hurt me," she begged.

The staff was immediately withdrawn. Free to move again, she took a glance at her captor to see that a hood concealed her face as well. Her? She thought. Out here? Long blonde hair was all she could see...

"You're a woman," he said, surprising her, removing his hood. This was no woman, but a man she realized, with unusually long hair. Long-but only in the front, she noticed. Strange.

"Forgive me, my lady," the man said. "I mistook you for a thief or an animal. I certainly did not mean to strike you. Are you hurt? How did you come to be out here alone?" he asked. "Could you kindly remove your hood?"

Val obeyed, trying to remain calm. Wary, she watched her new captor carefully, her face now fully visible.

Her hair was much longer than his, long on all sides, and black. She appeared younger than he, but certainly no more than a year or two. She was pretty, if not beautiful, with dark brown eyes that accented her hair color. Her figure was short in stature, medium build, attractive, her bosom a bit large for her small body. She wore what appeared to be a darkly colored dress, slightly exposing her cleavage, but this she immediately covered with the cape she wore over her ensemble.

Her captor stared for only a brief moment, seemingly disappointed. He spoke again after a moment.

"Forgive me for striking you, I beg. I truly meant no harm. Seeing as you ignored my other two questions, might I at least know your name?" he asked, offering his hand. She took it reluctantly, alert for foul play but allowed him to help her to her feet. He made no aggressive motion.

"Your name?" he repeated patiently.

"V-Val," she said. "My name is Val." He nodded.

"Why were you running, Val? A bit late for that, yes?" he questioned after a moment.

Could she trust him? She wondered. He was certainly not a large man, quite short and small himself, but he had been swift with that staff of his. The small knife she had concealed would certainly pose no threat to him. He might even have a knife of his own...

"Why were you runni—" he started to ask again but an anxious bray from his donkey cut through the night, distracting him.

"Shit," she swore, at the sound he had not at first heard. The donkey brayed again and pawed the ground. This time, he heard it too. Someone else was approaching. He gripped his staff tighter with suddenly sweaty palms.

"We have to hide," she said quickly, giving no reason.

"Who is following you?" he said, recognizing the look on her face.

It was fear...and a feeling he knew all too well.

With no answer forthcoming, he pulled his hood back up, concealing his face, those distinctive long blonde bangs hanging free as before. He quickly started to collect all that he could, food, blankets, anything that he could carry. He moved about his camp meticulously and silently gestured for her to do the same.

"B...Bandits." Val answered at length, selecting one of the bags containing food. "Evil men. Thieves," she finished, drawing her hood to conceal her face similarly. She had no choice now but to trust him and he the same, relying solely on her word.

Yes, he thought silently as the sounds drew closer. It sounded like more than one. Unmistakably human...for they were being far too bold and noisy.

"How many?" he quickly asked, offering his hand again.

"At least three. Maybe more," she said, taking it. His other held his staff and multiple bags of supplies were slung over his shoulder.

"Can you climb?" he asked and she nodded in response. "We climb then. We haven't much time."

He pulled her along with him deeper into the forest, desperately searching for a suitable tree. Uncertain how much time remained before they were seen, he chose one hastily, dropping his staff. Unfortunately, the lowest branch was too far for her to reach.

"I will have to lift you," he said, his voice coming in a whisper. Val nodded again, trust no longer an issue. She simply had no other choice.

He moved behind her and placed his hands on her hips and lifted, picking her up easily.

"I can almost reach it!" she said, looking for a grip and he responded by lifting her higher. "I got it!" Almost too loudly, as one hand found purchase; soon followed by the other. "Only...I cannot pull myself up," she whispered, immediately correcting her volume. "I think I need a bit more help."

Having no other option, he placed his hands on her bottom, giving her a solid push. She reached a bit further and managed to pull herself up the rest of the way, her weight no threat to the sturdy branch.

"Climb higher," he instructed and Val nodded again in response.

But having now to make his own climb, and realizing he could not carry his staff with him, he quickly called to Val once more.

"Wait. Val. Can you reach my staff?" he said, extending it upward. She nodded again, finding it easy to reach and took it with her free hand, relying on the other to keep a firm grip. This was no time to fall by accident or through sheer carelessness.

"Hold it just a moment," he said, suddenly springing up from the ground, both arms finding the branch easily. He climbed up a moment later to join her only to signal that they needed to go higher still. And then, seemingly by no coincidence, even as they continued their ascent, they were able to see from their vantage point a total of three men enter the small camp. They had had just enough time.

Val's companion had taken back his staff and he motioned now for the two of them to be very still. Val nodded in agreement, needing no verbal directive. Once they were as comfortable as they could be, given the circumstances, both gazed out towards the small camp which was not difficult to see, largely due to the small fire that still burned there. The men were already scouring the area, tearing the small camp apart while Merlin brayed piercingly, making the men's voices somewhat difficult to hear.

"Bah! The girl's not here. But it seems to me, that someone else aint here either." The tallest one sneered. He was lanky, thin, and carried a small sword. The two others, one a small portly man, the other lean but no taller, nodded in unison. The tallest one spoke again.

"Looks like 'our someone else' don't care about this here donkey either," he laughed, moving towards the animal. The donkey was kicking about. Afraid.

"Oh, I'm not going to hurt you, you poor creature, but I am going to take you," he snickered, grabbing for the donkey's reins. Merlin was restless, hysterical even, resisting the foreign hands.

"Help me, damn it! Both of you!" he shouted to the other men. They dropped what belongings they had taken, following the order immediately.

They tried to calm the animal with soothing words and calm tones but the donkey was bitter, restless, and kicked about for several minutes. Finally, due to exhaustion and at long last accepting defeat, the donkey settled down.

"I led them straight to you," Val whispered sadly to her companion. She realized then that had this man wanted to betray her, he could have already done so. She knew she trusted him, at least to this extent, and she suspected she could find herself confiding in him further. After all, he had helped her escape, risking his own life, along with his possessions, never hesitating to trust in her warning .

"Those men are evil, as you have said," he whispered back. "And they would have cut my throat regardless of us helping one another."

He obviously recognized these men as dangerous, and no doubt had appreciated her advanced warning. Had she not appeared, they might have searched here anyway...and he would have been helpless against all three. Furthermore, had he been caught unawares, they would have easily overpowered him and taken the donkey regardless. And while she may have likely saved his life, she could not help but feel responsible for bringing her troubles upon him. She wondered then what recompense he might take up with her after the trio was gone, provided they could stay hidden. His face, however, remained just as hidden, concealed under the hood he wore, along with that of his emotions.

The thieves made ready to leave shortly after, having looted what remained of his belongings, along with the donkey, but both still managed to breathe a sigh of relief. And once they were long gone, clear out of sight, he turned to Val once more.

"We shall stay here tonight, taking turns on watch. We should be safe enough, at least under the cover of night, but we should take no chances, thus one of us must always remain awake. I think it's safer to move about during the light of day, and by that time, let us hope they do not return."

Val wasn't so sure about that.

"If it suits you, I shall take the first watch, so take some rest if you are able. I will alert you if our situation changes."

"I'm not really tired," she confessed, no longer whispering.

"Neither am I," he returned after a moment. "Which is why I offered to go first."

He slowly removed his hood then and took a moment to sweep back his long bangs but they simply fell back in place, extending to nearly halfway down his chest, his hair parted perfectly down the middle. He tried to offer an encouraging smile, knowing her to be in an uncomfortable position, and remaining in the tree would effectively prevent any restful sleep. She smiled back briefly only for his smile to abruptly disappear a moment later. Noting he now wore a serious look, she suddenly feared for her safety. Was he going to try something?

"Who were those men?" he asked, unmoving. "You said they were evil and to that extent, I believe you. How did you come to be running from them? Did they harm you in any way?" His voice was calm, gentle and he waited patiently for a response.

The truth was, Val did not know how to answer. Did she dare tell the truth? This stranger had initially attacked her, yes, yet he also had not offered her up to the men, nor had he tried any further aggressive actions. At least not yet. He seemed to recognize her hesitation.

"You still don't know whether or not you can trust me," he gauged.

"Yes," she whispered back softly. Her dark eyes quickened.

"Yet, I still don't know what your business here is either. For all I know, you may be a thief yourself." He paused only briefly to let his words sink in, seemingly testing her reaction. "However," he started again, "I believe you *not* to be a thief, and so if you will permit me to make clear my position..."

Val held her breath.

"You are not my captive...and I have no intentions of bringing any harm to you."

Val felt immediate relief, for he had answered the most important question.

"You are free to go, as you wish...and likewise my order to stay low for the night was merely a suggestion. In our haste, I failed to mention that." He paused again, pondering a solution. In a moment, he spoke again. "Do you wish to leave?"

Val considered. She had trusted this stranger thus far, and no harm had come to her. Now he was giving her a choice. Was this some sort of trick? A test? Would he swing the stick suddenly if she decided to move?

Cautiously, she began her decent from the branch that held her and though the man looked disappointed, he made no attempt to stop her. She proceeded all the way down to the lowest branch while the man continued to remain still. She paused to collect her thoughts.

If she hung from the branch and dropped to the ground, she would need his help to climb back up. But if he harbored other intentions, perhaps he would make them known then. She decided to continue her rouse.

She clung to the branch as she had done earlier, getting a good grip before lowering her body down. She did so easily, hanging for a moment, then gently dropped to the ground. She made a small noise from the impact but managed to land on her feet. She then brushed off her dress, merely to stall, but the man remained in the tree, refusing the bait and continued to watch her impassively. She pretended to walk away then, moving a short distance but no attack came from behind. He had given his word that he would not harm her and he appeared to be validating the statement. She even then dared to walk far enough away as to be out of his eyesight, careful herself now for any other threats. If the thieves had hidden to wait in ambush...

She stopped. This was far enough, she thought to herself. She decided to wait several more minutes, just to be sure, but heard not a single sound. Convinced she was safe for the moment, she retraced her steps, back to the tree that they had climbed. The man, of course, was still there, perched up high, perfectly still, his hood still clear of his face. Val decided upon one final test.

"I will need your help to climb back up," she called up to him, cautious not to speak too loudly.

"I thought you were leaving," he returned in an equally quiet tone. It was hard for her to tell, but it looked as if he was smiling.

"I-I decided to stay," she said, firmly crossing her arms.

"As you wish," he politely agreed and started to make his way back down, leaving his staff behind. "What made you change your mind?"

She did not yet respond, instead finding herself preoccupied with how quickly he had moved about the tree, for in a moment he had already reached the same branch she had used to jump down. He clung to it with both hands only to swing his body free. He dangled now, needing only to let go but instead swung a few times, as if it amused him, before dropping to the ground, landing in a tight crouch. He then rose to stand before her.

"What made you change your mind?" he asked again, a serious expression on his face.

Time for the final test, she thought. Before he could react, she suddenly reached for his face, pressing her lips against his own in a kiss. If he tried something now...

But he did not. He instead backed away sharply, wearing a confused expression.

"What did you do that for?" he asked, sounding mildly annoyed. Val stood still.

"I...I had to test you," she said, no longer doubting him.

"Test me?"

"To be sure you had no other intentions," she put in for him.

"Other intentions?" he asked, puzzled. "You still don't trust me?"

"Trust is something earned," she retorted solemnly. "And also in short supply these days."

He nodded, understanding.

"Maybe now we can really talk," he offered. "My name is Zekiel...Zekiel Raven."

Chapter Twelve

"So tell me, why were those men following you?" I asked the woman, very much interested.

Coincidentally, this 'Val' was seemingly as mysterious as the first woman I had stumbled upon only...only now Merlin was gone, due to this chance encounter.

I privately wondered if the two women were somehow connected. As if it were more than sheer coincidence that had orchestrated these two strange events. Coming across a woman alone at night, in a forest of all places was certainly not common. But to meet two? Only days apart? Was this woman going to suddenly vanish as well at some point? I waited patiently for an answer.

"I think it would be best if we were back in the tree," she suggested, ignoring my question. "You said yourself it would be safer."

"Of course," I agreed, realizing she was right. The tree would be safer.

"You're going to have to give me a push as before," she said, already lifting her arms. There was no mischief at all in her voice.

I lifted her exactly as I had done before, first by her hips, then following with a solid push to her posterior. She climbed up just as easily as she had done earlier, almost as if she had prior experience. Such a skill was uncommon for a woman, leastways from my experience, and I could not help but to remain curious.

Once settled in our previous locations, I repeated my question.

"Why were those men following you? And for that matter, may I ask what are you doing out here all alone?"

"Couldn't I ask you the same thing?" she asked with raised eyebrows.

"I'm sorry," I apologized, feeling chastised. "Please forgive my rudeness. I tend to be very direct…and you are under no obligation to answer any of my questions. And if you must know, I am but a simple traveler, on my way to York."

She hesitated then, seeming to linger on her thoughts but after what seemed to be a dreadfully long pause, she opened her mouth to speak.

"I was their prisoner," she confessed. "Captured not two weeks ago." Another long pause. "Those men, as I have told you, are evil."

Her face suddenly flushed with anger and while I did not doubt her words, I got the impression that she was not yet telling the whole story.

"How did you come to be their prisoner?" I asked, wanting the full tale.

"First, you must tell me something of yourself," she stipulated. "When I find cause to trust you further, perhaps we may speak more freely." I nodded, understanding her proposal.

"Let us play a game then," I offered, remembering a game that Simon and I used to play. I had been a child then, and it had been more of a guessing game but perhaps it would suffice.

"What *kind* of game?" she asked with raised eyebrows.

"Please allow me to explain," I quickly answered, noting the suspicious expression on her face. "This is a simple game, a game of questions. *Just* questions," I felt the need to add. "I want to know about you and you want to know about me. That much we can agree upon, yes?" Val nodded back, seemingly interested, and so I went on. "We take turns, one question each. Simple questions at first…"

"And what if I encounter a question I do not wish to answer?" she interrupted.

"Then I will choose another. There is no need for us to get too personal. We answer only what we choose *or* feel comfortable with, but we still take turns until both of us are satisfied. Does this seem fair?"

"What if one of us decides that he or she no longer desires to ask more questions, leaving the other still wanting to ask more? What be the penalty for that?" she inquired.

"There be no penalty in this game. And since I believe I have nothing to hide, you are likely to yield first," I said with confidence. "There are no questions that I am afraid to answer."

"So confident you are," she said, eyeing me carefully. "Do you so easily discredit me?" she asked in a sly tone.

"No. I don't. I am simply well aware of who I am," I responded, attempting to defend my statement.

"Then let us find out, Zekiel. Let's find out who you are. Everyone has secrets…" Val said, narrowing her eyes, more than ready to begin. "First question. What's with your hair?"

"What?!" I asked surprised, stifling a laugh. "That's your first question?"

"You said simple questions first and this one is simple enough. Now answer. Or do you yield?"

She certainly knew how to play this game! Fortunately, I thought myself to be witty on occasion as well. "I will answer your question," I said, accepting.

"When I was found by Simon, only two years old or so, my hair, or rather my bangs specifically, were as they are now…albeit not quite as long, while the rest of my hair was cut short, as was the fashion at the time." I turned my head for a moment then, to give her a much better look. "Upon finding me," I continued. "Simon felt inclined to cut it but he tells me I protested. Quite a bit actually. My parents, whom I do not remember, had obviously cut it this way and I have kept it long in their memory, a memory I cannot recall. I know this all must sound very strange and I know it looks peculiar but…I am actually quite fond of it."

I realized, having finished my explanation, that I might have said too much. I had a habit of rambling.

"What do you mean, you were found by Simon?" Val questioned, appearing to be keenly interested. I almost went on to explain, but I focused, regained control of my position, and realized that it was now my turn.

"My question first. Remember? Then you may ask another," I quickly stated.

"Oh. Sorry," she apologized, embarrassed. "It is your turn," she admitted, wearing a serious look again.

"How did you come to be their prisoner?" I asked.

"You said easy questions first."

"Is this question not easy enough?"

Val paused before answering, perhaps not accepting my argument, and was looking far more guarded. Maybe I had pressed too hard. Too soon. She remained silent a long, long while.

"In time, we will come back to that question, yes?" I inquired. "And perhaps too, you were right. I will ask a different question." At that statement, Val seemed to visibly relax again, my first question apparently too personal to answer.

"Tell me, where are you from?" I asked.

"London. But I was born in Ireland, actually."

"Ireland? What brought you to London? And if I may further inquire, are we not some ways away from your home?"

"You had your question. It is now my turn, remember?" she returned with a smile. It was my turn to be embarrassed. I relaxed, nodded, and waited for her next question.

"What do you mean, you were found by Simon?" she asked, no doubt curious as to my previous response.

"I never knew my parents," I said, finding myself a bit saddened by recalling the memory. "Long ago, again when I was around two years of age, well; at least Simon thinks I was at least two. I could have been three. Regardless, Simon found me in a small basket on the shores of Scarborough, overlooking the North Sea, abandoned by whoever had brought me there. Simon recalls finding me sometime in the early morning while taking a brisk walk when he spotted the basket from afar. It was old and in poor shape and I was wrapped only in a few dirty blankets. He immediately inquired of everyone in our small village, but no one had any clue as to where I had come from, nor did anyone attempt to lay any claim to me. So, Simon did. And not by any coincidence, Simon happened to be our village's priest. Father Simon, everyone calls him. But to me, he was always Simon, and for better or worse, my father." I paused then, remembering again how I had left him. Left him to pursue my own desires...

"You're a preacher's son?" she asked surprised.

"It is now my turn."

"Of course." She conceded with a smile.

"What brought you to London? England, for that matter?"

"I came here when I was only a little girl," Val began. My mother died of complications during my birth, my father I never knew. Not even his name. My aunt and uncle took me in as one of their own, and they lived and still live in London. They have another daughter my own age but we were never treated the same. I was always the burden, always the cause of various problems...according to my uncle. I hate him."

In her voice there had been anger, depression. And while I trusted her words and believed her story, I felt myself wanting more details. But after a long pause, long enough to once again calm herself, I realized she would say no more on the current subject.

"It is now my turn," she finally said softly.

"Ask your next question."

"You are a preacher's son, yet you appear to be quite proficient with that staff of yours. Does a preacher not study the works and doings of the Church? Or does he spend his time practicing for battle? It would appear you are not all that you seem. Tell me more about this life of yours."

She was certainly as curious as I was and I realized I liked that about her. "Is it true what they say then, about the preacher's daughter?" she went on. "Only in this case, a son? Is it true that they are almost always the opposite of what their parent represents? Do you get into a lot of trouble, Zekiel?" she asked, flashing a mischievous smile.

"That was actually many questions, but I will answer. Simon taught me how to read, write..."

"You can read?" she exclaimed, then quickly corrected herself. "Oh, sorry. Go on."

"As I was saying, Simon taught me many things. The ways of the Church of course, but also the ways of the world. The ways of the country. He educated me with all that he knew and yet oftentimes we did not always see eye to eye. We had many arguments in the course of my instruction. I was always asking a lot of questions and sometimes disagreeing with his point of view." I smiled. Val smiled back.

"I guess in a sense I did not seek conventional ways. I admit to getting into mischief as a child, and even more so as I grew older. But you see, Simon had a singular view when it came to all things. Many things I could not accept, such as his insistence that my place was with the Church, regardless of all else I fancied. I rebelled, quite naturally, and sought out my own views and in due course, found myself interested in the study of weapons. Envying the knights, the warriors you would hear about in tales. Simon disapproved of course, and said that a preacher's life should not be spent fighting, but teaching. Teaching the works of God." I paused only briefly, glancing in Val's direction, to see if I still retained my audience. I was surprised to see that she was still listening intently and so I went on, unabated.

"I believe in God of course, along with the ways of the Church, but I also believe in something else. A different point of view. More or less that there's more than just a black and white way of looking at things. I longed to know of different beliefs, different people. 'Do knights not protect the Church?' I inquired of Simon many times. 'Does he not protect it by battle?' And just because I be the given son of a preacher, does that give me leave to run away from battle should I find battle on my doorstep? Do I not protect this Church in which I pray ? Simon would not listen of course, nor answer, calling me foolish as well as naïve. He forbade me as a young youth to meddle with weapons and/or warfare. Naturally, I refused to listen and practiced as much as I could without his knowing. I had no sword of my own of course, but I made do with what I could find, using simple things such as a stick. A long branch. Soon after, I developed a love for crafting wood. Only weapons, you understand, but I made many different things; swords of various lengths, a few staffs, I even once made a bow. The bow never worked," I added with a smile. "Have you ever seen a jester?" I asked her. "This is not my question to you, just so we are clear," I added with a smile.

"Is this similar to…to a performer? Somewhat like a minstrel?" she asked, searching for the right term.

"A minstrel be one that sings. A jester does other things for entertainment. Such as turning tricks. Somersaults, various acrobatics. Such groups of performers typically never stay in any given location for long, traveling to earn a living. I bring that up because on one such occasion, we had such a troupe in our village to give us all a performance. I was amazed. Simply amazed at what some of these people could do. Sorry, am I boring you?"

"No," she laughed sincerely. "Please continue."

"Very well. But you are to stop me should that change. Agreed?"

"Agreed," she replied, then making a slight adjustment to make herself more comfortable.

"As I was saying, I was simply amazed at what some of these folks could do. Soon after they left our village, I found myself out in the woods, practicing all that I could remember from the performance. I wasn't very good at it," I laughed. "Oftentimes landing on my head but I entertained myself well enough. Simon would find bruises on my arms, my legs, on more than a few occasions and my reply was always that I had fallen out of a tree and that I would try to be more careful the next time I was at play. My excuses seemed to keep him at bay...for the most part, but on most occasions, he simply left me to myself...during the free time I had, of course. I honestly never really got along nor played with the other children in our village, most of them labeling me as the village bastard...naturally behind adult ears. They would tease and taunt, always when I thought myself to be alone. 'Look!' They would say. 'The bastard thinks he is a girl, for look at the way he dances!'"

"Only you were not dancing. Were you?" Val asked.

"No. Thus I tried to pay them very little attention, content to play in my own private world. Alone. Seldom did anyone see me with my make-shift weapons or practicing my tumbling, which was always misconstrued as 'dancing' and thus when they *did* see, or bear witness, I never let on and would immediately stop whatever it was I was doing or working on. I was actually growing quite proficient after a time, or at the very least, certainly thought I was. I confess to you that I honestly have no idea for I had nothing really to compare myself to...although, I will have you know that I was landing on my head far less frequently."

Val smiled.

"I never did consider myself to be much of a warrior. Certainly, no knight. My imagination, I'm sure, was well beyond any actual *skill* I possessed.

"And in terms of combat, I confess...I honestly believe myself to be somewhat of a coward. I talk a lot and think too much. The thought of a man rushing me with a blade turns my blood cold, for who would not be afraid to take a sword to the gut? Or the thought of a dozen men surrounding you, only to cut you down? I have only enough mind to envy it and to admire braver men who have no such fears. I want that courage. To not be afraid of such things. To be strong both in the Church and to be strong at arms. I admit, often have I fantasized of doing battle and or to take part in one, but the truth of the matter is, likely I would lose all nerve should I find it at my door. A twisted fantasy is all it is." I paused for a moment for the words to sink in, not only for Val, but also for myself. I did, in fact, daydream much too often.

"You need to understand Val, that I swung at you out of *fear* and nothing else. It was purely instinctual. Nor do I think I could do such a thing again. It was just a lucky blow and nothing more. Ha! Look at me, I fear I have said far too much already and I believe I gave you answer enough. For if you give me the time, so grateful am I to have a listener, I could easily talk the night away. But alas, I want to hear more things concerning yourself and those men, and perhaps what has happened to my dear friend, Merlin. Does my answer suffice?" Val nodded. I would ask my next question.

"What became of this life of yours? With your uncle and aunt? Did you run away? Will you answer me this?"

Val nodded again, growing more comfortable in my company. She would answer.

"My life, much like yours was mostly spent alone. That's how I know how to climb. I went off a lot when I was only 6 or 7 or so. Not very far, mind you, but far enough to explore the edges of the nearby forest. I am certainly not as agile as you appear to be, but I can certainly take care of myself. For the most part." She paused suddenly as if remembering something. Something she looked unsure how to say. She even took a deep breath.

"When I was a little older," she continued. "My uncle started to demand more and more help from me in the kitchen, along with countless other duties, while his own daughter was allowed to do as she would please. He scolded me often for being late at times to his summons, but I always did what I was told...that is, until he decided to change everything."

"What do you mean, decided to change everything?"

"Understand Zekiel, I was growing older then, becoming the young woman I am now. My body was changing...and...and he *noticed* these changes. Took an interest."

"Val? What are you saying?"

Val paused again. She was evidently leading up to the answer to my question, taking her time to do so and her face became sad suddenly. A second later she spoke.

"He started to rape me, Zekiel. I could not have been more than 15 or 16, but the bastard raped me!"

She wept suddenly, and almost lost her balance. I reached out for her but she was quick to steady herself and made a gesture that she was fine. She continued to weep, no longer speaking any words, and I began to understand what I had at first feared.

"Those men," I said in a low voice. "Was one of them your uncle?" She shook her head 'no.'

"Then you ran away, did you not? That is how you and I crossed paths?" I asked, continuing my line of questioning. To this, Val nodded 'yes.' "They found you, these men, didn't they? Found you all alone in the wilderness?" Again, she nodded 'yes'. Her crying continued but I could not stop my inquiry now. I had but one more question.

"How long have you been with these men, Val? How long have you been trying to escape?" But Val continued to say nothing, her head now buried in her lap. "They took advantage of you as well, didn't they? Didn't they, Val?" I asked, my voice rising in volume.

"How long have you been with these men? How long?" I demanded, my anger growing. Not for Val, but for these men, these horrible, despicable men…along with her bastard of an uncle. I believed her tale, honest and true, for there had been no lie in her eyes, and it was obvious that this young woman needed my help.

"How long Val?" I asked a final time, and so serious was my tone that only then did she slowly raise her head, her sobs becoming far more controlled. She had only but to speak.

"Three weeks," she replied. "About three weeks."

The night was quiet around us and neither Val or I spoke another word. I could hear only the faint sounds of small animals rustling here and there. Scampering along in the dark.

I think it was fair to say at this time, that this part of our conversation was now over.

Chapter Thirteen

WHEN VAL AWOKE she was sore, her body felt stiff. Rubbing her eyes and then letting out a great big yawn, she soon found herself to be completely alone. The man 'Zekiel' was nowhere to be seen. She looked idly around while still clinging to her branch but saw no sign of him, nor heard at all any sound. His staff was also gone and he had left not a single trace. Not so much as a clue. How long had he been gone? She wondered. Had he simply left her? Even after all that they had discussed the night before? Would he have done that?

"Good morning," a voice called from below, nearly shaking her loose from her limb. A quick glance told her it was Zekiel and he had several pieces of fruit in his hand. His staff, nearby on the ground.

"Good morning, I said," he repeated. "Or do they not say such things where you are from, Ireland was it?" He inquired with a warm smile. Relief rushed through her, having been only momentarily startled and she smiled back in return feeling the sudden need to respond at once.

"Good morning," she returned and immediately began to make her way down. She made the climb easier, much easier in the light of day and in a few short moments stood before him. Now that she could see him clearly, under the bright sun, she found him to be a rather good-looking man. Even with that strange hair, she thought.

"My camp, they raided and took much of what I had," he began. "But they missed some fruit, so I thought we might as well have breakfast. I know I cannot speak for you, but I'm starving. I found some bread too. Seems they missed enough for a meal in the dark. Thankfully for us, since York is still some ways away."

"You mean to take me with you?" she asked, surprised at this notion.

"Of course," he said, as if the answer had been obvious. "Is it not right to help someone in need?" he asked with a small smile.

"I suppose so," she responded carefully. "But what do *you* need, if I am to gain this protection of yours?" she asked in a mischievous tone. She was by her own reckoning starving herself, but welcomed this new conversation while a brighter light was in the sky. The light of the day seemed to make all things better and she welcomed the feel of the warm sunshine on her face.

"I don't know about protection. Didn't I tell you I wasn't much of a fighter?" he responded. "Besides, all I really want is a little company on the road. If you'll come to York with me, we might be able to find you some help. Maybe work. And I might, though I doubt it, find some way to get Merlin back. I mean to go further than York but come, and let us eat like civilized folk. You must be hungry too, right? And whatever plans you have, for I do not wish to assume, can wait until we've had a small meal, agreed?"

"Agreed," she said, more than grateful for his continued kindness.

Breakfast was better than she had guessed. Zekiel had found some cheese as well, and along with the bread, it turned out to be a finer meal than Val had seen in months. She ate the fruit greedily, juices spilling forth down her chin, pausing only momentarily to wipe her mouth of the sticky substance. After this, she ate the bread and cheese which seemed to fill her body with a new strength. Her joints had loosened a bit and she found herself looking forward to taking to the road with this unexpectedly kind stranger. He still appeared to be more than he seemed, but he was kind, polite. Having finished his meal first, he then patiently waited for her to finish before he addressed her again.

"By my reckoning, though I cannot say for sure, York is still a good 20-30 miles from where we stand, but keeping the way is difficult. But if we keep a good pace, I gather we can reach York in less than a week's time. More if we face bad weather. There isn't much to carry and I will take most of it since it does belong to me. Oh, I almost forgot, you must be quite thirsty. Luckily, I kept my canteen on my person." He then produced a medium-sized water bag from under his cloak and offered it to her at once. She accepted this with many thanks and took a long draught.

"Better save some for the road," he cautioned, and upon hearing this, she pulled the bag away from her lips.

"Oops! Sorry, Zekiel. I forgot," she said, feeling rather embarrassed.

"Take another drink if you wish, but try not to take more than that. I'm guessing we might get thirsty again before our road ends." He took the offered water bag back but upon replacing it, wore a peculiar look. As if he had forgotten something.

"Forgive me," he said, addressing her. "I presumed you would travel with me...though I did not formally ask nor give consideration as to your wishes."

Val smiled, offering no objections and Zekiel nodded his accord.

He turned away then and went off to collect the few items that remained. The thieves had left most of his clothes but had taken most of the food. They had also left an empty bag behind and he used this to gather all that remained. He soon finished and came to stand in front of Val once more, a few bags now slung over his shoulder.

"Well, we best be getting off now...and hopefully, we won't meet any other dangerous folk on the road. We should still be careful, if their camp is near as you say...and should probably travel quietly as well, although I'd welcome any soft conversation. Be cautious and walk beside me. We can travel at a comfortable pace."

He certainly was direct she thought, as she moved next to him taking their first steps together. His gait was a little fast, but comfortable enough, and she soon found the pace to be rather enjoyable. Fresh air was moving in and out of her lungs and she breathed the morning air freely. Many times as a girl she took such invigorating walks...when she was able to steal away from her uncle, that is. All at once she seemed to remember everything. Not only her uncle but the thieves, the weeks which she had lost, this new stranger...along with everything she had confided in him last night.

Had she told Zekiel too much? Revealed too much? He said that maybe he could find her some help. But what help did he think he could give? Escorting her to York was one thing, but what would become of her after that?

"Zekiel..." she asked tentatively. "What help in York do you think you will be able to find for me? A new home? Work? I don't get it."

He remained silent for a few moments while their pace remained constant. The scenery, around them, unchanging.

"I don't really know, Val," he confessed after a pause. "I guess it was more of a notion than an actual well thought out plan. What I mean is, is that I mean to do for you what I can but tell me, what were your plans before you came into trouble with the thieves?"

"Are we playing that game again?" she asked. "Do you *want* to play that game again?"

He shrugged. "If we must. But not too intense this time. Simple answers will suffice. Agreed?"

"Agreed," she said, almost pretending to sound like him. He was so dreadfully serious all the time.

"Very well. Question," he said.

"Answer," she replied with a light air.

"What were your plans before you came into trouble? Where did you intend to go after you left your uncle?"

"You like to get to the point a lot, don't you?" she asked. He merely threw her a glance, his brows raised. "Alright..." She relented giving in. "The truth is, I didn't know where I was going. I guess I was trying to get away...from *him*. I guess I thought I'd think about that once I was far away. Very far away."

"That was your plan?" he asked sincerely, his tone not at all disrespectful.

"I didn't leave without any food, silly. I had enough sense to at least pack. Now it's my turn, where the hell are you going? And what's your reason?"

This seemed to give him pause and he said nothing for several minutes. His head was now facing the ground as he walked, obviously in deep thought or reeling from some form of shame. Val merely kept the pace and waited for his answer.

"I'm looking for someone," he said at last. He said nothing more for a few more moments before Val could not help herself.

"That's it? That's all? 'I'm looking for someone?'" she blurted out. "You'll have to do better than that," she finished.

"Very well." He shrugged. He seemed to do that often too, she noticed. "To tell you the truth, I don't have a plan either," he admitted. "Yes, I am looking for someone but I don't expect I will ever find this person. That in itself is only one reason."

"And the other?" she interjected.

"The other is that I desire to see other things. Other lands. My life has been a good one, and Simon has ever been kind to me, but I want more. In my heart I just want...more."

"What do you mean more? Specifically?"

"I don't know. Maybe a wife, a child someday? And yet even this is not my truest desire. I want more than anything to have a purpose in life. A place where I belong. Perhaps a place where I might even find courage. A life with...I don't know. Purpose."

He stopped suddenly and after a moment, Val knew he would say no more. She reasoned that he, himself, did not fully understand his mind and yet she could hardly blame him. She too had begun her own journey for similar reasons, seeking the unknown, seeking change, simply seeking for that which she did not have. A different life.

And yet, Zekiel had not by his own admission, had a hard life. True, he had never had any friends or any lasting relationship, at least so far as she knew, but he had had Simon, who at least treated him like a human being. *Not like me*, she thought. Still, she was not jealous nor resentful, and found herself starting to rather like him as a person. He just seemed honest. Both with himself and his outlook on life.

"Is it my turn again?" he asked softly after a time.

"Ask your question," she said without hesitation, both of them still maintaining a comfortable pace.

"Did you ever figure out what you wanted in life? I mean, what it was that you were hoping to find?" he asked in that same serious tone of his.

"Honestly, when I was captured, the only thought on my mind was to find some way to escape. And to be perfectly honest, it's still a little difficult...a little difficult to be around a man. I mean, after all...after all that has happened."

"If I may ask," he interrupted. "Am I making you uncomfortable? Asking such questions?" he inquired politely.

"No, Zekiel, no." She responded immediately. "It feels...it feels refreshing actually. It's just not at all something that I am used to. Conversing like this. I'll also have you know that you have been nothing but kind to me and that in itself has helped a great deal. It really has. Having someone to...you know. Really listen."

"I'm just sorry for what you've been through. I really am." he said sincerely. "But tell me, Val, what about before? Before you were captured? What were you hoping to find?"

"Before that, as I have said, I honestly hadn't had much time to think about it. I only wanted to get away from the life I had...kind of like you, I guess. But now you tell me, who is this someone? This person whom you wish to find?"

"You didn't really answer my question," he returned, sounding more as if he were stalling, attempting to delay her next question.

"Oh, yes I did," she countered. "I *told* you. I don't know. And that's the truth, Zekiel. I really don't know. Now...who is this person, whom you wish to find?" she asked deftly, proving that it was once again her turn. He paused a good while before answering.

"I met her only once. Three nights ago to this day," he said, barely audible, his voice not much more than a whisper.

"She?" Val questioned. "She must have been quite some woman to ensnare a saint like you."

"I am no saint... nor am I a preacher. Simon's the preacher."

"Come on, Zekiel," she responded playfully. "You're lying, and I thought preachers weren't supposed to lie. You *are* a saint, or so you appear, despite your minor indiscretions. When have you done any wrong?" she pressed.

"I was not at all raised as Simon wanted to believe," he began slowly. "I had my own thoughts, my own desires, aside from the Church...where most of my time was spent. I desired, and still desire a woman like any other man, but a lot of what Simon taught me, good values, good manners, the gospel? A lot of it I did believe. I still do believe. But you see, he thought me to be an angel, despite the many arguments we would have." He sighed. "But most of those arguments ended by me driving the poor man to tears."

"What were your arguments about?" Val asked.

"Most of the time it was merely his insistence that I was to follow in his footsteps. That my place was with him, with the Church. But it was something I simply could not accept, despite his greatest efforts to convince me otherwise. It just wasn't for me, you see. That's not at all to say I was ever ungrateful for what he was able to give me, but after a time, I realized that Simon could only teach me so much, show me so much. And so behind his watchful eyes, I pursued all else I would know. Regrettably, while I will always love my home, understand that our small village only had so much to offer. How was I then able to accept my place, by his side, without knowing all else I might be? To serve the Church is more than a noble profession and there is much satisfaction in helping those in need." Zekiel took a deep breath.

"But when two nights ago, when I met this woman, this strange, strange woman, I knew then it was time to leave. Not that I thought I would likely see her again, but I knew I could no longer stay. I took it all to be a sign. The push that I needed to leave. But don't you see Val? That is how I have sinned. I turned my back on Simon; I turned my back on the Church, my village...all to pursue my own desires. I have to ask myself then, what kind of person does that make me? I've long known that I was never worthy to be a priest, despite all the good I know I could have accomplished, nor is it Simon alone whom I have abandoned."

"It sounds to me as if you are carrying an unnecessary amount of guilt," Val observed.

"How can I *not*? I left those who would have come to depend on me, such as when Simon would reach the age he could no longer continue his work."

"But be that following in his footsteps was not at all what you desired, is it fair to burden yourself which you know is not in your heart? Some may see you as selfish...but I don't."

"But that's *exactly* what I am. Selfish."

"No," Val insisted without doubt. "I think people misuse that word. Or rather use it for their own selfish desires."

"What do you mean?"

"You said it yourself, Zekiel. It's *not* the life you wanted. And while some may call you selfish, aren't those people equally selfish for demanding from you what they want you to be?"

"I did not take you to be a philosopher," Zekiel weakly attempted to joke.

"Ha!" Val laughed. "I am far from that, I am sure. But do you want to know what I think?" And when Zekiel did not immediately respond, Val went on. "I think that had you not left, had you not left to follow your own heart, I wouldn't be here, free as I am now."

She stopped then suddenly and turned Zekiel to face her.

"If it hadn't been for you…" she continued.

"You give me far too much credit…and *did* just as easily climb a tree in which to hide."

"I would not have thought to do so," she argued. "Nor would I have been able to keep my wits about me had you not taken control of the situation. In many ways, I owe you my life."

"Again, you give me far too much credit."

"I disagree," she stated matter of factly. "And you want to know something else?"

"Do I have a choice?" he mused.

"Not at all," she replied with a smile. "Not unless you would like to remove yourself from my company?"

"The thought did cross my mind…" he quipped.

She smacked him then in the arm, wearing the same playful expression and started to walk away at once, only for Zekiel to quickly rejoin her by her side.

"The day is far too bright to dwell on whatever past we have left behind. Don't you agree?" she asked, looking directly ahead.

"I honestly could not agree more," he concurred, finding her contagious smile more than enough to lift his spirits.

Chapter Fourteen

THE PAIR CONTINUED to walk long into the morning, making very good time. The weather was pleasant, the sun was bright, and the path had been easy and sure. Birds were chirping, a pleasant breeze was in the air as if spring had officially arrived. But as the hours wore on, even on a beautiful day such as this, Zekiel could see the need for rest.

"This appears to be as good of a place as any to stop and take a short rest," Zekiel said, eyeing the sun. "Looks to be about noon to me. You hungry, Val?"

"Starving." Up until this moment she hadn't realized how hungry she was, for she was simply enjoying the company of this new-found stranger while also enjoying her newfound freedom.

Zekiel laughed. "Good," he added after a moment. "I was beginning to think I was the only one getting hungry. We don't have much, of course, but I suppose it will have to do."

He went about making a hasty camp and produced the contents of his sack: A few pieces of fruit, bits of bread, and a container of what appeared to be either stew or soup. Val couldn't tell which and decided it didn't matter. Zekiel's makeshift lunch looked delicious.

"I meant to give you some of this stew last night but I couldn't risk making another fire," he apologized. "I don't have much left but there should be enough for both of us. Of course, it's all cold now and that just won't do. Let me see if I can get a fire going so we can eat this nice and hot."

Val couldn't contain her eagerness. Again, this kind man was taking it upon himself to handle everything and being appreciative of his kindness, Val volunteered at once to help.

"I can make a fire as well as any...if only you would gather some wood, Zekiel. I would offer to go look myself but..."

"Say no more. I'm not comfortable with you going off alone and I can be back before you know it." He threw her a wink which unconsciously made her blush but hurried off before he could even take notice.

As promised, he returned within a few short minutes carrying a small bundle of sticks and these he set down where Val had dug a shallow hole.

"There. This should be enough," he said. "Now to make a fire." He started to go about this task when Val interrupted.

"Please, Zekiel. Sit. You've done enough for me and I would like to make myself useful. Please take some rest while I prepare the meal."

"Very well," he said, looking pleased as he sat himself down. "Thank you." Val smiled back, only this time she blushed openly. But whether or not Zekiel noticed, she couldn't tell. And then another thought struck her:

She *wanted* him to notice.

After the meal had been prepared, they ate in silence and afterwards, Zekiel found himself stretched out on the cool grass, arms tucked behind his head.

"A man could get used to living like this. On the road, traveling to God knows where, simply enjoying the sunshine."

"You seem entirely too easy to please," she remarked, throwing a playful smile his way.

"Is that so?" he joked. He paused then as if in reflection. "Simon raised me while providing only the basic needs. He taught me early on not to be wasteful and to always be happy with what you have...but I suppose that what I am doing, my leaving the Church...contradicts that somewhat," he lamented.

"Everyone deserves to be happy, Zekiel," Val reminded him. "Despite the expectations we are sometimes burdened with. And I think it's unrealistic, as well as unfair, to live one's life that way."

"I know. I guess what I meant is, without getting into it again, is that I don't aspire to have material possessions nor even a great deal of money. I simply want to enjoy life. And despite my leaving Simon, as well as the Church, I am not ungrateful for my lot."

"Then you are different from most men, to be sure," she replied. "All the men I have known have wanted either money, power, or both."

"Then I do not envy those men," he answered. "Being raised by a preacher, food was always provided and I always had a warm bed in which to sleep. For most folk, that's more than what could be hoped for in these times."

"But tell me, Zekiel, if you don't mind my asking. If all those things are enough for you, and I speak not about being ungrateful, then what do you hope to find? Out here, I mean. On the road?"

He paused for several moments. "Honestly?"

"Of course."

"Honestly, I don't know. As I've told you, I don't really know what I'm looking for. Yes, my life back home was pleasant enough, but deep down there has to be something more. More than the comfort and security that Simon would have had me boxed into. And it's not as if I am searching for either riches or power, as I've told you, just more to life itself. I just...I just wasn't *happy*, Val. And selfish intentions or not, which is not the same as being ungrateful, I mean to find my happiness. And so, I stand to believe, that if I never venture beyond the walls I have built around myself, then I risk missing out on all that may lie beyond. This is the mystery I hope to solve."

"You want to find that woman." She responded somewhat irritably without meaning to. Why did she care?

"I...I don't know what I hope to find, Val. And truthfully, finding this woman was only a pretext to exploring the open country. To find my place in the world. Yes, I admit I ventured off because of her initially, hoping to find her...but now? Now I'm not so sure. That search seems to be in vain," he finished, casting his head down.

"Well, I hope I'm decent enough company while you search for your answers," she said with no small amount of jealousy. Jealousy? Why was she jealous? Was she starting to develop feelings for this man? After such a short time? But Zekiel, as always, seemed oblivious to her true meaning and she couldn't help but to admire these innocent qualities.

"I know we haven't known each other for much more than a day, but I am glad to have met you, Val," he said after a moment. "And I hold to my earlier promise of trying to find you the help you need. You've been an attentive listener to all of my ramblings and I couldn't have asked for a better companion on the road."

"Is that so?" she said, moving closer to him. What was she doing???

Well," he laughed. "You are certainly better company than Merlin."

"Who is Merlin?" she asked, lying down beside him in a similar fashion. "You mentioned that name before."

"My donkey. Simon's donkey."

But once he said this, he seemed to recall that the donkey was no longer with him. Merlin had been stolen, along with his meager possessions, leastways possessions he no longer had on his person. His face grew sad and Val took notice immediately.

"I-I'm sorry about your donkey, Zekiel. I'm sorry for Merlin," she said, her emotions taking over. "Maybe...Maybe I should just leave you alone altogether. I seem to bring nothing but trouble." She immediately rose to her feet, intent on leaving. Zekiel rose as well.

"Val," he said calmly, but she was no longer taking notice of him. She had even turned her back, was literally preparing to leave.

"Val," he repeated, a bit more urgently. "Val!" he abruptly shouted with far more volume than he had intended.

Val cringed from his harsh voice while memories of the bandits arose in her thoughts, triggered suddenly by his tone. She was all at once both fearful and uncertain about what to do.

"Val," he said a fourth time. This time slow, patient, kind. This seemed to break the spell for she finally turned to him, stared deep into his eyes; and after seeing the look upon his face, she just knew, though she wasn't sure how, that Zekiel could never cause any harm.

"I'm...I'm sorry, Zekiel. I didn't mean to become so agitated. I'm still having a hard time...knowing that I am free again. The memories of where I was..."

"Don't apologize. I shouldn't have gotten angry with you and there's no need to explain with what you've been through. Come..." he said, starting to break apart their small camp. "A walk will do us both some good. Clear our thoughts. Are you fine to resume our journey?"

As always, Zekiel seemed to find a solution. She did want to get moving again.

"Of course," she answered. And then as an afterthought: "If we ever get the chance to get Merlin back..."

Zekiel stopped. He was thinking about something, probably the lost donkey again, but Val didn't think that was it.

"Look, Val," he started, turning to face her. "I want you to understand something." His tone had shifted to that of his serious voice again. A voice Val was beginning to like. He was commanding without meaning to but there was flexibility within his tone. He was direct, but not oppressive. Calm, but very serious. It made him seem larger than his short frame should have allowed and he resumed his speech very carefully.

"I wish I still had Merlin, this is true. But the reality, as I see it, is that I would not be alive if it hadn't been for you. Nor would I have had the opportunity to make your acquaintance."

"I still caused you lots of trouble, Zekiel."

"No more than I would have found on my own. They would have killed me, Val."

She nodded, not disagreeing.

"And besides..." he resumed thoughtfully. "You smell much better than Merlin, thus your presence here is more welcome than his."

Val burst out laughing, enjoying the joke.

"Both of us smell like shit, Zekiel," she remarked, using a derogatory word for the first time.

He looked at her quizzically, having not expected such a comment and suddenly burst out laughing himself, unable to keep a straight face.

"I suppose I haven't bathed in days and sleeping in trees doesn't help. Nor does walking all day under a hot sun," he said after composing himself. "Do I really smell like shit?"

His response similarly threw her off and together they shared another laugh.

"I thought you said you were a preacher's son," she challenged him. "Simon certainly wouldn't approve of that language, now would he?" she teased.

"There are a lot of things that Simon would not approve of," he continued to laugh. "But what Simon doesn't know can't possibly do him any harm."

"I suppose not," she agreed. "But neither have I been able to wash up in days either. They..."—and she said this with a tinge of anger— "they let me wash up every other day or so, but it was for their benefit more so than mine, as they used these opportunities to leer at my body."

It wasn't something he intended to do, but Zekiel took a long hard look at her. At her body. And his eyes unconsciously lingered on her large breasts. Val noticed immediately and the chastised Zekiel stumbled. He tripped very neatly over a rock in his path and found himself falling to the ground, meeting it fast.

"That's what you get, preacher's son!" she scolded with laughter. "Did you get a good look?"

"I'm...I'm sorry, Val. I didn't mean to stare. I'm...I'm ashamed." He looked away from her then, even as he tried to collect himself, staring hard at the ground. He was clearly embarrassed.

Val knelt down beside him.

"I'm not mad, Zekiel," she said sincerely.

And that was the truth. She wasn't angry at all. In fact, she had welcomed him looking. And then she realized that she had actually *enjoyed* him looking. And while this thought was somewhat foreign to her, it wasn't an unwelcomed thought either. Zekiel was just so presumably innocent, so impossibly shy. It was a complete reversal of roles for her. At least what she had grown accustomed to.

For as soon as Val had been old enough to be considered attractive, she had always had a hard time discouraging the advances of men. She was naturally beautiful, noticeably endowed, and even more so than what would have been considered typical. And through it all, she suffered their looks, their generally unspoken desires, along with much-unwanted attention. And while she rejected all those who stared at her long enough as to make her uncomfortable, along with those advances, she had no such feelings she realized when it came to Zekiel.

She certainly had not known him for long, under a day no less, but from what she was able to determine, desire did not overrule his thoughts. In fact, he had been nothing but kind, understanding, respectful, and conscious of her feelings, viewing her instead as a person as opposed to an object. He would ask before he would do, suggest rather than demand. Apologize when he felt he had done any wrong.

No, she didn't mind him looking at her at all. In truth, she was quickly discovering that she was enjoying his attention, along with that of his company. And then, just as curiously, another thought struck her. She very much wanted him to look at her again. She wanted him to find her pretty. And along with finding him to be a bit of an enigma, she also found him to be quite attractive as well, handsome...more so than she even dared to admit.

And while he still had not done anything out of the ordinary to convey those same feelings towards her, she understood that men were going to glance at her, even a shy individual like Zekiel. But just because he possibly found her attractive as well, it nevertheless failed to indicate whether or not he would do anything about it.

With Zekiel, she felt as if she was still in control, a feeling she was coming to enjoy. She liked the idea of gaining a reaction from him and she liked how his glance had made her feel, even if it was presumably innocent, though intentional. He simply wasn't objectifying her and she was smart enough to know the slight difference. There was just something about him. Some connection between the two of them. Something she couldn't quite put her finger on. Almost as if she were quickly being drawn to him for reasons she couldn't explain.

"Question," she asked, helping him to his feet.

"Answer," he said after a moment, still wearing a look of embarrassment.

They walked for a few moments before she asked her question, his patience with her never an issue.

"Have you ever been with a woman, Zekiel? I mean, *really been* with a woman? Is it ok that I'm asking you this?"

He didn't rebuke her but hung his head low as he walked. He then simply shook his head 'no' as a response.

"I see," she said, going silent for a time. After a brief moment, a sudden impulse came over her. And before she even realized what she was doing, she stopped walking, turned to him, and planted a firm kiss on his lips.

This time, he didn't resist. In fact, he gradually started to kiss her in return, but to her surprise, after such a brief moment, he was already pulling them gently apart.

His eyes bore the look of confusion but he didn't appear to be angry. He even wore a small smile.

"Why did you do that?" he asked in all sincerity.

"I..." she stammered. "I...I wanted to thank you for helping me. Properly I mean."

"That's the second time you've done that," he pointed out.

"The first time was a test, Zekiel."

A moment of silence passed. All was still. But a moment later, Zekiel spoke.

"Well, that was...quite the thank you, but not at all what I am accustomed to...for helping someone in need, I mean."

They both burst out laughing, breaking the momentary tension.

"You certainly have a way with words, Zekiel."

"As do you...but tell me, why did you really do it, Val?"

"Is that a question?"

"Aye."

"You didn't ask properly," she countered with a smile.

"Oh. Right. I apologize. Question."

"Answer," she said teasingly.

"Why did you really kiss me?"

Her playful banter could afford no more delays, but she was hesitant to answer. No, not hesitant. Unsure. In truth, a great part of her kissed him simply to see what he would do. How he would react.

She certainly felt comfortable around him, surprisingly so to say the least, especially when her unfortunate past was always weighing upon her decisions as well as her judgment.

She wanted to believe that part of the reason for kissing him was simply a test. A test to see if even now, he would try and take advantage of her. But as the moment faded, and presented with such a specific question, she realized that testing him hadn't even been on her mind.

She knew for certain that one reason for kissing him had simply happened by reflex. It wasn't something that she planned. After a long moment and feeling the need to say something, she finally offered the best answer she could.

"It...it just felt like the proper thing to do, Zekiel. I guess I was just living in the moment."

"The moment?"

"Living life, Zekiel. Just taking experiences as they come. I'm honestly not sure why I kissed you. I simply...felt the need to do so."

He reflected on this for a bit and then resumed his walk while Val took up her place beside him.

They didn't talk much after this, both content to be alone with their thoughts. Thankfully, it was not at all awkward and both enjoyed the lingering silence. After all, the sun was still shining bright, the skies were clear, and it was all together a very pleasant day; and neither would be quick to spoil it.

After some time, they spoke here and there but nothing of any real importance. Their conversation was light in nature, there were no more flirtations, both simply enjoying each other's fine company. They took regular intervals of rest and encountered no signs of trouble, nor was there any indication of pursuit. Something Val was silently thankful for.

They covered many miles that day and hiked long into the evening. By nightfall, Zekiel gradually slowed his pace, looking for a suitable place to camp for the night. The clouds were becoming thick and dark and the fine weather they had enjoyed all day began to turn. The wind was picking up, the temperature rapidly dropping, and both drew their cloaks around themselves tighter.

They had just made their way down a gradual slope and here the land appeared to level off. It was here that Zekiel paused.

"This should give us some shelter from the wind...and we should still be able to make a fire. I'm afraid we don't have much for supper though, as I only have a few pieces of fruit. I think a little bread yet too. I'm sorry I don't have more to offer, Val." She was certainly hungry, starving in fact, but under the circumstances, they were lucky to have anything.

"Maybe I can catch something for us to eat," Val suggested.

"You can hunt?" he asked.

"No," she laughed. "But I do know how to lay a simple trap. If we are lucky, perhaps we will be fortunate enough to catch a rabbit."

"How can I help?" he offered. "I've always been fortunate enough to not have to catch my supper. That makes me sound rather useless and perhaps even a bit spoiled."

Val tried to sympathize. "None of us can predict the life we will be given, Zekiel. You didn't ask for the life you have, so how is it fair to judge?"

"How has life been fair to you?"

"I got to meet you."

Zekiel smiled. But as an afterthought, he differed, "That was very kind of you to say Val, but I'm not sure I see the truth in that. I don't have anything for us to eat besides what very little we have, nor can I provide a roof over our heads. And judging by the look of those clouds..." He paused, looking to the sky. "It looks like it will soon rain. Our supper might have to wait."

Chapter Fifteen

ZEKIEL WAS RIGHT. The rain came swift and hard, as if a portion of the sky had opened up to let the onslaught through. The day had been warm, if not pleasant, but any warmth brought on by the day was erased in the next few minutes. The air grew chill and the rain only increased its barrage until before long, both of them were thoroughly soaked.

"We need to find shelter, Val!" Zekiel had to shout, his voice fighting against the wind.

Val could only nod. She was cold, miserably uncomfortable, but where could shelter be found? The storm only seemed to be getting worse.

Zekiel took her hand then and led them on. He had no idea where he was going and he couldn't see a dwelling anywhere. Strikes of lighting had begun in earnest.

"I'm...I'm cold, Zekiel," Val admitted after a while, unable to contain her discomfort.

"I am too, Val. I am too."

They continued to make their way through the storm and direction soon became irrelevant. They were slowly getting off course from their original path, as the road itself was swiftly becoming a ruined mess of mud. The going was slow and the footing treacherous but they pressed on as quickly as they were able, having no other choice.

After what felt like an unbearable amount of time, for it was impossible to guess how long they had been out in the storm, they came upon a steep, rocky hill with no possibility to go around. At least not now when their visibility was getting worse by the minute. They had no choice but to struggle upwards, bit by bit, only to face a steep decline. With nowhere to go now but down, and no promising shelter behind them, they worked their way down carefully, even slipping a few times (fortunately suffering no injuries), to at last reach the bottom where they were at once instantly rewarded.

Directly behind them, against the stone outcropping that they had just descended, appeared to be a shallow cave, perhaps formed from centuries of rain itself. The opening was just large enough to admit one person at a time and with a bit of slight hesitation, again having no better option, they carefully made their way inside.

The cave, if it could even be called that, was impossibly small. It was dry, which was the most important thing, but neither could fully stand as it was barely large enough to admit six adults at most, tightly packed together, albeit hunched.

After a quick surveillance, and ensuring that the small hole wasn't already occupied, or went any further beyond that which they could see, they both threw themselves upon the cave's dry floor, completely exhausted. The ground was a mixture of both dirt and rock and while the ground wasn't flat or even very comfortable, it was a far better shelter than they could have hoped for. After catching his breath, Zekiel started to rummage through one of the bags he carried.

"I have a few blankets that are still somewhat dry," he began. "But I'm not sure how warm they will keep us, seeing as our clothes are thoroughly soaked. These blankets aren't very thick."

"We'll have to remove our clothes, Zekiel," Val suggested, taking control of the situation. "We could become fairly sick if we don't. We will have to use the dry blankets to cover us as best we can." Zekiel could only nod his accord. They didn't have any other choice.

It was difficult removing their rain-soaked garments in such tight quarters but they finally managed and were soon both naked. Zekiel even took their wet clothes and piled them in a way as to block the entrance as much as possible, and thus, deflecting a good deal of wind. It was dark inside the cave, darker still with the entrance partially covered and neither could really see the other, thus preserving what little modesty they could. They then draped the blankets over themselves but found they were still shivering.

"We will have to sit closer together," Val suggested, again not shying away from resolving their current problem. As it was, both were simply sitting side by side, stretching the blankets over them as widely as they possibly could. At Val's suggestion, they pressed closer together and gradually their bodies started to warm. They didn't say much after, focusing solely on sharing their combined heat until gradually both became very tired. It had been a long day and much energy had been expended from navigating through the storm and they had eaten very little.

"I'm not sure how much rest we will get but I think we should be relatively safe here," Zekiel commented, trying not to shiver. "With any luck, the rain will be gone in the morning and we can see about getting something proper to eat. I don't think we strayed very far from our path but I expect tomorrow to be difficult...but hopefully no worse than where we find ourselves now. I guess we should try to get some sleep."

"Zekiel?"

"Yes?"

"I'm still very cold."

"I'm sorry. I'm cold too. The blankets are helping but I wish there was more I could do."

"Would you..." she started to ask. "Would you be kind enough...to...to..."

"To what, Val?"

"To hold me? To share warmth I mean."

"I..." he started to say.

"This...this is fine the way we are," she continued. "But you feel warmer than me, and if it's not an inconvenience..."

"I could use the warmth too," he agreed. "How...how would you like me to hold you? I mean, that's to say, how would you be the most comfortable? I won't try anythi..."

She silenced him once more, again by taking control of their mutual problem by gently putting herself in his arms. He was suddenly very much aware of her feminine form and he felt her press her large breasts against him. She guided their bodies down as far as they could comfortably go, allowing them to almost lie completely flat on the ground, their backs slightly raised against the uneven floor. When she finally settled into a position that was comfortable for them both, Zekiel found her face only an inch away from his. And because of the closeness of their bodies and bare skin, Zekiel couldn't help but to naturally have a reaction. As it was, he was pressed as firmly against her naked form as much as could be possible, and immediately felt embarrassed and chastised himself silently. She felt this, of course, could even feel his tension, but didn't say a thing, acutely aware that he was in no way trying to force them into any sexual act, instead choosing to spare him any further embarrassment. In fact, she even managed to somehow push herself even tighter into his embrace and when she did this he slowly started to relax. She was keenly aware that his body desired hers, even if he had no intentions of his own. But by indicating that she was not at all uncomfortable, and by drawing herself closer, Val hoped it was sign enough, at least she had hoped he would view it as such, that she would not hold him at fault for that which he could not control.

It was hard to believe that she had met this man, this 'Zekiel' only the night before, and yet here she was, completely naked with him and trusting in him fully.

And before she could even stop herself, once again obeying her instincts, she sought his lips for the third time in a little over a day, giving him a soft kiss on the mouth, and as before he gradually, but slowly, started to kiss her in return. His body flushed with warmth but his arms remained where they were, firmly behind her back and he simply held her close.

"Goodnight, Zekiel," she simply whispered, and no more words were said. She then tucked her head into his warm chest and for once in her life, for as far back as she could remember, fell asleep with a smile on her face.

Chapter Sixteen

When I awoke the next morning, I found myself alone in the small cave covered with just one blanket. Where was Val? Where had she gone?

I immediately began to panic, fearful that something had happened to her and grabbing the blanket, quickly made my way outside.

The rain had given way to what appeared to be another beautiful day and gazing up at the sun; I knew it was going to be hot. But first things first. I had to find Val. I had to figure out…

"Good morning, Zekiel," a voice called from somewhere to my left. I turned immediately but due to my surprise, I lost hold of my blanket. I struggled to catch it, but the damage was already done and I found myself standing in front of her, fully exposed. I was relieved to see her of course, but not so happy with my sudden carelessness. I tried to retain my dignity while I quickly sought to cover myself. I think Val smiled.

"I was beginning to wonder when you were going to wake up," she remarked, and I noticed that she had the other blanket similarly wrapped around herself. It did nothing to hide her curves. I tried not to stare and for the life of me, I could not think of anything to say. Looking at her in the bright sunshine, I couldn't help but notice how truly beautiful she was. How did I not notice this before? Was I that daft? I tried to shake away the last remnants of sleep.

"Little quiet this morning, aren't you?" she asked, a hint of curiosity in her voice.

"I'm sorry, Val," I finally managed to say. "I didn't mean to sleep so long. After last night..." And then it hit me. I started to remember. We had been naked together, we had shared a kiss...

"After last night what?" she inquired, snapping me out of it. "What were you going to say?" I knew what I wanted to say but I was a little more than embarrassed to admit it.

"Question," she finally demanded.

"A...Answer," I blurted.

"After last night. You were about to say something. Say it." I was caught.

"I've never..."

"You've never what?" she asked, crossing her arms.

"I've never...I've never held a woman before. I didn't...I didn't mean to....to react. If I offended you in any way or acted inappropriately..." Val cut me off.

"We did as we had to under the circumstances. We could have gotten sick otherwise."

"I know. And it's not that. It's just...I mean...I'm sorry. I'm embarrassed," I confessed.

"Don't be embarrassed. We provided each other warmth and no harm came to either of us."

"Then you're not upset with me?"

"No." She smiled. "You really are a saint sometimes, aren't you?"

"I suppose I inherited some of Simon's manners."

"Such as lying with naked women in the middle of the night, in a cave of all places?" she laughed.

"Not quite. You know what I mean."

"I know what you *meant*, Zekiel." She laughed again. "Sorry. I'm having fun at your expense. That's not very kind of me. You're always so serious all the time."

"Is that a bad thing?"

"No. And do you want to know something?"

"What?"

"I like that about you. It makes you different. Look, Zekiel, you were the perfect gentleman last night while any other man would have tried something. Would have tried to take advantage of the situation. You didn't. I thank you for that."

But what did that mean? Did that mean that she would have been upset *had* I tried something? And what about that kiss? Was she just being appreciative like before? I felt overly confused. But why? Why did I care? None of this was within my realm of experience. I struggled to change the subject. "As long as I did not offend you..."

"You did not." Again, a smile.

"As long as I did not offend you," I emphasized, this time attempting to smile myself. "Then we can carry on as before. No harm done, as you said."

"Agreed." Another encouraging smile. I began to wonder in earnest if I would ever tire of seeing that. That smile on her face. That face that I...what? Found attractive? I desperately tried to focus.

"Our cloaks..." I began again, seeking to solve our most immediate problem.

"I hung them on those trees." She pointed, indicating where she had placed them. "They should be fairly dry soon enough, along with the rest of our clothes. We can't much cross England in nothing but blankets," she joked. "But what about breakfast? Have we anything left to eat?"

"We have very little. Wet bread mostly and a small bit of cheese yet. It will hardly be a good breakfast."

I gathered what I could from what we had left. Most of the bread was ruined and the cheese was meager at best. We ate in silence those next few minutes trying to savor every bite. We would need our strength to resume our journey and hunger was soon to become a more serious problem. After we had sufficiently rested and retrieved our cloaks (which were almost dry) I took up my staff to resume our journey.

Val and I walked long into the morning. We talked here and there, tried to maintain our spirits, but with no food and very little water left (I should have thought to place the water bag outside to collect the rain which would have been perfectly suitable for drinking), we had no choice but to take frequent rests. The sun was no help either, blazing unusually hot above us.

We tried to backtrack at first, attempting to find the road we had been on, but having lost our sense of direction in the storm, even with the sun's movement to indicate east and west, we still could have easily missed the road by less than a mile...and most likely *had*, since we found ourselves in nothing but open ground. Nothing but the gently rolling countryside and pockets of forest in every direction. I knew we had to make our way relatively south-west, but with no road, we had no real sense of where we were in relation to York.

I made the decision then to head towards the only thing we could see: the forest...of which in England, there seemed to be no shortage of. At the very least, I hoped, the trees would give us some much-needed shade. I had no intention of going much further than just the woods' very edge, as I still held out hope we would eventually find a road. But as the day wore on, the landscape very much unchanging, we decided to make camp for the night while we still had light left.

"I'm hungry, Zekiel," Val finally admitted while we were both gathering firewood.

"I know, Val. I am too. Say..." I remembered. "Do you think you could try and set a trap?"

"But with what?" she asked. "With no bait for a lure, no trap would do us any good."

I couldn't argue with her reasoning. I felt rather silly then, misplaced hope and all, for failing to see the obvious. It was almost as if she knew I felt bad for even asking, because she even offered me a slight smile, telling me as much. I was trying, trying to think of solutions...but I just felt awful.

We did manage to get a fire going, and by propping my cloak up with sticks secured in small holes (dug using my hands, no less), I did manage to create a small tent, which made for a rather crude shelter.

"It's not quite big enough for both of us," I wryly observed. "But you should be comfortable enough."

"Comfortable? But where will you sleep?"

"Just outside, of course. Someone has to keep the fire going...as well as keep an eye on things."

"Well...then at least let us take turns," she offered. "Or at least allow me to keep you company."

"It's fine. I don't mind...and one of us should get some sleep. There's no telling what tomorrow may bring...and we will need to be rested. More than anything, we need to find something to eat as well as water to drink." Val looked like she wanted to say something more but I cut her off.

"You sleep. I promise that I will take some rest or wake you if there is need. I'll be quite comfortable here in front of the fire. Now please, get some rest if you can."

Val obeyed, albeit reluctantly, and made herself comfortable inside the shelter I had provided. Many minutes had gone by, it was hard to tell how much, but after a while, I couldn't help but notice that she was stirring quite a bit. "Zekiel?" she called out only a moment later.

"Yes?"

"Do you think we will be ok? Find a town?"

"We will be fine. And surely our luck is bound to change," I tried to assure her, speaking as confidently as possible. But the truth was, I didn't know. I was doing everything I could for us, but had no idea if we had made any progress. If we didn't find something soon…a town, better shelter, food…

"Zekiel?" she called out again.

"Yes?"

"I'm having a hard time sleeping."

"Are you cold? Is there anything I can do?"

"Maybe," she said. "But I'm not really cold."

"Then? What can I do, Val?" Here she hesitated and a long moment of silence ensued. I turned from where I was sitting and faced her directly.

"Val?" I asked again, unsure as to what I could possibly do.

"The fire is not likely to go out for quite a while…right?" she asked.

"Well, no. I just added a few logs. Should suffice for quite some time."

"Then that should keep any animals away. Right?"

"Animals, probably. I'm not so sure about anything…or rather anyone else."

"I see," she lamented. "But…" she went on. "Do you really think we are in danger from anything else? At this time of night? I mean…do you?"

I thought about it. It was late. That much I knew. And the likelihood of anyone being about was pretty scarce. When my camp had first been raided, the sun had just set. It had been fairly early. But now? It was likely well past midnight. At least. "Very doubtful," I finally agreed. "But I told you, no need to worry. I can sleep right here. Right where I am…and will do my best to keep watch. I'm a pretty light sleeper."

"That's not what I meant, Zekiel. I'm not…I'm not really worried about those things."

"Then? What's on your mind?" I asked, curious now as to where this was going. "Just say. There's no reason not to."

Even from the small fire I had going, I could see her bow her head a bit. She was hesitating.

"Val. Say whatever is on your mind. Please. I beg."

"Zekiel."

"Yes?"

"Would you mind...mind lying next to me again?" she pleaded. "Just to sleep, of course."

Admittedly, I was caught off guard. "I...is there enough room though? I don't wish for you to be uncomfortable," I said stupidly.

"If you don't want to..." she started to say.

"No...it's...it's not that at all."

"Then?"

I got up, having no other response and moved towards the tent, then tried to work my way inside. It was extremely tight and I wasn't sure where I was supposed to go, where she wanted me. I think she noticed my struggles.

"Just lie behind me, Zekiel," she suggested.

I did as she instructed until I was behind her, facing the same direction now, arms at my side. She managed to cover us both with the few blankets we had and I felt her nestle in a bit closer, pushing herself into me, making for a tight fit.

I wasn't very good at this sort of thing and I didn't really know what else to do.

But once again, Val took control of the situation. She reached behind then, took my arms into hers, and gently but very deliberately put them around her. "See? Much better, right?" she asked me.

"I...yes," I agreed uneasily.

I admit that I was growing confused. True, we had lain together the night before, naked no less, and here we were again. And though she was no longer facing me, as she had the night before; this, being like this with her, felt no less intimate.

I realized too that I wanted this. I wanted this very much. And despite our mounting problems, the need for food, a way out of the situation we were in, there was no other place I would have rather been. I guess what was truly bothering me, is that I didn't know how to feel about it. About her. And for that matter, how did she feel about me?

Were we simply companions? Struggling together? Banding together to accomplish a common goal? Sleeping like this out of comfort? Or...did this mean something else? Then, as if I wasn't confused enough, Val took my hand. And whether this was a conscious act or not, she moved my left hand, which had only been around her, and placed it directly on her breast and there held my hand fast.

I couldn't prevent myself from becoming aroused again, and surely, if she was still awake, felt that too. But at that moment, hungry and exhausted, I forced myself to relax, held her just a bit tighter, and decided our problems could surely wait.

When I woke in the morning, Val was once again up before me. She was sitting by what was left of the fire in silence, arms around her tucked legs.

"Did you sleep okay?" she turned and asked, having heard me stir.

"Yes. Thank you," she nodded back. "Well..." I rolled out of my blanket, thinking to waste no more time, and hearing the growling of an empty stomach. "We best be off and on our way." Val once again nodded her accord and in only minutes, we broke our small camp and were once again on the march.

The problem was that our current situation was very much unchanged. I still had no clue as to how far we had strayed from our original direction, and unless we came across a town soon, or at least a path in which to lead us, I knew we could potentially starve. I was fairly certain that starvation would take more than several days, but it was still something to consider. Especially since I knew we were both very hungry and traveling all day drained our energy. My bigger concern was thirst and finding clean water. Under the noon sun, we would soon become desperately thirsty and have to rest often, much as we had to do yesterday, in order to conserve our strength. That would, in turn, delay us further while doing nothing to solve our immediate needs.

We continued to walk for several hours and before long, my fears were realized. It was getting hot, dreadfully so, and both of us were soon sweating and had no choice but to drink what we had left, which was little over a mouthful apiece. Val, for her part, never complained once and simply trudged along beside me, both of us saying very little.

We moved on, exhausted, following no discernible path and I knew in the hours that followed that we were hopelessly lost. The afternoon wore on and it became hotter still, and surviving was soon occupying my every thought. Even Val's beauty, which even the sun and rain could not diminish, could neither put me in better spirits. It had to be mid-afternoon, the sun still unrelenting, when Val suddenly stopped. Her sudden action caused me to fiercely grip my staff, fearful that danger was near. But as Val didn't seem the least bit alarmed, I loosened my grip tentatively and bade her at once to speak.

"What is it? Do you need to rest?"

"I do need rest, Zekiel, but that will have to wait. Can't you hear it? The sound of running water?"

I closed my eyes to focus, trying to locate the sound, but I was unable to hear anything. "Perhaps your ears are better than mine for I hear nothing but the wind. Are you sure you aren't mistaken?"

But Val was no longer listening to my words. Instead, she grabbed for my free hand and began leading me through a thick grouping of trees, her pace fast and swift. After a few moments, I started to register the sounds as well. It sounded like a river, perhaps even a stream, and as she attempted to trace the sound to its source, the distinct sound of rushing water became abundantly clear. My throat, alerted to these sounds, ached for a drink.

"Let us just hope that what we find is drinkable," she said, trying not to get our hopes up. "Despite how thirsty we are, drinking foul water would not help us." She continued to lead us forward.

After much searching and retracing our steps several times, we finally located the source: a long winding stream that looked pristine, undoubtedly clean for its water was crystal and clear. I could hardly believe our good fortune. But was the water really clean? Appearances could be deceiving and we couldn't risk getting sick. Getting down on my hands and knees, and giving Val a hopeful look, I cupped my hands and took a very small taste. The water was clean. It had to be.

"The water is good. Clean," I said, verbalizing my thoughts. That was all Val needed to hear. She threw herself down beside me and took some water in her own hands, caring not at all how much she spilled. With such an endless supply in front of us, we both drank deeply, quenching our thirst. I filled our water bag as well.

"We've managed to solve one problem," I said. "And I think I can solve the other."

"What do you mean?" she inquired. But before I decided to answer, I had to confirm my suspicion. I ran along ahead, following the stream, looking very closely at the water, trying to decipher the best spot. If I was right…I was. The water was teeming with fish.

"Zekiel?" she called, racing to catch up to me.

"Look at the water. What do you see?"

"I see…" Here she paused. "What am I looking for?"

"Fish. Look closely. Stare at one spot." She did as I instructed and after a few moments, her eyes confirmed the same.

"I see them, Zekiel! I see them! But how do we catch them?"

"With this!" I exclaimed, a bit too loudly, producing a hook from my pack. I brought out my line as well and began attaching it to my staff with a series of loops.

"But how did you know?"

"Scarborough, the place where I am from. We are a fishing village first and foremost and nearly everyone, boys and girls alike, are all taught at an early age how to catch a dozen fish with a single line and hook...but more importantly," I felt the need to add. "*Where* to look and *where* to cast your line. I may not be very adept at surviving in the wilds, but if there's one thing Simon taught me, it was how to properly catch a fish."

"But what about bait? What will draw the fish?" she asked concerned.

"That part is easy. We simply dig for worms. Like this." I used the butt of my staff then to crudely till the ground until the ground began to give way. I then got on the ground and started to dig a shallow hole. "We were fortunate that it rained the other night, for the worms should still be close to the surface," I explained. Val simply stood and watched but I could tell she was anxious to see if this was going to work.

It did. Before long, I had three plump worms in my possession and I presently placed one on my hook and cast my line out as far as I could.

Luck was with us, for within the hour I managed to catch not one, but two nicely sized trout. Val was impressed and clapped her hands repeatedly. I would have had three fish altogether, but one managed to get away, taking the third worm with it. Still, it was a nice catch and I felt very fortunate. We would eat well this night and our stomachs would be full.

"I think it would be best if we camped here tonight. Or at least around this general area," I suggested, taking another look around to locate a suitable spot. "With any luck, we can catch a few more fish in the morning and drink all that we can before trying to regain our original path. I know we somehow strayed from the road, but if we simply make our way south, we are bound to come across a town. At least then we might gain our much-needed sense of direction, and that in turn should guide us to the path we seek."

Val, at this point, had started to become very quiet, from the time I caught the fish. In fact, now that I was thinking about it, she hadn't said much today at all. Even after I made clear my plan, she only nodded in accord and made no comments at all regarding the decisions I was making for us both. Before we had seemed to work in tandem and I wasn't sure why she was being so unusually quiet now.

I fetched what we needed for a fire, but upon returning, much like before, she bade me to rest, still saying very little. She cooked the fish, and quite well actually, but we proceeded to eat in silence. She seemed deeply disturbed about something, but I couldn't imagine what it could be.

We hadn't had a single sign of trouble, with the exception of our one rough evening in the storm, and of course, having to go hungry for a time. And yet, as this day of good fortune drew to a close, she seemed to draw deeper and deeper within herself. I finally grew very concerned and as I prepared our camp for the evening, I tried to engage her in some light conversation, but she wasn't very talkative. Perhaps she was growing tired of being with me? My company? But what then of my own feelings? What about the kiss from a few nights before? And hadn't she wanted my company last night? Those few other times as well? Had I done something wrong?

The evening was still quite warm, but pleasantly so, and as long as no new storms appeared, we would probably be fairly comfortable, even so far as not requiring any shelter. I still used our cloaks to provide some sort of roof over our heads, as I had done the night before as I figured it to be better than nothing.

At present, we simply sat outside our crude shelter, on the cool grass, both remaining disturbingly silent. We sat like this for at least an hour when she finally broke the silence.

"Was she pretty?" she asked abruptly, keeping her head low, averting her eyes.

"Was who pretty?" I asked rather surprised. And then I understood. She was asking about the woman I met several nights before.

"Was she pretty?" she repeated.

"It…" I began, trying to recall. "It was very dark that night. I could barely make out her face."

"But you saw it," she accused.

"I...I suppose I did. Briefly at best."

"Was she *pretty*?" she asked again, this time a distinct irritation in her voice. I felt compelled to tell her the truth.

"She was."

"Was she prettier than me?" But when she asked this, she looked directly at me, straight into my eyes and I felt nearly locked in place.

I didn't want to answer. Not because I was afraid to tell her the truth, but because at this given moment, I was honestly unsure. Val, in her own right, was undeniably beautiful, stunning in fact, and as I tried to think of an appropriate answer, I struggled to understand the meaning of all of this.

"She was, wasn't she?" she finally said, tired of waiting for a response.

She got up suddenly as if she meant to leave. But instead of leaving, she spoke again softly, her back now facing me. "When we reach York, assuming we eventually get there... what then? What of me? What of you?" Here she paused and turned to face me directly.

"What becomes of *us*?"

Chapter Seventeen

ZEKIEL REMAINED SILENT for some time, occasionally poking at the fire. He finally shrugged, not knowing what to say. Val finally spoke again.

"When you figure out the answer, be sure to let me know." And then clearly annoyed, added. "I'm going for a swim."

"Now?" he blurted. "At this time of night?"

"Why not? Can you give me a reason for that?" she asked irritably.

She started to get undressed, right there in front of him and in a moment stood stark naked before him. But unlike the night before, when they had been inside the cave, the fire now enabled him to see her form fully and completely. He instinctively drew his eyes away, feeling it impolite to stare.

"Look at me," she commanded. "Look at me, Zekiel."

He slowly raised his eyes to meet hers, taking in the complete view of what stood before him. She was impossibly beautiful, every last inch of her, and at that moment he felt a longing for her that he hadn't recognized before. Both the past two nights he had reacted, quite against his own will, but had he desired her even then? But he knew the answer to that as well, despite trying in those moments to deny it, and the truth was that he had. But what man wouldn't react to a sight such as this? To a woman such as this? What man could look away? Was it simply lust he was feeling now or something more? Her sudden nakedness left him very much confused and he struggled to find his thoughts.

In their short time together, they had started off as companions but as the hours and days lingered on, that quickly became a friendship, and then just as quickly after that, that friendship had no doubt developed into something more. Was it love? Was this what love felt like? Was this what he had been subconsciously searching for? Hoping for? To find a wife of his own? To start a family of his own? The very thought of viewing her as a marriage prospect started to put things into clarity. And at that moment, his responsibilities to the Church, the mysterious woman who had started it all, Simon, Merlin, none of it no longer mattered. All that mattered now was her. Was Val. To be with and to be loved by Val. He simply did not know how to say this.

Yes, he knew loved her, could not bear the thought of being apart from her, but just didn't understand the emotion. He couldn't put it into words. And with no answer forthcoming, Val decided to address him again.

"As I said, I'm going for a swim. When you find again the desire to speak, kindly let me know."

She left him then to ponder his thoughts while she, in turn, began to ponder her own. She walked away slowly, deliberately, to give him a lasting view of her backside, and made her way to the water's edge.

The water was cool, only slightly uncomfortable, so she slowly inched herself in, little by little, but in moments she grew accustomed to the temperature. The night was unseasonably warm and the water, by comparison, felt refreshing. It wasn't as deep as she supposed, shallow enough in which to stand, and once comfortable in the water and now treading very lightly, she once again addressed her own thoughts.

She knew in that moment that she desired him. More than any man she had ever met in her life. She knew this with absolute certainty. It wasn't just his kindness nor his innocence, although these were qualities she surely admired. No, there was something else about this man, something she couldn't quite define. Of course, she found him handsome, incredibly so, and realized in this moment of clarity that she had never remotely felt this way before.

For until Zekiel came along, no other man had ever been good enough for her, nor had any man forced her to explore these new, strange and growing emotions. No other man had ever made her feel like a *person*, treated her like a person, instead of an object for their lust. And what Val desired more than anything, as she went over these facts in her mind over and over, was to know if Zekiel felt the same way…because at this moment, at this exact moment in time, she knew herself to be in love.

But how? How was that possible? She had scarcely known him for four days and yet she was sure, somehow absolutely sure, that she wanted to be with this man for the rest of her life. It was almost as if he had been destined for her in some way she could not yet fathom, and her intuition was leaving no room at all for error. She loved him as completely as if she had known him all her life, and no matter how hard she tried to convince herself otherwise, found that she could not.

With Zekiel, she felt like a completely different person, removed completely from the life she had led before.

And yet, there was still so much more she wanted to tell him. So much more she felt she obligated to share and she debated internally if this was indeed the time, for she had not been completely honest with him. Not at all.

But then Zekiel surprised her. He was coming into the water himself now, and she knew he was naked as well. Her heartbeat began to quicken as he gingerly drew himself closer. It was obvious the water felt cold to him but he never slowed his approach and in a few short moments stood before her, the water up to his waist, her full breasts above the water.

"Zekiel?" she asked tentatively, wondering where this encounter would lead.

"I'm not going to leave you when we get to York," he stated matter of fact.

"You're...you're not?"

"I'm not even sure we should be going to York. Not anymore."

She wasn't expecting this. In fact, she had no idea what might happen next. She was visibly becoming flustered and felt her body trembling. She could tell he was equally nervous, so very, very nervous, for his own body was shaking in turn, not at all due to the cool water that he no doubt had already grown accustomed to.

"You said 'we'," Val started carefully. "Do you still in...intend to...to take me with you?" she stuttered.

"I..." he struggled to respond. "I don't know what I'm doing here. I have no idea where I am even going." He sounded hurt, full of despair, as if he couldn't quite collect his thoughts. He tried to go on. "I left my home in haste to chase after some woman I do not even know. My intention and quest was to *find* this woman...but I think of her no more." He paused, drawing in a deep breath. "No more, Val."

"Please, Zekiel. Go on..." she implored him.

He took yet another breath. "As I said, I no longer have any desire, no desire whatsoever to seek that which I once sought."

"You...you don't?" she responded, her eyes quickening.

"No." He was doing it again. Using that serious voice of his, and the sound of that voice, that voice directed at her, nearly made her lose control.

"Please understand," he began again. "I had plans to leave Scarborough regardless. She, that woman, I fully admit was the catalyst, but not the true reason for my journey. I understand that now." Another deep breath. "And while I don't understand what fate has brought you and I together, nor what the future holds, I know I am where I am supposed to be," he finished, his voice strong, confident.

"Where...where are you supposed to be?" she whispered.

"Here. Here with you. If..." He paused.

"If what?"

"If...if you will have me." He cast his eyes down, toward the water then, afraid of any negative reaction, of rejection. "I do not know what you see in me, if anything," he continued. "But I know what I see in you. I confess I am not a rich man, nor do I even have much money, much less value it beyond my most basic needs. And to be perfectly honest," he went on, resigned to be nothing but truthful with her. "At present, I...am rather quite poor..." he attempted to joke.

"I don't care about money. I don't care about how poor you are." she responded immediately. "I...I don't care about any of those things, Zekiel."

"I know, Val. I know."

"Question." And there it was, this was the question. This was where it was all leading.

"An...Answer." he stuttered.

"Will you...will you make love to me, Zekiel?"

He was suddenly kissing her fiercely, his restraints completely lifted, and she immediately began to kiss him back in a fury. He started by touching her face, tracing his fingers across her cheeks until he had no choice but to place those same hands around her waist. He drew her closer to him in mounting passion while Val slowly wrapped her legs around him. He proceeded then to carry her from the water.

Near the fire, he put her down gently and rolled himself on top of her, letting his emotions guide him in what he wanted to do, what her body was begging for him to do. He lightly stroked her body, using his hands tentatively until she could no longer suffer his soft touch. She wanted to be handled in a completely uninhibited manner, and seized the opportunity to take control by rolling herself on top of him. Again, he lightly touched her perfect, full breasts until she placed his hands there roughly, deliberately. Zekiel nearly swooned. He started to kiss them, gathering and caressing them with his hands and mouth while she slowly placed him inside her. His lips then met hers, both desperate now for the act, and they found their bodies shaking uncontrollably. Val had to pause then, momentarily breaking their kiss, before things could go any further, as if they had not already crossed several sacred barriers.

"It has to be for love, Zekiel. It can only be for love," she whispered, wanting nothing more than to continue, but desperately needing to be reassured of his feelings for her.

He responded with a kiss so passionate, so emotionally charged...no words were needed.

Their lovemaking was intense but brief, and when their combined passion had been expended, Val collapsed on top of him, breathing heavily, her energy nearly spent.

"My husband..." she managed to say between heavy breaths and her words gave Zekiel pause. He too was exhausted, but at this moment in time, was happier than he had ever thought possible, wearing a smile of bliss. And though he had heard her voice, he had scarcely registered her words, so delirious was he, that he bade her to speak again.

"What...what did you say? What did you call me?" he asked, attempting at that moment to sober, as if drunk.

"My husband," she confirmed. "For that is what you are. And I..." She smiled. "I am now your wife."

"My wife?" he asked, more than a bit confused.

"In Ireland, when a man shares his bed with a woman, this constitutes a valid marriage. Is that not the custom here?" she questioned, still smiling.

Zekiel took a moment to sort this out. "I do believe that custom holds here as well. The Church would demand a formal ceremony, as well as a dowry from your family to mine, but I think we violated those requirements by what we have just done." He paused, searching his memory for further details.

"Do you regret what we...what we have done?" she asked a little concerned. Zekiel could only smile.

"I regret nothing. I've never been happier in all my life, nor did I know that this kind of happiness was possible."

"Neither did I."

"I'm sorry it was so...so...so brief," he apologized.

"It was perfect."

"No. I can be better. It was only..."

"Only your first time. I know." Her smile more beautiful than ever.

They held each other for several long moments. Held each other in silence. Simply savoring the moment, the obvious and apparent love between them.

"Do you want to know something?" Val finally said, pulling back just a bit, still within his arms.

"Speak."

"I was lost in you, Zekiel. I am still lost. Lost in your love for me. I've never felt so...so fulfilled. So loved."

"Nor have I..." he answered sincerely before his face suddenly bore the look of mischief. "Do you think we could...?" he started to ask, once again beginning to stroke her face.

"Now?" she asked incredulously.

"Yes." A small laugh.

"Are you sure you ca...oh. I see that you can." She laughed again, sensing his renewed readiness. "But will you still love me in the morning when your passion is no more?" she teased, kissing him softly.

"Ask me in the morning. And then ask me again. And again. Until you no longer feel the need to ask me any more. That is how certain I am...of the love I feel for you."

"I love you more," she breathed, already initiating the act.

"Let us see." He spoke with confidence. "Let us see."

The second time was much longer, but no less intense, and Zekiel took the opportunity to re-explore her body. He deliberately tried to move at a far more controlled pace, establishing a rhythm between their bodies while slowly working up to the moment. He was far more aware of her gratification this time, which very much surprised her, for she could not have imagined anything more pleasurable than what had happened only moments before. But as what was starting to become routine, Zekiel had surprised her again. Not only was he naturally good at what he was doing, but she could feel his passion. She could feel his love...and she loved the feeling of his hands upon her. And when the moment finally came, she climaxed not once but twice, and then finally an impossible third time, all in rapid succession. And when Zekiel finally exhausted himself, their cries mingled as one, he finally let out a breath of absolute joy.

They laid together for quite some time, engaging in whispered promises and oaths and of dreams to come, and hopes for the new life they would have together, until they both slowly drifted off to sleep.

Val was first to rise again in the morning and still treasuring the emotions of the night before; she engaged him once again after he had practically just opened his eyes. And just as before, the passion and love between them was no less intense, and Val would have sworn that their love had grown even greater still.

They were deeply in love, full and complete, and the bond that was made, they would learn in years to come, would never, and could never...be broken.

Chapter Eighteen

That day, shortly after noon, it began to rain again, forcing the couple to abandon the special place where their love had been consummated. It was painfully hard to leave, especially with fish so plentiful, along with clean water to drink, but they desperately needed a roof over their heads. And if not surely now, certainly for England's cruel winters.

At first, the rain was a mere drizzle but before long, they both knew that a stronger storm was imminent, for the clouds were thickening and the afternoon was quickly growing dark. Neither wanted to leave what would always be a fondly remembered place and they promised one day to return, provided they could find it again.

They set off shortly after, not knowing where to go and without any sort of plan. Val had suggested they make for London where more work was available, or possibly even traveling further beyond, perhaps even as far as Ireland, where she was from, but the problem facing them still was that they had long ago lost all sense of direction. They could estimate whether they were traveling East or West, North or South, but not knowing how far they had strayed from the road could either lead them further away from their goal or just as easily pass it by. Out in the open country, with no visible beacons or landmarks, one guess was just as good as another. On they went.

Before long the rain came, strong and swift, and again they found themselves miserable, with no choice but to go on. They would need shelter and soon, or risk facing the same problems of the night before, when they been fortunate enough to find the cave. But one thing that Val kept on reminding him of was that at least they had each other, and relentlessly put forth a positive attitude.

There was even a brief discussion about heading back to Scarborough, where Zekiel insisted they could have a home, but they still faced the same problem: they didn't know how to navigate and the trip could take days, possibly weeks, and perhaps they wouldn't be able to find it at all.

Luck was finally with them, for at that moment a huge bolt of lightning brightened the entire sky, and in the distance, barely visible, Zekiel thought he could make out a few wisps of smoke. Most likely from a chimney, he surmised.

"I think...I think I see something, Val. I could be wrong, but there looks to be a house or settlement some distance away. Perhaps even a shed of some sort. A little over a half-mile ahead if I'm guessing correctly."

Val placed a hand above her eyes, shielding her vision from the storm. She was unable to make out what Zekiel had seen, as the lightning's illumination disappeared just as quickly as it came, but she trusted Zekiel implicitly. If there was even a slight chance that shelter had been found, she would have gladly taken refuge anywhere, including another cave.

But they were finally in luck. For while Zekiel could confirm as to have seen smoke likely issuing from a chimney, the constant barrage of rain had prevented him from making out much else. As the two companions drew closer, they discovered that they were actually on the outskirts of a fairly small town.

Numerous houses were arranged in much the same fashion as Zekiel's village in Scarborough. He could also make out what he believed to be the town's church, and instinctively thought to go there. But when they arrived at the small place, soaked and freezing, the door was securely locked. It wasn't that late in the night, but there was little reason for the town's preacher to be immediately available, much less the church itself, and Zekiel assumed the cleric had probably retired for the evening, or perhaps was even now taking his supper.

The thought of food pained them both and they quickly pursued other options. It was Val who spotted what appeared to be the town's small tavern, more than likely the only tavern, for most of the houses that lined the road were darkly shuttered, save for a few candles that burned in windows. They made their approach as quickly as they could manage and within moments, Zekiel was opening the door.

The rain and thunder had drowned out most of the noise from outdoors, but inside the place was surprisingly lively with music, a reasonable number of patrons, and from the looks of it, plenty of ale on hand. They were noticed the moment they entered; being strangers in this town, and curious locals were taking customary glances.

Zekiel went mostly unnoticed and was hardly given a second look. He still drew a few stares owing to his odd-looking hairstyle, but once confirmed to be male, the looks he received did not linger.

Val, on the other hand, was being gawked at by every man in the room. Even after having been on the road a few days, along with appearing completely soaked and miserable, this did little to diminish her appearance. In fact, many of the guests inside the tavern couldn't help but stare at the way her rain-soaked garments clung to her body.

"Excuse me, sir," Zekiel prompted the barkeep, trying to conduct his business quickly and moving directly to the bar. "But do you happen to have a room for the night? Perhaps a meal for tired and hungry guests?"

"Have you any coin?" the man asked in return. He was older than Zekiel by at least twenty years, clean-shaven but balding, and his portly physique suggested to Zekiel that the man was doing quite well for himself. He was short, much like Zekiel himself, and presented a warm enough smile.

"I don't have much..." Zekiel slowly answered, trying to retain his meager coins for as long as could be possible.

"One silver piece for you. Another for the lass."

Zekiel sighed. It was more than he cared to spend, as Simon had only given him so much, and he felt the price unreasonably high. Val seemed to notice his worriment at once and moved to join Zekiel at the counter.

"We will pay one silver piece for the two of us," Val attempted to bargain and at this, the barkeep raised his brows.

"Two coins of silver. And that's my one and final offer," he countered, the warm smile disappearing from his face.

In the short time it took to dispute the cost of what was probably an overpriced room, several of the patrons had made their way to the bar as well, looking to replenish their drink. Val capitalized on the situation.

"You seem a servant or two short tonight," Val replied, scanning the room to observe the one and only female attendant. She was a few years older than Val, not at all unattractive, but worn. Her employment here no doubt kept her quite busy, both during working hours with perhaps a task or two after dark. She hurried back and forth, collecting empty mugs, working as fast as she could to replenish her paying customers. Recognizing she was overly busy, the barkeep now smiled at this thought in a new light, clearly anticipating Val's coming proposal.

"If you will allow me..." she began. "I will work for your establishment tonight, earning our room and board. You will also provide a light meal and dry clothes for us both. We will pay you one silver coin and not a shilling more. And I should add," she said in a commanding tone. "That this seems a fair bargain, considering how busy you appear to be tonight. Wouldn't you agree?"

At any other time, the barkeep would have fought for any additional coins. However, he was exceptionally busy tonight and could surely use the extra hands. Already, his lone female servant was exhausting herself and he hadn't survived this long on poor service. Additionally, Val was attractive, something the barkeep could hardly miss. Perhaps her good looks might encourage certain customers to stay a bit longer, as she had already, from the moment she entered, captured the eye of every last man in the room.

Zekiel, not so ignorant of those looks now, debated if this was the wisest course. He naturally wanted no trouble, but could also see the attention that Val attracted, and only hoped they would not attract anything more than long lustful glances.

"Well?" Val asked after a moment. "What say you?"

"Aye...I accept," the barkeep said, extending a hand to both Val and Zekiel. "You drive a tough bargain but I could use the extra help. I have a spare outfit for...what did you say your name was?" he asked Val.

"I didn't say." she responded smoothly.

"We prefer," Zekiel cut in. "To keep our names to ourselves. We won't be here for more than a night, thus are hardly worth remembering."

"Suit yourself," the barkeep responded. "But if either of you are in any sort of trouble..." he clearly warned.

"We are in no trouble, other than being cold, tired and hungry," Zekiel responded. "We simply prefer to keep to ourselves."

"Trust that I meant no offense, young master," the barkeep remarked. "And I will trouble you on this no more. I would, however, prefer to refer to my staff by name, but I give you my word that I won't repeat it. Provided she does as she is told."

"Anna," Val interjected. "You may call me Anna."

"A fine name, Miss Anna...and I give you my word it shall not be repeated," the man responded with a smile. "Off you go then. You will find your room at the top of the stairs, first door on the left. I will have your supper provided shortly. After you have eaten, and I ask you not to delay, please join me downstairs to serve my customers at once. As I have said, I have some spare clothes for the lady, but will have to find something else for your...brother?" he inquired slyly.

"He is not my brother," Val immediately replied, once again taking the lead.

"We are companions..." Zekiel started to say but Val cut him short.

"Companions?" she interrupted. "Is that any way to refer to your wife?" she demanded of him. Zekiel, caught off guard, stumbled to find something to say.

"You two are...married?" the proprietor asked. To this question, Val threw Zekiel an unmistakable glance. A glance that implored him to remain silent. She wanted to handle this.

"Yes," Val stated, reaching for Zekiel's hand. "He is my husband. And an excellent one at that," she added with a mischievous smile.

"I see..." the man said sadly. "I did not mean to presume, but a lass like you could make a lot more coin if you were willing to..."

Now Zekiel caught on.

"She is *not* willing," he stated far more defensively in tone than was necessary. Val couldn't hide her smile.

"I am...flattered, to be sure," Val replied carefully. "But I don't share my bed. And I'm quite certain," she said, looking again at Zekiel. "That my husband would not approve of me being...'handled' by another man." As she said this, she pressed herself against Zekiel's side persuasively and the proprietor literally smiled with jealousy.

"A shame," the man said, clearly disappointed but amicable. "You are a rare beauty in these parts and I am most honored to have you with us this evening. I do expect you to work hard..." he said wagging a finger.

"And so I will," she promised.

"All is well then and please forgive me, for I can afford no more delays. Join me immediately after you have supped, I beg." Zekiel promptly produced the single silver coin and quickly followed on Val's heels, anxious to end the conversation.

Upstairs, their room was poorly furnished, but at least they had procured shelter. It was a simple room with a single area for sleeping and while crude overall, it was warm if not comfortable. There was but one chair, rounding out the room's only other piece of furniture; a bed with a coarsely straw-stuffed mattress, where tonight they would hopefully be able to claim some undisturbed rest.

"It's not much…" Zekiel started to say sadly. "And undoubtedly overpriced. I'm sorry I couldn't find something more comfortable, but we had little choice due to the storm. You didn't need to offer to work, Val. I would have paid the extra coin."

"Absolutely not," she stated. "I know you don't have much and we will need everything you have. I don't mind working to pay for our room and should a different opportunity have presented itself, I know you would have done the same."

"Of course. I'm simply not used to…to not doing anything," he lamented, no doubt wishing he could have done more.

"You have done quite enough," she said coming over to embrace him. "Allow *me* to help this time. And besides…" she added slyly. "You will need your strength again tonight."

Chapter Nineteen

ZEKIEL TOOK ONE of the few empty seats at the bar and absently ordered an ale. He didn't really intend to drink it, but didn't want to sit in their room while Val worked either, nor did he want to draw any further attention to himself.

The place wasn't terribly crowded at the moment, but the ale was flowing heavily and before long, most of the patrons were either drunk, or very close to being so, some even ready for bed.

Val, for her part, took the job in stride. She hurried back and forth, keeping pace with the other servant, and together they served the ale so efficiently that the place remained very much content. She would throw Zekiel a glance here and there, and it was always her smile, that loving smile that told him she was happy...and by those intimate looks alone, more than happy to be his wife. She was feeling extremely useful at that moment after everything Zekiel had done for them on the road, yet it wasn't at all about paying him back, for there was no debt to be paid. She simply volunteered to help because a shelter is what they had needed, and she fully and willingly intended to support her new husband.

With Val very much occupied, Zekiel turned inward to his own thoughts. Where would they go next? What work could they find? Where did they intend to live, and on what income? He wanted to provide for her, much like she was providing for them now, and he wanted more than anything to have a place of their own. He became so lost in these thoughts that he hardly registered the person taking the empty seat next to him at the bar.

"That your wife?" the stranger politely asked, ordering an ale in turn. He was considerably older than Zekiel and appeared to be a bit older than the proprietor. He wore a full beard with shoulder-length black hair, beginning to turn a bit gray, his physique a bit on the heavier side.

"I'm sorry...what did you ask me?" Zekiel asked a moment later, breaking away from his internal thoughts.

"That woman over there. That your wife? She keeps looking at you, son. You'd be wise to look back sometimes, a beauty staring at you like that." Zekiel laughed.

"She is. My wife, I mean."

"Hmmm."

"I beg your pardon?"

"Aw, nothing. Just can't shake the fact that I think I've seen that gal before. Not around these parts, you understand. Either of you ever been to London?"

"My wife is from London," Zekiel answered, curious now as to where this was going. He didn't think it wise to reveal too much, but at the same time, he was hardly finding cause to fear the old man.

"I hate to be so rude," the stranger continued. "But I rarely forget a pretty face. And your wife, well...you're a very lucky man, Mr..."

"Raven. Call me Mr. Raven."

"You from around here, Mr. Raven? Please...forgive me if I'm being too nosy. We do get quite a few outsiders passing through these parts...certainly frequently enough that I do enjoy trading stories. I suppose the traffic helps keeps this place in business too."

Zekiel didn't see the harm so answered. "I'm from Scarborough, actually. Are you familiar with the place?"

"Fishing village, right? Haven't been there myself but hear it's a nice enough place. What sort of work do you do, Mr. Raven?"

"My father," he began. "Rather, my adoptive father, wanted me to join the Church."

"Can't say I go much myself," he confessed. "Probably should. Well, you're obviously not doing that seeing as you are here. Was it the lass?" he asked slyly, throwing Zekiel a wink.

"She had a part to play, but no," Zekiel smiled politely. "The decision was my own."

"Well, Mr. Raven, a pretty lass like that certainly can turn some heads. Married you said, right?"

"That's right."

"I tell ya, some men have all the luck. Well...sorry for bothering you, Mr. Raven. You looked like you could use some company and I'm a man who likes to talk." He got up, ready to leave. "I best be getting home now," he said, draining what was left in his mug. "Got a wife and a few children of my own. Got any children yet yourself?"

"Not at present."

"Ah, but you have plenty of time for that. Wish you and your wife the best of luck, Mr. Raven. Thanks for sharing words and your time with an old man."

While inquisitive, the stranger seemed like a nice enough fellow Zekiel decided, and had to admit that it helped occupy some of his time. He still had quite a bit to think about, especially concerning his and Val's future together, though the sudden interruption from such thoughts and deliberations had certainly not been unwelcome.

"Who was that, love?" Val asked him, coming to stand by his side.

"Just some old man looking for conversation. He thought he recognized you from somewhere but he must have been mistaken. How are you doing?" Val paused, for a moment, and spared a passing glance at the door.

"I'm a little tired from serving..." She said, drawing herself close enough to whisper in his ear. "But not too tired to show my husband...how much I love him."

"I...don't trouble yourself over me, Val. You've been working hard. If sleep is all you desire this evening..."

"It is not," she replied sternly. And to accentuate her point, she deliberately clasped his face in her hands and kissed him passionately in front of everyone in the tavern.

"You're making every man in here very, very jealous," Zekiel warned, momentarily breaking away, unable to hide his smile.

"Let them be. I'll not have their jealousy impose on our happiness."

One man did abruptly get up then and found his way to the exit but neither paid him any attention.

"Ahem," the barkeep subtly called their attention, pretending at the same time to clear his throat.

"I have to get back to work," Val whispered, starting to draw away. She risked yet another quick kiss and then was off, just as busy as before, happily tending to her work. Yes, Zekiel thought to himself. I am a very lucky man.

After all the guests had departed for the evening, Val took the empty seat next to Zekiel, thoroughly exhausted from her work.

"You did well tonight, lass," the barkeep remarked. "So well in fact that it would be wrong of me to demand payment for your room. Here..." he said, passing the silver piece back across the bar. "This belongs to you. You earned it. The room is paid for and I wish you both a good evening." He tossed them both a wink but stopped short of the stairs. "If you have no other plans or aren't in any sort of hurry, I'd like to extend the same offer for tomorrow night as well. Hard workers are difficult to come by these days and we could always use the help. There would be no charge for the room of course, and I'd give the both of you two solid meals...*plus* a shilling each. Granted, it's only the lass who would be working." He then addressed Zekiel directly. "You'll forgive me for I have no tasks for you, young man. But should you decide to stay on an additional day," he resumed, before returning his attention to Val. "I'd gladly make it worth your while." Both Val and Zekiel looked at one another, silently debating this generous offer.

"Make no decision tonight," the barkeep put in. "I'm no worse for wear if you tell me in the morning. Be sure to come downstairs shortly after dawn if you would like to join me for a quick breakfast. The name's Henry, by the way, so don't hesitate to call me such. I'm off to bed." And with that, he departed up the stairs.

Chapter Twenty

We didn't make love that night, despite Val's earlier promise, for I knew she was tired and had simply wanted to please me. Her concern was hardly necessary. Instead, we simply laid together, talking quietly for a few minutes before I felt her slowly nod off, drifting away into a comfortable sleep.

I wasn't yet very tired myself and laid there wide awake for some time, simply collecting my thoughts. I was happy, undeniably so, but I was anxious about the future and was pensive as to where our lives might lead. I knew we couldn't stay here indefinitely, for Val's offer of employment would hardly be year-round, and knew I too would need a job. The problem was, I didn't know what I could do.

I had very little experience with any kind of gardening or raising crops. Nor did I have any real skill in carpentry nor blacksmithing which were also trades very much in demand. I knew how to fish, which was perhaps the only practical thing I knew how to do, but I didn't much see myself as a fisherman. Naturally, I knew how to pray, and could probably even lead a mass, but when I laid there and thought about it, I realized that beyond these things, there wasn't a whole lot I could actually do. Unfortunately, my life hadn't provided me with many opportunities to master other skills.

I started to become depressed, and as I turned to look at Val, so peaceful, so content, I knew I had to think of something. She was depending on me to provide just as I was depending on her now, and I silently prayed for a solution. I suddenly realized that I hadn't even bothered to pray in some time. From the day I met Val, in fact, something I now felt slightly guilty of.

I prayed for forgiveness then, both for my silence and the sins I had knowingly committed, but I also gave thanks for Val, for our continued health, for getting this far, and for the happy life I was hoping we could have together.

I fell asleep shortly after and before long, dawn was upon us. Again, Val was the first to rise and wasted no time in trying to make up for last night. I tried, to no avail, to tell her that this was unnecessary...but my argument died on my lips. She insisted quite firmly after that, and we proceeded to roll each other around in such an uninhibited fashion, that I lost all desire to ever leave that humble room.

"Will it always be like this?" I asked her, completely out of breath.

"I'm afraid so," she laughed. "But it is your fault, you know, that gives me such an appetite."

"Speaking of appetites..."

We hurried downstairs after that and joined Henry for a much-needed and welcomed breakfast. I was still hungry from the night before, as I'm sure Val was too, and we were treated to a very hearty breakfast of steaming scrambled eggs and bacon. Easily the best meal we've had seen since enjoying the last of Simon's thick stew.

After we washed up, Henry once again repeated his kind offer. We accepted of course, or rather, Val accepted, as we had yet to make further plans. But as the majority of Henry's business, and thus Val's duties, weren't to begin until early evening, we had a pretty open day ahead of us. We presently stepped outside to what was starting out to be a cloudy day. Still, the air was refreshing and

I felt a sort of longing to return to the open road. I think Val did too. While we were certainly appreciative having a roof over our heads and a bed on which to sleep upon, there was great satisfaction in taking care of ourselves out in the wide world, something almost primal about it.

Out there, on the road, everything was simple yet difficult at the same time. We didn't have to answer to anyone, but that's not to say we were without any responsibilities. Finding food for one thing, finding shelter another, but there was a certain satisfaction to that too. I think we both just enjoyed being outdoors.

We wandered around the small town for a bit, just to take in our surroundings, as the night before had offered very little in the way of sights. The town, while unremarkable, was certainly well maintained, but there wasn't anything particularly impressive about it. It was much like my own village, though smaller, and just large enough to provide for everyone, for it seemed as if everyone had a job to do, a unique place in maintaining the community. It made me realize at the same time how much we desired a place of our own.

The day passed uneventfully; the two of us even took a nap mid-afternoon (and coincidentally made love again), but before long, Val was needed to begin her evening's work. Henry's establishment was steadily getting busier, with mostly the same folks from last night, and the tavern was soon just as lively as before.

I took up the same seat at the bar and contented myself with an ale, this time which I intended to drink in enjoyment. I was happily about to order another, for saw little harm in doing so (on the house, Henry assured me), when I noticed Val conversing with a particularly loud individual. He was tall and lanky, about my age, but appeared to have a mouth too big for his own good. He was sitting down at present and Val was standing close. I attempted to overhear their conversation.

"And I told you," the man said. "I'm sure he's your husband tonight, but what about tomorrow night, Val? What about tomorrow? I'll be around at least that long. Or..." he continued. "How's about he just lets me borrow you for an hour or so now?

Didn't think I'd ever see your pretty face again and I think an old reunion would do us both some good," he finished with a chuckle, attempting to slap her rear. But Val moved deftly away, avoiding his dirty hands.

"Why now," he began again, sounding disappointed. "It hasn't been that long, now has it? A few months? Two at best? My memory's not so good these days. But surely you ain't forgotten a fellow like me. How many times have we been *acquainted* now? At least twice, sugar? Sorry. Husband and wife?" he taunted. "Is that what the whores are calling it these days?"

She whispered something to him, probably begging him to keep his voice down, but I had heard enough. I didn't know who this man thought she was, but I could see he was making Val very uncomfortable. I didn't understand any part of the conversation I had overheard, and which certainly required an explanation...but nevertheless, I intended to resolve this conflict as peacefully as possible. I calmly walked over to introduce myself.

"Excuse me, Sir. I don't believe we have met," I said, attempting to be amicable.

"Oh. This must be the 'husband'," he said mockingly.

"That's right. And you are?" I asked, offering to shake his hand.

"Zekiel...don't," Val softly warned.

"No, no, no, Val," the man interrupted. "Surely you can introduce me to the man you are sharing your bed with these days."

"What is he talking about?" I asked Val, starting to lose my patience.

"This...this is Will," Val hesitantly responded.

"An old friend?"

"A...business associate," the man she named as Will sneered back. "I was just telling your...your wife here..." And at that, laughed. "How much I would desire her company again. Surely you can understand."

"What kind of company? Speak clearly," I demanded.

"He doesn't know?" Will asked, raising an eyebrow at Val. She shook her head no, eyes to the floor.

"Forgive me if I spoil your little secret then," he addressed her, then turned back to me. "Your wife has been in my service before, you see. I was only inquiring if she would be so delighted to...to share in my company again."

"Zekiel...there's something you should know," Val tried to interrupt.

"Zekiel? That's your name? Well then, Zekiel...let me put this to you as cordially as possible. Your wife has certain...*assets* I wish to enjoy. I'll pay the usual price of course," he finished, once again facing Val. He produced a few silver coins in his left hand. His right still tending to his ale.

"I'm...I'm not for sale," she replied softly, then straightening to assume more confidence. "I'm married now."

"Sure. Married," he mocked her with laughter. "We've been married before too. Twice. Like I said. So let's do it again, Val. Let's get married a third time and fuck like..."

"Enough!" Val screamed at him and I struggled to understand what he was saying. What he had just more than implied. My entire body started to shake. And then Will laughed again.

"I...I think you should leave," I said to him, attempting to sound braver than I felt.

I had never had a serious confrontation before, not like this, and could feel a sudden tension rise in the room. I tried to remember who I was, the gentle manners Simon taught me, and I knew that if he were here, Simon would have demanded this conflict be resolved peacefully. "I think..." I started again, for he had yet to answer. "I think it would be best if you were to...to leave us in peace. Or at the very least, I would ask that you leave my wife alone."

"Or what, Zekiel?" he challenged, his words taking an angry tone while quickly rising to his full height. All eyes in the room snapped to stare at the three of us and every conversation came to a stop. No one moved, not so much as an inch, and I was keenly aware that no one would come to my aid.

"Or what, Zeekieel?" he scoffed again, mispronouncing my name. He squared off against me and before I could react, gave me a threatening push, forcing me back a few steps.

He was a considerably taller than me, no doubt stronger, and I didn't know what to do. I knew humiliating fear and felt at once a coward. It was almost as if he could sense my unease because he advanced, pushing me again, this time even harder, and I stumbled back only to collide against the nearest table, which was thankfully empty.

I wanted to hit him. I really did. I wanted to hit him as hard as I could, right then and there...

But I had no courage. It was nowhere to be found, and I knew I was simply afraid of being hit in the face. Or worse. As it was, I just continued staring at him. Not doing a thing. Not saying a word, and it was obvious that he wasn't the least bit afraid of me. Even Val had backed away then, knowing a fight was imminent, giving us plenty of room.

"You ain't going to do shit," he accurately predicted, closing the distance between us. He pushed me a third time, and I immediately lost my balance, falling to the ground in a pathetic heap.

"Leave him alone!" I think Val shouted, for I was still recovering, shaking my head. And without thinking, I foolishly started to get back up.

"Please," I found myself asking him. "I don't wish to fight...."

"Coward. What a fucking *coward!* I can't believe this beautiful woman here wants to be with a pussy like you. You won't even fight to defend her honor. But does a whore really have honor? I mean truly?" he asked the room, spreading his arms wide. "If a whore beds more than one man a night, what honor there be in that?" He laughed. "That's right. Your wife's a *whore*, Zekiel... and an expensive one at that! But I suppose that's at least one honorable thing about her...she doesn't settle for cheap, nor ever turned a trick for free! So, this is what I figure," he continued. "You must have a *lot* of money, Zekiel...and I suppose every bitch has her price."

I swung at him. My temper boiling over, I swung at him. But he, clearly anticipating my reaction, my anger, easily dodged the blow, only to leave me wide open. He immediately returned with a devastating punch of his own, connecting squarely with my jaw and dropping me to the floor.

Val screamed.

He kicked me once, then twice, landing both strikes to my midsection until I was neatly crumpled over, curling myself into a ball. He kicked me again. And again. Until Henry finally intervened on my behalf.

"Leave. Leave this place now!" he demanded. "I won't tolerate any fighting in my establishment."

"A pity," Will said, spitting on me. "We could have been good friends, Zekiel. If only you weren't so selfish as to deny me the pleasure of your beautiful wife. No man should be that lucky. Especially not a fucking coward like you. Why she now prefers the company of fools and unreasonable men? I cannot say."

"Will, you are to leave at once!" Henry shouted, his voice rising for the first time.

"Last chance, Val," Will said, tracing a finger down her face. She drew away sharply and I made an attempt to stand.

"Bastard. You fucking bastard!!!" I screamed, only to be kicked to the ground once more. Val immediately came to my side protectively.

"Get out!!!" she screamed at him. "Get out!!!"

Will laughed again. "Sorry to spoil such a lovely evening, Val. I truly am. I trust you know where to find me? Should you change your mind?"

"Get...out!!" Henry emphasized, coming to stand by Val and my painfully hunched over form.

"I'm going. I'm going," Will said, and finally made his way to the door and left.

"Zekiel," Val pleaded. "Zekiel...I'm so...so sorry."

I got up and fled up the stairs. Alone.

Chapter Twenty-One

It took a few minutes for the excitement to die down and Val hurried to serve her patrons, all the while fielding questions about what had just happened. She politely declined to answer each person in turn until everyone once again had a full ale in hand, along with Henry's apologies, and before long much of what had transpired had been quickly forgotten. She excused herself then, much to Henry's ire, but demanded to speak with Zekiel in private.

She was fairly certain that he wasn't seriously injured, but hated herself for not telling him the truth. The truth which could have possibly prevented such an intense encounter in the first place. Or, at the very least, avoided a great deal of embarrassment on her part, as well as humiliating the man she had come to love. She had hoped not to come across any person or dealings from her troubled past, always knowing it to be a possibility, but it seemed as if her past wasn't yet ready to relinquish its lasting grip.

Finding herself at the base of the stairs, she tentatively took the steps, slowly, one at a time, until she stood before the door to their room. Val hesitantly pushed the door open and stepped inside the waiting darkness, the gloom scarcely illuminated by the room's only dimly lit candle. It took her eyes a few moments to adjust until she made out a solitary figure standing in the furthest corner. His back was turned to her, facing away from the door.

"Zekiel?" she called falteringly, but the figure did not respond.

"Zekiel?" she tried calling a second time. "Are you hurt? Are you...?"

"When were you going to tell me?" he interrupted, his voice almost a whisper, but intense. "*When were you going to tell me?*"

He had turned his head slightly to address her, the candlelight highlighting the fall of his long bangs, his eyes completely covered. She took a few cautious steps towards him, to better see his face, but was instantly met with resistance.

"Stay back," he warned. "Keep your distance." His voice was cold, hurt.

"Zekiel...please. Allow me to explain," she begged.

"I think your friend Will explained enough," he nearly spat.

"Oh? Is that *so*?" she fired back, starting to get angry. "Have you no sins from your own past?"

This gave him pause and he took a moment before responding.

"Sins I have, yes...but I never would have lied about it."

"Always the saint," she responded bitterly.

"You mock me?"

"No, Zekiel. But how can one live up to your standards?" she demanded. "Have you never committed a crime? Is there nothing in your past for which you wouldn't seek forgiveness for, or even seek to erase?"

He stumbled to say something more, then must have thought better of it and retained his silence. Val addressed him again. "Does your own Church...not teach forgiveness?"

"How dare you use the Church against me!" He flared, turning to face her for the first time. She started to back away then, but as she caught Zekiel's eyes, illuminated by the candle, felt herself frozen in place.

Long moments passed in awkward silence, during which Zekiel admonished himself. He didn't relish getting angry and instead searched deep within himself, praying for much-needed patience. For understanding. He closed his eyes again, seeking to cool his temper and when he felt his anger slowly dissipating, he addressed Val again, this time in a normal tone.

"I would have you tell me the truth," he started slowly. "Tell me what I must know...even if it will surely pain me. I believe you owe me that much." His voice, while calm, was fraught with emotion and Val felt her defenses melt away.

She wasn't upset with him, but rather angry with herself, and knew she had simply lashed out in self-defense. She also recognized that the blame he had placed upon her, as well as his anger, had been fairly well deserved. She also hadn't meant to use the Church against him, having made the remark out of anger, and resolved not to do so again.

"I'm not sure...I'm not sure where to begin," she started tentatively, while carefully taking a step closer despite his earlier warning. At this, he turned and faced her squarely, revealing a bruised face. His lips were also swollen, bloodied, and she felt immediate concern. Forgetting his demand that she keep her distance, she crossed the remaining space between them, and placed an arm to lightly rest upon his shoulder. He allowed this, though still said nothing.

"Zekiel...what have I *done* to you?" she murmured with great concern, attempting to touch his face. He recoiled but slightly, suffering her soft touch, but cast his head down, unable to meet her in such close proximity.

"It's...it's not as bad as it appears," he claimed, but even her light touch on his face exacerbated the pain and he winced slightly because of it.

"All of this is my fault," she started to explain, but with no argument forthcoming, she led Zekiel to the bed and bid him to sit down. She then sat down beside him and pondered where she should begin and they sat for a moment in silence.

"Is...is it true what he said?" Zekiel started, taking the initiative. "What Will said? That you are...are a..." he tried to ask.

"A prostitute?" she finished for him. He nodded.

"I was." And then. "I am," she confirmed, tears starting to form in her eyes. "I...I had thought I left that part of my life behind when...when I first met you."

"And those men. Whom you fled. Did they...did they force you to? Or did you...?"

"Let me start at the beginning, Zekiel...so that I am sure you understand."

He nodded his accord and patiently waited for her to speak.

"It began with my uncle, whom I have already told you about," she began a moment later, digging through her memories. "When I first came to live with him, he treated me very kindly. Granted, I was but a girl then.

My aunt was also a nice enough woman but their daughter, as I have said, was close in age but we never became like sisters, nor did we ever grow very close. At any rate, my uncle..." And when she referred to him as such, there was an obvious revulsion that she practically spat the word. She even had to pause, taking a deep breath in order to resume.

"My uncle, as I said, initially treated me kindly, was respectful even, and seemed an honest and decent man. But when I started to get older," she went on, her voice becoming angry in tone. "Everything started to change, and he began to look at me...in a different light. He started to stare at me, Zekiel...and not at all in an appropriate manner...especially after I started to...*develop* into the woman you see now before you," she said, deliberately gesturing to her breasts.

"It was gradual at first," Val continued. "Something I tried to ignore. And it always when my Aunt wasn't around or paying much attention. But as time went on, there could be no mistaking his inappropriate glances. He lusted after me. I was certain of it. Day and night, week after week, I suffered these glances until one day he started to make small comments.

They were fairly innocent at first; mostly about how beautiful I was, how lucky my future husband would be...but gradually these comments started to make me uncomfortable. I tried to take these 'compliments' innocently, tried to dismiss them...I really did, despite how they made me feel...until the day he made his intentions perfectly clear.

He told me then that I was far too beautiful to belong to any one man, and that if only he were a bit younger, and perhaps not my uncle, that even he would ask I be his own, thinking this the only barrier between us. He referred to this as his 'undeniable love for me'."

She paused then, no doubt recalling these horrible memories, and it was obvious that the retelling was very difficult for her. Zekiel remained silent, and patiently waited for her to resume.

"Then one night, maybe but a week later," Val began again, taking another deep breath. "On a night I will never forget...my uncle came home, obviously quite drunk. My aunt was away, caring for a nearby relative who had been ill, and my cousin had already gone to bed for the evening.

He entered my room, Zekiel, clumsy and stumbling, and before I knew what he was doing, I was being pinned down upon my bed and he attempted to climb on top of me." Val started crying then, as the history of her past was painfully relived, so vivid in her thoughts and Zekiel couldn't help but drape his arm comfortingly across her back. To his surprise, she didn't recoil like he thought she would, but instead drew herself closer, reassured by his touch.

"I didn't know what to do, Zekiel. I didn't know what to do!" she sobbed. "I've...I've never told anyone this story before. Not even Meg, who befriended me shortly after. But I'm getting ahead of myself..." she said between sniffles. "I'm getting ahead of myself."

She took a deep breath, then another, her body visibly shaking.

"He tried to force himself upon me, telling me he had no other choice. I had vexed him, he said, his loins were burning, and that he could not control himself. He kept saying he had no choice. He kept saying that over and over. He struggled against me, tried to work off my clothes, all the while justifying his behavior." She paused. "But he was strong, Zekiel, so much stronger than me, and so I did the only thing I could. I screamed for help." She paused again, taking in another deep breath.

"Thankfully my cousin heard me, thought there was an intruder in the house, and came bursting into the room, not the least bit expecting the scene before her. And she saw my uncle, her father, breeches down to his knees, fully ready to engage in the act. *'Father!'* How *could* you? How could you!!!' She screamed. He sobered then," Val went on after a pause. "Being the only sensible thing he could do, and quickly retrieved his pants, all the while shouting his innocence. 'She bewitched me!' He claimed. 'Your cousin tried to seduce me!' But his daughter had already fled from the room. He started after her, more afraid of what she would tell her mother, his wife obviously, and I took that opportunity to flee. That very moment and not a moment longer. I took what I could, what little food we had, and ran out into the night…never to return."

Zekiel, having been silent this entire time, slowly digested her words. But with a long silence prevailing and uncertain what she would say next, if anything, felt inclined to finally speak. "What you did…leaving like that? You did the right thing, Val." he said, trying to sound comforting. "You did the right thing." A pause. "Did he…I mean…before your cousin entered the room. Was he able to…?" He wanted to ask. She slowly shook her head no.

"It…" she began again. "It would have happened, Zekiel. I know it would have happened. Had my cousin not intervened when she did…"

"But then…" Zekiel wondered, sounding very confused. "Why did you not tell me? Why did you lie?"

"I didn't know you then, Zekiel. For all I knew, you could have been like him. So many men are, you know."

"But Will called you a prostitute. Is that not true? What happened after you left? Surely after you came to know me, you should have known I could never do you any harm!" he pleaded.

"I know. I know that now, but I didn't know that then. And when I finally came to truly know you, when I finally came to *love* you, I wanted to forget, Zekiel. I didn't *want* to remember," she confessed, allowing the words to sink in.

"After you left your uncle's house," Zekiel began hesitatingly. "Is that when you became the...the..." He was finding difficulty in saying it.

"The prostitute? A prostitute?" Zekiel nodded.

"I met Meg shortly after. Out on the streets of London. She gave me food. She became my friend. She even provided a roof over my head, along with a few other girls...and that's when she taught me how to survive."

"By becoming a prostitute? After what happened with your uncle?" he asked, incredulous.

Val slowly nodded, determined to resume her narrative.

"Meg told me I was pretty. She told me I could make money. Lots of money. She told me I could choose. She told me I would be in control. That was the biggest difference. I could accept or refuse any man I wanted, Meg said. I could say where or when, and even how much. I didn't have any other choice, Zekiel. At the time I didn't...I didn't have any other choice." She paused to wipe her tears.

"We needed money. We needed to earn a living. Every girl had to do her fair share. And because I was pretty, or so I was told, more than even Meg or any of the others, I attracted those with money. Those with a *lot* of money. And Will...Will was one of those men." At the mention of his name, Zekiel was instantly on his feet, clenching his fists in anger.

"Please, Zekiel. Sit," she bade him. "*Please* don't make this any harder for me. I've never...I've never told anyone this before. No one but Meg, of course.

The two of us were very close. I realize now that what I did, especially after what had happened with my uncle, makes no sense. But Zekiel...I was *starving* before I met Meg. I had no money, no home, *nothing*!" Zekiel was still unmoving, silently cursing the man's name, prompting Val to stand.

"Please, Zekiel. *Please.*" She beckoned him again and he gradually turned in her direction, nodded, took a deep breath himself, and slowly sat back down. "In a few short weeks," she resumed. "I was sharing my bed with only one man a week and always with a man of my own choosing. Never for a relationship, you understand, as that was against the rules...but that wouldn't have hardly mattered anyway. In my line of...work, I wasn't...I wasn't exactly attracting 'nice' men."

"But after everything with your uncle," Zekiel started to protest. "How were you able to...to prost..."

"To prostitute myself?"

"Sorry. Yes. Am I using the correct term?"

"As I said, I had no choice, Zekiel. And I had been convinced by Meg and the others that it was either that...or starve."

"But surely..." Zekiel started to argue, but Val cut him short, knowing full well what he was about to say.

"I tried to get other work. I did. But after what I *had* to do?" she said, looking at him directly. "That's one of the things that attracted me to you, Zekiel."

"I beg your pardon?" he asked, confused.

"That word. Pardon. What you just said. How you said it. You're the first man that's ever treated me with any decency. The only man who didn't try to take advantage of me."

"Are you saying it was as simple as that? My mere kindness?" Zekiel answered in shock.

"No, Zekiel. Of course not. It was everything," she whispered, turning to face him. "*Everything.*"

"I'm not sure I understand," he said flatly.

"Did I ever ask you for money, Zekiel?"

"No. Of course not. You know that," he said, starting to get visibly angry, not understanding. "What does money have to do with it?"

"Don't you see, Zekiel? Do you not understand?" she demanded, her voice rising in volume. "Money has everything to do with it!" she exploded, suddenly getting up herself, clearly agitated. Hurt.

She took a long moment to calm herself, and Zekiel could verily see the toll these recalled emotions, this entire experience had had on her.

He wanted to say something. Anything. Especially after failing to understand at first what she then had to make perfectly clear.

He fumbled a good while, searching for words, but it was Val who spoke again first.

"What I did," she eventually said. "What I did with those men. With Will? Do you think it was easy? Do you think it ever got easier in time? I did it *only* for money, Zekiel. I did it to survive. I did not do this for pleasure...nor did I ever do it for love. *Never* for love," she said, turning to face him. "I could never love a man like that."

"Then..." Zekiel started to say.

"Then what?" Val asked.

"Then why me, Val? Why me? You say it was because of everything, possibly because of everything I did for you. For us. Are you telling me that had any man shown you kindness..."

"You would doubt my feelings?" she asked, no ire in her voice, but instead sadness. Confusion. "You think I do not know my own heart? And what of your own feelings? Do you ask me this because of who I am? What I am? Don't you *see*?" she asked, now exasperated. "Are you so quick to forget what we have done? What we have already shared?

"I will never forget..." he started to say. "My...my,"

"Your what?" she demanded to know.

"My wife. I mean...I mean, if that is to still be what we are."

"Is that what you still want?" she asked him urgently, her tone having never been more serious.

"What do *you* want?" he whispered. Val suddenly threw herself upon him, kissing him frantically, forcefully pushing him down upon the bed. And just when he thought they were going to proceed with the act, even at this incredibly awkward time, she slowly but purposefully drew back, leaving Zekiel breathing heavily. His lip still partially bleeding.

"I'm...I'm sorry, Zekiel. I'm sorry if you weren't ready for me to do that. I...I just wanted to make *my* intentions clear. My feelings...and I think you know what I want," she clarified. "But is it what *you* want?" She begged.

Zekiel knew the answer but was hesitant to respond. He knew he loved her, even after what she had told him, but there were still missing pieces to the story. Especially concerning how they met. "The men you ran away from," he redirected, gently trying to change the subject.

"Why did I run away?" she guessed, and Zekiel nodded.

"One of them was paying me," she began to answer. "One of them was what I would consider a...a regular. A man I saw as often as his money would allow. I did not know at the time how he made his living, for conversation was rare with any of the men I met, but soon after I came to be in his...service," Val went on distastefully. "This man made me an offer that was impossible to refuse. He offered to pay me night and day, not solely for sex, but also for my company. He wanted me exclusively, and perhaps, wanted me for his own twisted version of love. He offered me three times more than what I could make in a single month and he promised to pay me this ridiculous sum one week at a time.

Meg told me to go. The other girls considered me lucky. Told me I would never find a better opportunity. But as always...there was a catch. I had to be with him at all times, night and day, and I was to leave the home I knew. Not long after I had entered into his service, I discovered what this man did for a living. His name was Jack."

"Jack?" Zekiel interrupted. "Was he one of the men that raided my camp?" Val nodded.

"Then you know what he does and unfortunately, he's very good at it.

Jack and his men, of whom there were few, always took things by force or what they could easily steal. But what they lacked in numbers, they made up for by planning, how they would operate.

They would camp out near the road, men on both sides, waiting for unsuspecting fools. They never attacked when the odds were not in their favor, and Jack held to that. Most of the time.

But when the money started to dry up, his band became far more ruthless, far more reckless, and before long, every last one of them had blood on their hands. They became more than just petty thieves, and I knew it was just a matter of time before they would kill out of necessity again.

They frightened me, Zekiel. Especially Jack. He had an especially bad temper. Had I known who they were, what they were, I never would have left Meg. I never would have left the others. I didn't just lose my dignity throughout all of this, Zekiel. I also lost my freedom...and I lost myself," she finished with a bowed head.

"But then..." Zekiel interjected.

"But then...I would have never met you," she finished for him. "We wouldn't even be here. Even as we are now. Eventually," Anxious now to finish her tale, for surely it was wearing on them both. "Eventually the money *did* run out and when I demanded my payment, as what would have been proper, Jack refused. Told me he would pay later.

And so when I demanded to leave, sensing my only opportunity, Jack became very angry. Very angry indeed. He told me he had paid more than enough...and that I was now rightfully his. And at the time, I knew even Jack was starting to have feelings for me, though I would have hardly called it love. But he was hurt, Zekiel. Hurt that I wouldn't share my bed. Hurt that I wouldn't share myself for free. Jack thought he had earned that, thought he had paid enough. Thought he had paid for my love. And on the very next night, when I refused his advances, he tried then to take me by force. That's when I ran away. That was when I took my chance...and that's when I found... that's when I found...you."

Val said no more for a time, having fully completed her tale and they both sat quietly on the bed. Zekiel was still sorting through the details, absorbing all that she had told him. Strangely, despite trying to accept her past, which was not at all easy for him, he found that he wasn't angry. He wasn't upset at all. How could he be? And when he came to this realization, he broke the silence.

"I understand why you did not tell me the truth when first we met, but why did you not confide in me sooner? Were you that afraid of my reaction? Do you think I have the capacity to judge, much less pass judgment?"

"I wanted to tell you, Zekiel. I really did," Val confessed. "But I was afraid...afraid of how you would react, how you would then view me.

Obviously, I couldn't tell you when we first met, for fear you were a highwayman yourself. But as I gradually got to know you, began to fall in love with you, I came to see my mistake. I just wanted...I just wanted to leave my past behind. Surely you can understand that." She paused. "When I met you, I thought I had been given a second chance. A chance to change my past. A chance to be who I wanted to be. I thought I had gotten away, escaped from it all. But then Will...Will has now ruined everything."

"You say that as if you never intended to tell me...had Will not exposed your secret. Is that what I am to believe?" Zekiel had to ask.

"I'll understand if you no longer want anything to do with me," she said, casting her head down.

"You didn't answer the question," Zekiel came back.

"The truth?" she asked after a moment, fearful now of his reaction.

"The truth," he demanded.

"The truth is...the truth is I don't know," she replied honestly.

"You don't *know*?" he came back sharply.

"What do you want me to say?" she pleaded. "How is it even possible to answer? Had Will not interfered..."

"You are saying you would have kept it from me?"

"I don't know, Zekiel. I honestly don't know." She started to sob again. "But could you honestly blame me if I had? Knowing the risk I face now? The risk of losing you?"

"You speak as if you had a choice," he said with a scowl.

"Do you know what it felt like, what it *feels* like, Zekiel? The way you looked at me? Before all of this?" Val pleaded. "You didn't see the prostitute. Didn't see *me* as a prostitute. This whore! Do you have any idea what that *meant* to me? Do you?" she demanded. "And had I told you...would you still have fallen in love with me??"

Val started to sob again but Zekiel had no response.

The truth was, he couldn't begin to know what that had felt like for her, couldn't pretend to know, nor could he even begin to put himself in her shoes. Not after everything she had been through.

As for falling in love with her, would it have made a difference, knowing the truth beforehand? Was it possible to know? Now that he *did* love her?

A long silence passed before Val recovered. And with Zekiel not yet saying a word, Val went on.

"A moment ago, you claimed that I had no choice. No choice but to tell you the truth." Zekiel looked at her, curious.

"I could have lied. Could have made something up," she argued. "I could have said Will was drunk. That he didn't know what he was saying. That he had obviously confused me for someone else...but I did not."

"And I no doubt would have believed it," he said, desperately trying to understand her position, had their roles been reversed.

"Please believe me when I say that everything between us, everything that has happened has been true, Zekiel," she continued to plead. "All of it. In that, I told no lies. I only hope in time you can forgive me...should you still desire to keep my company."

There was another long moment before either spoke again after Val's full and complete tale, which no doubt had not been easy for her to relate, but had at last been laid bare. Zekiel reflected upon everything, tried to digest it all.

He knew it had not been easy for her to tell the truth, nor had it been easy for her to share her troubling past. He knew too she could have continued lying, but had not. She had trusted him, ultimately, but it bothered him that had Will not intervened, it's possible he would have never known. That bothered him more than anything...but there was a part of him too, that understood why she had kept it from him.

Would he have judged her differently? Perhaps even unfairly? Was it even fair to judge when her past had nothing to do with him? When he had not been involved in her life at the time? Was he even now, in this moment, in fact, judging her?

Yes, she had lied. But given the circumstances, given everything she had been through, he also understood how cautious she had felt inclined to be. But even after the fact, he did lament that she had not confided in him without practically being forced to. And for better or worse, he told himself, that was something he would either have to accept or decide to hold against her.

Had he been in her situation, would he have decided to tell her? Would she have judged him differently in turn? And being that her past was none of his business, at least initially, he reasoned, did she not deserve the opportunity to define her true character, without past or unfair judgments?

And so, it all really came back to her decision against revealing the truth earlier, and the possibility that perhaps, she never would have. The question he then kept coming back to was-could he forgive her? And perhaps more importantly, could he and *did he* trust her going forward?

As for falling in love with her, would it have made a difference had he known? Would that have changed anything along the road?

Zekiel took a long hard look at Val, though it was hardly necessary for he already knew the answer.

"It is I who should apologize," Zekiel offered, finally standing up. "I should not have gotten upset, nor do I have the right to remain angry. It pains me that you did not confide in me sooner, and realize that I may have never known...but I also can understand why you kept this from me."

"You do? Do you truly?" she begged. "I never...I never meant to hurt you. Nor would I ever keep anything from you again. Never, Zekiel. Never. I would have you know everything."

"I know," he responded truthfully, for in his heart, he did honestly believe her...and knew he loved her too much not to.

"But...but...what of us?" she asked softly, and truly the question gave him pause.

What of us?

"I told you before that I don't know what you see in me, Val. Truly, I don't," Zekiel said, turning to head for the door.

"Zekiel...don't."

"And because of this," he went on, ignoring her. "I have to at least question why you decided to tell me the truth."

"I told you because I love you!" she pleaded.

"That I do not doubt."

"Then?" Val asked confused.

"I know you love me, Val. I do. But what I don't yet understand...is why," he said, nearly choking on his words.

"Do you even now not know what I see in you?" she asked, exasperated.

Please, let me finish," he requested. "For I too feel the need to be truthful as well," he said, pausing to gather his thoughts. "Surely there are other honorable and decent men. Handsome and even respectful. Strong and hard working. And many, I would gather, in a much better position in which to care for you. And so, I don't understand what makes me different. *Why me?* When a woman, such as yourself, could have any man she desired.

"You saw everyone downstairs. The way they all *looked* at you. Bad intentions or not, and regardless of where you go or even what you do, or even that of your troubled past, most men would look past that just to be with you. You are beautiful, if not gorgeous, and a kind person with a good heart. And thus, any *decent* man, for surely they exist, would be hard pressed to find your equal. And so, I ask you again, Val. Why....*me?*"

"Zekiel...I told you," Val pleaded.

"No. I'm asking you to be more specific. Say the two of us had never met..." he continued. "Say you somehow still managed to escape Jack and his company. And so, what's bothering me is, what would have prevented you for falling in love with the first man who was decent towards you? Or if some other had come along to assist you? And if not the first man, then quite possibly the next. I need to know *why*, Val. Why me, when a much better man could be found? You told me it wasn't just a matter of kindness nor the fact that I happened to be there when you needed someone. And so I need to know *why*."

"Zekiel..." Val tried to explain. "I know not how love truly works. How the heart decides upon those that we go on to love. That I cannot answer. But what I *can* tell you is that I have never felt this way before. And while this may seem like a generalization, I can assure you it is not.

I feel a connection to you, Zekiel. A longing to be with you. To be near to you. It isn't simply because I find you handsome, which surely you are, nor is it your kindness...though these are certainly qualities a person may look for as you have already said. Yes Zekiel...surely there *are* good men out there. Men who are caring, honorable. And I tell you honestly...despite the things I have done, and the poor company I have kept, know too that I *have* met men who possessed those qualities. The good one's I mean. Men who would have surely cared for me."

"But before..." Zekiel interrupted. "You told me that no one has ever treated you that way. Like I have."

"Aye. And all that is true," Val assured him.

"Then? I'm not sure I quite understand."

"Any man...nay, any *person*, has the capacity to do good. To be a good person. But as I told you before Zekiel, mayhap not in these words, but even those with a strong desire to do the right thing, can falter. And so perhaps, even this very evening, there were good men among those like Will, perhaps the older man you spoke to earlier."

"I didn't honestly come to know much about him," Zekiel confessed.

"That's besides the point," Val continued to explain. "The point I am trying to make is that even a good man, even those I have met, have failed to measure up to that which I see in you. For even good natured men have looked at me under a different pretense. And much like Will, have been known to have that same lustful look in their eyes."

"But can you honestly blame them?" Zekiel protested.

"I can...and I do," Val answered.

"Just for being attracted to you?"

"Were you attracted to me?" Val asked him. "When we first met?"

This gave Zekiel pause, as he consulted his memory. "Under the circumstances? Having to spend the night in a tree? I don't think I gave it very much thought."

"But what about the next day? Or the day after that?"

"That's not really fair. You know now that I did. Find you attractive, I mean."

"No, Zekiel. I did not. I did *not* know. For you never gave even the slightest indication. And I dare say even then, you had no intentions other than to help me. Would you say that much is true?"

"Yes. But I still don't see what you are getting at."

"You viewed me as a *person*, Zekiel. Attracted to me or not, for that is not the point either, you still viewed me as a person, without so much as wanting anything in return."

"But how am I any different now? From those very good natured men you mentioned? For I desire you much now like they do," he admitted.

"The difference is where and how those feelings came to be. And I know that your feelings for me come from a very different place. A place not at all common, Zekiel. I know that what you feel comes instead from your heart. And believe me, perhaps due to my past, I very much know the difference. You ask me why you? Because no other man *is* you, could ever *be* you. I said before it was everything. And everything is what I meant.

From the way you've always looked at me, to the way you have always treated me. Spoken to me. This very conversation, even. And yes, even the way you *touch* me.

You asked 'why me?' Because for me there is no other. No other quite like you. Not for my heart. And surely not for me. There is only *one* Zekiel Raven. And it is he, and he alone whom I choose, along with what I *know* to be true and *feel* within my heart."

Zekiel was quiet for good long while. Pondering over all that was said. But as he slowly turned to regard her, to lock his gaze with her own, perhaps for confirmation, he felt as if he finally understood. And yet, after but a moment, his own face betrayed but one more thing he was afraid to ask, and unintentionally turned away.

"Zekiel?" Val questioned him, knowing there was more he wanted to say.

"Downstairs. Before. With Will."

"What about it?"

"You realize you keep present company with a coward. Will was not wrong to label me as such. And if you are to love me, truly love me, then it seems only fair that you know even those things I hesitate to admit."

"No!" she argued. "You are not. You stood up for me, Zekiel. You stood up for me! When no one…when no one has ever done that before."

"I did nothing. And as far as I can tell, the only thing I managed to do was get punched in the face."

"Zekiel…"

"I was afraid of him, Val," he confessed. "I was so afraid to face him. So why you seek to be with a coward such as I…despite all that you have said…"

"I don't know what fate brought us together, my love. But I see no coward here. And there is absolutely nothing wrong with being afraid sometimes. Everyone has fears...and perhaps too, I know this better than most."

"It doesn't change what happened. And if I found myself in the same situation, more than likely we would see the same outcome."

"I don't believe that," she answered truthfully.

"But I do. I bring this up because if we are to be together, there's a chance that something like this could happen again. And when that does happen, how will I be able to protect you? What could I do? I know nothing of fighting...nor do I have reason to believe I can even defend myself. Much less being able to protect someone else."

"Then let us face these challenges together."

"You would stay with a coward?"

"I would stay with the man I love," she said, coming to stand by his side. She clasped his hand and turned to face him. "Zekiel. Zekiel, I cannot lose you. *I can't*," she cried, her eyes still wet with tears.

"I...I don't want to lose you, either," he stuttered, overwhelmed with just how much he honestly loved her.

"Make me a promise," she demanded.

"You have only to ask," he verily whispered.

"We never speak of the past again, unless it is our own. Yours and mine. Let us never speak again of times better off forgotten."

"Agreed."

"Let nothing ever come between us, Zekiel..." she continued. "Nothing. And let us never keep from each other what we truly feel. Who we are. Even our fears. Can you make me this promise?"

"Aye. Only if you will promise me something in return."

"Anything."

"Truly?"

"I am drawn to you, Zekiel. From the moment I met you, I was drawn," she whispered, inches away from his face. "Even here. Even now. I...I can't bear the thought of being without you." She paused. "What must I promise?"

But the pair was interrupted. For in that moment, someone could be heard coming up the stairs, approaching their door and coming fast.

"Zekiel. The promise?" she pleaded.

Henry suddenly burst into the room.

Chapter Twenty-Two

"I'M SORRY TO INTERRUPT..." Henry blurted, rushing through the open door.

"I'll be downstairs in a minute, Henry," Val responded, not at all happy with the interruption. I, however, sensed something different. Something was wrong. Something other than waiting on tables. Henry was clearly in distress.

"It's not that Miss Anna...or is it Val? It doesn't matter," he said shaking his head. "I've just received word that England is under attack."

"Under attack?" I asked, incredulous. "By whom?"

"We, as of yet, do not know. But they are coming. An invasion is coming!" he said, raising his voice again.

"Please, Henry," Val asked. "Please calm down. Tell us what you know."

"I don't know much and I've sent all of my patron's home. Most left on their own. Please," he begged. "Join me downstairs where we can talk more comfortably."

Val and I followed on his heels. Once downstairs, the establishment was as he said. Empty. Everyone had gone home. Henry politely asked us to sit down together, and his other servant was there also. Her name, which I had never bothered to learn, was

Lucy. She was clearly worried too by the look on her face, but as of yet had not spoken, other than to offer us both a nod of courtesy.

Once we were all seated, I bade Henry to tell us more of this news. "As I said," he began. "I don't know much. But it is bad. Very bad indeed for us all." Though I didn't know Henry well, there was no mistaking the look on his face. We were in danger. All of us. That much he made clear. We waited impatiently for Henry to continue.

"These foreigners, no doubt, seek to dethrone the King, to take our lands, for what other purpose would an invasion serve?" he asked, not seeking an answer. "I hear even now the King is making ready for war. A war that will no doubt prove devastating to us all." He took a deep breath and then sighed. "Many do not think we have the power to repel them."

"How many are in their forces?" I asked. "Do we know who comes?"

"Again, we do not know. There is so much yet we do not know. Everything I have learned came second hand. A man entered here, an informant of mine, not long after you both went upstairs, and in that brief time we learned that the invaders were here. Here right now. Making their way inland."

"My God," Lucy gasped, covering her mouth with her hands.

"My information comes from one most trusted and reliable, for I like to have a fair idea of what goes on beyond my doorstep," Henry continued. "But some people are fleeing their homes. Others are off to join the war. I bid you both now to find safe refuge."

"But we have no home!" Val pleaded. "We have nowhere to go!"

"Then I am truly sorry," Henry commiserated. "I would invite you both to stay, for you seem like decent enough folk and I extend that invitation to you now, but…"

"But what?" Val questioned.

"I simply cannot pay you. Either of you. For there will be no work, nor business, I fear. At least for a time. I wish there was more I could do…"

"But how would you feed us? Feed yourself?" Zekiel asked.

"I do not know. I honestly do not know. I have some stores, dried meat, supplies to last the winter, of course, but I don't have much. I did not have any reason to prepare much further beyond."

"Zekiel?" Val asked, looking to me for guidance.

"We cannot stay with you, Henry," I decided at once. "But we thank you for your generous offer." Henry nodded, looking partially relieved.

"But Zekiel!" Val pleaded.

"We cannot impose on this man, Val. We cannot," I told her. "We would drain what little food and resources he has and he will need to take care of himself. Just as we will. We must not abuse his kindness, nor put his life in any further danger."

"But Zekiel..." she pleaded to me again. "What danger?"

"The danger of starvation. For that may soon become a reality. I'm sorry Val, but we will have to take care of ourselves. Agreed?" I knew she wanted to stay, but also that she understood the truth of my words. What little food Henry claimed to have would be gone before winter's end, perhaps even before. I was not about to repay this man for the shelter he had provided us by drawing on what limited resources he had remaining. Val finally nodded her agreement. "But where will we go?" she asked with a concerned expression.

"We may have to return to Scarborough. I don't know where else to go. But in Scarborough, we would have shelter. Food. A place to stay." Again Val nodded, not disagreeing with my logic.

"I'm sorry..." Henry interrupted. "Zekiel, is it?"

"I apologize, Henry. I should have told you our names. Yes, my name is Zekiel. You obviously now know my wife to be Val."

"Yes, yes, of course," he answered courteously. "But I'm afraid I must bring you even more bad news. News of Scarborough. Is that where you said you are from?" he asked gravely.

"It is. But...but what news of Scarborough?" I demanded. "What news?"

"I'm sorry, Zekiel. I am truly, truly sorry. Scarborough is where they landed."

A sudden shock passed through me. "What news then, Henry? What more news of Scarborough? Tell me!" I pleaded, growing more panicked by the second.

"It's just that..." He paused. "I'm so very sorry, Zekiel. So very sorry..." he said, wiping his eyes for he was starting to cry. "Scarborough has been burned to the ground."

I was already moving. I didn't know what to do, but I was already moving. Heading outside.

"Zekiel?" Val called after me. I didn't stop. Had to get some air. I felt like I couldn't breathe. I practically collapsed passing through the door and stumbled my way outside, where I fell to my knees and began to vomit. I was hyperventilating, clearly so, and could do nothing but think of Simon. If Scarborough had been burned to the ground, then what had happened to Simon? I think Val came to my side.

After I had emptied the contents of my stomach, I tried to draw in a deep breath, but as it was, I was still heaving, simply dry heaving, for I had purged everything else. Val tried to wipe my mouth. "I...I have...I have to get back to Scarborough..." I panted between breaths.

"We'll get there, Zekiel. I promise. I promise," she assured, looking grim and very concerned for me.

Henry and Lucy soon joined us outside. "I'm sorry to have had to be the one to tell you, Zekiel. I truly am. Lucy..." he said addressing her. "Please bring us some water. Could you do that?" She nodded, then headed back inside while Val tried to get me back on my feet. I continued to take labored breaths.

"I can't go...I can't go on foot. Take too long," I struggled, trying to formulate a plan. I needed time to think.

"No. No, you cannot. And with soldiers about, walking is far too dangerous," Henry put in. "How long did it take you to reach us here?" he asked. "On foot?"

Val took the liberty to answer for me. "At least a week. No more. I joined him very shortly after he had left." This statement seemed to confuse Henry a bit for he scrunched up his eyebrows. He didn't know that Val and I had scarcely known each other for only six days. It didn't really matter. Lucy soon came back with a full mug of water and handed it to me. I took a good long pull and in another moment, swallowed the rest.

"I'll go on foot if needed," I announced, able to speak again. "I'll run as much of the way as I can. I don't see any other choice." But Henry was already shaking his head no. What was he thinking?

"I won't let you go alone," Val put in, and I knew she meant it. The only problem was, I was already viewing her as someone who could potentially slow me down...and I needed to make all speed. I didn't want to leave her...but what was I to do? *What was I to do?*

"Let me proffer a solution," Henry suggested, surprising me after clearly noting my distress "I have a horse. At home. Not far from here. Just down the road. He is getting older but still quite spry. I would lend him to you..."

"Henry...I...I don't know what to say. Would you really do this for me? But why? I've done nothing to deserve this."

"In times of war, all of us must stay together. And that's just what a good neighbor does!"

"But can your horse...can he carry us both?" Val asked with concern.

"I'm afraid not," Henry confirmed sadly. "The horse would be overburdened and you wouldn't get very far. I'm afraid he's not a very large horse, nor a very young one, but I will gladly place him into your service if it will help you reach your home. Traveling alone you could make the trip in but a few days."

"Then I must make for Scarborough at once. I must. If anything has happened to Simon..."

I was starting to panic again, but in my haste, I was forgetting her. I was forgetting about Val. I had to protect her too. But how?

"You're concerned about your wife," Henry said, interrupting my thoughts. Was it that obvious?

"Zekiel?" Val asked. "What...concerns do you have?"

I didn't want to do this. I didn't want to leave her. But I had no choice! I left Simon all alone, the deep guilt and weight of that decision now finally upon me. He could be hurt. He might need help. He might even be...

But I couldn't finish that thought. I could not. I had to stay positive. I had to believe that he was all right. Surely someone in our village would have seen to him. Cared for him. But I also knew that this responsibility was mine and mine alone. His welfare was very much in my charge, and at that moment I felt nothing but despair. Complete, and utter despair.

I tried to tell myself that I could not have known of the coming war. I couldn't have known he would be in danger. I couldn't have known nor foreseen any of it. "Zekiel?" Val asked again, snapping me out of it. Thankfully, Henry answered for me. "He needs to go alone, child. Don't you see? He cannot take you with him."

"Zekiel? Is what he says true?" Val asked in a rising panic.

"Please..." I implored Henry. "Give us a moment." Henry nodded, took Lucy by the hand, and together they went back inside.

"My love?" She asked, and was already starting to cry.

"I need you to listen to me, Val. I need you to understand," I began, trying to sound as comforting as I could, taking her hands in mine. "Simon is my responsibility. I must know how he fares. If something has happened to him..." I lingered, still refusing to assume the worst. "I simply would be unable to forgive myself. Do you understand what I'm saying?"

"I do, Zekiel. I do...it's just that..."

"Yes?"

"I fear..."

"You fear what?"

"I fear you won't come back to me," she admitted at last.

"Of course, I'll come back," I said, attempting to sound convincing. But the truth was, I didn't know. I didn't know how any of this was going to turn out.

"It's not that. I know you will return when you can...*if* you can. It's just...I fear for your safety."

"I'm more concerned about you," I said sincerely.

At that moment, Henry came back outside and waited patiently by the door, not wanting to interrupt. He appeared as if he had something else on his mind that couldn't wait...so I couldn't help but address him, my curiosity getting the better of me, though I surely could have used more time with Val. "Henry?"

"I'm sorry. I don't mean to interrupt."

"It's fine. Did you forget something?"

"No, no. I just wanted to say that...that one additional mouth is far easier to feed than two. Lucy and I talked it over just now and we would be more than happy to have Val stay with us while you are away. As I said, I won't be able to pay you," he said, addressing Val. "But I suppose we could find you a few things to do and I'll see that your stomach is full. Likely we won't have many patrons for a bit I'm thinking, but here..." he continued, looking again at me. "Here she would at least be safe. Safe as one can be under the circumstances."

"Again, Henry, I thank you for your kindness...but I do not wish to impose..."

"It would hardly be an imposition," he disagreed. "The moment business picks up, I can assure you she will more than pay for what I offer."

I had to admit that Henry was making a generous offer. I still didn't feel comfortable leaving Val behind, but saw little choice.

"The decision is for Val to make," I said after a moment, not wishing to speak for her.

"My love?"

"Listen to me, Val. Here you would be safe. Here you would have food." She suddenly threw herself into my arms and buried her head in my cloak. She was sobbing uncontrollably and I tried to hold her still. I turned again to Henry, such as I could.

"If Will comes back..." I said, stating my most pressing fear.

"He will not be welcome," Henry said with finality. And to this, I nodded back in appreciation.

"What of the horse?" I asked, trying not to sound too eager for Val's sake. "How soon would I be able to leave? Can he be ready this night?"

"It is already late and it would be difficult finding the way in the dark," Henry explained. "Within a mile, the horse could become lame, unable to find good footing. No. The best option would be to leave at first light. At dawn. And besides," he added. "The rest would do you some good. By horse, Scarborough is at least a few days' journey. I would advise this course over any other. Yes. Leaving at dawn would be best. For man *and* horse."

"Then I give you thanks and accept your generous offer. I promise to repay you of course..."

"Think nothing of it," Henry said, waving a hand dismissively. "I know an honest man when I see one and I take you at your word. Now let us all go inside. I'm sure all of us could use some sleep. I'll have Lucy prepare you breakfast in the morning and the horse will be saddled and waiting. You can depart as soon as you are ready."

"Again...I thank you." I bowed. Henry simply nodded and stepped inside.

I lingered there a moment with Val, who was still holding on to me as though I was liable to disappear that very second. We stood there for some time, embracing one another, and I took this opportunity to ponder my options. I knew I was about to embark on a dangerous journey, especially considering there was no knowing where the enemy forces were at present, but my responsibilities to Simon demanded the risk.

Wasn't it worth the risk? I asked myself silently. Could Val and I instead stay together? Wait for the threat to possibly pass? No, I finally concluded. I, myself would then have to depend on Henry, and as it was, he was already being more than generous to almost complete strangers. Besides, if I later learned that there had been something I could have done for Simon, or possibly someone else in my village, the guilt would linger and I would never forgive myself. No. I had to go. I had to. So why did some part of me still think...no. *Feel* this might go terribly wrong?

"Come...let us go inside," I said, tired of my own internal debate. It had been a long enough day, tomorrow promised to be even more challenging...and both of us were exhausted.

Chapter Twenty-Three

Once upstairs, I placed my cloak on the single hook by the door and started to get ready for bed. But while I was going through the motions, washing up and packing my meager belongings, I recalled that Val had never given me a decision. In my haste to secure a way to Scarborough, I had simply assumed she agreed, when in truth, she had agreed to nothing. She had made no decision at all.

I suddenly felt guilty for not asking for her opinion, and I immediately sought to make this right. I was just turning to address her, who was already in our bed, before noting that she was naked, having made no effort to cover herself at all. "But...but your decision..." I protested, realizing what she had in mind, only to be hushed.

"You already know my decision...even though it pains me," she responded to my thoughts, already working off my shirt.

"Then...then you'll stay? With Henry and Lucy? Even if..."

"Please, my love," she begged. "Let us not waste what little time we have remaining...with words."

She proceeded to help me work off the rest of my clothes, but again paused before proceeding with our lovemaking, similar to what she had done before. Positioned above me, she admonished me.

"You don't need to do this..." she whispered. "With me."

"But why ever would I not?" I asked, feeling exceedingly confused, very much wanting to proceed.

"Then you still seek to be with me? Knowing what I was? What I am?" And then she whispered into my ear, barely audible, "The whore?"

"You already know *my* decision," I answered, eager to initiate the act.

"Are you sure, Zekiel?" she asked, already starting to breathe heavily. "Are you sure...? Even...even after everything? Even when you return? Even then...you will still...still desire me? Desire to *be* with me?"

"Just as you would stay with a coward?" I asked, burying my face in her breasts. I lingered there long, simply enjoying the taste of her. The smell of her. The way her body yielded to my hands, my lips, my mouth. Before long, she had already begun to quicken the pace, the two of us becoming more and more frenzied. Desperate.

"Before..." she panted between moans. "Before you had mentioned a promise. What...what must I promise?"

But I, completely lost in her, completely lost in the act, was no longer in a position to answer.

She didn't ask me again.

I was awake before dawn and, not wanting to disturb Val, silently made my way downstairs. As promised, Lucy was already there, just starting to set the table.

"Good morning, Mr. Raven," she said kindly. "I hope you slept well?"

"I did, Lucy. Thank you. Is Henry...?"

"Henry should be along any moment," she quickly answered. "Please," she went on indicating one of the small tables. "Take a seat and make yourself comfortable. Breakfast will be served shortly."

"Again...I thank you," I said, taking a seat. Before long, a hot steaming plate of bacon, sausage, eggs and toasted bread was placed before me. As if on cue, Henry entered through the front door, just as Lucy was setting down a second plate; the girl having practically prepared us a feast.

"Ah, Zekiel. Glad to see that you are awake. I would have roused you should you have slept much later." I nodded and took in a mouthful of eggs.

"The horse?" I asked, not wanting to be rude but eager to be on my way.

"The horse is fed, saddled and waiting. Provisions I have packed also. I trust you've ridden before?"

"Enough so I'm able to manage. We didn't have many horses in my village, but Simon, my adopted father, insisted I have some experience around them. I took any opportunity to not only ride several decent saddle horses, but also learned some about their care and feeding, as well as how to tack up properly. I certainly feel reasonably capable and confident that I can return him to you...no worse for wear."

"Of that, I do not doubt," Henry said, taking a bite himself. "But tell me, Zekiel. What road do you plan to take? Are you familiar at all with your direction?"

"I can follow the sun well enough and know the general direction in which Scarborough lies. And once I reach the shore, which I am bound to do, rest assured...I will find my way."

"Just stay to the East," Henry suggested. "And take the road out of town for as far as it can lead you...or as long as it remains safe."

"Don't worry, Henry. I will. And thank you. For everything, I mean.

"I just wish there was more I could do," he lamented. We quickly finished breakfast, or rather I did, for Henry and Lucy hadn't quite finished but sensing my haste, Henry excused himself and no sooner was bringing the well packed horse around.

Once outside, and with the sun just beginning to rise, Henry handed me the reins. But as I leapt up into the saddle, thinking I had not a moment to spare, the guilt of leaving Val...without so much as saying goodbye started to weigh upon me heavily.

I had just wheeled the horse around, trying to get accustomed to the beast when Val came rushing out of the inn, gasping for breath.

"Zekiel? Zekiel!" she cried, spying me on top of the horse. Henry threw me a glance and I knew that I was trapped.

I promptly dismounted, handed the reins to Henry, and barely managed to maintain my balance when Val slammed into me full force. I struggled to hold her still.

"Were you just...just going to leave? Without so much as a goodbye?" she cried.

"I didn't wish to wake you." I fumbled, speaking the first thought that entered my mind. "No," I corrected. "The truth is...I...I didn't want to make our parting any more difficult than it already is."

"You'll come back, Zekiel. I know it," she said, holding me fast.

"Of course, I'll return," I said, trying to reassure her. "Of course I will."

But the truth was, I didn't know. There was no way I *could* know. So much was of yet uncertain. But for Val's sake, and perhaps even my own, I tried to put on a brave front for us both. "Listen to me," I said gently, pulling her slightly away. "I know not what lies ahead, nor what potential dangers I face. What all of us face during these difficult times..." Tears were already forming in her eyes, making this all the more difficult.

"But I do know this," I continued. "As soon as I know that Simon is all right, as soon as I know he is well, I promise to return with all speed. I won't delay a single moment..."

"I know, Zekiel...I know..."

"Then let us despair no more." I separated myself then, with no time left to linger and quickly regained my mount, knowing that time was short and that I had already been delayed far too long.

I offered Henry and Lucy a quick parting glance, unable to look at Val again. If she only knew how difficult this was for me...if only she knew how much at that moment I simply wanted to take her in my arms.

"*Zekiel?*" she called again, just as I made to leave, her tone desperate. I wheeled the horse around once more and to my surprise he obeyed, making the sharp turn with ease.

"The promise, Zekiel. The promise! What must I promise?" she begged.

Oh. The promise! In my haste I had nearly forgotten! Thankfully, I indeed had an answer.

"You asked me if I still would have fallen in love with you, had you told me the truth sooner," I began. Val's eyes grew wide.

And here I tried to smile for her, to say what words could not. But instead I found tears forming in my eyes. Because the truth was, I loved her. I loved her more than anything. And had I not fallen in love, had I judged her unfairly, then I never would have known that the happiness I felt whenever I was with her was even possible. I tried to tell her these things, desperately with my eyes alone but I knew that would not suffice.

"The promise be this..." I started again, trying to keep my voice steady. I knew what I wanted to ask, had long been thinking about it, but the coward in me was afraid.

Always afraid. But this I had to ask, I had to...and somehow, though I do not know how, I managed to carry on.

"When I return, whenever that may be...you and I...as soon as time allows..."

"Yes?" she said desperately. "Yes?"

"You and I are to be properly wed." Val gasped. "That is of course...if you will have me. Is that desire enough?"

Chapter Twenty-Four

I RODE AS HARD as I dared, covering the seemingly endless miles as fast as my horse would allow. We traveled both day and night, enduring occasional driving rain and subsequent treacherous going, resting only when absolutely necessary. Stopping only when both man and horse required sustenance or sleep. Forced to continue long after the road could no longer be seen, ever on guard against thieves or invaders, and searching for the coastline that would unerringly guide me home. I could ill afford a single delay, even despite Henry's earlier warnings.

When in less than three days' time, I somehow managed to reach the borders of Scarborough, I was completely unprepared for the nightmare that awaited. Not at all anticipating the horror and utter destruction that stood before me. Scarborough, my home, had been completely destroyed. Every last house, gone. *Everything* was gone. Nothing now remaining but ash and debris.

I screamed. Alarmed, my horse nearly threw me and I promptly dismounted then, body shaking, to inspect what I could of the remains. I found it odd that there were no villagers about. None. And for all I knew, dead. Murdered. But then...what of my home? What of Simon? Where was Simon?? I slowly made my way towards the small church and our adjoining home, holding my breath as I stumbled through the debris. In every direction I looked, destruction and smoke surrounded me. Nothing remained...nothing but an eerie, lingering silence along with the stench issuing from the rubble that yet still burned.

When I finally came upon where the church, my home, should have stood, I immediately fell to my knees and wept. My home, of course, was no more...and had been burned along with the rest. Nothing remained at all. Nothing. Nothing but crumbled rock and stone.

I grew frantic then, verging on panic, while memories of all that had been my home, my life, began to filter through my mind.

I was besieged by these thoughts, assaulted by vivid memories, what this place had meant to me, and they came at me at such an alarming rate that I nearly collapsed due to both grief and mental exhaustion. All the while asking myself, where was Simon?

WHERE WAS SIMON???

My imagination was running rampant, wild, wondering how and *why* this all had occurred. Who could have done such a thing? Suddenly, jolted from my thoughts, I noticed a solitary figure steadily approaching, only to recognize the man an instant later. John. A man of my village. A fisherman.

"*Zekiel*?" he cried, no doubt recognizing me the moment he came within range. He quickened his pace.

"John!" I shouted back, though hardly necessary, for he drew near. But I was desperate, in shock, rising to my feet at once. Surely John would have answers. John would know what had happened. John would know where I could find Simon.

"John!" I exclaimed, grabbing his shoulders to steady myself, leveling all of my questions upon him at once. "John, tell me what has happened. Where is Simon? Where are all the people?"

"Few survived," John nearly whispered.

"What do you mean, few survived? Who survived? Where is Simon???" I asked, my eyes wide with fear. "Where is Simon???" I demanded again.

"Zekiel..." he began slowly, but the answer was already in his eyes. A look of dread. And I knew even at that moment, without him having to say another word, knew what he was about to say.

"Please don't say it, John. Don't," I pleaded, my voice breaking.

"Zekiel...I am, I am truly sorry. I'm sorry to be the one to tell you this. Simon..."

"No," I said, my face and heart literally breaking. "No," I said again, only this time it sounded more like a wailing moan. "Please John, no." I sobbed, and I think I just kept repeating this, having completely lost it. But underneath the screams that came next, and despite the volume of my cries, even I heard what John said next.

"Simon is dead, Zekiel. Simon is dead."

Chapter Twenty-Five

THE FRENCH ARMY was easy enough to follow, for that is who I learned was responsible...and after ten minutes of questioning John, mostly about the direction in which they were headed, I was already on my way. Naturally, John had protested. Told me I was mad to dare go after them. That he, and what few survivors were left needed me. But in those first moments of agony, I had not been thinking clearly. Still was not thinking clearly.

"But Zekiel!" John had argued. "What do you intend to do?"

"What do I intend *to do*?" I asked, as if the answer had not been obvious. "Why, I intend to *kill* as many of the fucking bastards as I can."

"But Zekiel," he then tried to reason with me. "This...this is so unlike you. You are supposed to be a man of the Church! All of us are suffering. Surely you can see that. *All* of us have lost someone. All of us. And so I say to you, this is madness! Have you thought at all about what...what Simon would say?"

"Simon? What would Simon say?" I returned, my teeth clenched in rage. "*Simon is dead*, John." And when John had made to grab for my arm, begging me to reconsider, I had given him the coldest stare I could conjure, assuring him in no uncertain terms that those who had been responsible would pay. All of them would pay with their lives.

I departed immediately though it was likely I now rode openly toward my own death, but that thought neither slowed me down, nor would I alter my course. John said that the army had gone by way of water, a fleet so large, that with any luck, unburdened by the currents in which they sailed, I was certain to catch up to them soon, possibly even that very night.

But it was not to be. Exhausted by the pursuit, I rode long into the night until both man and horse could go no farther. We took what rest we could, sleeping a mere few hours before I woke only moments after dawn, refreshed, replenished and fueled by my hatred.

We rode on.

However, when we finally reached our destination, having ridden countless miles, catching up to the invaders at last, those I knew to be responsible for Simon's death, nothing could have prepared me for what I witnessed. Even from what I thought to be a safe vantage point, what did my eyes behold? The most horrific sight I had ever seen.

Men were being stabbed, slaughtered by the hundreds, if not thousands, and the coward I am insisted I turn away at once. All thirst for battle, revenge, gone in an instant. And yet I stood transfixed, unable to look away, surveying the gruesome scene before me.

Heads were decapitated, limbs were lost, and the blood; my God, there was so much blood, and I could no longer fight the urge to vomit and so I did.

Our own army had met them of course, were even now challenging these invaders, and no doubt had been assembled under the command of our king. I tried to locate him, searching for a royal banner or some other indication he was here, even now engaged in battle, but there were far too many soldiers to sort it out, for it was the largest gathering I had ever seen.

My horse gave a nervous snort, even as I managed to wheel him around, back the way we came, my eyes having seen more than enough, when I noticed we were suddenly being flanked on both sides.

Shit. Two men were running, approaching us on foot, one brandishing an axe, the other a crude spear, and I roughly kicked my horse forward, begging for all speed, only to narrowly dodge them both. I was nearly thrown then, so panic-stricken was my horse, and quickly realized that my mount had not at all been trained nor bred for battle. And who could blame him? In a land long having found peace? For all that we had witnessed, what we still witnessed, and what we now sought to escape from, should have driven any sane man or animal bolting for the hills.

I had to make a decision then, for there was very little time to ponder my options. My choice was to either fight or flee, join the battle or run. For to remain on the poor beast left us both an easy target, and it was simply only a matter of time before we would both be shot down.

This was it then. The moment. The life or death moment in which to decide. "Fight or flee, Zekiel," I whispered to myself. "Fight or flee."

I had allies here, I tried to remind myself. I wouldn't be alone. And here at last, I finally had the chance that I had asked for. To be the man I had always wanted to be. And with that thought, I tried to strengthen my resolve...only to find that my will wasn't strong enough. And so we ran. Terrified, we ran. I hit my horse on the flank as hard as I could and galloped off like the coward I was.

But no sooner were my worst fears realized as my horse, Henry's horse was suddenly shot out from under me and both man and horse went crashing to the ground, the enemy already upon us.

He came in the form of a single lone archer, having left our prior enemies behind, and even now he was attempting to fit another arrow to his string with a bow he leveled at my gut.

On my feet at once, the decision was then made for me. Without even thinking, without so much as a conscious thought, I made directly for him, running as fast as I could, deftly snatching a fallen sword that laid directly in my path, a sword already covered in blood. Its former master lay nearby I noticed, even as I sped past him, eyes wide from his recent death...and thus would hardly need the short blade again.

I don't know if all fear had deserted me, or if it was fear itself that drove me, but I managed to run faster still.

The archer had by now managed to refit a second arrow and steadily tried to take aim, even as I moved to engage him as fast as I could, madly darting left and right. My speed and boldness no doubt made him nervous as his hands appeared to be shaking, wildly unsteady, but he managed to take a deep breath to steady himself, and fired the arrow loose with an audible twang.

The bolt sailed wide and clear, having not been even remotely close, and I barreled into the man with my blade, full force, without so much as a second thought. I impaled him deeply, thoughts of Simon on my mind, and before I could even register my actions, before I could consider what I had just done, his eyes rolled back into their sockets.

I think I smiled, a strange but not unwelcomed feeling starting to come over me. He slipped from my blade then, collapsing upon the ground, only to land in a pool of his own fresh blood.

And no sooner did I clean the blade, wiping it upon the grass, hand visibly shaking from the excitement, when I realized I was being attacked again. And then again. Until I began to kill anyone and anything in my path. In those moments, I no longer knew fear. I no longer feared death. It was kill or be killed and the only option left was to fight, and so I fought, I killed, I maimed...and I did all of these things with a disturbing passion, a passion rivaling something close to ecstasy.

I began to lose count then, of how many lives I had already claimed, and yet every time I severed a man's head from his shoulders, every time my blade dug deep into another man's flesh, I felt a rush of satisfaction, elation, unlike anything I had ever known. And I wanted more.

My face I knew, was now a constantly contorted mess, teeth clenched while spitting undecipherable words and growls. Words of revenge, curses full of hate. But as I launched myself into each and every new attack, every stab, every cut, every man I laid low, I felt as if I had finally arrived home. Felt as if I had finally found my purpose, my place. And not only that…but I was eerily and surprisingly good at it. But perhaps most importantly of all? I had at long last found my courage.

And I wanted more.

Blood now covered my entire body, my clothes soaked in gore, torn to shreds, yet I could not have cared less for I was reveling in it all, and had at long last joined the ranks of my English allies.

Following the voices of our commanders, we were led into great surges, where we English, would boldly rush the French, concentrating our forces in hope of gaining a decisive victory or at the least forcing their retreat. Though I had never been a soldier, nor was officially a part of this army, all of us stood together as one. Farmers, carpenters, and soldiers alike.

But the French stood firm. Over and over, they stood firm. And as much as we pressed, as fiercely as we fought, the momentum ever shifted back and forth, both sides ever-pressing for surrender or even utter annihilation.

Even with dead bodies piled across the battleground, choking warriors with the stench, the bloodshed only raged on.

When I had but first arrived, it had been just past high noon, and yet somehow it was now dusk, for the day had grown darker and both sides had long since grown weary of the conflict.

We fought another sort of battle then, a battle of our own madness, for it was arising in each and every one of us, infecting us all, much like a disease. And as the hour grew later still, this contagion only took greater hold, for men from both sides began to rush half-crazed into battle, with cries of pure insanity, foolishly discarding their armor, for it had grown too heavy only to be cut down by one equally gone mad.

My limbs were exhausted and numb, my legs threatening to collapse beneath me, and what earlier had been movements filled with rage and purpose had now become clumsy and slow.

I held two blades by then, having rightfully gained another at some point, but for the life of me could not remember when nor how it had come to be. But did it even matter? I had no need of a shield, I *wanted* no shield, for I felt as if I were immortal, exhausted as I was. With two swords, I simply reasoned that I could kill twice as many.

I cried out myself then, stumbling forward much like the rest, thinking only of who I was to kill next.

And I knew then too that I was losing it, falling prey to this insanity, becoming crazed myself, and that the madness of the moment...had fully taken me.

Chapter Twenty-Six

A MERE THREE miles from where I stood, I knew a place existed where there was no violence. No pain. No death. Just three miles away from where I fought, there was peace. There was quiet. There was no such knowledge of this senseless violence, things as evil as those taking place in front of my very eyes. But the greater shock still that now passed through me, even as I slaughtered my next victim, was that *I, Zekiel Raven, was fully part of this evil.*

I knew in that moment that I was a slave to it, a slave to this madness. It was kill or be killed. Fuck or be fucked. And I was fucking these bastards up.

My strength was my hatred, and my hatred was my tool, and my tools were my weary arms along with the blood stained weapons that I possessed. I was an instrument of death, a living reaper, and lived only to stab, to maim, to kill…

To kill, to kill, to *kill*.

Kill, keep killing. Kill, keep killing…

I found myself screaming out loud, half out of my mind, as I finished off my next unfortunate victim, a lad no older than myself.

Blood gushed out before me as I yanked my blades free from his chest, mutilating his form in the process, though such a thing had now become routine, practically second nature.

I would not stop killing, *could not* stop killing, less I collapse from exhaustion, and no sooner did I whirl around to face the next man brave enough to cross my path.

He was a heavy-set man, significantly larger than myself, this newest foe who carried a double-bladed axe. I think I may have even shrugged.

For at that moment, it hardly mattered who he was, how big he was, for he would inevitably soon be dead.

Kill. Keep killing. Kill, keep killing...

I ducked his first swing easily, a strike aimed at my head, but he had foolishly made it clear how slow and clumsy he was with such a formidable weapon. The weight of his axe combined with his powerful but unproductive swing provided an opening and I lunged in with both blades, drawing deep red lines on both of his weary arms.

He dropped his axe in pain, even had enough sense to turn and flee, but with a second criss-crossing stroke, my blades had found his throat, splattering blood all over my already wet crimson face. He collapsed to the ground like a fat sack of shit, leaving yet another man dead. Another one for you, Simon.

Not a moment later, I was keenly aware of yet another enemy racing up fast behind me and likely thinking me unaware. And so I turned with little effort, wearing a wicked grin, thinking that this fool was simply the next in line to die.

I made ready to dodge which felt natural by now, thinking him utterly predictable, only to be impaled by a sharp spear point, which drove deep into my right side, slightly below my ribs.

I stared at the weapon embedded in me, felt my eyes going wide... as if both surprised and unwilling to accept what had just happened. But it had. And as I looked my assailant in the eyes, man to man, I knew that I had erred, knew I had been too slow, too confident, too careless. But I was tired...just so very, very tired.

Both blades fell from my hands as my initial shock passed, my sheer disbelief in the moment.

"Bblaaattgh," I gurgled, as blood erupted from my mouth, and I keeled over in horrific pain. The spear then slid out of me, the exchange having taken all but a second, and I hit hard against the ground, clutching at my side in agony. I waited for the final blow...waiting, just waiting...but the killing stroke never came...for my assailant had already moved on. Thinking me dead, there was no point in lingering for no doubt he had countless more enemies of his own to kill.

Kill. Keep killing. Kill. Keep killing.

That was what we were there to do...right? *Right?*

Blood continued to gush from my gut and my hands desperately scrambled to stem the flow, but I could not control the bleeding. I knew then that this was it. I knew my luck had finally run out...and that I would die.

I was going to fucking die!!!

No God, no. Please, God no, I silently begged. Please do not allow let this to happen.

Do not let this happen!!!

I struggled to remain conscious, but the pain was becoming unbearable. Stay alive damn it, I told myself. I have to stay alive. I had to avenge Simon! And what about...what about Val? My God, what about Val? Where was she? In my madness, I had until this moment nearly forgotten her. Consumed by my blood lust, consumed by my rage...I had nearly forgotten the woman I loved! The woman, who at this very moment was waiting desperately for me to return.

How could I have forgotten her?

How could I have forgotten the woman I loved???

But I had. In my quest to avenge Simon's death, I had. And through this madness, this disease I had whole heartedly embraced...I had lost sight of everything. *Lost...everything.*

My God, what have I done?

My God, what have I done??!!

My thoughts, proceeding of their own accord, then turned to that of the mysterious woman, the one I had met so near my village. That brief encounter that had seemingly put all of this into motion.

That one moment had changed my life, that moment had led to everything that happened since...my thoughts now wandered vaguely everywhere at once.

I struggled to call for help, having no sense of how much time had passed, but could see nothing but dead bodies. So many dead bodies...so many dead around me. Surely soon I would be joining them.

"Someone...help. Someone...p...*please*..." I tried to call out, but it may as well have been a whisper.

Though the battle still went on, raged on all around me, it was as if I had already ceased to exist, for none had come to my aid.

"H...h..." I panted. "H...help! HELP ME!" I managed to shout.

Nothing. Again, there was nothing...nothing but the sound of war in response, and I knew no help would come.

I knew no help would come...

Countless hours went by. And then at last, long into the night, the sounds of battle gradually faded away and an uncomfortable silence hung in the air.

I struggled to look around me, such as I was, but my vision became blurry and my body had gone cold.

I still clutched at my side out of instinct but beyond this, I could no longer hold onto any clear thought and knew I was finally losing consciousness, my life blood nearly at an end.

"Val...V...Val. For...forgive me...please forgive me for what I have..."

But I was unable to finish the sentence.

And as I drifted off towards death, perhaps through even the darkest of dreams, I could have sworn a shadow passed over me...

My eyes closed.

Part Three

The Book of Zekiel

Chapter Twenty-Seven

THE VAMPIRE MOVED swiftly across the littered field of battle. It was dark, well past midnight, but the vampire could see as clearly as if it were day.

Bodies were piled and lying about everywhere. Dead bodies mostly, some already beginning to rot, while others still fought death itself, desperately clinging to life by a thread.

The vampire sought such an individual now. She carefully combed the field of battle, the scent of blood assaulting, threatening to overwhelm her senses, yet the vampire moved with purpose, having no desire at all to feed.

She was searching, carefully searching, for someone very special...and she only hoped that she was not yet too late. Was it possible that she, that *they*...had been wrong? She wondered. No, she quickly reminded herself, for they had never been wrong before. But while their proven history and uncanny accuracy did little to silence her mounting concerns; what if this was the one time they had failed? What if they had miscalculated? What if she had simply been too late?

A lone black raven crowed, momentarily drawing her attention, and she watched as it pecked at a particularly large corpse, the bird eagerly taking its fill.

She scolded herself then, as she could ill afford to be distracted, but as she lingered and stared but a moment longer, both eager and ready to resume her search, she couldn't help but notice that there was a second body to be found underneath the first, buried underneath the remains in which the raven was perched upon.

It was him! Without any regard for the corpse on top of him, or the squawking raven who was forced to take flight, she flung the dead thing away at once, not giving it a second thought, for nothing else mattered at that moment...except him. Nothing except for him. The one that she had come for.

She quickly felt for a pulse and to her astonishment, the man still breathed, if faintly. His heartbeat was weak, barely perceptible, but the human was still very much alive...though her keen senses were telling her...that she had made it just in time.

The human suddenly coughed. Free of the weight that had been lying on top of him, he coughed again, several times, breathing now all the easier.

But when the man attempted to speak, even though his eyes remained closed, the vampire wore an even greater expression of relief.

"V...Val," he barely got out. "V...Val. Wh...where? Where are you? My...my love..."

He spat up a mouthful of blood then, directly into the vampire's face, but the mortal's eyes remained firmly closed. Any lesser vampire would have lost it. Would have given into that primal part of the brain. The very nature of her being. For the smell of him, the very scent of his blood on her face, almost drove her into a frenzy. Almost.

"Val," he repeated, this name over and over. He seemed delirious, quite unaware of anything, though the vampire couldn't help but to wonder if this "Val" that he spoke of, was going to present a problem.

And for as long as she had waited, how long she had sought out this specific individual, had watched over him, the vampire could ill afford to take that chance, nor would she allow this woman 'Val', to interfere with her plans.

But who was she? The vampire wondered. Who was this person that the mortal would not shut up about? The vampire saw no choice then but to enter his mind. It was not something she was particularly fond of doing, nor was it something that she had planned. Regardless, something had to be done. She hadn't traveled all this way just to deal with a mumbling fool, and the vampire thought it paramount to understand the extent of that relationship.

And so she searched through his mind then, carefully going through his thoughts, his memories, until she came upon the one he called Val.

She was beautiful, this human, her features striking, and it was a wonder the vampire had not come across this vivid image of her at once.

This 'Val' apparently existed throughout his mind, seemingly everywhere at once, his thoughts practically reeking of her scent...and it was clear that he loved this human dearly. So dearly in fact, that the depth of that love nearly had the vampire overwhelmed. His love for her was pure, his emotions impossibly deep. And this human knew, before he had foolishly ventured to nearly die in a war he could not begin to understand, he knew his beloved still lived. And that, the vampire decided, was a problem. An unexpected, complicated problem.

But it need not be, the vampire reminded herself, and so she used her considerable powers to work herself in deeper, ever deeper into his mind.

His mortal ties had to be removed, his past reconfigured, if he were ever to be of any use to her at all. She gathered his most recent memories, for therein lay the vexing emotions in question, and by using her inherent vampiric power, combined with that of her strong will, the vampire, in this one moment, with but a single stroke, altered the memory of that relationship...

...Altering his memory of Val.

Chapter Twenty-Eight

"DON'T TRY TO MOVE." A female voice instructed me. I tried to open my eyes.

"Don't try to move, Zekiel," that same voice repeated. "You've been wounded very badly...and you aren't out of the woods just yet. So the expression goes."

I was struggling to wake up, my vision still cloudy, and I could not yet make out this person who was somehow with me. My right side ached with incredible pain, such incredible flaring pain, but I did, however, realize one thing...

I was still alive.

"I am relieved to see you awake, truly, but please don't try to move," the female speaker warned a third time.

Her warning was hardly necessary.

For while I was still obviously breathing, I would not have been able to move even if I had wanted to, despite her repeated warnings.

Wait. *She?* Where exactly was I? I could no longer hear the sounds of battle and clearly, I was no longer outside. But more importantly...who was I with? Was I safe? Had I been captured? Was I..."Aaaaahhhggk." I moaned in agony as I became more and more lucid. The wound in my side felt as if it were burning, burning both inside and out.

"You're lucky to even be alive," the female voice remarked, only this time, her voice had been directly next to me. Momentarily startled, for I could have sworn she had been some distance away, if but a second ago, but perhaps too, I was simply groggy and not thinking straight. I craned my head in this new direction, off to my immediate left to better view my mysterious benefactor, my vision thankfully coming back into focus. And to my greater surprise, I recognized this woman immediately.

Her. *It was her!* The woman from the very beginning. That beautiful woman I had met just outside of Scarborough. Who had captured my heart and had gone on to become the very reason that had placed me upon this quest in the first place. The very reason behind all of this, for all that had transpired. It was *her!*

I desperately tried to concentrate, still reeling from the shock of having seen her again, but the pain in my side was as yet too great, my mind still foggy...and my eyes closed again.

When next I awoke, I could not at all begin to guess how long I slept, and had not the slightest clue as to whether only minutes had passed, or perhaps even days. I tried to remain conscious...

"Zekiel...be still," her now-familiar voice said softly in the darkness, for that voice was unmistakable. But was she really with me? Here with me? I started to wonder...but then I felt her cold hands touching me, tending to my wound. Was I dreaming? Was I imagining all of this?

"You went to sleep on me again, my brave one," she said in a soothing whisper.

"How...how long? How long have I been out?" I wanted to know, struggling to form the words.

"Days..." she replied evenly. "Days and many nights," she corrected, the same whisper in her tone. She said no more and continued to dress and clean my wound. Her touch was soft, comforting and sure, but strangely cold.

Colder hands I had never felt, but perhaps the sensation was due to my weakened condition. I suddenly had many questions. Wanted to know where she had come from and how, naturally my condition and how I fared, even her hands...but all was becoming dark suddenly, for my eyes were closing once again.

I could not stay conscious...I had to stay conscious...

But I could not.

Chapter Twenty-Nine

I IMMEDIATELY FELT like closing my eyes the moment they had opened again, but I somehow knew that I was not alone. I just felt it. Much like when you get the odd sensation that someone is behind you. And though disorientated as I was, there was simply an unmistakable presence in the room...*if* this was even considered a room. It felt more like a crude shelter (was that a breeze I felt from time to time?), though I could not say for sure. I struggled to stay awake.

How much time had again passed, I could not ascertain. Several times I felt as if I had woken up, albeit briefly, but the time had been fleeting. And during those times, I had barely been conscious, almost as if I had been in a trance. Just completely and utterly detached from the world. Sometimes I think I dreamt that I had been fed, bathed, cleaned even. Sometimes it felt so real, at other times I was not so sure. But always she was with me, always there in my dreams, always whispering words of comfort, telling me not to worry, bidding me to be still. But whether or not it had all been fabricated by my mind was impossible to say.

Before I could manage to speak, to question these things among others, I heard her voice again. That voice that had now been my constant comfort, my only friend, the presence that kept me from despair.

"How do you feel, Zekiel?" she politely inquired and somehow, I knew then that I had not imagined a thing. This was real, my wound was real. She, her voice, *all of it* was real. And I found myself once again thankful for I was miraculously still alive. Even the pain in my side, where I had been stabbed, seemed to have lessened considerably, but I knew I was yet in no condition to move. I knew that beyond any doubt.

But might I still die? Was I even now... slowly dying? Were her efforts simply prolonging the inevitable?

"How do you feel, Zekiel?" she patiently asked again, demanding my full attention.

"I feel...I feel..." How could I describe it? What could I say?

"It...it still hurts like hell," I responded at long last, barely able to complete the sentence. Even speaking out loud seemed to take considerable effort.

"But do you feel better or worse? You need to tell me. Tell me *exactly* how you feel," she asked, the last question sounding especially urgent.

"I feel...I do feel better," I managed. "But far from able to stand, I think. But...but how did you manage to rescue me?" I wanted to know, desperately trying to stay awake.

Every moment I lay there, attempting to stay lucid, seemed to consume a great deal of energy, energy I did not have, energy I could not sustain for long. My body just wanted to sleep.

"How? How did you save me? Find me even?" I forced myself to repeat when she had not answered in turn.

"Not as important as *why*," she replied.

"What?" I was perplexed. "I don't...I don't understand."

"*How* I saved you is not important. And as far as being 'saved', there's still no guarantee of that. You choose your questions unwisely, Zekiel. Or, I should rather say, you lack the proper knowledge to ask questions that are far more imperative."

"What questions should I be asking?" I said, a bit irritated.

"For now, Zekiel…you need your rest. And in the meantime, I will care for you as best I can, tend to you as often as possible. The worst I think has passed, but you lost a lot of blood, suffered a deep wound, that mind you, took all of my considerable skill to address… and soon? Too soon you will once again need your strength."

"My strength? Whatever for?"

"To witness the events that will soon take place."

"What events?" I asked, every moment growing more confused. More tired.

"The events…. sadly, which will plague this country a second time," she responded cryptically. There was a long pause of silence as if she were considering her next words very carefully, and so I took a moment to examine my current surroundings. From what I could gather, lying down such as I was, we appeared to be in a crude shelter of some sort (confirming my earlier suspicions), constructed from simple materials, wood most certainly, but I was unable to determine what else. Because the room was illuminated by only a single candle, off to my right, it made everything difficult to see. Made *her* difficult to see.

The mysterious woman always kept to my left, I realized, always opposite the light, her face constantly cloaked in shadow.

More than anything, what I desired most was to see that face, her face in the light. More than anything…I simply wanted to see *her*. As it was, I had only caught glimpses here and there, and only, I was starting to suspect, when she allowed herself to be *seen*. The long pause of silence continued.

When at last she spoke again, I listened closely, making every effort to concentrate on her words. I was still so very tired.

"You see, Zekiel…" she started again slowly. "Another war will soon take place. Even now the pieces have already been set into motion."

"I don't…"

"You don't understand. I know. You tend to say that a lot."

I don't know why, but her last remark made me smile. And strangely, I couldn't even recall the last time that had happened, something so simple as a smile. I tried to stay focused.

It was true that I would have liked to know more about this so-called war that had as of yet not happened, if I understood her properly, but another thought then dawned upon me, and I felt a fool for not asking sooner.

I was still in quite a bit of pain, but the answer I had spoken earlier had certainly been true. Yes, the pain had lessened dramatically, but I still wanted to know: Would I still live? Was I slated to die? All I seemed to have were questions, so many questions…and yet, no answers.

But she did.

And yet somehow, someway, for I did not know how else to explain it, I felt as if…as if the injury I had sustained, the horrible wound I had taken…I oddly felt like it had happened for a reason. A reason I had not yet found the answer to.

Would she have still come to my aid had I not been in need? And suppose I had never been injured. Would we still be in this place? Wherever we were? Simply under better circumstances? Furthermore, did I even know her name? Had she told me at some point and I simply could not remember?

"What is your name?" I asked her suddenly, ignoring her previous statement. She almost seemed relieved that I did.

"Ah, Zekiel…" she seemed to say with a smile. "But you ask of me that which I hold most dear."

"Your name?" I asked in disbelief.

"Yes, Zekiel. My name. A name gives a person a face, you see. And my face…is not meant for most good men to see."

"Your face?" I was dumbfounded. "But…but you're beautiful," I admitted before I could stop myself. She laughed out loud then, triggering my memory of that first encounter. Our first encounter. When we had first met.

I suddenly wanted to know everything about her. Everything about this extraordinary woman, whose fate was somehow intertwined with my own. If only...

"You will know, Zekiel," she said oddly, no pretext, catching me quite off guard. Had I known better, it was almost as if she had responded to my very thoughts, but that was absurd.

Wait, I tried to recall. Had something like this happened before? I couldn't at that moment remember.

"What will I know?" I decided to ask, bringing forth my growing suspicions.

"You will know...*everything*," she breathed, her voice once again a whisper.

"Are you always speaking so? Forever dodging the actual question?" I complained, once again growing irritated.

"For now, Zekiel...your health is all that matters. *All* that matters," she repeated, emphasizing the word. "That is...*if* I am right, of course."

"Right about *what*?" I snapped back in a tone I immediately wished I hadn't used.

I figured at once to apologize, but I felt as if what little energy I had, had all but been spent. Everything around me was becoming blurry once more and I knew I was losing consciousness.

I could feel my eyelids growing heavy, could feel my awareness fading as I vainly struggled to keep myself awake. Fighting against this overwhelming exhaustion that was destined to soon consume me.

I think I heard her speak once more.

"I have questions too, Zekiel...questions only you can answer."

But I was gone.

Chapter Thirty

When next I opened my eyes, I sensed that something was different.

Something had drastically changed. I struggled to shake off the last of my clouded dreams, but I was having a hard time getting my bearings. A hard time collecting my thoughts.

I think I felt a breeze...but I knew I wasn't in the room, nor in a bed. I was lying down on what felt like soft grass and after a quick check with my right hand, I knew it to be certain.

I was outside. Or rather, I should say, *we* were outside because I knew at once that she was with me. How I knew this, I could not be sure.

Much like before, I simply *felt* it.

When my vision at last came into focus, all before me was confirmed...but it was getting dark, the sun having just set I reckoned, which was easy enough to tell from the sky. I still had no idea as to where we actually were and yet...I started to hear a familiar sound. Sounds of...

"Be still for a moment, Zekiel. We have traveled a long way," her voice said softly beside me.

She suddenly had my full attention, but I very much wanted to know the source of these sounds for they were familiar to me...but sounds I could not yet place. I still felt somewhat groggy.

"Where are we?" I asked, thinking that the most pertinent question. I wanted desperately to sit up then and even made a weak but deliberate motion to do so.

"Lie still just a moment, Zekiel," she repeated.

She was then kneeling down beside me, inspecting the bandages that covered my wound, her hands gentle and warm, when I finally caught a glimpse of her face up close. And for that moment, all I could do was...was...

Stare. My God, she was beautiful. Possibly the most beautiful woman in the world. Certainly, the most gorgeous woman I had ever laid eyes on. And now here she was, at long last, as I had first remembered her.

For a long while, I had no words. No words came to mind with which to describe her beauty, nor what I felt when I looked upon her.

When I was finally just able to see...*her*. Clearly. Up close.

And then just as suddenly I realized something else...that something else had dramatically changed. Her hands had been *warm*.

"How do you feel, Zekiel?" she asked, demanding my focus once again.

"I...I feel...I...I think I can get up."

With her offered hand firmly in mine for support (and again I took note that her hand was indeed warm), I started to rise halfway into a sitting position, but quickly realized I could go no further, not yet able to stand. Not without causing serious discomfort. Or worse still, aggravating my recent wound.

I was well aware that I was obviously not paralyzed, for my legs weren't the problem. But the wound, however, was in such a place as to make standing incredibly difficult. As it was, it pained me a great deal simply to sit up, and knew my limitations were a direct result of my still, as of yet, weakened condition. If only my wound would heal, if only I could...

"Ugnnh," I involuntarily moaned. Just sitting up like this was a tremendous burden, took enormous effort, even though I did honestly feel much improved. Far better than before, even compared to just a day ago.

"Your body knows what it can and cannot do, Zekiel. Trust it. Sitting like this will suffice for now."

"Suffice for what?" I wanted to know.

"Are you able to stay awake?"

"What?" I replied, ever confused by the manner in which she spoke. The way she never directly answered a given question.

"Are you able to stay awake?" she repeated, a slight ire in her voice. "Why am I always repeating myself so?"

"I...yes. Yes, I can stay awake," I responded, starting to become irritated myself.

But something else was then distracting me. The sounds I continued to hear around us. Somewhere off in the distance. And these sounds were becoming far more pronounced. Far more...intense. I then became fully aware of what I was hearing and recognized those sounds for what they were.

Sounds of metal against metal. The thuds. The scrapping. The sound of cries, and yes, I could now even clearly hear the screams.

They were the sounds of war. Sounds of death. I knew right then and there that I would never forget them. That they would forever be kept in my memory. And upon hearing these sounds once again, so soon, made me feel...

I think I clenched my free hand, instinctively making a fist.

"I need to turn you a bit, Zekiel. Try to be still. I don't wish to disturb your wound."

I did as she instructed, keeping myself perfectly still, wondering what she intended to do. And then suddenly she had her arms under me, was starting to lift me! Moving me! But how? How was this possible? And yet, she now had me cradled in her arms, displaying no effort at all!

I tried desperately not to panic, despite knowing that this should not have been possible. Not for a woman her size. But then, just as quickly as she had picked me up, she was already gently setting me back down some distance away from where we had just been.

However, all of this was nearly forgotten as I found myself gazing upon that which I had no doubt been brought out here to see...

Another war. Another bloody and senseless war. I immediately wanted to look away. I wanted to be away from this place...along with the memories that were even then, starting to flood back to me.

"Witness it, Zekiel," she demanded, noting my discomfort. "Witness now the folly of men," she directed, crouching down beside me. "Witness the destruction they wreak upon themselves. Witness the hate. The pain. The very substance of mortality. Witness...witness now the death."

"But it...this is horrific," I whispered, unsure if I should have spoken.

"Ah, Zekiel, but you only speak the truth. Or at least, a part of the truth."

We remained a fair distance away from the battle, a battle already well in progress, but a battle I could see well enough...and yet still far enough away to be considered relatively safe.

We were perched on a very steep ridge, a good ways above the battle going on below, and yet distant enough to go unnoticed, especially concealed by the darkness as we were. And yet, despite how strange all of this was, the two of here together like this, and despite the horrific events I was now bearing witness to, I knew that with *her*, we were somehow safe. I simply knew it. And as crazy as that notion was, I could not help but feel oddly protected, as if for as long as I remained in her presence, no danger, nor harm would come to me. But *how* I knew this, I simply did not know.

But *who* was she? And why were we here?

"Focus on the battle, my brave warrior," she spoke again, interrupting these thoughts. "Focus on the lesson that you were brought here to learn."

"Lesson?" I replied in shock. "What lesson can I learn from this? What possibly can be learned from this, this stupidity?"

"Are you so quick to forget where it was that I found you?" she accused. "Furthermore, is it not wise or even prudent to defend oneself when other agreements cannot be reached? When someone seeks to take that which is yours by force?" she asked, always some riddle to be deciphered from her questions. "Observe for now, Zekiel," she bid me. "Simply watch...and let it all unfold."

Again, I heeded her words, even if I did not properly understand their meaning.

There was no mistaking what she wanted me to *observe* but...but what was it that she wanted me to see? To learn? How senseless war is? Was? I didn't for the life of me understand.

What I was able to witness in front of me, or rather far below, was a sight I recalled all too well. A sight I was not at all enjoying. Not at all. But as I could not move, not without her aid, I forced myself to take in what details I could.

The two armies were clearly very distinctive. The English, of course, were known to me, while those they fought were obviously foreign. But oddly enough, they bore no resemblance to those I had fought an untold amount of time ago. Was this a third army then?

I briefly wondered how long I had now been in her care, not knowing neither the month or day at present...but at the moment, I found myself with far more pressing questions to address.

"Who are they?" I wanted to know. "Who are they that invade these lands? For they are not whom came before. Of that, I am certain."

"Who they are will soon not matter. Not to you," my guardian answered in her typical cryptic fashion.

"But, why? You never tell me why," I protested, confused as ever. She did not answer straight away and instead continued to survey the battle for several long moments. She looked pensive, unsure for once how to answer. I looked again to the battle myself. Painful as it was…

"For now, Zekiel, you are but to watch," she reiterated. "To study that which you see. I need for you to understand."

"Understand? Understand what?"

"For one, that some things are *worth* fighting for. Did you not fight yourself to avenge the one you loved? To fight for your home which was destroyed? To fight for your very people? Think carefully before you answer."

"But how? *How* do you know these things?" I wanted to know, wondering how it was possible that she somehow implied having knowledge of Simon, and that of what had happened to my home.

"You…you spoke quite often. Quite a bit actually during the times you have been asleep, if you must know."

"Truly?" I asked, raising my eyebrows.

It sounded like a lie. As if she had fabricated her answer that very moment…and yet, I had no just cause. No cause, nor proof to dispute her claim. I turned a suspicious eye in her direction.

"You doubt me." she accused.

"No…I…"

"No? Now who is being dishonest?" she countered, as if she had been able to read my exact thoughts. "Must we continue to talk about trivial matters or can we continue our discussion? Would you believe me if I told you that *how* I know of these things is irrelevant to that which we discuss?"

When I could come up with no suitable response, she having effectively placed my growing suspicions on hold, she prompted me once more, as if our most recent exchange had never even occurred.

"I would have you tell me your cause for entering the battle," she began again. "What were your reasons? And were those reasons worth fighting for?" she reiterated carefully. "Again, I advise you to take your time before answering. I…trust we can now move on?"

I took a deep breath before answering, resolving to perhaps...discuss the prior topic at a later time.

"Very well," I began after a pause. "At the time, I admit that I had rushed headfirst into the battle, although I would argue that I was hardly given a choice."

"You did not answer my question. What drove you, Zekiel? What made you...plunge 'head first' as you so eloquently put it?" she mocked. "Was it simply to avenge those that you had lost?"

I thought again of the horrible battle. The battle that I had taken part of. The battle that had nearly claimed my life. That *still* might claim my life, for I knew other men surely died having suffered much less due to infection or worse.

"Zekiel?" she prompted.

"As I said"—thinking carefully—"I was not given much of a choice. I was attacked on sight upon my arrival."

"Had you no other opportunity to escape?" she pressed.

"I...I don't know," I said honestly. "But I confess that...I confess that once I had committed myself, committed myself to the battle, after that first man I killed..."

"You what?"

I took another deep breath. "I had no intention of leaving." I finished, casting my head downwards, feeling ashamed then of my actions, of what I had felt during those moments.

"Go on, Zekiel. What drove you? What prompted you to stay?"

"Initially? Revenge. My motive had been revenge."

"You said 'initially' as if there is far more to it. Far more reasons for your actions. I would have you tell me those reasons."

"I don't...I don't know," I lied.

"Ah, but you do. You do know. Tell me," she insisted.

I think I sighed. "As I have said, my motive had been revenge, but I realize now that revenge had...revenge had simply only been the start. But as time went on, even revenge, which should have been reason enough, had become...revenge had become the furthest thing from my mind. And I found myself becoming..."

"Becoming what?"

"Senseless. Completely senseless. As if...as if I were in those moments without *feeling*. Without any remorse at all for those I had slain, nor for those I had gone on to kill."

And then came the darkest thought of all. The truth at that moment that I was even then trying desperately to deny. The truth I dared not even speak out loud. And yet, somehow she *knew*. *Somehow, she knew!* Almost as if she had been able to read my every thought!

"Say it, Zekiel. Say it!" she insisted. "Say it!" she dared to shout.

"I enjoyed it!" I finally admitted. "At one point I found myself actually *enjoying* the slaughter. Is that what you would have me say?" I asked, exasperated, defeated.

"What are you more afraid of?" she came right back. "That of my judgment...or that of the truth?"

I took another deep breath. "I'd like to believe that I did it for Simon. That much, at least at the beginning, that much was true. My own private pain, driving me forward. Driving me to kill.

When I had first committed to the battle by choice, after the very first man I killed, even while my mind was yet my own, before the madness that surely took me, I realize now that Simon was merely my justification, the name I gave to my rage, my hatred. An excuse, almost. The reason I had entered the battle. It was not, however, the end result, nor did Simon long stay on my mind."

"And what was the end result?"

"Nothing. I accomplished nothing...except to discover that I am perhaps not the man I thought I was...and in more ways than one."

"Did you at least fulfill your thirst for revenge?"

"No. No amount of killing could have brought Simon back. I know that now."

"But was it worth it? Worth killing your fellow man several times over? Worth killing your race?"

"I don't want to belong to any race that does *this*," I said, gesturing towards the current battle. "Not anymore," I concluded somewhat defensively.

"And yet, how are you to know if their own reasons are just? Those who fight now? Perhaps for their own homes? Perhaps for others, they too have lost? But come, let us speak of the battle you fought in."

"That was purely self-defense...and therein lies the difference. These folk came here to bring death and destruction. We made no hostile act against them."

"You don't know that."

"Do you?" I countered.

"Yes. But you are correct. This country made no move against them."

"Then I find myself not guilty of anything. Leastways, I will not hold myself responsible for the lives I took. My conscience is clear."

"Do you not feel any remorse? Any remorse at all for those you have slain?" she questioned.

"Yes," I admitted after a short pause, determined to be honest both with her and myself. "Yes, I feel remorse. And yet, everything I did, these acts that I committed...somehow it all felt unavoidable. And yet, justified...as much as it pains me to admit."

"How so?"

"It almost felt as if...as if I *had* no choice. As if I was *meant* to *be* there. As if I had been charged with a duty. To fight for those unable to defend themselves. Much like my village. But I suppose that doesn't make any sense, does it? And yet I have to ask myself. What choice did I really have? It was kill or be killed! Any sane man would have done the same. Any sane man would have fought for his survival."

"Yes, Zekiel. Yes. That is it."

"That is what?"

"That is one of the lessons you were brought out here to learn. Remember it. All of it. Everything that we have spoken of."

"I don't think I understand. What lesson am I to learn? And how could I ever forget both the event you brought me out here to witness and that of the battle I recently took part in?"

"No. No, you will never forget," she said, more to herself, once again ignoring my questions. "And perhaps in time, no doubt, you too will one day understand. But what you said earlier...kill or be killed. Do you still feel this way after witnessing these events? Would you come again to those in need?"

"As I said before, what I did was for my own personal reasons. And yes, I openly admit that I enjoyed it. And even despite of my losing sight of things, when I found myself consumed by it all, I had gone to war for Simon. For my village. And yes, even for myself. And to that I hold...despite my later actions and motivations."

"I remember what you said, Zekiel," she said firmly. "I recall every conversation we have ever had, every last word spoken. However, did you, or did you not, also come to another's aid once upon a time? Possibly a young girl, perhaps...for reasons other than your own?"

My mind suddenly reeled. She knew! Somehow, she knew! She knew about...

"Val," I said out loud before I could stop myself. How did she know about Val?

"I know much, Zekiel. Far too much to tell on a single night," she answered, again seeming to know my every thought, my every action. "This Simon of yours..." she continued as almost an afterthought.

"What about him?"

"He seems to have taught you many valuable life lessons. These lessons too, you are not to forget."

"I will never know a greater man. Nor a better father. But tell me, how do you know of Val?"

"One day, Zekiel, you will become wise enough to know again the right questions to ask. How I know of her is also irrelevant to this conversation. What *is* relevant is the fact that you helped her but for no reason other than because it was the right thing to do. Am I mistaken in that regard?"

"No. No, I suppose not...and she was in danger. She needed my help."

"A completely unselfish act. And while most people would think themselves kind enough to help those in need, very few of those same people would have had the courage to *do something* about it.

People oftentimes think too much of themselves...and more often than that, give themselves far too much credit. But you are different. You are special...and that is why I have chosen you."

"What?" I asked, dumbfounded.

But I found at that moment that I had no more strength in which to debate. And that suddenly, everything that she was saying, our entire conversation, had swiftly gone beyond my comprehension. It was simply too much for me.

For the need for sleep was then descending upon me, beckoning me even, and I knew that my precious time awake was nearly at an end.

But before I could even begin to tell her of my weakening condition, even as I struggled to keep my eyes open, she once again seemed to sense my need before I could even speak the words, seemingly able to extract these thoughts from my very mind. It was almost then as if I could feel her...inside? Inside my head?

I wanted to ponder this further, reflect on all of these odd occurrences at length, but my strength had been all but spent.

"You have learned enough this day," she said, even as I was fading. "And many more lessons you will learn in the years yet to come. You have done well tonight, my chosen. Take now the rest you deserve."

I once again closed my eyes.

Chapter Thirty-One

"Zekiel, do try and stay awake long enough so that you are able to eat something. We have had a long journey."

As I began to rouse myself, which always took considerable effort, I knew we had returned to the small cabin. I was warm, bundled under several blankets, and as I opened my eyes, she was there as always, standing by my side, this time with what appeared to be a steaming bowl of soup in her hands.

"Please, Zekiel. You need your strength," she said, offering me the bowl.

Once again, I brought myself to a sitting position, taking note that this was becoming less and less of a strain, and took the bowl into my hands. It was warm, so comfortably warm, and the delicious aroma filled my nostrils.

"How long have I been asleep this time?" I asked after putting the first spoonful into my mouth. It tasted as good as it smelled. Better even.

"The time will come for conversation. Finish the soup first, please," she instructed.

I did as I was told without question. I was hungry, starving even, and managed to finish the entire bowl after a few short minutes, anxious to talk to her once more.

Afterwards, she took the empty bowl from me and took a seat next to the bed on the only available chair within the small chamber. Which, aside from a small table, and of course the bed in which I slept upon, were the only pieces of furniture in the room.

She waited several moments before speaking, as if debating how to proceed.

"The war is over. At least for now. The English...have lost," she said all at once, no emotion in her voice whatsoever. Nothing.

I was certainly shocked to hear such news, but felt oddly detached from it all, as if this news hardly mattered. My life had become a broken shell of what it once was, and with Simon having been taken from me, as well as the only home I had ever known, I did not at that moment hold our country, leastways our government, in the highest regard.

"Is England to be doomed then?" I asked, thinking more of the people than any impact this had on me. "Are the people to lose their freedom?"

"No. The people will come to accept it. They want nothing more than to live in peace. A new king will soon be crowned, but he will not be a king of this land."

"I don't quite understand. What was the point then? Of so much bloodshed?"

"There's nothing to understand. Nothing here that we will continue to discuss. I was merely relating the condition of your country. It matters not to me, nor will it soon matter to you. I only thought you would want to know."

"All I know is that I no longer have a home," I bitterly remarked. "It was destroyed...and not by those that are here now, but by those who came before. What's more, I am having a hard time caring for a country that can't even protect its own people."

"Good," she stated.

"Good?" I exclaimed. "What good do you speak of? Tell me what good has come of this? For I have only witnessed death, and much by my own hands, no less. And with Simon now gone and no home in which to return to, what do I have left? What kind of life am I to have? I was wounded and nearly killed in a war I did not start, and now lie here helpless with no future that I can see. Tell me then," I asked, changing the subject and wanting instead to know where this conversation was headed. "What is to become of you once I get better? *If* I get better? What is to become of me?"

"Ah, now those are good questions, Zekiel. However, those answers are yours to give, not mine."

"How so?"

"You are meant for more, Zekiel. But only if you *want* it. And the time has now come for me to tell you of the choices you now have before you."

"What choices do I *have*?" I demanded bitterly. "My home is *gone*, my village completely destroyed, and I find myself completely homeless. I still do not know why you saved me, or how, nor why you continue to help me. You tell me nothing of yourself, only to speak in riddles, and while I am not ungrateful, I confess I don't know what any of this really means."

She laughed. As if amused by it all, she laughed, while I could do nothing but lay there, completely helpless.

"Why do you laugh?" I asked her, clearly irritated.

"So much you do not comprehend, but I suppose I have only myself to blame. I know I owe you an explanation…for all of this, I know, but trust that the answers, *all* of the answers, are coming."

"Tell me then of my choices."

"You really *are* impatient at times," she sighed.

"What is your point?" I replied flippantly.

"Patience is a virtue," she came right back.

"Is that so? Well, it would appear as if that is one virtue of many, I do not have nor care to possess."

She laughed again, and this time I had to laugh myself. As much as these conversations drove me mad, I *liked* this woman. I liked this woman a great deal. There was something so odd about her, something so different, yet something entirely special too. And despite my constant confusion, even disregarding my current condition, I would happily go on like this forever, if only to be with her. To *know* her. That much at least was becoming clear, and perhaps the only thing I knew to be certain. I even began to fear then that if I were to lose her again, if she were to suddenly leave my side, I would almost surely go mad with grief.

Even as these feelings for her continued to grow, for I still knew so very little about her, my feelings for her were undeniably growing into something deeper still. A feeling I could not begin to understand. Even looking upon her face now, it was almost as she could sense this, *felt* my growing desire for her, and yet how she was able to do this I feared I would never know. She merely smiled in return, that knowing smile of hers, never revealing more than she wished.

Admittedly, the more time I spent with her seemed to arouse my curiosity further, and I wanted so very much to know everything. Everything about her, all that I could know.

"And I want to tell you, Zekiel. All of it," she spoke again, seemingly out of nowhere, as if it were impossible to keep anything from her. Again, how she was able to do this, or seemed to do this…I had no idea, nor even cared anymore.

Who she was, where she was from, how she was able to do some of the things I had seen her do…none of it held much meaning. Naturally, I still wanted to know these things but more importantly, I just wanted to *be* with her, loved by her, and found myself constantly distracted by her beauty, leastways when she allowed me to see her face.

"You find me attractive?" she asked, again seeming to respond to my innermost thoughts…though I had admittedly been staring. She even leaned in a bit closer.

"I…I…" I stammered, blushing.

"I find you handsome as well," she admitted, already pulling away. "But come now, Zekiel. We have far more important things to discuss…and my personal feelings must not get in the way."

"Get in the way of what?" I demanded, a flood of emotions rushing through me.

"Our destinies," she sighed. And at that moment, she bore a look of utter sadness. An expression I had seen only one other time. That night on which we had first met...and that face pained me deeply. What was the reason behind that face, I wondered? Such obvious...I don't know. Despair?

"Why do you care so much, Zekiel? Why do you care so much for someone you don't even know?" she suddenly snapped. "I've known you to have done that before. Before with that girl. Val, I believe is what you called her."

Val. How did she know about Val? And how could I have been so quick to forget that only days ago, or weeks, whenever it had been, that night we had witnessed the battle, she had spoken of Val then also. But how? How did she know?

Perhaps more importantly, for my mind was once again reeling with a rush of memories, I was forced to recall the circumstances in which Val and I had been separated. So suddenly, so abrupt, and I found myself feeling somewhat guilty now for I had not given Val a second thought since I had been wounded. Nor even after the day I had left her side.

Caught up in my own personal battles, I felt a profound sense of guilt, this feeling that I had abandoned her. And God only knew where she was now...or even if she was still alive...

"You cared for her a great deal," she said, obviously taking note of the distressed look I now wore on my face. "I can also see that you still do."

"I..."

"Tell me this, Zekiel," she interrupted. "Did you love her? *Do you still* love her?" she asked me flat out.

"I...I certainly care for her."

"That's not what I asked you," she came right back.

"Then...then, no. I do not love her...nor *did I* love her.

"You sound as if you are unsure."

Was I unsure? Was I honestly asking myself? Why did it feel as if...as if I were not quite thinking clearly? Almost as if...something were missing? Perhaps even out of sorts when the question had been simple enough? Did I really have to think about it? I mean...Val had only been a friend. Right? A very close friend, even a dear companion. But love? Why then...why did that thought feel like...like an internal debate?

"Zekiel?" she prompted.

"I found her attractive, that much I can admit," I answered after thinking carefully. "But we were from two different worlds, two very different people...nor did anything ever happen between us. More importantly, I never sought anything other than friendship with her. Nor did she."

"Good," she said, sounding pleased.

"What do you mean, *good*?" I pressed, feeling very much confused. "What did you mean?"

"Why nothing more than a friendship?" she countered, ignoring my questions.

"I guess..." I said after a pause. "I guess I meant that, well, although she was as fair a woman as any man could ever ask for, we just...neither of us wanted, nor desired to take our friendship any further. Perhaps too, she just wasn't *the one*."

"But why? What type of woman do you seek, Zekiel? Is there such a one for you?"

"I don't know," I admitted. "I've always been attractive to those far different from myself. And for whatever reason, I confess I've always found myself drawn to the mysterious."

"All women have the potential to be mysterious, Zekiel," she laughed. "Surely it is more than that. And based on what you said only moments ago, you said you were attracted to those who were different."

"True." I managed a chuckle. "But what more can I say? Other than to trust that which is in my heart?"

"Tell me more about the one," she insisted. "Your idea of the one."

"Why are you so interested?" I asked, curious myself as to the reason behind her questions.

"I'm only making conversation," she said, dismissing my question with a smile, that wonderful smile of hers. I would swear sometimes that it could light up the entire room, dark as it was.

"Let us change subjects then, if only for a time," she suggested, interrupting my thoughts.

"What would you like to talk about?"

"What I would really like to know is...what did you hope to find when you left your home that fateful day? When you set off alone to venture off into the wider world?"

"That's a difficult question." I stalled, thinking carefully as to how I should answer. Did I dare tell her the truth? Would she think I was mad?

"Why? Is being honest with me that difficult for you?" she asked with raised eyebrows. "Just be *honest*, Zekiel. Ever do we make things far more difficult, when simply being honest saves not only time, but prevents misunderstandings, confusion as well."

I didn't answer for quite some time. I didn't want to. I don't know if it was fear, dreading her reaction...or also because I knew it wasn't as simple of an answer as she was making it out to be.

"Zekiel," she prompted with that utmost patience. "Why did you leave? Put the thoughts you are having now into words."

I think I sighed.

"Zekiel. Just *say*," she demanded.

"I wanted to find you," I finally admitted. "I left my home in hopes of finding *you*." And there it was. That had been the reason. "Regardless of whether or not it was even possible, finding you I mean, much less any *hope* of finding you," I dared to go on. "That had been my motivation...along with the desire to explore different things. Different lands and customs. Experience life in a way apart from what I had grown accustomed to. I still don't know if I ever would have left...had it not been for you."

"I am flattered, to be sure, Zekiel...but you also speak with wisdom," she observed, again with a soft smile.

"You call that wisdom?" I questioned wryly. "I would call it foolish. Not only could I not find you on my own, but as you can see, I ended up nearly getting myself killed."

"Again, Zekiel, you speak with understanding. And you at least understand...as well as reflected upon the decisions you have made. I like that about you...impatient as you are. That in itself is a rare combination. Be not so quick to judge yourself. Instead, learn from thyself. For that is how we truly grow. But tell me, while you did not find me initially, why did you seek me out in the first place?"

"It was more than that." I spoke now without hesitation. "You were certainly the reason behind my motivation to leave...the push I needed." Smiling a bit ruefully then. "But to be perfectly honest, while I hoped and prayed to find you, as I have said, I think I was also searching for something else."

"Another person, perhaps?" she asked slyly.

"No." I laughed. And at that moment I realized something else.

I honestly felt better. Physically so. Like I was finally on the mend. Maybe even ready to walk soon.

This time spent in her care had been both the most painful of my existence, and yet easily the most fulfilling.

It was not just the fact that she was beautiful beyond comparison, for I knew there was more to it. Far more. She was deep, she was understanding. And much like Val, happened to be a fantastic listener.

Few, I think, go through life without finding such a person. Without ever knowing such a person. Someone willing to just hear you. Feel you. On an emotional level that nearly speaks to your heart. And that, I was coming to understand, was a large part of what I had been searching for. A mind and heart to rival my own. A person just as inquisitive. Ambitious, even. Not that I was some exceptional scholar, for I certainly was not, but I had always felt different from everyone else. I had always had different aspirations, greater than what our simple village could offer. And while a simple life could have and *should* have been enough, deep down I wanted more out of life. I just wanted...more. No. Not necessarily *more*. Just not what I *had*.

"So, what was it that you were looking for? Still looking for?" she asked, seemingly always in tune.

"Something different," I lamented. "I don't know how else to put it."

"Am I something different?" she asked mischievously.

"Yes. You are certainly that," I laughed.

"What else? Besides me, of course. Be specific, Zekiel."

"It's hard to explain."

"Try."

"Very well," I briefly laughed. "Have you ever at any time of your life...wanted a different existence, other than the one you have?"

"Yes." She answered in all seriousness, and strangely her tone had changed, as if I had just asked a question of great importance. Nevertheless, I continued. "Then you know what it is to search, what it means, to search for something that you don't even know what you are searching for."

"Oh, so much more than you know, Zekiel. So much more..."

"Then I feel as if the unknown is what I am searching for. A different life than the one I now possess."

"Do you truly, Zekiel? *Do you truly?* Sometimes, the unknown can be far beyond our imagination. So much more than we could ever dream. Sometimes for the better, sometimes for the worse. Often times, for the *worst*. Leastways, so it has been for me."

Finally. The first time she had ever truly revealed anything about herself, as if she were finally beginning to open up.

Please, my eyes bade her silently. Please, tell me more. Tell me more of yourself. And then, I knew I had to ask. I had to...for long had it been on my mind. "When we first met," I started tentatively. "That is, if I may...why were you crying so? Will you, at last, tell me?"

Silence. Complete silence in the room. Had I gone too far? Was I asking too much? It seemed a simple enough question, only I had no idea how personal the answer was to her. Not a clue.

After a lingering uncomfortable silence, she leaned in very close.

"I want to tell you, Zekiel. I do. But my tale is one that would take nights to tell. So many nights...and furthermore, my story is one that I fear even you would not understand. You, whom I would share everything with. Even that which I should not. Even that which I...I..."

Without warning, she stood up. Seemingly uncomfortable now with the conversation at hand. I even feared she was going to leave, fearing that I had upset her.

"Please..." I started to say. "Please do not leave me. If I have upset you in any way..." I pleaded, voicing my fears out loud.

"Maybe this is wrong," she said in all seriousness. "Maybe this is all wrong. Perhaps I have been too selfish."

"*Selfish*?" I questioned, in a rising tone. "You saved my life!"

A long and cold silence ensued.

"*Did I*, Zekiel? Did I *really*? You know not what you say."

"Then explain it to me!" I demanded in desperation. "How could you manage to cause me any harm? From what I can see, you have shown me nothing but kindness, asking but nothing in return! Nothing at all!"

"There is something I would ask, Zekiel." She deliberated after another long pause. "But something I am beginning to realize...I should not have thought to ask in the first place."

"Ask it," I demanded. "Ask anything of me and I will do it. Anything at all. You have only to name your request!"

"No!" she almost shouted. *"No!!!"* she repeated more forcefully and this was surely a side of her I had not seen before. She was visibly angry. Furious even. Her tone clearly indicating there was no room for debate.

"I...I...I need to be alone for a while." She spoke in a broken tone, obviously attempting to calm herself. "Yes. I need some time to myself."

I bowed my head in response and watched her turn to face the door, having no words left in which to argue. Nothing. Nothing that I could think to say...

Was I just going to let her leave? Just like that? Without so much as a fight?

"Wait!" I called out before I could stop myself. "Please...I just want to know. When...when will you return?" I verily begged, my voice caught in my throat.

"I...I don't know. I...I simply must...Zekiel, I need to go," she replied sadly, turning to face me.

"Please...just talk to me. Stay but just for a moment," I pleaded a final time.

And then? For the second time, I witnessed what I would never be able to explain. Would not have believed had I not seen it.

Standing almost directly in front of me, at the foot of the bed, she suddenly disappeared. As though she had never been in the room at all. Just as she had on the night we first met in Scarborough's woods.

She simply...vanished.

Chapter Thirty-Two

SHE DID NOT RETURN that night. Or the night after. Or the night after that.

I found myself utterly alone and in mounting despair, constantly longing for her presence, only to discover I was absolutely ravenous. I had to find some food, water, anything.

I worked my legs to get out of bed, for the first time since suffering my wound, but they failed to support me and I fell hard to the floor. I was not at all off to a good start.

I took the time then to rub my legs vigorously, knowing they'd had no exercise and little to no circulation, all the while trying to give myself some proper motivation. At first, all I was able to manage was wiggling a single toe. Then my foot. Then my ankles. It was a bit of a slow process and I grew exhausted from the effort, but at long last, was finally able to stand.

I was quite unsteady and took a few small steps, my stomach continued to ache painfully, but I otherwise appeared to be in surprisingly good condition.

Making my way slowly to the crude wooden door, I gingerly stepped outside. I had no idea of the day or date, nor how much time might have passed, nor how long I had spent inside the little shelter.

It was cold and very windy, and couldn't have been much past noon. I was always fairly accurate at guessing the time based on the location of the sun and had no reason to doubt myself now, even though the day was overcast, the skies filled with thick grey clouds.

The sun was well hidden, along with its welcome heat, and I took note that I hadn't bothered to dress appropriately before stepping outside. Until then, I had hardly been aware of the thin, dirty tunic that I wore.

Chastised by the cold, I wanted to go back inside, but delayed just a moment longer to examine my surroundings.

From what I could tell, there were no other dwellings in the area and the region was thick with trees. And thus, this place my mysterious benefactor had chosen was obviously remote and very well hidden, as there was no path or road to speak of. Nothing.

"Where *are* you?" I whispered into the wind, wondering in earnest as to where she might be. "Why did you leave me?"

Feeling drained from this short ordeal of being on my feet, even for those few minutes, I felt another great wave of dizziness, threatening to overtake me. I was still in no condition to do much of anything, much less stand, and this feeling of helplessness and uncertainty regarding when or if she would return made me despair. I lumbered back inside, still feeling quite hungry, and collapsed upon the bed.

Without warning, the small door to the crude shack I was resting in was suddenly rendered to pieces. It sounded like thunder and I awoke with a start, knowing that I had slept through the day, the room now completely dark. I craned my head from my prone position and was able to make out two figures silently entering the room. Fear gripped me from all sides…and I was still in no condition to move, much less defend myself without considerable effort.

"Where is ssshee?" one of them hissed. "Where is the bitch? Herrrr ssscent is everywhere."

"She's obviously not here," the other replied. "Search the room for clues," the other answered back.

"Who...who are you??" I stammered from the bed. "Why are you here?" I asked, attempting to sound braver than I felt.

"Well...what do weee have here?" the first one sneered. "I thought I sssmelled a mortal. I thought my keen sssenses were beginning to fail me, brother."

"Indeed."

Suddenly, both were standing over me, one on each side of the bed, having somehow moved across the room in the blink of an eye when a moment ago they had surely been near the open door. They had moved *just like her*, unnerving me further, though likely the least of my concerns.

I could now smell their rank breath directly above me, but as the room was completely dark, I couldn't make out their faces. I didn't know what to do.

"Thissssss one is almost dead," the second one chuckled. "Hardly fit for a meal."

"He will have to do," the first chuckled. "He will have to do."

I panicked. I didn't know who these men were, or more importantly, *what* they were. All I did know is that these intruders, whatever they were, were not here on amicable terms. The second one bent low and gave me a sniff.

"He will hardly do for the two of usssss...and I have no desire to drink from a corpse."

Drink? What were they talking about? What the hell was going on? I gripped the side of my bed and attempted to sit up. But before I could even register the movement, I was pushed back down with a strength that appalled me. And with only one hand restraining me, I couldn't even begin to move.

"Let me tassssste him first," the second man went on. "You had your fill from the last one."

"Very well," he said, removing his hand from where he had it on my chest. "But see that you don't suck him completely dry. But first..." he reflected. "Let us devour his mind. Surely he knows where she is."

"Indeed."

And suddenly I felt it. Before I could even think of trying to get up again, I felt it. The mental intrusion. I felt these creatures, or whatever they were in my *head*! I could feel what felt like invisible fingers, searching and groping my mind. Taking all of what was there and scrutinizing every piece, every last memory, every tiniest detail. I desperately wanted to shut them out but did not know how. I didn't know such a thing was even possible! I didn't know what to do!

It felt as if I had other people sharing my brain, almost as though a separate conversation was taking place between them, and I could feel them searching, scouring my memories of...of Simon, Merlin, of Val. Of *her*!

"He doesn't even know the bitch's name!" the second one screeched, and I felt at once that the mental grip had lessened considerably, though their combined presence remained in my mind.

"And yet, she has cared for this pathetic human. Tended to him," the other put in. "And from the looks of it, even cleaned his feces! Disgusting. Even now this mortal is so pathetic that he cannot even stand. So fragile. So weak. Why would she do this?"

"He doesn't know when shhhhhhe will return either," the other responded. "He doesn't know anything...and as to why she has spared this human? We will simply need to ask upon her return."

The mental intrusion ended abruptly, and I felt the oppressive foreign presence gradually leave my throbbing head.

"But in the meantime, he will know pain," the first one laughed.

"Yessssss," the second one agreed. "And he will feel his life being sssssslowly drained away."

He reached for me with clawed hands only to suddenly stop and here he paused, almost as if...as if he sensed something? The other creature hesitated as well and I knew...somehow in that instant, I knew that *she* was here. It was almost as if I heard her voice in my head, much like their mental intrusions, but instead of hearing actual words, I felt a certain reassurance. A reassurance that I was safe. And I knew she now stood within the door.

"Touch him again and you will perish. Both of you," she warned, and there could be no longer any doubt that she had arrived.

But what could she do?

"Ah....so the Master's bitch is indeed here. In this...pathetic England," one hissed at her, both of my tormentors turning to face her squarely.

"Come back quietly and we will let the mortal live," the other put in. "We care not one bit for this morsel. Only that you return to the Master at once."

"I will not be going anywhere with you," she said in a tone of finality, one that left no room for debate. "But you are both more than welcome to try."

At that moment, I could feel the sudden tension in the room. It felt charged. As if infused with some sort of physical energy crackling in the air. I feared for both of our lives.

I craned my head to see what was going on as the two creatures surrounding me were for the moment, considerably distracted and I saw her assume what appeared to be a fighting stance, a state of readiness, and she didn't appear the least bit concerned.

"Come now, sweet bitch," one of them said. "Don't make this difficult. The Master has promised to treat you kindly upon your return, provided you return with us now."

She laughed. "Treat me *kindly*? Show me this supposed kindness," she said mockingly.

"Enough games, you fucking cunt! Come with us or your pathetic mortal dies!" he promised, whirling around to raise a claw over my face, threatening to strike but once again stopping just short.

"Wait..." he started to say.

"What is it?" the other asked in turn.

"Don't you see what is going on here? She means to turn the mortal!!" he suddenly screeched.

Turn? Turn what? None of this was making any sense.

"Answer us truthfully and I will honor our original bargain. Do you mean to convert this mortal?"

"He is none of your concern." And with that, I heard the distinct sounds of weapons being drawn.

"Don't make this any harder than it hasssss to be," one of them stated. "We have no desire to kill you."

"Ah, but I," she countered. "Desire to kill you very much. Very much indeed."

From the corner of my eye, I saw that she held what appeared to be two short swords. Possibly long daggers. They glinted faintly in the darkness.

"Those blades..." one of them remarked. "We have been searching for those. The Master, and particularly Azuul, would like those back very much."

"I suppose we owe you a bit of gratitude then..." his companion chimed in. "Everything we have been searching for, neatly packaged, all in one room."

"Don't forget the mortal," the first one joked. "She provided a meal for us also."

"I tell you one last time," she interrupted, raising her blades threateningly. "Leave this place. Leave while I let you go freely. As I've said, I *very* much desire to destroy you, and so if you value your pathetic immortal lives, you will heed my warning. Depart this place and begone."

Immortal? What in God's Earth was going on here? Who were these men? How do they all know one another?

Be silent, Zekiel. A voice suddenly commanded from within my head. *The answers are coming. Close your mind for they can read it. Close your mind!*

It was *her* voice, inside my head! Just like them! My God, just like them!! But how could I close my mind? How was I supposed to do that? All I could do was stare at the action unfold in front of me.

"You have committed far too many crimes for us to depart in peace, sweet bitch," one of them said. "The Master has...requested your return and we *will* complete our task. And surely, as I'm certain you can imagine, the Master would prefer we not...damage his prize."

"Then the 'Master'..." she mocked. "Should have sent someone else!"

She suddenly disappeared from my view and what happened next became a blur. Even the men that stood over my bed had equally vanished. Gone. As though they had never been there at all, but I knew it was not so.

I could still feel them around me, even hear their pitched voices, but could see nothing with my eyes. The room sounded as if it were being battered from all sides until the battle became deafening. I couldn't make out anything and yet I knew all three were still there! I couldn't conceive how this possible, but they were all still there, somehow all around me. And somehow...fighting one another?! But how? How was any of this possible?

More importantly, I was becoming increasingly aware that the tiny shack was being ripped apart by supernatural forces. Destroyed.

The beams that I guessed to be supporting this place began to steadily groan and crack, the fragile walls beginning to shake...and I felt that at any moment, the place was going to collapse and bury me in the process. I tried to remain calm but at that moment, I was completely in a panic. I was certain that the roof was about to give way and trap us all within.

Already I could see holes blasted into all sides of the room, seemingly appearing of their own accord, letting in the faint moonlight and giving the room an eerie glow. This did little, if anything to improve my vision for I still could see virtually nothing, nothing of the battle that was surely taking place…and the roof was about to come down. The damn roof was about to come down!

Suddenly, without any warning whatsoever, in a moment that happened within an instant, I was instantaneously *outside*, cradled in her arms and she quickly, but gently was already setting me down upon the cold winter grass.

"Lie still just a few moments longer, Zekiel," she whispered. "Don't try to move. We are not free of danger just yet."

The tiny cabin, that which had been my home for untold months, fell to ruin with one final groan, collapsing, but a heartbeat later.

None of it made sense. None of it! She stood over me protectively and I saw those men once again, only several yards away. I was breathing heavily, my mind…struggling to understand. The mental exertion of this ordeal, wearing me out.

"You fight well," one of them complimented her, pointing a blade in our direction, the other similarly armed. But my protector was armed too, with those two short but vicious looking blades, of a make I had never seen before.

"How long has it been since we have seen you last?" the other questioned. "Centuries at least."

"See me well then," she commanded. "For I shall be the last thing you see!"

"Oh, but we do enjoy a challenge sweet, bitch. Our dear sweet…sister. Our dear sweet…

"…Amparo."

Chapter Thirty-Three

Amparo knew these two well. Knew how well they fought, how well they had been trained. But she was equally confident in her own abilities and even considered herself strangely fortunate. Neither of them was Cain.

"I see that your Master was wise to send two of you…Kabaal…Guma. Oh yes…I know you both well," she teased, starting to advance, the blood lust evident in her eyes.

"Ssss…stay back, bitch…" Kabaal warned, retreating a few steps. Guma did the same, but she slowly came on. Stalking even. This was not at all what they were expecting, Amparo taking the initiative, nor were they aware that they were doing exactly what she wanted them to do. Providing some distance from Zekiel.

She knew he was a liability now, a potential target that required protection, and so her primary focus was on him and solely him, for so much depended on his survival.

She led them on, constantly advancing, taunting, drawing both further and further away. But while they could still reach him, quite easily in fact, even in but a second, Amparo was, at the very least, putting him out of their view, hoping to direct all of their attention on herself.

"She leads us away from the human!" Guma cried, noting the deception and both vampires stopped in their tracks.

Amparo swore.

"Don't make us kill you, Amparo," Kabaal warned, once again pointing his weapon. "Come now...save yourself. Ssssave the human."

"It is *you*, both of *you*, who should be fearing for your lives!" she cried. "Be gone at once...and I promise to spare you."

Both vampires laughed. "We know you are old, Amparo...but everyone says you are weak."

It was Amparo's turn to smile. "That's simply because I've never displayed *my true power*!" she screamed, and they both cringed. They recovered after a moment, clearly more than embarrassed, and made ready to resume the fight once more.

"I'll admit, you have a way with wordssss, Amparo...but that is aaaallll you have," Kabaal said, trying to regain both his courage and a measure of pride. In truth, her claims had made them both question how powerful she truly was. Or...was it simply a bluff?

"I want...I want to seeee thiss. Thisss...power of yourss," Kabaal slurred, bolstering his confidence.

"Come with us now and return to the Lord Cain!!" Guma demanded.

"Never!" she cried, and with that proclamation, the battle commenced.

She rushed Guma first, who was directly to her left, her daggers poised and ready.

But her opponent hadn't anticipated her, hadn't anticipated her incredible speed, and she struck fast and hard, quite nearly taking his head. And while it hadn't been a fatal blow, significant damage had been done.

The vampire began bleeding profusely and fell to his knees, two identical deep lines of crimson, drawn just below the neck.

The blood flowed freely at first, swift and plentiful, but in a moment the flow slackened and the dark blood dripped no more.

The vampire remained where he was, however, resting, *healing*, eyes darting about, expecting another attack, but Amparo was no longer there.

Her second opponent, having witnessed this initial assault, was far more prepared, but was still as of yet, not quite ready enough.

Amparo was on him, faster than he deemed possible and he managed, only at the last possible second, to parry just in time.

But only in time to stop one blade. The other blade he felt, for it had been buried deep within his stomach, and he gurgled a generous amount of blood to his lips, his eyes going wide in pain.

Amparo then pressed herself in closer, bringing them face to face.

"How does it *feeeeeel*?" she mimicked, pushing her sharp blade in deeper, her other still pressing his sword.

Kabaal couldn't believe her strength. And finding no way in which to match her physically, he hissed in place of words and spat directly in her face. In response, she cruelly drew the embedded blade out...only to strike again, this time plunging the blade deep into his left breast.

"Gooooooo...to hellllll!" he growled and Amparo only smiled.

"I've already resided there long enough. With both of you. Most especially with *him*," she spat. "The one you so easily call, Master!"

The first vampire she had attacked, the one known as Guma, had now fully recovered. He was even then already on his feet and approaching fast, hoping to attack her unaware, but Amparo, never losing focus, easily sensed his movement from behind.

She disengaged with her right hand, which had been effectively pinning Kabaal's sword, and faster than he could react, much less parry, used the freed dagger to strike for his face, stabbing the creature in the eye.

He screamed in complete agony and stumbled back a few paces, but even she knew this vampire was still very much alive and would need only moments before the eye would once again be as good as new. Nevertheless, her non-fatal strike had still served its purpose, for at the very least, it had bought her some much-needed time...and Guma was coming.

She pivoted away from the grievously wounded Kabaal then and glided deftly back, moving so very fast, impossibly swift, and the attacking vampire missed his target easily. Amparo then quite abruptly shifted her feet, bringing her movement to a dead stop, spewing up dust from the ground due to the sheer force of the redirected momentum change, only to catapult back in the other direction, back at the vampire who was still trying to slow himself down. He had no time to even turn around.

Her blades entered his back and the vampire collapsed to his knees, howling and shrieking in pain. She literally ripped him apart then, piece by piece, and so appalling was her strength, so deadly were her blades, those immaculate, impossibly sharp blades, that his back was soon gutted and mutilated like a fish. Blood and gore was being flung everywhere, the vampire now very near death.

"And now I take your head," she declared, and her tone was that of absolute finality. And even though the vampire, as hideously mutilated as it was, was already attempting to heal, Guma closed his eyes, resigned to accept this fate. His immortal life, having lived for centuries, had finally come to its end.

True to her words, Amparo took his head clean off with a vicious crisscrossing stroke of her blades and the bloody thing fell to the ground, landing with a dull thud.

The headless corpse in front of her then spontaneously ignited, becoming a figure of flaming ash, until the bloodless remains became a dark grey husk. The solid ash figure, that had once been Guma, then broke apart and crumbled, only to be scattered by the very next breeze.

Amparo, whose work was hardly done, wasted no time and immediately started to scan for the other...but Kabaal, the one she had stabbed in the eye...was no longer to be seen. And then Zekiel's voice cried out.

"Zekiel. Oh my God, *Zekiel*!" She whirled around only to see the vampire she sought, holding Zekiel close.

No. Not just holding him. The vampire Kabaal was drinking his blood, his mouth pressed to Zekiel's throat.

Amparo was upon him in but a moment, having crossed the distance in a mere instant, and Kabaal was forced to disengage, much to his dissatisfaction.

Kabaal had seen her coming of course, and could have easily torn the human's throat, which had been Amparo's greatest fear. For so strong was the lust in those moments, so strong was the hunger, that he drank until the last possible moment, taking all that he possibly could. Only instinct and a will sharpened over centuries had made him brace for Amparo's attack and pull away, though no vampire in that moment, possibly not even Cain himself, could have stopped what happened next, for her timing and execution had been nothing short of perfection.

She collided with Kabaal with all of her force, and when she brought him to the ground, planted firmly above him, his back had been instantly broken, his spinal cord having been severed in half.

Seizing her advantage, she drove both of her blades deep into both of his wrists, neatly pinning the vampire to the ground, leaving his neck clear and exposed. It hardly mattered. The vampire was paralyzed, essentially nailed to the ground and even though his broken bones would eventually heal, Amparo wasn't about to give him that chance.

Allowing her very nature to take over, she immediately bared her own fangs and viciously clamped herself to Kabaal's throat.

The taste was liquid bliss. She went on to drink greedily, savoring the taste, absorbing the strength of one so old, though not nearly as ancient as she. Still, he was powerful and had sired only one other, but that had been many centuries ago, and thus his full power had been nearly restored.

For when a vampire is sired, Amparo, of course knew, the maker was very slow to recover the strength he or she passed on, for it was known to take centuries, *at the least,* to properly create a second offspring nearly or possibly just as powerful. Time was their ally and yet, also their greatest curse...and Cain had sired far too many. Fortunately, Amparo had been only his fourth.

Still, it was satisfying, deeply satisfying, to drain this one before her. She reveled in the moment, relishing every last drop as the vampire Kabaal moaned quietly, now under her complete control, unable to do anything other than yield his potent blood.

Zekiel started to groan. Zekiel! She had forgotten about Zekiel!

Lost in the trance of taking one of her own kind, she had been a victim to this dark embrace, hypnotically entrapped by her own blood lust, reveling in this new found strength gradually rising within her.

This was the inherent benefit of feeding upon one so old, for their power was added to your own. And through no fault of her own making, she had been lost in this feeling, lost in absorbing it all, lost in a feeling nothing short of ecstasy.

But remembering Zekiel, and thus recalling her all-important task, she finished Kabaal off quickly, draining him unto his death, and was but a moment later at the young man's side. But from the looks of him, Amparo didn't know what to do.

Much like when she had found him on that battlefield, Zekiel was coughing and spitting up blood...only this time, not from any outward injury. No, she knew. This had been the work of Kabaal...and the vampire had drained him deep.

Amparo began to panic, for it wasn't supposed to be like this. Not like this. *Not like this!* There was still so much that needed to be done...but Zekiel no longer had that time. His eyes, which had been closed, opened at last and desperately focused on hers.

"H...h...help...me," he barely managed to whisper.

"Zekiel!" she begged. "You have to hold on. Just a few minutes more. Please! *You have to hold on*!" she cried, trying to keep herself composed for his sake.

"Heeellllppp..." he whispered again in response.

"Zekiel! Zekiel, you *must* tell me *now* how you wish *to be*. How you wish to be...*for all time*."

But he had no idea what she was saying. Was barely conscious as it was. Amparo dropped one blade.

"*Zekiel. You have to tell me!!*" She shook him roughly, but Zekiel's eyes had already rolled back in his head.

Having no other choice, she knew she would have to enter his mind.

She did so then, breaching the way easily...but caution had to be taken for she had done this only once before.

She searched for specific images, particularly for images of how he saw himself, and they were much like when first they met. Long bangs, hair cut short in the back, cleanly shaven, very well-groomed. That was how he had to be...but this was hardly the Zekiel who lay before her.

He had grown a thick beard, his bangs were too long, and his hair had grown out in the back. Why hadn't she thought to handle these details before? Why hadn't she done more to prepare?

Yet she did know why. Because then, she had still been undecided, unable to make a choice, even though the blades had never once misled her.

Zekiel was *indeed the one*...and she knew it. The one she had been searching for, the one she had been led to, as well as the one she had waited centuries for...and now, here at last, the final decision was upon her.

Using the second dagger she still held in her hand, she began to cut his hair in the back, making it incredibly short, hardly aware of what she was doing or what this meant for them both. But her actions seemed answer enough...and she worked as fast as she could.

Such was the dexterity of vampires, so sure were their hands, that she made the cuts easily, precisely, moving as no human possibly could while she simultaneously continued to soothe Zekiel with her mind.

She trimmed his bangs next, still working impossibly fast, for they had grown almost down to his waist. She decided to cut the bangs to fall halfway down his chest, leaving them quite long, and angled them to frame his face, for that is how he would want it, and that was how it had to be.

She also thinned his hair, but mostly his incredibly long bangs, giving both sides a razor-sharp edge. The bangs were thinnest and longest at their points, but gradually the hair thickened the closer it got to his eyes. She stopped to survey her work, while also checking Zekiel's pulse...

She was starting to run out of time.

She had to shave him next, but without any water, or soap to use, she slashed her wrist and covered his face with her blood. She didn't want to risk a cut to his face, nor did she dare leave a scar.

Knowing the blood would have to do and ill affording any delay, she worked just as quickly, using the same blade with amazing grace, turning it effortlessly over and over in her hand.

As an afterthought, she left him just a bit of stubble, giving his face a slight shadow, should he ever have the desire to appear older. He could still shave if he should wish, but each time he did so, the stubble would simply return on the very next day. Or rather, in a vampire's case, the very next night.

This was in turn, why his hair had to be just so, for he would very much want an appealing appearance. It would be ghastly to awaken each night having to give oneself a haircut, to make oneself look presentable, and for eternity no less, should the vampire never perish. And Zekiel, had she not intervened, would have been frightful indeed.

Thankfully, he was quickly starting to resemble the impressive vampire he could become: handsome, dynamic, graceful...provided Amparo succeeded in time.

Zekiel's shallow breath had begun to quicken, but thankfully her task was almost done. Again, she inspected him, quickly trimming his fingernails, his toes, until she was at last satisfied with her work. She finished by wiping his face clean with her dress, wanting to be sure.

Amparo smiled. He looked perfect. Every bit as perfect as the vision in his mind.

Coughing, he suddenly sat up then, spat up another mouthful of blood, but by now Amparo was calm. She could not afford to rush the process.

"*Look at me*," she commanded softly, but Zekiel could not obey. His body had slumped back to the ground, eyes still closed, and he started to go into shock.

Amparo lunged for his neck. A connection had to be made.

She bit into him deeply and sought to connect their minds, for once a human was locked in this trance, a vampire could then communicate on an even deeper level and using this unique ability, she further attempted to calm his mind.

Zekiel had little blood to spare, for Kabaal's feeding had nearly killed him, so she would have to be swift, would have to be in total control. Fortunately, Amparo had seen this done many times before.

She knew how it had to be done.

Over the course of centuries, Cain himself had gotten sloppy, having conducted several rushed transformations, but at this particular moment, she couldn't help but to be silently thankful, for in her case, Cain had taken the time to craft her well. Far too well than he ever should have allowed.

For when Cain had created Amparo, he had done it to near perfection, and perfection is what Amparo desperately needed now, the moment now finally upon her.

With Zekiel now nearly drained, she fought savagely against herself, desperately searching for the will to let go, to free herself from the thirst, the very taste of his being, to disengage herself from the kill.

But the hunger was strong, so very, very strong, and she wanted very much to drain him, to kill him. For that was her natural instinct, her very nature, the sort of creature a vampire *was*.

Calling on her greatest strength and fortitude, she forced herself free of the feeding trance, fighting against those urges, and pried her bloody fangs free, effectively shutting down her hunger. With a slight growl escaping her lips, Amparo focused, promptly regaining her self control.

Zekiel, once free from her mind, started suffering through fits of paroxysmal coughing and it seemed as if he was trying very hard to speak. His eyes, which he'd opened somehow, stared at her blankly, threatening to roll back again.

He was nearly out of time.

Amparo addressed him at once, her tone completely calm. "Zekiel...you are dying. And in minutes, perhaps even seconds, you will be dead," she confessed to him.

"H...help...help me..." he pleaded between coughs, and likely the only words he could think to say.

"You have a choice, Zekiel. The choice I did not have. The choice I offer you now," she went on, pausing only long enough to make sure he was coherent enough to understand. She also spoke telepathically to his mind, these same words echoing in his head.

"You have the choice to be with me. To be with me for all time." she continued. "Free of mortal burdens. Free of the human life you have led...

You will never become sick, nor will you ever grow old. Every wound will heal, and you will remain as you are, unchanged for all time...but as always, my Dark One, there is also a very high price that must needs be paid."

"A...anything!" he managed to cry. "A...anything to be...to be with you. Anything...anything...to take away the pain...!" he gasped.

"No, Zekiel. What I offer must *not* be to ease your pain," she scolded. "That, I simply cannot accept. You must choose to be in this darkness, this darkness with me, for you will never again see the sun. And *that* is only a *part* of the evil curse I carry, Zekiel, this infection if you will, and then? And then there is also the thirst. Yes, Zekiel, the thirst...the internal, *eternal* thirst for mortal blood, and this you will need in order to survive. To sustain yourself.

For without blood, be it animal or human, without *accepting* this, you will no doubt perish, or at the very least, become a wretched and decrepit *thing*," she paused to let her words sink in but remarkably, Zekiel was starting to calm.

But he was simply near death, Amparo knew, yet even his mind told her in no uncertain terms that he had understood every word. And so, Amparo went on, nearly now out of time. "You will become a hunter of men. A killer! A creature of the night. And *that* is the truth of what I offer. That is the truth of *what I am*."

"Vampire..." he said. "Vampire!"

"Yes...Zekiel," she confirmed, pleased he had understood. "Vampir, in the old tongue, but always have we been called many names, and the many tales you no doubt heard as a child are true.

"Indeed, we *do* exist. But mortals do not see us. We never allow them to. Unless of course, it is our desire. They are food to us, Zekiel, sustenance for me, and that what keeps me alive, their blood in which keeps me young. And to you? I give you now the choice. I will let *you* decide. The choice I never had. The choice that was *never* given to me.

"Know that you will never again walk in the light of day, you will never know another dawn. Never. I cannot stress this enough.

"Think about what that means, Zekiel...to never again feel the warmth of the sun upon your face, trapped forever in an endless night. And then too...there is still more.

"My burdens will become your burdens...and I tell you now openly and truthfully, I carry the heaviest burden of them all.

"To be with me is to be hunted, hunted by my own kind. Marked for destruction by the one that did this to me.

"For you see Zekiel, even an immortal has enemies, particularly those who would seek to destroy them and my own life is fraught with constant danger. Immortality is not a given, not even to me, and I don't just mean the rising sun, which none of us may ever look upon again.

"For this is the existence we would have...and this is the life I offer. But together? Together we will find a way to survive. But only if you *want* it, Zekiel. Only if you decide to share this curse. This burden I have carried for centuries...

"For while you may have been searching for me for months, *I* have been searching for *you*...my entire life."

"I'm so...so *thirsty*," he mumbled, his body growing cold and starting to shake uncontrollably. Amparo remained calm. She had to time this perfectly. He had to be on the absolute brink of death.

Zekiel was wracked by a violent seizure then and was going into cardiac arrest and Amparo swiftly slashed her wrist, the dark blood spilling forth.

"*Choose, Zekiel. Choose!!!*" she shouted. "*You must choose now!!!*"

But with Zekiel saying nothing and her wrist already beginning to heal, Amparo was forced to slash her wrist again.

"*Choose!!!*" she demanded, and not another second could be spared.

"I choose...I choose *you*," Zekiel hoarsely whispered, suddenly coming to full awareness. His resilience, determination, were nothing short of stunning. But then his heart abruptly stopped beating...and he closed his eyes once more.

"So be it," Amparo declared, shoving her bleeding wrist into his mouth, her blood dripping down his throat. "Drink," Amparo implored. "Drink as much as you can. But you must drink from me, Zekiel. You must drink!!!" she cried. But the effort to do so was beyond him and she slashed her wrist yet again, bringing it to his mouth, this time pressing his lips wide.

Amparo started to panic, thinking herself too late...

Until finally...Zekiel began to swallow.

He was slow at first, gradually coming into awareness, but so thirsty was he, so parched, he cared not at all that he was drinking blood. Vampiric blood no less.

Amparo slashed her wrist again, enlarging the wound and again, pressed herself to his waiting lips.

And again, Zekiel indulged. On and on he drank.

"Yes...Zekiel..." she moaned, giving herself freely, all she possibly could. "Take it..." she breathed. "All of it. As much as I can possibly give..."

Zekiel was now sitting up, starting to take her in his arms. He continued to drain Amparo of her very life's essence, consuming what seemed every last drop of her being. And still, the feeding went on...and on...

Finally, when Amparo at last thought she could suffer no more, she growled at herself in protest, and resolved to give even more. And more...

But Amparo had taken it too far. For Zekiel was now draining her literally to death and Amparo no longer had the strength in which to stop him. If he did not disengage soon, her own life now starting to fade, Amparo's own immortal life would be lost.

"Zekiel..." she softly pleaded. "Zekiel...you must stop. Zekiel...you must *stop*!" she cried. "Please, Zekiel...*no more*. Please, Zekiel...*no more!!*"

And just when Amparo had thought her life at an end, only at the last possible moment prior to her own annihilation, Zekiel finally threw his head back, eyes wide with wonder, obeying his Master's command.

The transformation had begun...

Chapter Thirty-Four

THE BASTARD BIT ME. I can't believe the fucking bastard bit me! And then he started to drink my blood...the bastard *actually drank my blood!*

After that, *she* or rather...Amparo, was telling me to make a choice.

Amparo.

So that was her name. After all this time.

Amparo.

That was her name!

And then...and then I had agreed to something...a choice, something about a choice before me...

Something about life and death?

Wait.

Amparo had said something else. She had revealed something else...

I recall...

I recall that she made many revelations...had been telling me many things. Things that couldn't possibly be true...and yet, they were.

But none more important than...than...

Vampire.

Vampire!

Amparo was a vampire!

And then she had given her wrist to me. Because...because I was dying...and then I started...

Did I start to drink her blood??

I...I had been so thirsty.

I was still so very, very thirsty...

Oh my God.

What did I do?

Am I dead? Is this what death feels like?

What did I do???

And why am I...why am I still tasting blood?

Why is everything dark?

Why is everything black??

Why am I tasting blood???

"Zekiel..." a voice whispered, slicing through my thoughts.

Was that her? Was that Amparo?

Why am I tasting blood? Why couldn't I see anything?

Why am I still tasting blood?

And how? How do I even know what blood tastes like?

"Zekiel...you must stop," the voice said again. And it...it was her!

It was Amparo!

I suddenly opened my eyes. That had been the problem. That was why I couldn't see...

I now realized what was happening.

Zekiel...you must STOP!" Amparo cried...and now I knew why. I had her wrist pinned to my mouth tight.

I realized then what she had been asking. What she had demanded of me. Why she was asking me to stop.

But the taste...the taste was exquisite...*she* was exquisite...

And I never wanted this to end.

I only wanted to drink...

I never wanted this to end...

And I had never been this thirsty.

"Please, Zekiel...no more," she again pleaded to me and at that moment, I looked into her eyes and realized that if I didn't let go, if I didn't stop drinking, I was surely going to kill her.

Oh my God, I was killing her!

I was killing her!!!

But the thirst in me...this newfound thirst in me was in conflict with those thoughts, these emotions, struggling so very hard against them...and it was so hard to think rationally...with the taste of her, the very taste of her on my lips...

At this moment, I only knew the thirst. I cared about nothing else...and so my eyes pleaded to her...to let this go on. Please, Amparo...*let this go on*. Let this never end!

"Please, Zekiel...*NO MORE!!*" she cried. "Please, Zekiel *please!!!*" she begged.

My eyes had closed again involuntarily, if only to savor this as much as I possibly could, and yet unable to ignore her, I opened my eyes to look upon her once more.

Over and over she was pleading with me, desperately asking me to stop...and I knew that if I did not let go, that very moment, I realized with sudden clarity that Amparo was going to die.

Gritting my teeth and growling for strength, I finally found the resolve to pull myself free.

My eyes went wide then, feeling a sudden tightness in my stomach...

And then came the pain. Immediate and indescribable pain.

I fell back and collapsed to the ground.

Chapter Thirty-Five

AMPARO WAS LYING very still on the ground, on the very fringe of death. So impossibly close to death...

But even as she took in what felt like labored deep breaths, breaths she didn't even require, she still managed to turn her head, ever so slightly in order to turn her attention to Zekiel. He was starting to convulse again, writhing in spasms, and even as he began to vomit, even though he looked to be in indescribable pain, Amparo couldn't help but to shed a warm smile.

Zekiel was not vomiting blood. Instead, he was vomiting up his insides, anything that could be expelled. Everything he would no longer need.

She closed her eyes then, focusing for a moment on her own recovery, a recovery that was even now, ever so slowly, starting to take place. She was weaker than she had ever been, weaker than she had ever thought possible, for frailty was not common among her kind.

Pain was foreign. Pain was if anything, temporary. But pain she felt now unlike anything in all her years. She felt drained. Completely spent. For she had given the mortal Zekiel, everything. All but what she would need to survive.

She knew she had taken it too far, farther than she had ever initially dared, farther than she should have ultimately done.

And while likely in but a week's time, she would find herself much restored, she would be slow to recover the potency and strength of her blood and would likely need centuries to recover what she had lost. What she had given. What she had sacrificed…for she had gambled nothing less than her own immortal life.

But for all her pain, for all the suffering that she was now having to endure, and would endure, Amparo knew two things as absolute fact: She had been flawless. Absolutely flawless. And the process, as well as her execution, had been nothing short of perfection.

She privately wondered what strange fortune had befallen her, for draining Kabaal *immediately* before nearly sacrificing herself, had been nothing short of a blessing. Such a transformation, that she knew of, had never been accomplished quite like that. Not so soon after feeding on one of her own.

Certainly, Cain had been gluttonous before he would attempt to sire another, but for this he depended on mortals, whose weak blood was nothing compared to that of a vampire who was already many centuries-old like Kabaal, who was only a few hundred years younger than Amparo herself. And that blood, his ancient powerful blood, had instantly become a part of her. A part of her being.

For what had once been Amparo's own chemistry, derived from Cain's blood alone, had now mixed with that of Kabaal's, and even with what very little she had left, this powerful new mixture was already working to regenerate her body and pumping through her dry veins. For all but a few drops had been given to Zekiel, who now stood to inherit the blood of Cain, the unique blood of Amparo, and now even the blood of Kabaal, and all were now working together and binding within his body.

But even though he had been given so much, so much blood from Cain himself through Amparo, there was no foretelling what he would become. How powerful he would be. Nothing was ever certain during this most exacting, unpredictable and dangerous process, but Amparo had done it better than most. Had given far more blood than most. And she had even done it...better than Cain.

Now keeping a very watchful eye on Zekiel, she waited patiently, filled with so much hope...waiting to see what the dark undertaking would finally yield. Thankfully, the process, once it took hold, would not take very long...but for Amparo, those changes could not come soon enough.

He was done vomiting now, still on his hands and knees but thus, did Zekiel Raven start to noticeably change. Amparo noticed his arms first, for they were suddenly becoming strong, powerful, rather than the weakened limbs they had once been. As she continued to watch, much to her surprise, his arms actually seemed to swell, flexing out and then contracting, until his arms distinctly became more muscular than they had formerly been. Considerably more muscular than they had been even during the peak of his mortal life.

Amparo found that curious. Having witnessed countless transformations, this was something she had never seen before. He had been in relatively good shape before he had been confined to a bed for two months, but even Amparo could tell the difference in his arms.

The transformation, typically, would restore one to their best physical condition, but in most cases enhance only defects caused by malnourishment, an ailment of some kind, even repair a lame leg or broken arm. A minor restoration, basically.

But what Amparo saw in Zekiel appeared to be vastly different. He wasn't becoming overly muscular by any means, but his body was even now becoming far more impressive than what was typically possible. Almost as if he seemed to be endowed with a hidden strength that was slowly manifesting itself...

And the changes had only begun. Next, she noticed his legs and more specifically his calves. Visually, they were clearly looking more dynamic as well, those muscles appearing now slightly larger than what they had been only moments before. And while no mortal could conceivably see the slight difference, Amparo noted these changes well, with far more than a passing interest. For she had never witnessed an increase in muscle mass before, even on the smallest scale.

And yet, Zekiel continued to change.

Next, his hair actually *grew* another few inches, but solely his bangs, and Amparo nearly gasped.

How? Amparo wanted to know. Had he done it? Had he willed it to be longer? Had Amparo not witnessed it with her own eyes, she never would have believed it. And then Zekiel started to get up. No longer showing any physical pain, he staggered for just a moment before planting his feet to the ground, his eyes firmly closed.

His hair then, again seeming to have almost a life of its own, stretched itself impossibly straight, removing every last wrinkle, every last wave, until his hair fell effortlessly toward the ground.

Like all vampires, his hair would almost glisten with its own light, but even Amparo could already see that Zekiel's hair would be brighter than most. For the color of his hair had become blonder still, until it became a striking absolute yellow.

His ears, which his hair did not cover, were what Amparo noticed next. The ears would almost always become pointier for most vampires, while still retaining their basic shape, but Zekiel's were already becoming sharper than most, looking far more vampiric, while making him no less visually striking.

Even his face was becoming a bit more chiseled and yet smooth, his brows slightly tighter and overall, becoming far more handsome in the process. Zekiel had certainly been fair before, if not average in appearance, but the blood was crafting him into his very best. And while these changes were slight in the making, being such small things individually, when combined as a whole- Zekiel's transformation was making him perfect, in every sense of *how he wanted* to be viewed *himself.*

The next thing that Amparo noticed was the slight change in the color of his skin, becoming a bit paler in tone common to all vampires. It was already taking on a somewhat translucent sheen, still as yet almost imperceptible to most humans, unless viewed with the highest scrutiny. His fingernails would soon acquire a shine as well, appearing as though to be made of glass.

And while all these changes were happening simultaneously to various degrees; last but not least, was Zekiel's torso, and again Amparo witnessed what could only be described as an increase in mass, which added definition to his abdominal and chest regions, those muscles becoming far more pronounced.

A moment or so later, the transformation now nearly complete,

Amparo could only guess at what was going through his mind...

Zekiel Raven opened his eyes.

Chapter Thirty-Six

"How do you feel, Zekiel?" Amparo asked me. "How do you feel?"

I think I blinked several times.

I could see...

I could see in the dark.

I could see perfectly well in the dark! As if it were day!

And I could see...I could see...

I could see incredible detail. Every last possible detail. I didn't even know how this was possible...how to even describe this...but it was if I were viewing the world around me for the very first time.

From the dark clouds and bright stars above, to the fine distinct pattern of bark on a given tree. Even the leaves appeared different, full of color with their etched surfaces, the beating wings of a tiny insect, now clear to me with no discernable effort.

"Zekiel," I vaguely heard Amparo repeat. This time far more commanding...and I struggled to look her way, my senses overwhelmed.

The trees...the grass...I could see *every last detail*!

And I could focus my vision even tighter I discovered, by simple concentration alone. I even made out a rodent a fair distance away…scurrying and running about! Something I never would have seen otherwise.

And I immediately wanted to kill it.

"Zekiel!" Amparo snapped, and I finally turned her way. And then? I finally saw…her.

Oh my God…*her*.

Amparo.

Amparo…

With my new vision, I was seeing her as never before…

But she was lying on the ground and clearly hurt, even in pain! And I suddenly remembered that I had been the one who had done this to her!

Without thinking, with but my desire alone, I willed myself to her side moving faster than I could have possibly imagined, for I had somehow covered the distance between us in but an instant! How? What the fuck did I just do? My God, what the fuck did I just do? How had I moved like that? And what's more, it felt…natural, as if no effort had been exerted at all! But how?

But I had no time for such questions. Not when Amparo surely needed me. And not knowing exactly why, I gathered her into my arms, cradled her protectively and stood up, quickly and easily, her body as light as a feather.

What the hell was I doing?

"Zekiel!" she shouted, causing me to nearly drop her. "How do you feel?" she demanded.

I struggled, at a loss for words. "I feel…" I thought out loud, not at all comprehending what I was feeling. For I was feeling so many different things at once. But one thing I knew for certain. And that one thing was that I was feeling…nay…I felt…

Incredible.

"I feel incredible," I stated, repeating my thoughts out loud, as if confirming it, making it real.

And then I realized something else.

I felt no pain. I could no longer feel any pain!!! And instinctively I knew, just knew beyond any doubt, that the wound underneath my tunic...was completely gone. Healed. As if it had never happened.

I felt remarkably and incredibly in tune with myself. With my body. This body that I could *feel* just teeming with some newfound power. I felt strong, powerful, and no idea at all of what I was capable of...

And wanting to know the answer to that question very much.

So very, very much.

I felt...I felt as if...as if I had countless new senses, countless new hidden abilities, I felt...I just felt...

Completely overwhelmed.

"Zekiel," Amparo whispered, gently stroking my face, and I realized I was doing it again. Was becoming lost in my own thoughts, completely distracted, lost in these changes...but as I met her eyes with my own, I found myself silently pleading: When would these changes...when would they end? What was I becoming? What *had* I become? And if these things weren't enough to question, I could still feel myself becoming stronger still. As though some kind of energy that I couldn't begin to understand was even now surging and still growing inside me.

"When Amparo?" I finally asked her out loud. "When do these changes end?" But Amparo was doing nothing but staring at me. Staring at me with a smile.

"What is it?" I asked.

"Zekiel...you are...you look...amazing," she finally whispered. But she looked exhausted, drained, and her condition, among other things, concerned me a great deal. And despite these wonderous powers I was eager to discover, what I really needed to do in that moment was *focus*.

"Those other men. Other...vampires, I mean. What became of them?" I asked with concern, thinking of our immediate safety, still trying to piece everything together. With all that was happening to me, I had completely forgotten them.

"Dead, Zekiel. They will trouble us no more...though your concern for me is touching. Your eyes say as much," she managed a slight smile.

"Amparo," I addressed her firmly. "You're obviously hurt. So tell me what to do. You need to tell me what to do."

"Feed, my chosen...I need to feed. And rest. Yes. Much rest is needed," she answered with a whisper. She pressed herself in closer then, her head, form, now flush with my body. Pressed in closer so that she could...sleep?

Do we sleep??

Wait.

Am I? Am I like her?

Am I like...*Amparo?*

Oh my God.

I suddenly, and quite uncontrollably, started to sense the presence of a larger animal nearby. I could hear it. Hear it rustling. I could even smell it. And knew, from this scent alone, that what I had found was a fox. And a fairly nice sized one at that.

Tuning my senses, which took so very little effort, I quickly placed it mentally, and estimating it to be about 60 yards or so away. Amazingly, without any kind of visual confirmation, I simply *knew* where it was.

All other thoughts fled my mind at that point and I felt this sudden urge come over me. And not being able to control myself, I rudely dropped Amparo to the ground.

I was moving before I could think...before I could even register the thought.

And in but a flash, a mere instant...the fox was in my hands.

And before I could stop myself, before I could even consider my actions, I was biting the poor animal's neck.

Blood. I must have this creature's blood.

Blood...

Yes...blood. *The taste of this blood...*
I feel as if I *must* have blood...I *need* it.
And I felt as if...
Amparo.
Oh my God, I needed to help Amparo!

I reluctantly removed my teeth from the dying animal, which in itself was no easy task, for I had this nearly uncontrollable instinct, as well as what can only be described as a primal desire to simply *kill it.*

But Amparo. I had to help Amparo!

In but another instant, I willed myself back to her side, moving as I had before, and presented what was left. My movements again, unconscious. Happening by sheer reflex.

"Drink..." I instructed her, but Amparo needed no directive. The fox, what was left of it anyway, was drained in seconds.

But the blood seemed to have no effect. No effect on her at all.

Admittedly, the blood had been weak. Even inexperienced as I was, I could sense that in the taste...even though the taste had been pleasant enough. But I did start to feel something.

In the few minutes that had passed, I was of course still trying to grasp all the changes to this...to this new body, for surely this felt nothing like my own. But I do know that the fox blood was starting to have a positive effect on me...almost as though it had revitalized me on the smallest possible scale, as though I had taken its energy. No, it's very life force.

Amazing, these new senses. Amazing that these senses were allowing me...to feel these things. Especially from a creature so small, so seemingly inconsequential...and to feel something so distinct from the blood. And somehow...oh my God, somehow...I knew what Amparo needed. And what she still needed.

Blood. Amparo needed blood...and a lot of it.

Amparo must have blood...

As I...*as I must have blood?*

I didn't mean to snare the fox in my hands...I hadn't intended for that to happen! But I...I also cannot deny that I had enjoyed it. Enjoyed the taste of it. And had it not been for Amparo, had she not needed that fox more than I, than I surely would have loved nothing more than to have drained that fox dry myself.

Oh my God.

I need blood...I *like* the taste of blood.

...And I'm afraid I want more of it.

Chapter Thirty-Seven

AMPARO COULDN'T TAKE her eyes off of Zekiel. Even in her weakened condition. She just simply couldn't believe how incredible he appeared.

He was strong, oh she could sense he was strong...but how strong?

How fast?

How cunning??

Catching the fox had been nothing...for any vampire could have caught it just as easily. But Zekiel? Even for a task so simple, the way he moved, his speed, just seemed entirely too natural for him. Second nature, even. But first things first, she told herself. She desperately had to feed.

The fox had already been half-dead, hardly a mouthful, and it had only increased her thirst for more. Never before had she felt the thirst such as this. Not even after she had awoken after centuries of the deep sleep. Mortal blood could restore her...to a certain degree, but Amparo, in her weakened state, would require half a dozen. Half a dozen mortal lives at least.

Zekiel suddenly crouched down low beside her. He looked left...then slowly panned his head to the right. What was he doing? What had he sensed?

"Amparo," he said calmly, his head turning vaguely north. "I sense...I sense something...I?"

"Humans," Amparo answered, closing her eyes. "Two humans...no...three. Not more than 2 miles away." She opened her eyes and turned a puzzled expression towards Zekiel. "You can sense them?"

Zekiel nodded. "And now that you have identified them as humans," he began thoughtfully, "I should have no problem distinguishing them in the future. It is as you said, three...but I..."

"Speak, Zekiel," she commanded.

"I sense..." he started again and instinctively closed his eyes, concentrating. "I sense that...I sense that these men...I sense that...there is something not quite right about them. They...they have evil intentions. And I feel as if..." Zekiel's eyes shot open. "I feel as if I can read their thoughts! *Am I* reading their thoughts? Is that even possible? Is that what I am sensing?" he asked incredulously.

Amparo smiled. "You can, my chosen. You can. Indeed, you can read their minds if you *choose* to do so. Start with one. Yes. There is a larger one among the group. Can you sense that as well?"

Zekiel closed his eyes and in a moment he opened them again, and again he showed his surprise. "I can. Oh my God, Amparo...I can!"

"Concentrate, Zekiel!" she snapped. "Let this serve as your first lesson." And here she paused and incredibly rose to her feet. Zekiel was quick to follow, offering an arm for support but she stopped him with an outstretched hand. "You...Zekiel Raven. My chosen. *You*...are no longer mortal."

"I..." he started to respond.

"Be silent!" she commanded, more forcefully than she had intended. He obediently lowered his head. Eyes to the ground.

"I...I apologize." Amparo said, seeking to amend her harsh tone. "I meant no harm, Zekiel. It's simply that...you must understand." And here she became especially serious. "Zekiel." This time in a much softer tone, and ever so slowly he met her eyes. "You are no longer human. You are *vampire*, thus you must no longer think...as a mortal. Gifts you have now. Abilities, lessons you will have to learn quickly. Do you understand?"

He nodded. "Good," she said. "Then your next task be this. It is time for you to feed, but this time, not on a mere animal. And so you shall feed on human blood...starting with the three humans nearby."

Zekiel looked at her incredulously.

"Yes, my chosen," Amparo responded to the look on his face. "And yes, Zekiel, you must kill...but you will spare the largest one. That one you will bring to me. *Alive*."

Zekiel closed his eyes then and Amparo could not tell whether he was struggling internally with what she had asked, or if he was merely mentally trying to locate the men. Amparo held her breath and hoped for the latter.

Zekiel Raven once again opened his eyes and the look on his face, the wild smile planted there...was answer enough.

And not for the first time, and certainly not the last, Zekiel Raven surprised Amparo once again.

He disappeared.

Chapter Thirty-Eight

I WAS RUNNING as fast as I could, my legs pumping fast. Trying to discover the limits to this power.

My power.

This incredible, amazing power that was seemingly bursting from my fingertips. From my arms. My legs. My entire body...and I suddenly felt the urge, nay, the very *need* to jump.

I took a few more steps, moving now at what I thought was my absolute top speed and pushed off the ground to propel myself as high and as far as possible, the explosive power of my legs astounding me. I shot up, higher and higher, and even higher still until I felt as if gravity no longer existed, finding myself completely airborne.

Oh my God, oh my God, Oh my God! This incredible sensation!

I felt as if I could fly...

I felt as if I could fly!

But alas, I could not. Gravity seemed to have no effect on me one moment, but in the very next, was gently calling me back to the ground. Down, down, down to the ground.

Considering the sheer height of my descent, I admittedly felt a little nervous about a proper landing and even feared injury, but a moment later I touched down lightly, landing in a comfortable crouch. I had thought to do this, or rather my body did almost naturally, thinking to absorb my momentum.

I came to learn this was hardly necessary, for much like a cat, falling from some great distance, this body seemed to be simply designed for this. And I found myself very much wanting to do it again...

But I had been given a task. I had to locate my prey. My prey? And yet, this is what these men felt like to me.

Prey. And the only comparison I could make as to this predatory feeling surely coming over me, was that I had to assume that *this* had to be what a wolf or other predatory animal must *feel* when it is hunting for its next meal. And it was if, in that moment that my very nature had changed. I still felt like myself...but there were suddenly new instincts, impulses that were even now guiding me, compelling me into action and I felt inclined to listen. And what these instincts, what my *body* was urging me to do, was *feed*.

I opened my mind then, closed my eyes, and focused on this inner voice. This inner power...and listened.

The humans were already very close. Very, very close to where I had landed, no more than 200 yards away.

I could hear their conversation quite clearly, though I honestly had no interest in what they were discussing, other than to take note of my exceptional hearing.

Another four leaps carried me to the base of their camp, but what I found surprising is that, even without the added momentum of running, I was still able to leap an incredible amount of distance. In fact, I even felt the need to hold back for fear of leaping beyond their camp. Naturally, that still would not have been a problem, but while I had a task to complete, there was no sense in wasting time. Amparo was waiting for me, and now was the time to focus, for there would be plenty of time to sort out my powers later.

In fact, these humans, who were even now before me, would prove ample enough...for a very different type of practice. I desperately wanted to know what I could do in terms of combat. To what extent. And so brimming with newfound confidence, I boldly walked into their camp.

"Good evening," I greeted them, suddenly feeling very foolish for having left Amparo wearing nothing more than my dirty and soiled tunic. All three men turned to me in surprise. I didn't hesitate.

I lunged for the tallest one, wrapping my arms around his midsection, and before I could consider my actions, having simply gave in to this impulse that drove me, the sheer force of my attack brought us to the ground with me fully in control and on top of him.

I felt something within him break, likely his hips, where I had taken hold of him, but before he could even cry out in pain, before the others had even moved, I reached for his neck, fangs bared. Fangs? But then my teeth broke his flesh...and nothing else mattered.

A flood of blood started pouring down my throat and it was almost as if Heaven itself had opened. Unlike the fox, this was nothing short of bliss, and had I any willpower in which to stop, I surely would have let out a cry.

Mouthful after mouthful, this glorious fount went on and I felt nearly powerless against it. And as his blood continued to flow into me, it was then at that moment that I knew him. Knew everything about him.

His memories, his history, his entire life, even his most closely guarded secrets. All of it.

For his mind had been laid bare before me, it was all there in his blood, and I found myself savoring these details, and very much wanting to consume every last drop.

His heartbeat started to quicken, beating faster and faster...His blood flowing into me...faster and faster...until I felt absolutely roaring drunk.

Drunk with the taste of him, the taste of this rich, succulent blood. Possessed with rising power and vitality, and I wanted nothing more but for this to go on.

Yes. Like it had been with Amparo. On and on. I never wanted the blood to end. I *never* wanted the blood to end...but I could feel his heartbeat slowing, slowing along now with the flow of blood. The human collapsed in my arms then, powerless, lifeless, and all I could think about was that I wanted more.

I looked up from my first kill, blood covering my face, and I was swooning so much from his fresh blood, still-living mortal blood, that I hardly registered that the fat human was swinging a slow punch at me. So drunk I was on this power, so drunk was I on this feeling, the feeling of all that blood coursing through my veins.

Planting my feet upon the dead carcass, taking curious note of my ridiculous flexibility, I sprang off him backwards, almost lazily in the direction of my next attacker. Using my outstretched hand, I planted it on his head and pushed off to complete the rotation, landing clear behind him.

I think I laughed, for the motion had been so easy, effortless. And I also realized that I had given no thought to it whatsoever. It had been completely instinctual for me, my reaction and these acrobatic movements feeling entirely natural.

The heavy-set man turned around then, obviously finding me now behind him, his brain not quite comprehending what had happened. Remarkably, I was reading this directly from his mind and even knew what he was going to do next! And knowing what was coming, I simply stood my ground. As for the third man, he was even now trying to sneak up on me from behind.

Somehow, even though I had once again killed a man, killed a man in cold blood, I came to the instant conclusion that I was enjoying this. There was no sense in denying it...and I even found that I wasn't the least bit bothered by it. Whereas before, when I had been injured in battle, there had at least been a sense of remorse, no, not remorse...perhaps guilt, guilt that I had done something evil. Well, *fuck all of that*, to put it bluntly, for I carried no such moral dilemmas now.

These men were all *truly evil* and so I told myself that they all deserved to die and all would be better off because of it.

Even I had to admit that I found much enjoyment in killing that first one...and I very much wanted to kill again.

Kill. Yes, kill. I very much wanted to *kill*.

I turned ever so slightly, just to show the man behind me that I indeed knew he was there. "Yes," I purred, speaking out loud, eliciting a look of terror on their faces. "Come at me again. Both of you."

The heavyset man halted his advance, as did the other. Neither human moved, for fear had overwhelmed them, and it was in this brief respite that both were now able to see me clearly. And if I could have seen myself at that moment, could have seen the blood on my face, I would have been terrified as well, for these men had just come to the realization that both of them were going to die.

But humans are resilient. Proud. And even in the face of impending doom, most would try to defy what fate has surely laid before them. Scared, even terrified, but somehow finding a bit of courage, both men approached again.

I quickly moved behind the fat one and in doing so realized that he hadn't even seen me move. He was still looking ahead, dumbfounded, thinking I had vanished. But I had only moved faster than his human eyes could see! I tested this, placing myself in front of him once more, surprising the fat one again. If only he knew how surprised I was in return!

Overriding his fear, he somehow managed to swing at me but this time I noted the movement. This time I stayed perfectly still. My eyes followed how slowly his hand appeared to move, and when it finally came close to striking me, I intercepted his fist with my own hand, palm up, letting the full force of his fist hit my palm squarely. I heard a sickening crack and the man howled in pain, his knuckles and possibly a few fingers broken, whereas I had not felt a thing. Not the slightest amount of pain. I had felt the strike of course, but it carried the relative force of a small child's impotent fury, nothing more. Perhaps even less.

Curling my fingers over his outstretched fist, I gave a little squeeze, crushing every bone in his hand to mere powder. I couldn't believe my strength! The fat man crumpled to the ground then, the pain, rendering him unconscious. I turned my attention to the other one, ready to engage him, but having seen the short work I made of his two companions, he wisely turned and fled.

Slinging the fat bastard over my shoulder, who weighed absolutely nothing in my grasp, I took one leap, bringing me past the fleeing human, landing directly in his path. He tried to stop and turn, panic etched on his face, but tripped and fell. I think I sighed, thinking this too easy and flung my cargo to the ground, only to leap for him once more.

I caught him easily, even as he tried to scramble away, and proceeded to lift him above me with one hand, holding him by his tunic, taking care this time to not break the fragile thing. I drew him in close and on impulse attempted to read his mind, very much wanting to try this trick again. And as I had done from a distance, and also with the heavier man, I mentally reached out, this time amidst him shouting curses at me.

At first, I felt nothing…but a moment later, an invisible barrier seemed to come down. Down from inside the human's mind. He stared back at me in utter panic. But his mind to me? Was now perfectly clear.

He was evil. Oh my God, this man was evil. A murderer himself. A thief. Even an adulterer…and knowing he had done these evil things, knowing he had committed unspeakable crimes, his foul acts were sufficient enough. I felt absolutely no remorse for this man and I eagerly wanted to kill him.

"Don't…" he pleaded, seeking to break my grip. Panic stricken, he attempted to detach my single hand that was holding him aloft, using both of his hands to little effect. I felt only the smallest pressure, again like that of a child. I think I snickered.

"Please don't kill me," he begged, but I hardly even heard his plea, the very smell of him nothing short of intoxicating. I sought his neck then, driven again by instinct, and sank my teeth deep into the artery in his neck. And once again, the blood started to flow.

The mysterious connection between us returned, and I was able to read his thoughts even more clearly than before. But this time, I voided those images out, stopped peering into his mind and simply focused. Concentrating on the life force I was taking from him, and very much savoring the effects taking place inside me.

I was feeling stronger. Even stronger than before...and I began to wonder what might be the limit to this power. This power that seemed to increase with each mouthful of blood I swallowed.

What would five humans do to me? What about ten?

What about...?

Amparo. I had to get back to Amparo. And she needed this blood at lot more than me.

I tried to disengage but my body seemed to refuse. My body desired only to feed. To take this next mortal and be done with him. To consume him until he took his last breath. There was a sense of completion that came along with that, I realized that too, much like a wolf who won't relinquish his grip until his prey no longer moves.

But Amparo needed me. And she needed this one alive as well.

I growled, concentrated, and only with great difficulty did I manage to break myself free, collapsing with him upon the ground. I laid there, just for a moment, fighting hard against this urge to leap upon him again, his blood, the taste of him still on my lips. But I had to get back to Amparo. I had to stay in control... and luckily for me, the human was still very much alive.

Fortunately, my predatory nature was already beginning to fade, and I made the important discovery that this too could be controlled. I got up a moment later, thinking I had been gone far too long as it was, and set about to completing my task.

Once I had both men securely slung over my shoulders, again easily carrying their weight, I took to the air once more.

Chapter Thirty-Nine

"You have done well," Amparo told her fledging. Zekiel Raven could only smile back.

She could tell he was still feeling the effects of the blood. The effects of the kill. The *thrill* of making one's first kill.

Amparo was pleased.

She wasted no time to feed upon the first delivered victim, the one Zekiel could have killed, but to her satisfaction had left very much alive. And still very much filled with blood. But Amparo, due to her insatiable thirst, killed the human only seconds later with hardly so much of a groan escaping his unconscious form. Within moments, she was already draining the second man, the large fat one, while Zekiel waited in silence, looking on to see what effects the blood would have on her. And much to his relief, the effects were swift. In mere seconds after draining both humans, she was already looking much better and no longer showed any difficulty in standing. But Amparo knew even then that it would take more. A lot more.

Creating another of their kind was enormously taxing, and while a vampire could recover their normal strength in a relatively short time, provided the vampire fed often, that inner strength, that potent hidden strength built over hundreds of years and held in reserve, what every vampire used to create powerful offspring, could not be so easily replenished. That would take time, perhaps as many as another thousand years to regain and even then, Amparo could never hope to create one as strong as Zekiel ever again, for he had been her first. No vampire's second offspring had ever been stronger than their first; not unless the first had been made poorly, but that was a rarity and for the most part, such things simply did not happen. So while not impossible, for there were certainly other ways in which to produce strong offspring, the probability was incredibly low.

Amparo knew these things all too well. And because she had given Zekiel virtually everything, she also knew he would likely be her last. Because even if she could fully recover, she had no intention of ever siring another again. Nor would she have to...if Quest and Armageddon had guided her truthfully.

Quest and Armageddon...and suddenly she recalled the daggers. And for the first time since rescuing Zekiel, she was at last feeling well enough to use them, and perhaps now she had a reason to.

"Amparo?" Zekiel interrupted her thoughts.

"Y-yes?" she managed, needing a moment to focus.

Zekiel had been standing beside her, but suddenly, and quite quickly she noted, had crouched to the ground. He intently gazed left...then slowly panned his head to the right. What was he doing? What had he sensed this time?

"Amparo," he said calmly, his head turning vaguely east. "I sense...I sense something...it almost feels like..." Amparo started to panic. She started to vaguely feel it too. Another presence...

Another...

Vampire!

"Zekiel..." she warned, suddenly fearful now for them both. "I...*oh my God.*"

"Amparo?" Zekiel asked in confusion.

"I fear...I fear I am once again being hunted. Hunted again! Hunted by *more of our kind*!"

Zekiel stared back, eyes wide, and got back up. He kept his body low but showed no sign of fear.

"How many?" he asked and then: "Wait," he snapped his eyes shut. After a moment, he opened them again. "Two...two of our kind," he added, easily perceiving the approaching creatures.

"You can sense them?" Amparo was astonished. She too rose from where she had been sitting.

"Yes," was all he said.

Even now she could tell he was listening. Listening to *them*. Tracking with his new senses. Locating and reading humans was one thing. But reading the minds of other vampires? So soon? But was he doing it against their will? Or were their minds simply open and unguarded? What other abilities did Zekiel already possess? She wondered, but also knew she hardly had the time to ponder these curious developments.

"Zekiel...listen to me! Close your mind to them," Amparo instructed, trying to control her panic. "They will attempt to read your thoughts. Pretend your mind is a door. A door to all your thoughts. Keep this door closed," she implored. "Zekiel..." she repeated more urgently. "*Keep it closed*," he nodded.

But it was happening. Happening again like before. Just as it had with Silas and Kadar.

Silas and Kadar. Every vampire knew the tale well...

Silas...Amparo lamented in her mind. It was happening just as it did with Silas...

"Who is Silas?" Zekiel prompted, and Amparo displayed an even greater expression of shock.

"What...*what* did you ask me?" she asked breathlessly.

"Who is Silas? This man you think of? No...vampire. Is Silas a vampire?"

"You...you can read *my* mind?" she asked in wonder.

"I...I'm sorry," he said honestly. and she knew he hadn't meant any harm. But he had, in fact, read her mind *without her knowing!!*

"It wasn't something I consciously tried to do..." he continued to apologize, his expression one of embarrassment.

Without warning, he tensed suddenly and crouched to the ground once more. "They draw near..." he whispered and Amparo was forced to abruptly regain her focus.

Was Cain among them? Was he? She closed her eyes and concentrated deeply...

No. Cain was not among them. Who comes then? She scanned. Who comes for us? She wondered. *Who comes?*

"Amparo..." Zekiel whispered, and a sudden change came over him. His voice had been different...so too was his posture.

Amparo struggled to understand. How much could Zekiel sense??

"They are here!!" he cried out, and then Amparo understood. Understood what Zekiel had sensed what she had not, and watched in awe as he leaped and shot up into the air.

A solid 70 feet.

And then remarkably, his body appeared to stall for just second, a fraction of single second, but in that moment, he overcame his initial surprise, collected his bearings, and still managed to mark his arriving enemies.

Neither vampire saw him descending from above...

Chapter Forty

I CRASHED INTO the one nearest to where I touched down, a dangerous thrill starting to come over me. That same bloodlust I had felt in the war. The unmistakable thrill of battle...and I wanted this vampire dead.

Vampire.

It was hard to understand and accept that this is what *I was*.

What I am. What I had become.

Amparo.

What did you do to me??

What did you do???

What is this that you have given???

And yet...something...be it instinct or just a gut feeling, something coming from the deepest part of my being...was telling me.

Telling me that I was *meant for this*.

This was natural.

And I suddenly realized that I was finally...finally who I was supposed to be. Who I had *wanted* to be. As odd as all of this was. This creature, this, nay...vampire. This is what I am meant to be. This is the life I was meant to have...Amparo and I.

But why?

But the question would have to wait. So many questions would have to wait...

Amparo was already engaging the other vampire, something I should have been far more focused on, and that had been my first mistake.

The vampire I had collided with, whom I had initially caught by surprise, was already reacting swiftly, taking advantage of my hesitation. In one quick motion, almost faster than I could detect, he was pushing me off, kicking me free, with an extended powerful right foot.

I was launched through the air, a good 20 feet or more, but landed quite impossibly on both feet, needing only a single hand to balance myself and bring me to a stop.

Stranger yet...I had somehow known he was going to do that. Had almost been prepared for it. Anticipated it even. But how? And somehow...somehow, I had instinctively made the adjustments to land...almost as if it had been as natural as walking. And with only one hand? After being thrown so far? Had I even needed it?

But then I realized something else. Regardless of how natural it felt, adjusting to these new abilities, I *had* distinctly felt the force of that kick. And while the pain from that blow was even now miraculously disappearing at a rapid rate, I knew this creature was powerful, dangerous...and I knew I could be harmed.

Both of us paused then, a considerable distance away from each other, and I could tell he was taking measure of me, as I in turn was taking measure of him.

The vampire was scowling at me in a threatening manner, in the process of looking me over. He was taller than me, thin, lanky. His hair, short and black, as was his skin. A part of his mind then, which felt foreign to me, seemingly reached out to me, and without the use of a single word, he had imparted a message of utter disapproval and disdain. I readied myself.

A second later, almost faster than I could register, he was already upon me. *If* it had even been that long.

He collided against me with astonishing force, a force very much like his first kick and I was roughly brought to the ground. I growled in protest, my anger rising along with a sudden feeling of helplessness and I fought to bring my own strength to bear.

Roaring in rage against him, and again trusting my instincts, I managed to get a firm grip on my assailant and brought a tucked left leg up against his midsection and pushed, hurling the bastard backwards as hard as I possibly could. Like a projectile, I watched him fly far away until he abruptly struck a tree. But faster, again faster than what should have been possible, the vampire was already back on his feet, looking perfectly unharmed. Even across the distance between us, I could easily see that same scowl on his face.

Could I move that fast too? I wondered.

The vampire came at me again. But this time, I dug my bare toes into the ground, bracing for the impact and ready. But at the last possible moment, an instant before he could lay his claws upon me, I decided to try a completely different tactic, instead springing straight up from the ground.

Airborne, I watched him screech to a stop beneath me and foolishly thought I had gained a much-needed advantage. But then he did something I did not expect. He launched himself into the air after me.

Caught unaware, he snatched me into his arms even as we began to descend. I grappled with him then, still in mid-air, but I couldn't work myself into an advantageous position...and I knew I was going to hit the ground first, with him completely pinned above me. I growled, fighting hard against gravity, the force of his grip, and knowing I had to change the angle of our descent.

At the last possible moment, with a burst of strength...and a little luck, I managed to somehow turn us around, maneuvering him in line to hit the ground first. It happened so fast, in a mere instant, but the impact was jolting as the ground met us in unison. My positioning had surely saved me from the brunt of the impact, and I heard him gasp for breath beneath me. He was shocked far more than injured I quickly realized, if he had been injured at all. He actually seemed more surprised that I had been able to change our decent so unexpectedly. Against his will. And this time I took advantage of *his* hesitation by lunging for his neck...

But it was not to be that easy and I found myself being expertly thrown away from him again, his neck unharmed.

But even as these exchanges were occurring, I was becoming far more and more comfortable with this type of combat. I stopped myself again, easily finding my balance, and immediately launched myself right back, using as much speed as I could summon, trying to remain on the offensive.

He wasn't ready.

I barreled into him only this time, I neatly pinned him to the ground and went right into throwing a barrage of punches to his face.

I managed at least four solid blows, drawing more than just first blood before he twisted himself from under me while deftly throwing his left leg in a sly kick, seeking to dislodge me.

But I had seen it. I had noted the movement. Blocking with my right forearm, I made a grab for his foot using my left. I quickly added my right and now held his leg aloft with both hands. Without even thinking and without the slightest effort or hesitation, I screamed in defiance and brutally broke his leg in half. The vampire howled in pain.

Seeing my opening and seizing the moment, I lunged a second time for his neck, this time finding purchase.

The vampire thrashed for only a moment...and then went very still.

Chapter Forty-One

AMPARO WASN'T FARING nearly as well. She was still weak, yet recovering, and the vampire she faced was well aware of this, and pressed her hard.

Both were old, Amparo the far older, and normally, would have been well beyond his abilities. Hardly a worthy opponent. But in her weakened state, they battled on even ground, her opponent with but the slightest edge. But that small edge, Amparo knew, could easily spell her doom. Cost her immortal life. And right now, she needed every last advantage possible. Especially if there were more enemies to come. Others on the hunt. Possibly even Cain himself. For Cain surely knew what she had done, somehow sensed when another was created, and she knew as well as any, that Cain would be none too pleased.

That last thought only pushed Amparo harder, and she issued a primal growl as she and her opponent continued to trade blows, neither one committing to any risky moves.

Yes, she realized, this one was no novice to battle. Even showing a great deal of patience. Patient enough to hold out. To wait for his chance, wear her down. To beat her through sheer endurance, endurance he knew she did not have. And he knew she was tiring quickly.

To that end, he remained far more defensive, blocking more than striking, letting her purposely take the offensive, while he only struck occasionally, simply to let her know he would not be an easy target. He smiled then, an evil crooked smile, letting her know only too well that she was moments, perhaps even minutes away from being defeated. Seeking to end the battle quickly and decisively, Amparo played her last card, drawing forth her prized blades.

Her opponent, no fool, immediately took notice and paused in battle, offering her a look of surprise and respect.

"Those...those blades," he commented, speaking for the first time. "Where did you get those?" More than idly curious.

"They are none of your concern at the moment, but rest assured they soon will be. As soon as I cut your throat."

That set the vampire back on his heels, but just for a moment, during which he took the opportunity to wipe his long dirty brown hair away from his face. He was larger than the one that Zekiel had engaged, and only then did she manage to risk a glance in his direction. But Zekiel and the other vampire were behind her, outside her line of vision and she could not risk turning her back on this enemy. She could clearly hear them fighting, but she could not tell how he fared, nor spare the concentration to find out. The vampire Amparo faced addressed her again.

"Those blades," he repeated. "Yes. I have seen them once before. Long ago...if indeed they are what I think they are. And if I am not mistaken, they belong to the Lord Cain. Am I mistaken...*Amparo?* Oh yes. I know quite well who you are," he confirmed, ending his speech with a snicker.

Hearing her name spoken again surely increased her respect for this one, especially since she had never seen this one before. How many others knew of her? How many more were on the hunt? How long would Cain continue to pursue her? And how many other vampires might be closing in on them even now?

The vampire regarded her curiously, noting the pensive look on her face. Considering her next move perhaps, he gathered, or perhaps just stalling to give herself a brief respite.

Wanting to keep her moving, and knowing what a prize both she and the daggers would be to Cain, the vampire rushed her again without warning, hoping to lure her back on the offensive.

Amparo took the bait, meeting the vampire head-on and lunged forward with both blades, seeking a quick strike, but her crafty opponent surprised her again, at the very last moment pulling forth similar blades of his own. Surely, they were not at all of the same quality nor craftsmanship. She knew that without a doubt when their blades came crashing together. Could she use that to her advantage?

What she did know was that Cain desperately wanted the blades back and no matter what, even at the cost of her own life, she could not let that happen. Amparo fought on. Her opponent was skilled with his blades, and far more adept than most. His own daggers were just as long, nearly as sharp, and he wielded them with incredible dexterity.

Amparo would have to be careful. She launched her next combination, a feint with her right while seeking to score a quick slash with her left. But to her dismay, and despite her best effort, he parried the true threat expertly, even managing a surprising counter-attack. Starting to despair, and more than starting to tire, Amparo moved far too slowly to intercept, and his right blade deeply gashed her forearm.

The vampire laughed at her then, even as Amparo refused to cry out, doing nothing at all to stop the flow of blood. But of course, there was no need, for even in her weakened condition, her body was already beginning to heal, albeit very slowly. The blood stopped flowing only moments later, but Amparo knew she couldn't continue to take hits. Already the wound was healing far too slowly. The blood had stopped, but the fresh line on her arm remained. Her opponent noted this as well and came on again, seeking another opportunity to score.

He rushed forward with both daggers leading, seeking to skewer her midsection, but this lunge had been merely a clever bluff. Half-way into the attack, he abruptly stopped and took aim, throwing his right dagger directly toward her face. At such close proximity, the dagger came swiftly and only instinct had allowed her to duck just in time. But then the vampire threw the other, anticipating this action, and Amparo could not react in time.

Amparo staggered then, his dagger having found its way deep into her gut, and she doubled over in horrific pain, dropping her blades in the process. The vampire was standing over her at once, and though both were now weaponless, he still remained very much on guard.

She struggled to get up. Courageously attempted to remove the embedded dagger from her stomach. But Amparo was weak. So very weak now. The brief battle had drained her, taken its toll, her energy now nearly spent. Halfway into an attempt to get up, she collapsed to the ground once more.

"Don't try to get up, Amparo," he laughed. "There is no need. Do us both a favor and surrender now, while you still have your head." He started to bend down into a crouch which put him in line with her face. But she refused to look him in the eyes, refused to raise her lowered head. While she did not fear death, not in the slightest, if this was to be her fate, she was resigned to accept it with dignity.

"You think I'm going to kill you?" he asked, easily reading her thoughts. Amparo, clearly surprised, snapped her mind shut, and berated herself for carelessly letting down her mental barriers. She was just so tired.

"Closing your mind is pointless, beautiful one. There is no need. But to answer your unspoken thoughts, no. No, I will not kill you. Not when the Master so desperately wants you alive and well." Amparo, her indomitable spirit nearly broken, finally locked eyes with her enemy.

"Oh yes..." As he read the horrified look on her face. "The Master is indeed on his way...and will soon be here. The moment we discovered your trail, Kabaal called out to the Master at once." Amparo's eyes went wide.

"Oh, he is not here yet. Not yet in this place called England. That much I can assure you. But soon, Amparo. Very soon. Perhaps no more than a day. Two at most." The vampire laughed again, savoring his great victory, but sobered almost immediately as another thought occurred to him.

"Tell me then, where is Kabaal? And where is the pitiful Guma? I never did like that one."

"Dead," she spat.

"Dead?" He asked with new respect. "Slain by you?"

Amparo said nothing.

"I see..." he went on. "Commendable, Amparo. Even impressive. Kabaal was powerful. Powerful indeed. But not nearly as powerful as I."

"I highly doubt that," Amparo challenged.

He seemed to reflect on her words for just a moment before suddenly remembering the daggers. The daggers that were lying on the ground directly in front of him, so very near his hands. "If you don't mind..." Starting to reach for them. "I will hold on to these for the time being. At least until they are safe in the Master's hands once more."

"I don't mind," Amparo suddenly laughed. "I don't mind at all. But Zekiel might. And with your companion quite dead, surely you will need them."

"*Victor?*" the vampire called out, suddenly concerned, slowly beginning to look over his shoulder. In his moment of triumph, he had clearly forgotten. Forgotten that he hadn't come here alone. He realized his error then...realizing that the crafty Amparo had stalled him. As he completed his turn, looking to see how his partner fared, he was immediately punched hard in the face.

"I think she's had enough." the one Amparo had identified as Zekiel said casually, as the vampire crumpled under the heavy blow, which sent him sprawling to the ground. But the vampire, no novice to battle, rolled expertly with the impact, even absorbing a part of the hit. When he recovered enough to stand, still partially reeling from the blow he had taken, he quickly surveyed this newest opponent with open hatred.

The unlikely challenger, the one called Zekiel stood tensed, several yards away, long streaked blond bangs standing out against his rather slight form.

"Zekiel?" the vampire asked, wiping his mouth clear of blood. "Amparo's *fledging*?"

"It doesn't matter who I am." Zekiel replied sternly.

"You killed Victor?"

Zekiel smiled.

The vampire assumed his fighting stance then, pausing ever so slightly to offer Zekiel a nod of understanding, readying himself for the unavoidable battle. "If your sire was no match for me, what does a mere fledging think he can do?" the vampire teased.

"Let us see," came the reply as Zekiel crouched low to spring. He rushed towards the vampire a split second later, moving with blazing speed, but the seasoned warrior was ready, well accustomed to his kind's range of dangerous abilities and he easily dodged to the side.

But remarkably, Zekiel had somehow managed to stop mid-attack, knowing instantly he had missed his target, and changed his direction accordingly, his movements swift and sure. This time the vampire had to meet him, having no other recourse and the two began to grapple one another.

The old vampire was strong, nearly Amparo's equal. But as Zekiel gripped him tighter, starting to contest the old vampire's strength, the elder vampire, seeking a wiser course, attempted to hurl the fledgling away. But Zekiel, stubbornly refusing to let go, took the vampire with him and they both went tumbling to the ground.

They both disengaged then, seeking solid footing, and the two faced off once more.

"You think yourself *strong?*" the vampire mocked, looking for any sign of weakness. He hoped to engage Zekiel in conversation once more, seeking at the very least to distract him.

But Zekiel didn't take the bait. Instead, he came on, barreling into the vampire and taking him to the ground, faster and harder than the old one thought possible.

Zekiel started to pummel him, seeking to score a decisive blow, and the vampire found himself on the defensive. But the blows were coming too fast, the punches bruising his blocking arms, until with a sudden roar of fury, refusing to lose to the upstart fledgling, the seasoned fighter brought his right foot to bear and struck Zekiel hard across the face.

The blow sent him reeling, but only for a moment, and the old one wasted no time. He saw his opening, seized the moment, attacking with a series of devastating kicks, more than once connecting with Zekiel again.

But just when the old vampire started to sense his victory, even as he had his opponent staggering, Zekiel suddenly straightened and blocked the next incoming attack, another well-aimed kick to his face.

Zekiel smiled. For he had deceptively lured the old vampire in close, the earlier blows having little to no effect on him whatsoever. He had *purposely* taken those hits willingly, had even welcomed them, even then attempting to discover the limits to his power. The limits of his healing.

And the seasoned vampire had fallen for the ruse.

Relying on instinct alone, and having watched the old vampire carefully, Zekiel suddenly spun in a complete circuit, mimicking the vampire's earlier movements, and threw a devastating left back kick of his own, catching the vampire squarely in the face. The old one staggered, hands already reaching for his shattered jaw, his nose erupting in blood.

Zekiel came on then, having learned the lesson that all vampires heal quickly, and struck repeatedly with his feet, refusing to engage the vampire so close again. With each blow splattering more and more of his blood all over the ground, the old vampire realized he was losing, had in fact already lost, and instinctively covered his face protectively.

It was hardly effective. Somehow, blows were still finding him, punishing him, and the old one didn't understand how this was possible.

He was a veteran warrior, one of Cain's elite. But this *fledgling*...this impossibly fast and powerful fledgling...had somehow beaten him.

Was still beating him.

The vampire, now seeking any chance to escape, attempted to bolt, only to feel and hear a sickening crack in his right knee, effectively dropping him to the ground.

"No...no more..." the vampire cried for mercy, seeking any chance to stop the punishing assault, to avoid his own destruction. Zekiel did pause just then, hearing the plea, curious as to where this new conversation would go.

"H-how..." the vampire stammered, painfully recognizing that a number of his ribs, along with many other bones, had been broken. "How are you so...so powerful? How are you so fast? *How?*" he demanded, spitting up a mouthful of blood.

"She was *nothing* like this!" he screeched, pointing to Amparo who was just now extracting the blade from her stomach, gasping painfully in the process. "She was weak," he ranted on. "*Weak!* But I could still sense glimpses of her *true* power..." He paused, only to spit up more of his blood.

"But you..." he began again. "You are nothing like her!! How??" he screamed.

Zekiel stood by silently, not entirely understanding the question. He had been transformed only that night and surely knew very little himself, so all he offered was a slight shrug.

"I...I must know," the vampire went on. "I beg."

"You should be begging for your life."

The vampire looked up from his prone position, looking the fledging in the eyes.

"You...you would spare me?"

"Answer me this," Zekiel responded, abruptly changing the subject. "Would you have spared her, had she so asked?" he questioned, pointing back at the still resting Amparo. "Speak the truth."

The vampire took a moment before answering. "The...the Master," he began. "The Master desires her return...alive."

"Who is this...this Master you speak of?" Zekiel demanded, suddenly holding him aloft by his neck with one hand.

"How?? How do you move so...fast?" the vampire struggled, both hands working against Zekiel's one. "How do you move like this?"

Now Zekiel felt him. Those two hands working against his one, the old vampire futilely attempting to free himself.

It was time for Zekiel to try something else. Something he initiated purely on impulse.

Still keeping a solid grip on the vampire's throat, and suddenly crouching powerfully to the ground, which alone nearly snapped the vampire's neck, Zekiel launched himself upwards, utilizing what he thought was the extent of his power.

Zekiel and the vampire shot up. And up...well beyond the highest tree branches, until they were a full 80 feet or so off the ground.

He released the vampire then, whose head was already reeling back, and punched out hard with his right, sending the vampire shooting back towards the ground. Such was the force of his landing that a breaking sound was heard when the vampire's body hit, which even created a small crater in the ground, scattering dust and debris everywhere.

"Who is this Master of yours?" Zekiel demanded again, standing over the vampire once more. But the old vampire remained perfectly still. Said nothing...because he could not. As a vampire, he had never been rendered unconscious before, but that was precisely what had happened at the hands of this fledgling.

"*Who* is this Master of yours? Of hers?" Zekiel shouted, shaking him halfway back to consciousness. Zekiel's hand was on his throat again. How was his hand on his throat again? He felt himself pulled aloft once more, feet off the ground and though still dazed, he finally raised his head to look Zekiel in the eyes. He feared to be struck again and wondered through his many cobwebs what this enemy would do. He had never felt so out of sorts, had never in his long life been hit so hard.

"I'm going to ask you once last time..."

"Cain!" he gasped, speaking the secret name. "Our Master...her Master. *Your* Master! Cain! *Lord Cain!!*" he screamed, momentarily regaining his confidence.

And then the vampire was thrown.

Chapter Forty-Two

"My name is Jin," the vampire conceded, after gaining consciousness once more. Zekiel had begun to question him in earnest after that and the old vampire, having no desire to be struck again, nor thrown, readily offered information.

"Tell us, where is Cain now?" Amparo questioned, having recovered enough to stand by Zekiel's side. Jin remained on the ground, his face not yet halfway healed.

"I told you his location!!" Jin screamed. "Even now he crosses the sea. Can you not feel his presence??"

Amparo closed her eyes and sought out Cain's location for many moments. "Nothing," she finally concluded. "I sense nothing."

"Nothing?" Jin asked confused, only for a moment later to discover the answer to the riddle. "It should be obvious then. He deliberately hides himself from *you*! For I still feel him."

Zekiel closed his eyes himself, picking up only the faintest bit of energy. "I sense..." he began, startling them both. "I sense something. I do...*sense* something. But whatever it is, is still very far away."

"*You* sense him?" Jin asked, clearly astonished.

"I cannot be sure," he pondered, in response. "I feel as if this creature does not wish to be found nor discovered. But it appears to be very strong, this presence. That much I guess to be true."

Now it was Amparo's turn to gasp. How could that be? How could a fledgling vampire detect such a thing? What other abilities did Zekiel possess that she did not know about?

"What does this 'Cain' want with Amparo?" Zekiel asked. "With us?"

"She has stolen something very valuable that belongs to him. Yes, that is what he wants. That which was stolen to be returned." Jin smiled as he finished.

"What has she stolen? Tell me! And why do you smile? Do you wish to be thrown again?"

The vampire Jin immediately sobered. "Show the fledgling, Amparo. Show him what you have taken. And while you are at it, do tell your offspring the countless rules you have broken. So go on, fledgling. Ask her yourself."

"I'm asking *you*," Zekiel said sternly, his grasp tightening around his captive's throat. "What did she take that he's willing to cross an ocean for?"

"Show him!" Jin gasped, trying to loosen Zekiel's grip.

"He means these," Amparo announced, drawing forth the two daggers.

"Why does this Master of yours want a pair of daggers? Specifically, these?" Zekiel wondered, not understanding.

"Those daggers are...very *special*," Jin replied. "Very special indeed, but hardly the *only* thing the Master desires." He glanced at Amparo and Zekiel caught on immediately.

"If anyone so much as touches her..." Zekiel warned, and for a moment, Jin thought his neck would be broken, the grip painfully tightening around his throat, and yet curiously, a smile appeared on his face.

Suddenly Zekiel understood, having sensed the deception at once. "He is notifying others of our presence!" Zekiel gasped, easily reading Jin's mind. "Cain!" Without the slightest hesitation, and with Zekiel still holding Jin down, Amparo lunged for the left side of his neck. Jin screamed.

"Drink!" she shouted at Zekiel. He understood then, baring his own fangs and needing no further directive.

Both vampires found purchase, on either side of his neck and within seconds the vampire Jin was no more, his body already collapsing into smoking dark ash.

"What...what do we do now?" Zekiel asked, breathing heavily, already feeling the effects of the strong blood, Amparo similarly out of breath.

"D...Dawn comes," Amparo replied without hesitation. "We can do no more against the coming of the rising sun. Come, my chosen. Follow me, and be swift!" In an instant she was off, sprinting with incredible speed and Zekiel burst into motion behind her, easily keeping pace. Amparo turned her head his way even as she ran, and nodded in approval to the fledging that was easily staying close on her heels.

After twenty minutes more of constant running, and realizing there was but little time remaining until sunrise, Amparo abruptly came to a halt, satisfied with the distance they had placed behind them. But Zekiel, not slowing fast enough, shot right past her, quickly realizing his error, and abruptly took to the air, turning as he did so, to complete a perfectly executed aerial.

He landed hard, coming down in a tight crouch, his acrobatics having turned him completely around. And without hesitation, or so much as a running start, he immediately leaped again, easily crossing the distance, even turning a stalled and tightly controlled somersault mid-air only to land precisely beside her.

"How?" Amparo demanded. "How are you able to do these things?"

But the look on Zekiel's face displayed his confusion.

"Just now," Amparo started again, this time with far more patience. "How were you able to do that?"

"I don't...I don't understand. What did I do?"

"You stopped, turned a complete circuit in the air and then without the slightest delay, propelled yourself back to my side."

Zekiel was still confused.

"Are you saying that what I did was...difficult?"

Amparo laughed, delighting in his innocence.

"No, my chosen," she answered. "It's just that..."

"It's just what?"

"Was it instinct that guided you? Guided you into the maneuvers you did just now?"

"You stopped, so I stopped," he answered truthfully.

"But you didn't just stop," she remarked, again showing patience. "You altered your course, by jumping no less. Why did you do that?"

"Should I have walked?" he asked, genuinely still confused.

"No. I mean, I don't know."

Just then, Zekiel started to feel the slightest tingle. It made him uncomfortable and for just a moment, he nearly lost his balance.

"The sun rises, Zekiel. That is what you feel." Amparo informed him, even though it was still considerably dark all around them.

"I do not, not as yet, feel it as keenly as you, but heed that warning well. For if you do not." She paused, letting the gravity of her words sink in. "It will spell your demise." Zekiel's eyes opened wide.

"Yes, my fledgling. We, you and I, are creatures of the night. We do not belong, nay, cannot survive. Not in the light of day." Without another word, Amparo knelt down upon the soft grass and begun to dig a hole in earnest.

"What are you doing?" Zekiel asked, having just noticed that the spot where Amparo was digging had obviously been previously disturbed.

"Our first task was to put some distance between ourselves and those who would see us dead. Our second task," she continued, the hole already becoming substantial, her hands and arms working impossibly fast. "Is that we seek both shelter and rest, well hidden from the sun. Come…" She instructed him. "Help me dig. For in the Earth is where we will sleep."

"In the ground? But how will we breathe?" Amparo laughed but Zekiel still felt unstable. His legs buckled beneath him and he found himself on the ground beside her, quite against his own volition. "I feel…suddenly I feel…so weak. Tired."

"It is the rising sun, Zekiel. Warning us to take shelter. Please, help me dig."

"But air," Zekiel asked again, starting to work beside her. "How are we to breathe underground?"

"When we ran here just now, covering those many miles, did you or do you feel out of breath?"

"No…I…" And then he realized that his breathing hadn't been labored at all. Not one bit. In fact, he scarcely could remember taking a single breath.

"Because we do not breathe, my chosen. Even when we would draw breath, regardless of the occasion or reason, it is simply a human reflex, an old habit. Nothing more," Amparo stated, easily reading his mind. "Remember, Zekiel. To mortals and all other creatures of the natural world, we are not even alive. We do not age, we do not change. We do not eat and we do not tire easily. We feed, of course, we feed on the *living*, but that, of course, you already know. And by day? This is when we take our rest. For the sun is but for natural things, whereas the night belongs to *us*. But this, you must understand is where our similarities with mortals end. We are not like them, Zekiel. Nor will we ever be so ever again. It is important for you to remember that, for we no longer belong with their kind. Do you understand what I have told you?"

Zekiel could only nod, having no further questions, even though he was surely overwhelmed with all that had happened and all he had been told. What occupied his thoughts now was how exhausted he felt. He just felt so very tired, had never felt more depleted, save when he was almost slain which now felt like ages ago.

To think, he wondered to himself, the distance he had traveled, how far his journey had taken him, what new acquaintances he had made, and most importantly, what he had become. What he now was. What he would be...and as Amparo had stated, forevermore. His thoughts were becoming jumbled then, and he only wished to sleep. Yes, sleep is what he needed and he could scarcely keep his eyes open any longer.

By now the hole was very deep and large enough for them both. Amparo bid him to lie down and Zekiel climbed down easily. Once he was in place, Amparo climbed into the hole herself, now standing within to bring as much earth down upon them as possible. She burrowed her own way down afterwards and in but moments it was dark, black as pitch, the waning night sky and rising dawn safely removed from sight. Once they were both settled, comfortably lying side by side, Amparo, on impulse, took his hand in hers.

"And so, it will be thus, Zekiel. You and I. For all eternity."

But Zekiel Raven was already fast asleep...

Part Four

The Second Book of Ravens

Chapter Forty-Three

The tin pot that Val was washing accidentally slipped through her fingers and fell to the floor with a clang.

"I can't. I can't do this anymore, Henry. I can't."

Henry, who had been standing nearby, stocking a cabinet, paused in his work. "You can't do what, my dear?"

"This, Henry. This. I just can't." She began to weep.

Lucy, the only other person in the small kitchen, calmly walked over to comfort Val, who had sunk to the floor on her knees. "You miss him," Lucy guessed, easily sensing the obvious, putting an arm around her.

"I...I fear for him. It's been too long, Lucy. It's been way too long." Val managed between sobs. "The war has long been over and he should have returned. He should have returned by now."

"Val..." Henry interjected. "It hasn't been that long. I mean, perhaps Zekiel is even now attending to Simon. That was his name, was it not? You have to remember dear, that his home, Zekiel's home, has been burnt to the ground. Perhaps he has duties there, things he did not mention. Things he did not foresee. Others to help, perhaps. He was always kind, that one."

The mention of Zekiel's name sent a shiver down her spine, triggering a new round of tears. Surprising them both, she suddenly stood up. "I have to go, Henry. Lucy. I must. I simply cannot stay here."

"But Val," Lucy protested. "Scarborough is far away. Very far. We have no other horse…"

"I will walk."

"Val," Henry bade her. "Do not do this. You are being irrational. Please, take a moment to calm yourself. I'm certain he will return."

"No, Henry. I will not calm myself!" she said, raising her voice for the first time.

"Val," Lucy said softly.

"I'm sorry, Henry. I'm sorry, Lucy." Val sobered. "I did not mean to raise my voice."

"There, there, my dear," Henry said, coming to join the women. "Do not apologize. I know you care for Zekiel dearly, and surely you miss him. Neither I, nor Lucy can fault you for that."

"Please understand, Henry. I still have to go. I have to leave. I…I can't escape the feeling that something has happened to him. If something has…I don't know what I would…"

"Easy, Val," Lucy jumped in. "Easy. We will help you. Right, Henry?"

"Of course, of course, Lucy. Of course, we will help. Only…I'm not sure what we could do," Henry sadly concluded. "The only horse, the only means of transportation, I leant to Zekiel."

"I will walk," Val declared.

"It is a very long way, Val," Henry protested.

"It doesn't matter," she said firmly. "I have to *do* something, Henry. I can't stay here. I will walk all the way to Scarborough if I have to. If anything has happened to him…"

"I will go with you," Lucy decided, drawing a concerned look from Henry and a surprised look from Val. "Relax, Henry," she continued. "I won't go far and I certainly cannot accompany her all the way to Scarborough. But perhaps a few days out. I…I don't want you going any further than you have to all alone, Val. We've known each other a few months now and...well, we are friends now, are we not?"

"Oh, thank you, thank you!" Val nearly shouted and threw herself into Lucy's arms. "That is, of course," she said drawing back to look Henry's way. "If it's okay with Henry."

"I..." the man started. "Yes. Yes, of course. It would be the only right thing to do. Mind you, I will miss Lucy, for she helps me so very much, but it is, of course, the least we can do to aid you in your search. Yes. I trust, being that it is not quite midday...that you will insist on leaving at once?" he asked with a smile.

"Oh, Henry. Thank you!" Val cried and nearly knocked the man off his feet in a warm embrace. Henry blushed.

"Now just don't go and make a habit of it," he joked. "I will make preparations at once. But be careful. Both of you," he warned. "It is still quite cold out there and you will need to be mindful of the weather. Especially at night. They can be quite dangerous if you..." he paused, considering his words. "I don't suppose I could convince you to wait until Spring? The going would be a lot easier, as well as far less dangerous." Henry suggested.

"I'm sorry, Henry. I cannot. I simply cannot wait another day. I promise we will be careful. I am not unaccustomed to being outdoors."

Henry nodded, knowing the argument had been lost.

Within the hour, both women packed provisions enough for several days, Val carrying substantially more as her journey was sure to extend well beyond the distance that Lucy had agreed to go. And with the noon sun just underway, the two women set off, Henry waving long after they had disappeared from sight.

Chapter Forty-Four

I AWOKE THE FOLLOWING evening with the taste of dirt in my mouth.

Panicking, and quite clearly forgetting where I was, I instinctively struggled against my prison, clawing my way upwards until my left hand finally broke free, reaching the surface. I quickly scampered above.

I gasped for breath under what would soon be a night sky, forgetting again that taking a breath was no longer an issue, and flung myself to the side of the gaping hole, trying to collect my bearings...and then I remembered.

Vampire. I was a vampire! And then just as quickly, I remembered my companion. Amparo. Where was Amparo? I turned my attention back to the hole below. She was still there, of course, despite my having made a mess of the hole, covered in layers of dirt, my vampiric vision no less potent.

I called to her, gently at first, then louder when I did not get a response. The figure did not stir, not one bit, so I quickly climbed back into the hole. "Amparo," I whispered, removing the dirt that covered her face, but still getting no response. I started to panic, wondering what might have happened to her, what was potentially wrong. My mind raced through the possibilities. After what had to have been a half-hour at the very least, Amparo finally began to stir.

"Z...Zekiel?"

"Thank God. I thought you were dead," I said, breathing a sigh of relief.

"I don't understand." She wondered, becoming fully alert. "How is it that you are awake? So soon? The sun...it must have just set."

"Nay. I've been calling you. For some time. A half-hour at least. You wouldn't wake up, Amparo. And your body. Your body was so stiff I thought.."

"A half-hour? Are you certain?"

"The sun has only recently set. It is now fully dark as you can see...though when I awoke, there was still a bit of light in the sky."

Amparo thought about this for several moments before answering.

"I find this odd, Zekiel, and this be no minor issue. It is not normal, nay, it is unheard of that a fledgling would rise before his maker. Nor is it common for one of our kind to awake so early. I am an early riser myself, earlier than most among our kind."

"Do you doubt my claim?"

"No, Zekiel. I do not. Even without reading your mind."

"But I still do not understand, Amparo. Why is my rising before you an issue?"

"You will learn, Zekiel, in due time, all things concerning us...but at the forefront, the source of all our unique gifts, all of our powers, comes from *time*. From age. And a good deal from your Maker. But come, let us remove ourselves from this hole."

Amparo took one leap, clearing the hole easily and gestured for me to do the same. I followed, having no difficulty, landing nimbly by her side. "Oh! I almost forgot," she stated, looking me up and down before quickly dropping back into the hole.

"Amparo?" I asked, slightly confused.

She leaped out of the hole a moment later holding a large leather-bound trunk. "No fledgling of mine is to be seen wearing the rags you are outfitted in. Please," she bade. "Open the trunk."

"But where? Where did this come from?" I asked. And then I recalled the night before, this spot she had chosen. The earth had already been disturbed. She had rested here before then, I assumed.

"Yes, Zekiel," she confirmed, having read my mind. "Now close it. Your mind, I mean. Because know that if I can read your thoughts, so too can other immortals. Open the box."

I wanted to ask her more questions. Questions about these abilities of ours that I still knew so very little about. But perhaps too, that could wait. I knelt down to inspect the large trunk and opened the lid. Inside was a bright yellow tunic made of the finest material I had ever seen and I looked back at Amparo in disbelief.

"This garment," I gasped. "How did you come by something like this? I have never seen anything like it." For it appeared to be of a quality fit for a king!

"Put it on, Zekiel. Accept this as a gift. I had this specifically made…just for you. I trust it will fit." No doubt the soiled and ragged clothing I was wearing made me look ghastly indeed and I eagerly stripped off my old tunic to quickly put on the fine new garment. The fit was perfect.

"To match the color of your hair, of course," Amparo said. But look, Zekiel. There is more." She laughed. I inspected the trunk a second time and found an exquisite pair of black boots and a fine pair of black pants, again the quality unmistakable.

"Will you not put these things on?" she asked a moment later, noting my hesitation.

"It's just that…" I started to explain.

"Honestly, Zekiel," she sighed. "Let us get beyond this foolishness. Are you so quick to forget how long I took care of you? And in what manner? Do you honestly fear getting undressed in front of me?" Amparo laughed, though she hardly needed to read my mind to know that undressing in front of her was exactly what I had been concerned about. I nodded, indeed feeling very foolish and promptly donned both the pants and boots, all the while thanking her repeatedly. Thinking my ensemble was now complete, I just stood there not knowing what it was that we were to do next and also because she was just staring at me intently.

"Zekiel," she laughed again. "There is still one more item yet inside the trunk." I looked a third time and pulled out the finest, thickest black wool cloak I had ever seen.

"This *cannot* be for me," I gasped.

"It is. Put it on." She smiled widely. "Let me see you garbed like a proper vampire. You didn't think I would let you run about as you were, did you?"

I put the cloak on, complete with a thick hood (which I left down to fall behind my back) and couldn't help but marvel at how well it fit. My old black cloak had been nothing like this. Nothing like this at all, and surely, each and every one of these things had cost a small fortune. I stood in front of her once more, my new outfit complete.

"Splendid!" she applauded. "Everything is satisfactory, I trust?"

"Amparo...this is too much. I don't deserve this. I...I can't thank you enough."

"Don't be foolish. You are most welcome. Now if you are done admiring your new clothing..." And here she paused just for a second and I was certain she was mentally searching the immediate area. Searching for other vampires, I realized. I hadn't thought to do this myself upon awakening, but I probably should have.

"Yes. You should have," Amparo said, again reading my thoughts. "But it is good that you realize this. Make it a habit."

I nodded, resolved to not forget again.

"Now come," she began again. "Let us walk for a bit. I think at present we are safe."

I suddenly recalled the night before. My first night. My first battle. The other vampires...Cain!

"Do not concern yourself with Cain at this time," Amparo advised, my thoughts still open to her. "And while I can read your mind now...and in turn, you can read mine, *never* let down your guard. Even for me. From now on, make it difficult for me to do so, unless we are speaking freely. There are times when speaking mentally is simply far more convenient."

I nodded, but even as I was opening my mouth to comment, I suddenly felt a more pressing need. Something that was overriding all other concerns. Starting to tug at my insides. And found myself suddenly thirsty beyond measure. Thirsty for human blood.

"Amparo?"

"It is the thirst." she responded immediately, knowing full well my concern.

"Yes. I feel...I feel so thirsty. And I..."

"And you what?" she asked.

"I...I don't understand."

"It is our curse, my chosen. Passed down to us by Cain himself. All vampires require the blood of the living. Blood to survive. It is the blood that preserves us, it is the blood that gives us our strength. The source of all our power."

"But, Amparo..." I started again. "It is more than that, or rather, I understand what you have said. Much of this you told me last night."

"What then?" she asked curiously.

"I feel..."

"You feel what?"

"It's not that I simply desire to feed. I feel...I feel the need to kill."

Amparo smiled. "Come with me." She suddenly shot forward, leaving me where I stood, until she was well beyond my sight.

"Where?" I asked, having not reacted fast enough. I had no idea where she had gone. Hadn't been prepared for her to move so fast!

"Use your gifts now, Zekiel. Speak to me with your mind. Use your given abilities...to find me."

I concentrated, closing my eyes and reached out with my mind. In but a few moments, I found her, locked in on her location and knew her to be 500 or so yards away.

"Come to me then..." she teased. *"If you can."*

Smiling, I broke into a run and quickly navigated the thick forest we were in, dodging trees, leaping when necessary, until I knew to be almost upon her. Until she moved. I sensed this immediately, knew she was on the run again and the sudden challenge of the situation excited me greatly, and I pushed to increase my speed with every step.

"Good," she complimented mentally. *"Faster."*

I attempted to do this but found that I was nearing my limit, noting full well that she was still increasing the distance between us. But it wasn't that I couldn't go any faster, I sensed that I could, but the nagging thirst, my need for blood...was somehow imposing a restriction, preventing me from fully applying myself. Occupying every last thought in my mind. Perhaps in all truth, an annoying distraction. I knew I needed blood, at least some small amount, to deal with this terrible nagging thirst. This *need* seemed to overrule all else.

Discouraged, I slowed to a stop. I took stock of myself then, noting again that much like the night before, I was neither breathing heavy, nor experiencing any type of fatigue. Rather, I simply knew beyond a doubt that I could not focus beyond my need for blood. Had I reached my limit? I honestly did not know. All I could think about was blood.

All I wanted was blood. I scanned the area nearby, forgetting Amparo completely, searching for any creature I might devour...

"Zekiel." Her voice interrupted my search. I was annoyed then, overwhelmingly so, angry at this intrusion.

She mentally laughed. *"Are you so starved for blood that you would forget me?"* the familiar voice teased. And then just as quickly, the speaker was directly in front of me, commanding my full attention.

"I...Amparo." I stuttered, feeling ashamed now for my anger. It was quickly fading now, my temper already cooling, lost in the beautiful woman in front of me.

"If I lead you to food," she laughed. "Would you follow me then?"

"Lead on," I begged, though was confident I already knew the way.

With my instincts taking over, I tried to surprise Amparo by darting off in my chosen direction, but she had been ready, a moment later already running beside me and then even overtaking my pace. Within moments however, we came to a stop as in the very next clearing, and not yet perceiving our presence, were two large deer.

We both crouched low, slinking through the thick bush, a predatory like feeling coming over me. We acted as one then, both springing forth, tackling our prey all too easily, all other thoughts lost.

I drank then, losing myself in the animal, losing myself in this lust for blood, taking all that I could from it until the blood no longer flowed, leaving it dead in my arms.

It had been easy. So remarkably easy. And I knew at once that I wanted more, already feeling it's effects. *"And we shall have it,"* she responded, choosing again to speak to me telepathically.

"Will it always be like this?" I asked, attempting to speak using only my mind as she had done.

"Forever and always, my chosen."

"Chosen," I repeated. *"Why do you call me this?"*

For reasons I had yet to understand, her face became grim. As if I had triggered something within. Something she was desperately trying...to forget? *"You are attempting to read my mind,"* she accused, the politeness in her tone vacant.

"As you read mine?" I countered. "If we are to be thus..." I continued, wanting to speak out loud. "Then I would have you tell me. Tell me about us. About our kind. About you. About...Cain."

Amparo snarled at me then, and crouched low as if she meant to attack but instead suddenly sped off, moving at what I guessed to be the fastest pace she was capable of, for I had never seen her move that fast before.

We would see.

I sped off after her then, pumping my legs as hard as I could. Satisfied, at least for the moment of my need for blood, I felt both angry for having to chase her (since I was no longer in the mood), and annoyed for her continued hesitance to answer my questions. I worked hard on closing the distance, the fresh blood coursing through my veins.

But she was fast, impossibly fast, and I narrowed my eyes to focus. All I could see ahead of me was a blurred form, moving this way and that and I started to grow enraged that she would leave me behind, my patience wearing thin.

Purely on instinct, and quite tired of these games, I catapulted myself upwards, snapping off a sizeable tree limb with my bare hands to serve as a staff, and continued to launch myself closer and closer...closer to gaining on my target, determined to not let her escape.

Chapter Forty-Five

Henry was right. It was cold.

With the night well underway and a new snow falling fast, both women were beginning to question the decision to leave during such a brutal month.

Luckily, they had been able to start a fire and tucked themselves under a shallow overhang, but both the fire and the crude shelter did very little to provide them any heat. And due to the worsening conditions, it was a constant effort just to keep the fire ablaze.

"I'm s-s-sorry, Lucy," Val apologized, teeth chattering, both women huddled together tightly.

"We just n-need to make it through the n-night. With any luck, the dawn will bring the sun, making the temperature at least bearable."

They didn't speak much, concentrating instead on trying to stay warm and keeping enough wood on the fire. The task proved to be a difficult one for finding wood, much less dry wood, as it was very hard to come by under the thickening blanket of snow.

The women managed as best as they were able and while cold and quite miserable, they somehow made it through the night, although neither got much sleep. Thankfully, as they had hoped, the following morning brought lots of sunshine and warmer temperatures, and while it was still cold, the weather was at least tolerable and the snowfall had come to an end.

"Well, Val. I certainly do hope we can avoid nights like the one we just had," Lucy said, putting together a light breakfast of bacon and cheese. "We have certainly earned the sunshine."

"I agree, Lucy…and please, please know I am thankful for your company. Had you not accompanied me, I surely would have perished. I would not have been able to maintain the fire. Not on my own."

"Think nothing of it," Lucy replied, but she wore a concerned expression, and an expression Val did not miss.

"Lucy?"

"Yes, dear?"

"You cannot go much further than this. Can you?"

"I…I'm sorry, Val. I cannot. Another night, no more. I simply am afraid of not getting back to Henry safe. If I were to have a night alone, such as we just had…"

"I understand, Lucy, and I am grateful to you for accompanying me as far as you've come."

"But that's just it, Val. We haven't traveled far at all." And that was the truth. Because of the snow, every step had been difficult, and the two women had not made significant progress. Scarborough was still many miles away. Many more than Val had hoped to travel alone.

"Val, I know you do not want to hear this but I think you should consider heading back with me. Back to Henry. Being out in the cold like this, night after night, alone of all things…"

"I can't, Lucy. I cannot go back." And this is where Val took pause. Something about this whole situation, Zekiel's prolonged disappearance, had been slowly eating away at her. She couldn't explain the way she felt, but somewhere, from deep inside her being, she just *knew* that something had gone wrong. Something had gone terribly wrong with Zekiel's excursion to Scarborough. Call it a gut instinct or intuition, she just simply knew it was so.

"Look, Val," Lucy interjected, breaking the prolonged silence. "No one is telling you to not seek him out. Or to give up, for that matter. All I ask is that you do this under less trying conditions."

"He's my husband, Lucy. How can I not go to him? Look for him?" Val retorted, clearly agitated. "You don't understand, Lucy. You don't know him like I do. I could never forgive myself if any harm has come to him, especially if there was anything I could do about it. Zekiel has been gone for months, and it took us but a week or so to reach Henry's place. And when we set off, Scarborough was still reasonably nearby. And now for months to have gone by, and no word sent? It just isn't like him."

Lucy sighed. "Val, you have to understand that Henry and I only have your best interests in mind. We had hoped that Zekiel would have returned by now too."

"I know."

"All I ask is that you consider our predicament," Lucy said, gesturing around them. "What good will it do Zekiel if you cannot reach him safely? How would he begin to forgive us, if we do not do all we can to protect you?"

Val started to cry. "Oh, Val!" Lucy cried, putting an arm around her. "Please don't. I don't mean to upset you. Look. I will travel with you another day, no more. Let us make a decision then. But if these conditions should worsen, especially at night, I feel that it would be best to return."

"I told you, Lucy," Val sobbed. "I'm not going back. Whatever it takes."

"I see. Let *me* be clear then," Lucy started, trying her best to be both firm and understanding. "I have to be returning regardless, as I believe we were clear from the beginning about how far I would go. I do have to keep my own safety in mind, you understand. But as for you, I will not try to stop you, as you are free to do as you wish. In fact, I don't think I could stop you if I tried." She tried to laugh. "Just be careful, Val. You don't want to make the situation any worse than it already is. And, if I might add, should Zekiel happen to reach us first, what do we do then?"

Val had not thought of that. What if he did return? What if he returned only to discover that she had gone out searching for him? What then?

"Listen, Val. Make no decision today. Let us sleep on it, attempt to get as far as we can and when we wake up, hopefully avoiding another dreadful night like the one before, you can decide then. Is that fair?"

"Yes, Lucy. Thank you. And I truly do appreciate all that you and Henry have done. Come then," Val urged, anxious to resume their journey. "Let us keep moving."

Determined, the women moved on. They traveled much farther that day, making some good progress and found the way a lot easier. But as day turned to night, the cold came steadily creeping back, forcing them to soon halt for the evening.

They had tried to stay clear of the forest that was always to the East, making their way as Val and Zekiel had done earlier, but now both women agreed to venture just a short way inside, thinking the trees could offer a bit more protection from the wind. Before long, they found a suitable spot in a small clearing, but unfortunately it offered very little in the way of shelter. As it was growing darker by the moment, the women had no choice but to make due where they were. Thankfully, Val reasoned, it was not snowing that evening and there was plenty of firewood to be found.

"As long as we keep a steady fire and alternate watch, we should be able to at least get some rest," Val suggested, taking her turn in preparing their supper. I will take the first watch this evening, Lucy...so please, try and get some sleep. After this meal of course." She smiled encouragingly, trying to keep their spirits up.

After a decent meal of seasoned pork and a few cooked vegetables, Lucy climbed into her bedroll and attempted to get some rest. After some time, perhaps an hour, she stirred. "It's no use, Val. I can't seem to get any sleep! I just can't seem to get comfortable!"

she complained. When Val didn't answer, Lucy called again. "Val?" No answer. "*Val??*" Now panicked, this time fully sitting up.

"I'm glad you are awake, Lucy," Val finally responded tersely, and Lucy didn't mistake her tone. Something was clearly wrong and Lucy could see that she was brandishing a brand of fire, leaving her all the more confused.

"Val?" she questioned again.

"We aren't alone," Val almost whispered.

Lucy turned her gaze then, following Val's line of sight, only to see many eyes illuminated by the firelight, and screamed.

Chapter Forty-Six

Amparo couldn't believe it. How was the fledgling gaining? She glanced behind her, whenever she could spare the attention, and the young vampire was indeed steadily gaining.

How? How was this possible? She wondered. She tried to focus ahead, but couldn't stop herself from checking on him every few seconds, growing rather frantic now and yet couldn't help but marvel at both the speed and ease with which he moved. He even took leaps every now and then, and the height, the sheer height of those jumps! Each one bringing him closer and closer.

Amparo pressed on. Not far ahead, she saw what appeared to be an especially steep cliff, several hundred feet tall at least, rocky and jagged, and pushed toward it as hard as she could. When she reached the base a moment later, she crouched and sprang up from the ground, seeking to lose Zekiel in the long climb to reach the top. That one leap carried her a solid 45 feet straight up the cliffside and from there, Amparo immediately started to climb.

Zekiel arrived only seconds later and paused for just a moment to look above, attempting to gauge the distance. He crouched in a similar fashion, bringing himself impossibly low to the ground...and jumped.

Amparo, still clawing her way upwards was forced to stop in her tracks, for there above her, at least 20 feet ahead, was her fledging Zekiel Raven, easily clinging to the face of the cliff with a casually outstretched right hand.

"Impossible!" She swore. For indeed, it did not seem possible. But somehow the fledgling, in one leap, had cleared her own impressive jump, as well as the short distance she had climbed. Somehow, Zekiel, whose abilities continued to impress and astound her, seemed unbound by natural limits.

A fledgling was never, not in all of their history that she could recall, stronger in any ability when compared to their Maker. Not in speed, not in agility, nor in any other powers that the secretive race possessed. These things all took time to develop, and at the very least, considerable practice to master.

Surely, there were fledglings who were or became far more talented than others, occasionally even more gifted than their sire, but this was something that would only develop over time. A very long time.

"Impossible!" Amparo growled. Determined to prevent her fledging get the better of her, she suddenly took two back-to-back giant leaps upwards, the first taking her above and past the fledgling, and the second, accomplished with no discernible pause, bringing her all the way to the clifftop surface.

Gritting her teeth, and not quite understanding her rising anger, she pushed herself even harder, knowing Zekiel would surely be close behind, but also confident she had managed to widen the gap. Or so she thought.

But to her astonishment she saw Zekiel landing, somehow ahead of her again, his makeshift staff bared...and held before him defensively.

She knew she could still run, set a different course, but instead met him, her anger boiling over, the situation escalating quickly, spiraling out of control. "You dare attack *me*?" she flared, moving in close, drawing her own blades in a flash, more than prepared to put him in his place.

But the fledgling was ready, letting her cut his staff in two, and meeting her charge easily, parrying each blade with both sections of wood. Amparo redirected her attack then, coming at him from a different angle, and then yet another, but this time it was the fledgling's turn to make a mistake for he failed to recognize these blades for what or who they were.

Quest and Armageddon made short work of his already-severed staff, blowing them to pieces on the very next parry. Finding himself disarmed and in dire straits, Zekiel instinctively went into a back handspring, and then another, before he launched himself into a back-flip, rising high in the sky, seeking to give himself some breathing room.

But Amparo, the far more seasoned warrior, was starting to anticipate his movements and capitalized on his gravity-defying leap, using the time he was in mid-air to move into position, right where he was now landing. She timed her attack perfectly, both blades thrusting out and it was only instinct, Zekiel's finely attuned instinct, that sensed the blades in a fraction of a second, and he deftly twisted himself out of harm's way even as he was landing.

"Impossible!" she screamed, attacking again with blinding speed, only this time catching his forearm, drawing a deep gash.

But Zekiel was far from finished. He rolled with the blow, ignoring the cut and spun, thrusting a powerful left foot behind him which caught Amparo, still quite committed to her last attack, square in the face. The blow sent her reeling, the sheer force dislodging her weapons from her grip, and she found herself stumbling, trying desperately to regain her footing.

But then he was upon her, bringing her hard to the ground, and her mind became frenzied, wondering how it was all possible.

"Do you yield?" Zekiel demanded more than asked, his powerful arms pinning her, the weight of his body pressed against hers.

She knew she could choose to struggle, could even now continue to resist, but one look into Zekiel's eyes told her that he would not make it easy. Accepting defeat, she let her body go limp, exhausted now from her efforts.

"How?" she asked, finding herself calm again, having regained her composure.

"How what, exactly?" he asked, his face only inches from hers.

But Amparo did not answer and instead found herself staring intently into his eyes.

"Are you ready to answer my questions at least?" he probed.

But Amparo had her own questions. She wasn't sure what had come over her, nor why she had run from Zekiel in the first place. She wasn't even sure why she had gotten angry. "Zekiel?" Now seeking to sort through her thoughts.

"Speak."

"Zekiel...I owe you...I owe you an apology. I don't understand what came over me. Why I ran. Why we fought." She paused, considering her next words. "No...That's not true. I *do* know why." And the reason, she realized, was that she had developed personal feelings for him. Feelings she had tried to deny. Everything had just happened so fast. And with Zekiel, despite the quest she was determined to carry out, despite how resolute she had always been, she could not help but feel a sudden loss of control.

His face remained close to hers, the tension rising rapidly with their proximity to one another. Amparo, her resistance crumbling, felt herself being drawn to him, *drawn into* him, and she closed the distance between their lips, sealing his mouth with a kiss. He passionately kissed her back, very much wanting the same thing and before either could question what was happening, they were working each other's clothes off, their emotions having hit a feverish pitch.

"Amparo...I've never done this..." he briefly interrupted, wanting to confess.

"Shh," she silenced him. And before Zekiel could even ask if such a thing was possible, if making love was even achievable between immortals, she soon gave him answer enough by initiating the act.

Their pace was frantic, both of them fully committed, and as they neared the point of ecstasy, the pinnacle of their passion, Amparo drove her fangs into his neck. His body stiffened, on the verge of paralysis but again, solely relying on his instincts, his fangs sought the same, finding purchase on her own neck and Amparo softly moaned. She *wanted* this, in their mutual paralysis he knew she wanted this, and then the blood began to flow. The blood now flowing between them.

It was very slow, this exchange, passionate and with meaning, not at all intended to drain, or even drink, from the other. It felt more like a prolonged kiss, tender and subtle, and served a far deeper purpose than pleasure alone. What that greater purpose was, Zekiel was soon to discover, would be something for him to reflect upon for days, if not years, to come.

His mind exploded then, filled with countless images, visions she was sending him through a powerful mental and intimate bond. A connection only possible between fledgling and Maker, a bond of unparalleled closeness.

It had been created during Zekiel's transformation, a bond they would always share, but this second exchange for immortals was vastly different and far more intimate.

Gradually, their minds and bodies became one and the intensity of their bond only increased. Even in this shared paralysis, he continued to make love to her, and nearly released his fangs simply to cry out. Amparo similarly felt her body quicken, her hips pounding against his own, even as the blood continued to slowly mingle between their bodies.

Having shared so much in mere minutes, for this act went far beyond sexual love making, Amparo was finally ready to let go. To surrender what she had kept inside for so long.

She pressed in even tighter, the blood still passing between them, and she somehow managed to pull him further down upon her.

Amparo was ready. Ready to lift her restraints, now willing to allow herself to be far more vulnerable than she had ever thought possible. And so at last, at long, long last, her story, one she had guarded for as long as she had been alive, a tale she had vowed never to share, would finally be told.

Chapter Forty-Seven

Val was doing her best to keep the wolves at bay, but they were gradually inching their way closer, ever nearer the ring of fire that Val had crudely constructed.

"On your feet, Luce," Val ordered her companion, trying to maintain a sense of composure. "Grab a log, and get yourself at my back. I'm not sure how long we can hold them off. I'm running out of wood."

Lucy was nearly frantic, noting at least half a dozen pairs of glowing eyes, some yellow, some blue, but all with the same intent. She fumbled her first log, swore, then recovered, doing her best to comply with Val's demand.

There were at least six wolves in plain sight, flanking the small camp, working in tandem, looking for any opportunity.

Every so often, one wolf would lunge at them, as close as possible to the fire, only to be waved away by a burning brand. They were operating as any seasoned pack would, wearing down their foes, making the women constantly move, forcing them to face any incoming threat. And thus, this strategy, this cooperation, was how the pack retained stamina, how they executed their waiting game to perfection.

While one wolf would feign attack, drawing nearer to the fire, the others would rest while staying just close enough as to not be ignored. In this manner, the wolves could all take turns, causing the women to spin this way and that. It was an exhausting ordeal for both sides, but the wolves were patient, and wood was now in short supply.

Much of the wood that had been gathered for the evening was being used as a perimeter, in a circle as tight as Val dared, but the circle would not hold the night, and the cunning wolves knew it too.

The minutes passed slowly, then an hour, and as the dire situation grew, Val refused to give up even as one section of her fiery circle began to falter.

"I need you to cover me, Lucy!" she called above the constant growls and snarls being directed their way. Lucy, who had performed remarkably well, having long ago gained some much needed composure, whirled to defend her friend as Val placed the remaining wood at the weakest point. The failing fire sizzled back to life, and just in time, for one wolf had unwisely drawn too close, and got its paw singed in the process. It retreated, but only briefly, and came on again now absolutely enraged.

This time Val, her brand back in hand, reached out and struck the beast as hard as she could. It retreated once more, scampering back on all fours, and Val turned her attention to the next opponent.

The wolves were getting more and more brazen by the moment, driven by their hunger and wanting to end the conflict quickly. While Val knew that they were defending themselves admirably, making a courageous stand, each and every attack the two of them repelled was slowly but surely taking its toll. And it was clear to the wolves, and now simply a matter of time, before the two companions would fall.

Even now the circle they had maintained was failing, the wall of flames steadily diminishing by the moment, and barring some miracle, the women were nearly out of time. For once the circle was breached, there would be no stopping the onslaught of the hungry, vicious animals.

Val was panting now, much like the wolves that faced her, and could no longer deny that her attempt to find Zekiel, much less keep herself alive, had failed. For if one of them should fall, due to exhaustion or a breach in the circle, the other was sure to follow.

And then Lucy collapsed.

Chapter Forty-Eight

(AMPARO'S STORY)

AMPARO HAD NO IDEA how she had gotten lost. She only knew that she was, and that she had strayed much too far from her home. Night was falling, her sense of direction gone, as she squinted against the coming darkness, trying to place herself. Desperately trying to understand where she was in relation to home, the darkness only seemed to grow thicker.

That's when she saw...*him*.

"Hello there, dear girl," the dark figure courteously greeted Amparo, though startled her by seemingly materializing out of the night itself. "Are you by chance lost?'

Amparo was scarred. His voice was peculiar, his approach completely silent, and before she could even address this stranger, he was somehow, impossibly behind her...and she could feel him breathing on her neck.

"P...please. Do not harm me. Please..." she begged, turning around to face him.

"Harm you?" the man soothed. "Why, my dear. I have no intention of harming you." He laughed, further disturbing the frightened young woman.

"If…if you know where we are…" she bravely asked, seeking to overcome her fear.

"Know where we are?" he inquired. "But of course. I know exactly where we are."

"Then…then perhaps…" she began again.

"Perhaps I might…lead you to your home?" he asked slyly.

"Yes, sir. I mean, if you would be so kind. I'm…I'm afraid to admit that I am…I am rather lost, kind sir."

"Kind? Is that so?" he chuckled. It was disturbing to her how he spoke. How he insisted on repeating everything she said. How he knew what questions she would ask.

Amparo's every instinct urged her to bolt. To run. To run anywhere she could. Anywhere at all…if it meant escaping…him.

"If you would…that is, could you at the very least point out the direction of my home so that I might be on my way?" Ever polite and hoping somehow she had misjudged him. But something about him just felt off. Felt…evil. And at that moment, she had never been more terrified in her life.

"You are beautiful, you know," he remarked, ignoring her question. "So…very beautiful. Why, if you will forgive my boldness, the most beautiful woman I have ever seen…in all my long years."

Amparo swallowed hard.

"I have been watching you, you know," he continued.

"W…watching me?" she barely got out.

"Oh yes. I've been watching you for a very, very long time…my dear sweet…" And here he paused. "Amparo."

The mention of her name, his knowing her name, verily reduced her to a state of panic and she turned to run, only to see him standing before her, blocking her way yet again. It was impossible, she told herself. Impossible. But it no longer mattered. All that mattered was getting away. Far away.

"You would seek to leave me?" he asked, feigning as if he were truly wounded.

"I…" she started to say, but the vampire was already upon her.

Zekiel fought hard to maintain any composure. He saw these things, these memories quite clearly, as if he were there himself and keenly felt the initial exchange between Amparo and the Vampire Cain.

He watched in horror as Cain mounted her, consumed her, violated her, and sank his fangs deep within her human flesh. He felt Amparo's pain, experienced her anguish, her fear, always fear. Her sheer hopelessness.

He could even hear her cry out, struggling futilely against this impossibly strong opponent. Completely and utterly helpless.

She was dying a moment later, he knew that with certainty, for he recalled his own weakened state of being, clearly remembered how that felt, only the night before...but it had been nothing like this horror unfolding in front of him. Invading his own mind.

Tears were now spilling down his cheeks and all he could think to do was hold Amparo all the tighter. She was confiding in him, trusting him, and her tears mingled with his.

He could still see Cain clearly, head thrust back, lost in the ecstasy of her blood. He desired her, yes, this evil creature greatly desired her. Desired her body, her mind, all for his own. For his own sick and twisted pleasure.

She was a victim of her beauty, Zekiel knew that clearly, and shared at once the utter hatred she felt for this one, all while struggling against the will to live. For in those moments, Amparo had simply wanted to die.

But it was not to be...and Cain would not allow that to happen. With her body taking its last breaths, Amparo felt her resistance slipping, her will all but broken, and when Cain offered her his bloody wrist, Amparo had no choice but to drink.

Zekiel felt that thirst, felt her desperation, and knew that nothing could stop the exchange. He too had experienced that thirst and knew evermore that it would never, could never be quenched. Could never be sated. Would never cease to exist.

He watched her then, watched as she pulled the bloody wrist to her mouth, knowing she wanted nothing more than to drink. Cain only smiled.

At first, the exchange was slow, Amparo taking only small amounts, but as the exchange went on her thirst only increased, and Cain, evil Cain did nothing at all to stop her. He was now in a form of ecstasy himself, clearly enjoying this forced connection he was surely having with her, consuming all of her mind and devouring all of her secrets. They were one then, Amparo and Cain, and the exchange went on for some time.

After what felt like an eternity to Zekiel, Cain was breathing heavily, panting like a dog in heat, and he saw the old vampire press Amparo in even tighter, bringing her up to his neck, where he gashed himself, letting her drink from the very core of his being.

Agonizing moments later, Cain was finally finished, could withstand no more, yet still managed to laugh as he crumpled to the ground with her still in his arms, to witness the transformation already starting to take place.

Scenes suddenly shifted to years later, and Zekiel saw Amparo, no longer the young woman she had been, but now a vampire standing by Cain's side.

He was giving a speech to his ranks, scores upon scores of other vampires, and Zekiel surmised that there must have been hundreds, if not thousands, in this gathering, but it was impossible for certain to know.

They were all his children, he had so many children, and there Amparo stood, at the front of this assembly wearing a look of despair. She was to be and *was* his vampire Queen, destined to stand by his side while he would rule for all eternity, all been done by force, completely against her will, and she had long lost hope of finding a way in which to end it all. To be free of him, to be rid of him...But Cain would not let her die.

Several times, Zekiel even witnessed thoughts of suicide. Images and memories of Amparo's many attempts to end her own immortal life, but each time he was there, somehow always there to prevent her, to stay death's hand, laughing in her face.

"You can never leave me. Don't you see?" he would laugh. "You are *mine*, dear Amparo. *You are mine forever*. As I am forever, *yours*."

Zekiel was then transported to another time and place where he saw a rather handsome vampire, kind and compassionate, who Zekiel immediately knew to be the Vampire Silas.

This vampire was dear to Amparo, and Zekiel was briefly given a glimpse into their mysterious and very personal relationship. He watched Amparo meet with this vampire in secret, times far too numerous to count. He saw the mutual love that had grown, the secrets they had kept, and the devious plans they had made.

The visions swirled and changed yet again, and this time Zekiel's attention was drawn to the two mysterious daggers, those phenomenal weapons now known to him as Quest and Armageddon. He was shown through visions and images their mysterious history, how Cain had used them to build his vast empire, to wield them for his own evil purposes...and understood why Amparo had thought to take them.

These were the very daggers that Amparo now carried, and he soon witnessed how she came to possess them. The very night in which Amparo had risked her own life...to claim them for her own. He also saw what fate had befallen Silas, knew that he had been murdered, and knew that their plan to escape together, such a brave but dangerous plan...had ultimately failed.

He saw her running then, full of fear but also purpose, desperately trying to put as much distance as possible between herself and Cain. Running so very fast. And then he watched her dig, taking refuge deep underground where she would sleep for a very long time. Many centuries then passed, so much time had passed, and he watched as she finally clawed her way back to the surface from the deep hole which had served as her resting place for so very long.

He witnessed her travels from Egypt to Europe, and from Europe to Paris, and then on to England, all in accordance with the will of the blades.

All of this Zekiel watched, and somehow felt as though he'd been present; he was even now breathing heavily, still holding Amparo close, but nothing could have prepared him for what he witnessed next.

He saw her then in Scarborough, his own village, and there, through her eyes, saw a little boy. A little boy in a basket. She was not aware of where the child had come from, nor would the blades, those mysterious Quest blades, answer her many questions. They simply pointed to the child, a child who had yet to grow, and bid her to watch over him at all costs and remain patient until he eventually came of age.

He saw and felt her frustration, the utter confusion as she finally took the basket and child, placing it where she knew the preacher Simon would find it. And then, almost as an afterthought, Amparo showed Zekiel, through her vision, an image of her cutting his hair, marking him as her own...and this was the last known contact she would have with him for many more years to come. *It had been her!*

Amparo then watched the boy grow, always from afar, witnessing his many trials and tribulations as he was outcast and bullied, seeing his fear, lack of courage, all the while thinking that the blades had somehow erred.

She watched Zekiel mature, always taking care to never remain in the area for long, fearful that Cain would one day find her and put an end to the plan that she had so perilously put in motion. For 24 long years she waited, never in the same place, not always even in England, but faithfully waited nonetheless for the blades to tell her the time had come. And then came their first meeting, the fateful long-awaited meeting, where he had found her crying, on the very brink of giving up. On that same evening she had attempted...to take her own immortal life no less, thinking the blades inert.

And just when she thought their time had finally arrived, that the moment had finally come, she was once again forced to leave, instructed again by the blades to flee from other vampires, for there were always disciples of Cain in pursuit, lest her plans unravel.

Months later she found Zekiel again, directed by the blades, to a field of battle, discovering him on the verge of death. He watched her take his body, take him into her care, the two of them together at last, as she attempted to nurse him back to health.

And then he saw the other vampires, those vampires who had been in pursuit. Watched and they burst into the cabin. He saw them leering over his body, witnessed Amparo's daring rescue, finally culminating in his own transformation.

The last image he saw, as Amparo's history was coming to an end, was an image of the mysterious Quest Blades themselves. One blade flashed a soft blue, the other an angry bright red, and he watched as their colors quickly faded, their most recent appointed task, complete.

And what that objective had been, he realized with a shock, was to guide her across oceans, over mountains, even guide her over centuries for nothing less than one specific purpose. And that purpose...had been to find *him*. But *why*, he wanted to know. Why would the blades have done this? What exactly had Amparo asked of them? For a companion? What did any of it actually mean?

What Zekiel did know however is how long she had slept, how long she had lived, and perhaps most importantly, how long she had waited.

He knew how far she had traveled, knew how long she had been running. He knew all the risks she had taken...all of which had been taken to find...*him*.

He finally understood then that their first meeting had been no coincidence, no chance encounter. Not random at all.

No. It had all been planned, all carefully planned...by the Quest Blades themselves.

And then the final message was imparted to him...the climax of Amparo's vision...what Amparo had asked of the blades, what the Quest Blades had promised, and what he had been chosen to do...

Chapter Forty-Nine

Amparo finally broke the connection and I felt myself collapse, landing roughly on top of her. She wasn't hurt of course, and put her arms around me. She was crying, crying uncontrollably, and my mind tried desperately to make sense of it all.

Why did the blades lead her to me? What could I, a mere fledgling do? How was I supposed to stop, much less kill, this ancient vampire? How did she expect *me* to kill Cain???

Why me?

One thing for certain was that I hated him. I hated him not only for what he had done. I hated him for what he *was*. He had taken Amparo against her will, enslaved her, violated her, took *everything* he could from her. I clenched my fists, my anger nearly boiling over.

And I *knew him*. Somehow through this experience, I knew him as though I had met the old vampire myself.

But his power!

Such incredible power!

I was somehow keenly aware of this power and it shook me to my core that I was able to perceive, even from this distance, how powerful this being truly was.

I knew then why Amparo feared him and now I dreaded as well…and cringed knowing that this vampire would soon reach these shores. That this powerful and ancient vampire, this creature of unspeakable evil was even now, on his way here.

I knew Cain to be the first vampire in existence, of that there could be no doubt and no small thing in itself, but what Amparo had not imparted to me was *how* Cain had come to be. I had no clue at all as to *how* he had become a vampire himself, but at present, it wasn't a pressing concern. I was however curious about it and resolved to ask Amparo at a later time.

Furthermore, I was still in the process of sorting through all of the information I had received from our mental connection and was amazed how much I suddenly knew about our secretive race. I was well aware of our limitations, had knowledge now of several of our more common powers, and while I had much to digest and understand, none of that seemed to matter right now.

What really mattered, at this exact moment, was the woman before me. I suddenly knew…*her*. I suddenly knew…*everything*. It was like a spark had gone off in my brain, and my mind frantically tried to process all of this information.

"Zekiel?" Amparo whispered.

"Amparo? I…" But I had no words. My mind was overwhelmed and I found myself just staring at her, as if looking upon her for the first time.

She was staring at me intently too, waiting for any reaction, but I was truly at a loss for words. "Zekiel…" she asked again. "Please. Say *something*."

But I didn't know what to say. Not after such a staggering and emotional experience. She was getting back on her feet now and I followed, even offered a hand. We proceeded to get dressed in silence, as it seemed proper again to do, and moments later we stood awkwardly facing each other. Despite all that we had just shared both physically and mentally, I couldn't help but feel…to feel a very deep sadness.

"I...I had no idea, Amparo," I finally managed. "I didn't know. I...so much of this is new to me. I am so very sorry," I stammered.

I started to cry, tears swiftly filling my eyes, recalling again all of the horrible unspeakable things that had been done to her. Everything she had suffered at the hands of *Cain*.

"No, Zekiel," she said in a serious tone. "It is I who must apologize to you. You did not ask for *any* of this, nor can you understand, even after all that I have shared, what a tremendous burden I have placed upon you. Do not cry for *me*."

I looked up from my downcast position to look her directly in the eyes. And what I saw was a woman, such an incredibly beautiful and strong woman, and one who could do no wrong. I was in love with her, I realized. I knew that implicitly. And no matter how great of a burden she had placed upon my shoulders, regardless of the odds, no matter the opposition, I was resolved to stand with her for all time.

I no longer felt naïve to our existence. I knew what I was. What we *were*, and again I found myself pondering over everything that Amparo had made known to me. And what we had to do next, I realized was to figure out and decide our next move, make plans of our own...and I think I even knew *how*.

"Zekiel?" Amparo asked, noting the changed expression on my face.

"Show me the Quest Blades."

INTERLUDE

CAIN STEPPED OFF THE boat, or rather, glided over the water's surface, easily crossing the remaining distance to shore, refusing to soil his freshly polished boots.

Melchiah came second, a rather gangly looking creature with long black hair, and though his face might once have been called handsome, the expression he wore now was twisted and evil. He moved hunched over, almost beast like, and leaped over the water, not having Cain's ability, to stand by his Master's side.

"Welcome to England, My Lord," Melchiah greeted him, his voice deep and throaty.

"Hmm," was all the dark vampire said, as he distastefully took in his surroundings.

"Shall I send out scouts, My Lord?"

Cain closed his eyes and focused. Concentrated on the lay of the land. Honed in on his prey's location.

"She is here," Cain responded, a smile creasing his face. "Oh yes. She is indeed here." He fell into deep contemplation then, digging through his memory, thinking of that last encounter. When Amparo had so cleverly deceived him...

At the time, he found it odd that she had behaved so out of character that night, having sought him out in his private chambers.

She had entered scantily clad, enticing his senses, playing to his masculine nature.

She had coupled with him then, going to extreme lengths to satisfy the old vampire...and like a fool, he had fallen neatly into her trap. She even managed to exhaust him in a completely different manner that evening, and forced him to seek early rest, by slyly convincing him through her feminine charms to once again share his powerful blood.

She had won many favors that evening, taking from him a second deep drink, and by doing so, taking an additional dose of his incredible power. So very potent was the blood of Cain, in that one moment alone, her own considerable power had been virtually doubled. At the very least. Oh, but she had been clever, he mused. And then? *She had stolen his blades!* His single most prized possession. He laughed then at himself, despite being fooled and manipulated so easily, even silently congratulating her cunning and fearless treachery.

"Master?" Melchiah questioned, shaking Cain loose from his memories.

"It is nothing, Melchiah." Cain continued to laugh at his own expense, rubbing his bald head in a pensive gesture. "Yes," he added, once again surveying the land. "Do send out a few scouts."

"As the Master commands." Melchiah bowed low.

"Do be quick about it!" Cain suddenly snapped and Melchiah hunched down even lower. Cain laughed again. So easily his children obeyed. But even as Melchiah turned to carry out his orders, he gave pause and turned to Cain once more.

"Lord Cain?" Melchiah dared to ask, almost as an afterthought.

"You try my patience, Melchiah..."

"My Lord. Please. Forgive me. My fledgling..."

"Guma is dead," Cain answered bluntly, easily reading his mind. "Can you not sense this?" Melchiah concentrated, not wanting to believe Cain's words but as he scanned far and wide, as far as he could cast his mental net, he could not detect so much as a hint of his fledgling's presence. Not even the smallest trace.

"Slain by Amparo, no doubt. He was weak," Cain surmised. Melchiah bit his lip, for Guma had been dear to him.

"Kabaal too has perished. Jin and Victor also. Hmm. I will need to meditate on this. Yes," Cain said, speaking to himself.

"Shall I seek Amparo out myself?" Melchiah dared to interrupt. "I would very much like to pay my respects."

"You will do nothing but what I command!" Cain said in a sudden burst of anger. With a movement Melchiah could not even register, Cain's hand was suddenly on his throat. "You will do as I command, Melchiah. Nothing more. Do I make myself perfectly clear?"

Melchiah, unable to speak, nodded as best as he could.

"Good." Melchiah found himself released.

"My Lord..." Melchiah dared to say, now that he could speak again.

"I do not wish to destroy you, Melchiah...but you test my patience," Cain warned.

"Indeed, Lord, indeed. It is just that..."

"Speak!"

"Yes, my Lord. Yes. I only wish to ask if sending two scouts is sufficient?"

"Do you question me, Melchiah?"

"No, my Lord. No. I...simply do not wish to see my scouts..."

"My scouts!" Cain made perfectly clear. "What about *my* scouts, Melchiah?"

"Of course, My Lord."

"Send for them."

Within moments, two of Melchiah's most trusted servants were brought before Cain.

"Close your eyes. Both of you," the old vampire instructed and the two obeyed without question. "Search for her presence."

But after a few moments, both vampires looked to Cain, confused.

"My Lord...we do not sense her..." one dared to admit.

"*Weaklings!*" Cain shouted, becoming agitated. "She masks her presence, *fools*. Look...again."

"I still do not sense..." one scout began, but the other quickly cut him off.

"There is another of our kind here."

"Yes," Cain said with a smile, regaining his composure. "Very good. You can track *him*, yes?"

"Of course, Master. The fool does little to hide his location."

"Indeed. Do seek our newest family member out."

"And when we find him?"

"Amparo is likely to be with the fledgling. When you find her, you will notify Melchiah. He will report to me. But be mindful, my children," he continued. "She will not be taken easily, nor by surprise. She is formidable, that one. Do take all precautions and *do not* engage her until I give my consent. Melchiah will give those orders on my behalf." Cain paused to boldly stare at the two scouts individually, making certain they understood, for Cain would not tolerate any errors. He finally turned to Melchiah, who once again bowed low.

"Look at me!" Cain snapped and Melchiah verily cowered under his voice, though still managed to heed the command.

"You will not harm her in any way. Is that understood?"

Melchiah silently nodded his accord.

"I wish to deal with Amparo...*personally*. When you know her exact location, you will notify me at once. Do not delay in this, Melchiah...and do not fail me."

Again Melchiah nodded and bowed submissively, then turned to his scouts. With a second nod, they made ready to depart.

"And what of Amparo's fledgling, oh glorious Master?" one of the scouts dared, addressing Cain directly.

"Ah, yes. *The fledgling.* How careless of me to forget." Cain chuckled. Both scouts looked uneasy as Cain's face grew dark with anger.

"*Kill him.*"

Chapter Fifty

"Get up, Lucy! Get up!" Val screamed, chancing a glance at her fallen companion.

"It's no use, Val," Lucy called from her collapsed position. "We can't hold them off."

"*Get up!*" Val demanded.

The wolves were becoming ever more aggressive. At this point, it was only a matter of time before one would breach the circle.

Val struggled to be everywhere at once, turning constantly this way and that, feeling herself growing dizzy with exhaustion. With her companion still down and failing to keep an eye on the determined predators, one wolf, tired of waiting for its meal, saw an opportunity and leaped inside the barrier itself.

Lucy shrieked, and Val turned again, the warning having given her only a moment to react. Rows of sharp teeth were suddenly in her face and only her courage, and split-second timing allowed her to strike the wolf first, firebrand in hand, directly on its muzzle.

The wolf yelped, scampering back in surprise and pain, its nose burned, hair singed. It foolishly backed into the fire itself, furthering the damage before finally leaping clear.

Whew, Val thought to herself, trying to keep her wits about her. She had been extremely lucky on that last attack but knew she could not be pressed much longer. Her strength and luck were both running out.

"*Lucy!* You have to get up!" she cried and this time the woman finally stirred. She seemed to be in a daze, stricken with shock. The face she wore just looked empty and blank.

"Lucy! Snap out of it, *damn it!*" Val swore, risking another jab at yet another wolf venturing too close.

The fire was nearly extinguished now, barely keeping the wolves in check and with no more wood, Val knew that the ring was lost. That she and Lucy were finished, their only protection dying away.

But then, just as the wolves were ready to pounce together as one, even as Val whispered a desperate prayer, they heard the sound of many men shouting and coming their way.

Arrows suddenly started to rain down then, one nearly striking Val, but the wolves had already started to scramble for safety, while a few others were shot dead on the spot. The remainder of the pack broke apart, scattering in all directions, and Val breathed a huge sigh of relief. Fortunately, no other arrows had come close to hitting her and she quickly verified that Lucy was unharmed as well.

The woman was coming around now, waking from her stupor, as tears formed in her eyes. "I'm so sorry, Val!" she cried, throwing herself into Val's arms. "I'm so sorry. I don't know what happened to me. I was just *so scared!* Thought we were dead for sure!"

Thankful they had survived one danger, but Val couldn't help but worry that they now faced another, for their rescuers started to approach, albeit too quickly for her comfort. Keeping her eyes trained in the direction from which they came, Val's cautious nature was coming back in full.

Who would be out here? Wandering out in the cold? In the middle of nowhere of all places?

The men, whom she now counted as a group of four, were still coming toward them rapidly, bows still drawn and strung. It made her nervous and she silently hoped they were decent men, and perhaps their haste was due to concern that perhaps she and Lucy had been injured or were possibly still in danger. But two women, both attractive she knew, out on the isolated road alone, did little to calm her nerves.

The four men finally came into sight and while it was still quite dark, Val couldn't help but notice something strangely familiar. Was it the way a certain individual walked? Did she possibly recognize a voice?

Not but a moment later, the men now stood before them, each and every one wearing a hood over their heads. While that alone didn't frighten her, as it was cold after all, it was hard to ignore the multiple warnings Val heard screaming in her head.

Suddenly one of the men stepped forward, putting away his bow, and taking a torch from the man to his left. He looked the women over, enough to make Val feel even more uncomfortable, no one yet saying a word. Not even the slightest courtesy or greeting or to even ask if they had been injured.

He came even closer then, even leaned in, and in the light illuminating from the torch in his hand, Val gasped, recognizing the smile on his face.

The man then removed his hood, bringing his face into clear view and Val's greatest fears were realized.

"Why, hello there, Val," the man greeted her, quite pleased. He was literally beaming and making no effort at all to conceal it. "And here I thought I would never see you again. You left without saying goodbye."

"Val?" Lucy questioned. But Val ignored her, paralyzed with fear.

"H...How?" She questioned the man. Val was visibly shaking.

"Ah, a good question," he laughed. "We have a camp nearby and you don't see many fires out in the middle of nowhere. At least not around here. And when we came to investigate, thinking we may have found a...business opportunity, the last person I expected to find was my dear old Val, if that is what you were asking. That I'm afraid, was fate." He paused. "You never should have left me, Val," his tone now menacing.

"Val? Who is this man?" Lucy asked with concern.

"Oh yes. Do tell your friend who I am," he laughed. "Val and I go way back, don't we Val? So nice of you to be considerate enough to bring a friend. I brought a few friends too. One I think you will surely remember, although certainly, we are all friends here. Aren't we, Val?" He verily cackled, and gestured to one of his other companions. The individual stepped forward and a second hood was removed.

"I believe you know Will?" Val gasped again. Lucy did too, clearly recognizing the man.

"Oh, don't be too alarmed, my dear. Will here told us you were in the area. But that was months ago. Never thought we would find you, really. Henry refused to tell us where you had gone. Such a shame," he recounted stroking his chin.

"Henry?" Lucy asked. "You didn't hurt him, did you?"

"Nah, the man is fine," Will said, speaking for the first time. "Lucky for him, seeing as he did throw me out. Not good for business though. Especially considering I'm such a good customer, hey Luce? Amazing how things work out sometimes," he laughed. "You certainly are not as pretty as Val, here." At this bold statement, the other man assumed an agitated expression. "But under the circumstances," Will continued, "I am more than willing to...resume our...acquaintance. My friend here insists on having Val all to himself." He sighed. "But we will have fun too, right Luce? I am, after all, a most reasonable man." He laughed again and the other man nodded curtly, revealing himself as the ultimate authority.

"I will not do anything with you!" Lucy screamed at Will. "Never again," she spat.

"Oh...but I think you will," Will replied. "For I have already paid for your services by saving your life. And I do intend to get what I paid for, Lucy. I do."

"Val?" Lucy turned to her companion, seeking some way out.

"I intend to get what I paid for as well, Val. That was always our arrangement," the leader said, ignoring Lucy. "I can understand why you left initially, Val. No payment and all. But now?" he laughed. "You both owe us your lives. I think that buys me quite a bit, Val. Quite a bit, indeed."

"I don't know who you are..." Lucy started to say but Will grabbed her roughly by the arm and pulled her to her feet.

"Jack," the man responded with an evil smile. "You may call me Jack."

Chapter Fifty-One

Amparo placed the daggers on the ground so that Zekiel could view them clearly.

"How do they work?" Zekiel asked. "I mean, I understand the basics...due to the vision, but I wasn't able to see or determine *how* they function. How and why did the blades lead you to me?" he wondered aloud.

"Many things about the blades are unknown," Amparo replied. "They do not tell me why."

"You refer to them as if they could speak?"

"They can."

"I beg your pardon?"

Amparo laughed. "I can see your confusion," she said evenly. "And I can assure you, that they do, in fact, speak."

Zekiel's eyes went wide. This was too much to comprehend.

"They speak much in the same way that we do," she went on, trying to explain. "Only, they use telepathy. They have no audible voice."

"But..." Zekiel interrupted. "Why can't you ask them why they led you to me?"

"I can ask them. I *have* asked them. They do not answer. But mind you, they can and do speak. Typically, they reply with a single word, but regardless of this limitation, they understand what we are saying perfectly well. Whereas they choose to answer what they will, and often times again but with a single word, I can assure you they are listening now. Hearing our every word."

"Impossible!" Zekiel whispered in disbelief.

"I am afraid it is possible. It is. *They are*. They are here. In front of you, as you can see."

Zekiel tentatively reached for one then stopped.

"Are they safe to touch?"

"At this time, I would not advise it."

Zekiel retracted his hand. "How then did they lead you to me?" He asked after a moment.

"They work as such," she began. "The wielder may ask a question or make a request. They have the ability to track any object or person, or even complete a specific objective."

"I don't understand."

"Let me try to be more specific. I will use you as an example." She bent down to grab the dagger on the left. The one that displayed a pale blue in color.

"This is Quest," she said, holding the dagger aloft. "Quest is the seeker blade. The guide."

"The guide?"

"Stop interrupting, Zekiel," she half-joked. "I am trying to explain."

Zekiel's face grew serious then as he gave Amparo his full attention, resolved not to interrupt.

"As I said, Quest is a guide. Its purpose is to guide one to his goal. Not to be confused with *completing* the specific goal. That is where Armageddon comes into play." At this remark, she picked up the second dagger, holding the pair now in front of him.

Armageddon, while mostly silver in color, had a distinct red tint to it, much like the other was tinted blue. But unlike Quest, this second blade almost appeared...angry? Though Zekiel was not at all certain as to why nor how he seemed to perceive this.

"Ah yes, Zekiel," Amparo confirmed, responding to his thoughts. "Indeed. The blade is angry quite often. There is a certain malice attached to this one...though the cause for it, I do not know."

"How can a dagger have thoughts? Feelings?" Zekiel asked, momentarily forgetting his promise of silence.

"I do not know," she answered. "I have yet to determine that. But I do know quite a great deal about them. As I said, Quest is the guide. It can take you far and wide. It will lead you to your objective if such an object or objective *can* be found. It found you, Zekiel...before you were even born."

Zekiel gasped. "Impossible!' He cried, and again Amparo forgave this brief interruption.

"I don't know how or *if* the blades are able to see the future, for that is seemingly what they did, or rather, what Quest did...in leading me to you."

"How could it have known?"

"Honestly, Zekiel," Amparo scolded, losing patience. "If you insist on interrupting me at every turn..." But she stopped here and calmed herself. Reminded herself that it would be foolish to not have any questions. And perhaps, through Zekiel's questioning, she realized, they may together discover more answers.

"I am sorry," she apologized. "I understand this is difficult to understand, but I will do my best to answer. I do not know *how* Quest operates. Not in this regard. Nothing for certain. Perhaps, it cannot see the future at all. Perhaps, what Quest does is merely wait until the request can be carried out. This be only one of many theories. I only know what happened during our history together, myself and the blades mind you, and what I was instructed to do. You saw me take to the Earth. You witnessed the deep sleep."

"Deep sleep?"

"Ah. I can see we will need to speak of many things this evening. Even with the mental connection, certain things are difficult to explain or even interpret. We vampires need rest. Like any other creature, as you already know. However, there is a deep sleep unique to our kind...similar to an animal, such as a bear, hibernating to escape the long winter. But our sleep is different, Zekiel. In this state, we no longer need to feed, much like a bear will survive on its own fat, but unlike a bear come Spring, we can escape the need to rise. It is also a way in which to grow stronger."

"How so?"

"We are getting off-topic but I will answer. A vampire's strength, as you will soon come to know, is due to several factors, and the first is tied directly to the maker. In your case, that person is me. I have never brought one over before, never created another of our kind, and as you know, I have been a vampire for a very...very long time. Centuries, Zekiel. So, when I brought you over, the blood you took was already centuries old, as potent as could be possible, for again, you are the only fledging I have created."

"There are limitations then?"

"Yes and no. Even Cain's power wanes after creating so many. Each offspring or new fledgling born is a tax upon our power. Our very life source, though I can assure you, we remain quite immortal. But the blood, that pure, centuries-old undiluted blood which has been in my very body since the very beginning takes centuries to replenish, and never is a vampire created more powerful than the first...because the blood I carry, replenish henceforth will never be as old as what I *had*. You were my first. And so, if I should go on to create others, at this very moment, or even centuries from now, none would be nearly as strong as you. Not even half of what you possess. Perhaps, and far more likely, even less. However..." Here she paused, contemplating Zekiel's own creation. "You, Zekiel, are somewhat of a riddle. Your own strength already rivals my own. I have yet to discover why. But perhaps this is one of the many reasons I was guided to you. Another factor in determining our power is time. As a fledgling, any vampire you would create would likely be weak, for you have no time accumulated 'in the blood'. Do you follow?"

"I think so. But please, elaborate...for I now carry your blood, which already is centuries old."

Amparo nodded. "Yes, Zekiel. You now carry my blood. But it was *transferred* to you. It was not *of* you, and thus while I hesitate to use the word 'diluted' to describe what is now in your body, it is *my* body that aged the blood, and not your own. But in time, again over centuries, *you* will gradually age this blood, it now being a part of you. Naturally, the older the blood-the stronger the offspring, but once the blood is passed, each time this happens? Much of that potency is lost.

"Yet perhaps you may prove to be an exception to this rule, for I cannot help but wonder how powerful a fledgling of yours might be. As I have said, you are a bit of a riddle. An intriguing mystery, Zekiel. In time, we must discover that answer. But say, for example you were born as any other fledgling. What largely determines your strength is directly associated with how long the maker has been alive. His or her age. Time you see, is the essence of our power, along with the blood of the Maker. The two go hand in hand. How long a vampire has been in existence greatly influences the gifts any offspring may receive. I have waited centuries to do this. Centuries, young one. And remember, you are my first."

"So, had you created another," Zekiel inquired. "Several centuries prior. Would that affect how powerful I would have been?"

"Yes, Zekiel. You understand. We cannot create vampires at will. That is to say, we could, but they would be weak. Barely above the strength of a human. So you see, even we have certain limitations. A vampire does not create another of our kind without good reason, for it leaves the Maker weak as well. The blood of those we killed last night has certainly gone a long way toward restoring my former strength, but I am a fraction of what I was. A fraction of what I was before I created you. I still retain all of my abilities, and physically, after enough feedings, most of my strength will gradually return. However, the *potency* of my blood, which is perhaps the most accurate way to put it, is simply not what it was. Because I gave nearly all of it to you."

"Are you saying...I have caused you harm?" Zekiel asked concerned.

"Not any lasting harm, no. It will simply take me centuries to recover my former strength."

"*Centuries?*"

"Aye. Centuries. If not longer. That which is given is not easily regained nor replenished. It would take the blood of Cain himself to replace that which I have lost."

Cain.

Hearing his name again made Zekiel cringe. And then something else happened. Though Zekiel made no conscious effort, all at once he began to sense the legendary Vampire's presence. "*He is here!*" Zekiel confirmed.

Amparo scanned the area quickly, thinking Cain was upon them that very moment, but after a thorough search of the area using her own considerable power, she could not detect a single presence. "I don't sense..." Amparo began.

"He is here," Zekiel insisted. "Not *here*. Not in this general area. But he is here. Here in England. I feel...Amparo, I *feel* him. I..."

"Where, Zekiel?" Amparo asked concerned, never doubting him. "*Where* do you sense him? How close is he?"

Zekiel concentrated and many moments seemed to pass. Amparo began to grow restless, desperate for an answer.

"Zekiel?"

"He is far. Still very far from here...but his *presence*. Amparo, his presence here is unmistakable."

"I do not doubt you. What concerns me is how you are able to sense him whereas I cannot. This is strange...very strange indeed. If you can sense Cain..."

Suddenly, Amparo realized that she had made a crucial error. While discussing the history of the Quest Blades, in part distracted and not in any immediate danger, Amparo knew she had been careless.

"Close your mind!" Amparo warned. "*Now.*"

"Shit!" Zekiel swore, and did as instructed, immediately picturing his mind slamming shut like a door. "Amparo...I fear..."

"You fear he knows!"

"Yes."

Amparo nodded. "Come," she instructed. "We must travel at once. We need be far from here. As far as we can. We must put some distance between us."

She sheathed the daggers, ready to take off running that very second, Zekiel right beside her. Ready to run all night if necessary. Amparo hesitated then, as if another thought had crossed her mind.

"Do you sense any others?" she asked. "Look carefully, my chosen."

Zekiel concentrated once more, and when at last he opened his eyes, wide and full of fear, that had been answer enough.

Chapter Fifty-Two

THE TWO VAMPIRE SCOUTS, Morluun and Jeremiah, suddenly stopped in their tracks.

"His presence..." Jeremiah started, turning to his companion.

"Gone. Masked," Morluun finished. "Amparo has instructed the fledgling well."

"But how?" Jeremiah questioned. "How can we not detect a mere fledgling?"

Morluun, the far older vampire, was honestly not sure. "She does have the blades," he reasoned. "Perhaps she uses them to guard their location. His fledging mind should be no match for our own."

"What do we do then?" Jeremiah asked.

"We search. Look for clues. We wait for them to make a mistake. We know they are here. That is sufficient."

"But Lord Cain...he will not be pleased."

"What would you have us do?" he snarled at the younger vampire. "Admit our failure? Face Cain's wrath?"

At this, the other vampire fell silent.

"I will consult with Melchiah," Morluun decided. "Perhaps he can best judge what we are to do...but I will not report to him prematurely. We have been given a task. A task we will see done.

Should we encounter any extended delays, we will make our inquiry then. Is that understood?"

"Yes, Morluun."

"Good. Surely in time, we can pick up their trail."

With no more words forthcoming, the two vampires resumed their search.

Chapter Fifty-Three

Val and Lucy soon found themselves in Jack's mess of a camp.

Tents had been haphazardly assembled and random items were littered everywhere: clothes, blankets, even a stack of dirty pans and dishes. There were more men here, five or six at least from what Val could tell, all of whom were staring at her and Lucy intently.

It had not been a long walk, well under an hour, and Val quickly realized that had they not been caught, they would have likely passed through this very region anyway. It gave her a chill. That was Jack, all right, she thought to herself. Jack was always cunning. Always found the best location. Always kept himself and his band close to any main road. Close enough to catch and plunder any vulnerable travelers.

Val was filled with despair. She knew what was to come. What Jack would demand. And this time, he wouldn't take no for an answer nor be made a fool of. Would not let her so easily escape again. All of her possessions, even the small knife she carried, had been taken.

But what bothered Val more than her own fate, was the fate of her companion. What was to become of Lucy? And how could Val ever forgive herself for getting Lucy into this mess? What was to become of her?

"Hey, Val," Jack sneered, sticking close to her side. But when Val did not respond, lost in her own thoughts, Jack repeated her name and roughly grabbed her arm.

"When Will saw you that night at Henry's place. He said you were with another man. Claimed he was even your husband. You will explain."

Val didn't know what to say. How to respond. If she told the truth, what would Jack do? Could the situation possibly get any worse?

"I…"

"Explain!" Jack demanded.

Every man in the small camp now turned their way but when Jack returned their stares, everyone wisely returned to what they were doing.

"Tell me now, or…" Jack repeated menacingly, and she knew he would not ask again.

"The man…" Val began, the lie already forming on her lips. "The man was nothing. A paying customer. Nothing more."

"*Liar!*" Jack shouted and delivered a sharp slap to her face. Val reeled under the blow, felt the welt already forming on her face, but did her best to avoid showing any fear.

"I…I speak the truth, Jack," Val countered, bravely trying to stare him down.

"That's not what Will told me."

"Will knows nothing."

"Indeed," Jack responded, not easily fooled. "He told me this man was your husband. Said he had a funny look about him. Are you calling Will a liar, then?"

"No, Jack," She responded coolly. "Perhaps he simply…misunderstood. He was quite drunk that night."

"Oh, I don't doubt that. But I'm not for trusting you either."

"Let me ask you this, Jack," Val said, surprising the man with her confidence. "Did Will also tell you that he wanted me for his own?"

"Bah," he spat. "What man would not? We already discussed that. You heard that conversation."

"But did you hear *our* conversation? At Henry's place?"

"I don't know what you are getting at," Jack snarled.

"Then let me explain. Will wanted me for his own. *Still* wants me for his own."

"He has Lucy. And seems happy enough with our arrangement."

"That's what he told you."

"Don't play games with me, Val..." he warned.

"I play no games, Jack. But perhaps you would be wise to keep an eye on that one..." A pause. "Many desire what you have...Jack." She moved persuasively closer, hoping he would take the bait.

"Oh? And what do I have?" Jack asked, suddenly feeling quite aroused, and thinking of only one thing.

"You have *me*," she whispered, only an inch from his face. He almost fell for it then, nearly gave in. Almost believed every word she had spoken. And why wouldn't Will desire her? Lucy was fair, sure, but paled in comparison to Val. There was no one else quite like Val.

"Enough!" he shouted, breaking them apart, unwilling to accept her words.

"Suit yourself," she responded, maintaining a cool air of confidence. "Trust not my words. Not tonight. But mind you, Jack...every man wants more. And every man wants that which he cannot have. You may be in alliance now..."

"Will!" Jack barked, gaining the attention of the man who was only a dozen yards away. He came over to join the pair, clearly irritated.

"Jack," Will began. "While I...respect your authority here, I was just about to get...reacquainted with Lucy here. If you don't mind..."

"I *do* mind...and that fucking whore and *your needs* can wait."

Will paused as if he had something to say but wisely held his tongue. Jack was in charge here after all and Will thought it best to remember that.

"Val here was just telling me about her...recent adventures. At Henry's place. I want to know about this other man she was with."

"The coward?" Will laughed. "He was a worthless piece of shit."

Val bit her lip.

"Tell me about him. About the encounter," Jack asked.

"Shit, Jack. I wouldn't worry about him."

"*What happened?*" Jack nearly screamed. Will sighed.

"Was having a drink at Henry's. Typical night. That's when I saw Val."

"Go on."

"Well, I hate to tell you this Jack, but Val and I have been...um, acquaintances before. That's how I recognized her."

Jack visibly scowled.

"You have to understand," Will tried to put in. "Val here had a life before she met you, Jack. I mean..."

"Enough about that. Tell me about the encounter. About this... this supposed husband of hers."

"It's like I said, Jack. The man was a coward. A fool. I was attempting to arrange for...Val's...*services* for the night..."

"And did you?"

"I told you," Val whispered, but Jack cut her off with a stare.

"No. But it wasn't going to happen in any case because of the man she was with. Henry got involved in it too. The coward and I got to fighting and Henry threw me out."

"I wouldn't have slept with you. Regardless," Val added.

"*Quiet!*" Jack roared.

Val knew he was beyond possessive. Jealous of any man that came near her. If she could use that to her advantage with Will...

"Did this man claim to be Val's husband?" Jack asked, after he had somewhat composed himself.

"I suppose. But to what extent?" Will laughed, not being able to help himself.

"What do you mean?" Jack asked, his anger nearly boiling over.

"Come on, Jack. Don't be so naïve."

"Watch your tone, Will."

"Honestly, Jack. I don't see how it matters. Now, if you will excuse me..."

"No."

"I beg your pardon?"

"Explain to me what you mean. What you mean by 'it doesn't matter.'"

"Jack?"

"*Explain*," Jack said in a tone that left no room for debate. Will could only shrug his shoulders. He obviously wasn't getting through to the man.

"Right now, Jack, *you* are her husband. Well...not quite, if you catch my meaning."

Now Jack began to understand.

"In her line of work," Will continued. "Val here has a different husband every night. Isn't that right, Val?"

"What he says is true, Jack. The man I was with was a customer, nothing more," Val answered, thinking it was best to continue the lie.

"Remember when we were *married*, Val?" Will asked with a smile and only a second later did he realize his mistake.

Jack was swinging at him then, enraged, bent solely on Will's destruction. But Will fought back. Before long, both men were in a tangle, rolling around in the dirt and suddenly every man in the camp was rushing over to watch. Such excitement was a rarity. Even for highway bandits.

Chapter Fifty-Four

ZEKIEL AND AMPARO ran long into the night, running side by side, covering many miles. At the time, Zekiel was unclear how close the pursuit actually was, but Amparo insisted they take no chances. She communicated with him often, talking to him as they ran which proved to be a most welcome distraction for them both.

She told him more and more about their abilities, particularly about a vampire's mental prowess, and Zekiel proved to be an eager student.

"*But mind your mind. Always, young one,*" Amparo stressed as they passed through a particularly thick crop of trees, dodging them with ease, even at such incredible speed.

"What do you mean?" he asked.

"*When we communicate like this. Mentally. This is when we are most vulnerable to other mental intrusions.*"

"So...before," Zekiel communicated. "When I detected Cain. The scouts. Is that when I dropped my guard?"

"*I honestly don't know. I...I fear I was not paying close enough attention to this. I should have known, Zekiel. It was my responsibility.*"

"But how can you blame yourself if you, yourself could not sense them?"

Her student had a good point, and in all honesty, it was a legitimate question. How could she have known they were being tracked if she, herself had been unable to detect the other vampires?

No, Amparo told herself. By sharing the dark blood with Zekiel, she was solely responsible for his instruction. For his training. He was her responsibility. So even though she had been unable to detect Cain and his scouts, she still should have retained her discipline. She had been far too careless. Much too carefree.

Yes, she had warned Zekiel repeatedly. About how easily other immortals may seek to read his mind, even learn of their location. But with him being a new fledgling, only a few days old, it was far too much to ask. Becoming skilled in a vampire's unique abilities took time, as Amparo herself clearly remembered. And for Zekiel's part, he was learning quickly. Very quickly. She had yet to determine what her offspring was truly capable of, but reminded herself to remain aware of his inexperience. For now, the damage was done and it was time to prevent mistakes in the future, rather to regret or even linger over the past.

After Amparo felt they had gone far enough and with dawn no more than a few hours away, she finally came to a stop, only Zekiel did not. Instead, the young vampire vaulted into the air, latching on to a long horizontal branch and swung his body upwards and around, multiple times to build momentum before propelling himself even higher, backflipping twice in the process only to land nimbly on top of yet another branch, a great deal higher, where he then rested and perched.

Before speaking any more words to her peculiar student, Amparo surveyed the area carefully and cautiously. They could afford no more errors, especially now that Cain himself had arrived.

She reached out mentally, as far as she could cast her net, but could discover no other vampire's presence.

"Zekiel, could you…" she started to ask, looking upwards in his direction, but the young vampire already had his eyes closed. She smiled then, pleased with his initiative and had the utmost confidence that Zekiel would not error in this regard again. Confident that her fledgling would learn from his mistakes.

She studied him carefully then, and unconsciously whispered his name. "Zekiel Raven."

Raven. And she mulled over this name thinking to herself how befitting it was. How he even now appeared much like the bird itself, perched and draped in his black cloak, the sleeves almost appearing as if they were wings. He even moved like one, she mused, knowing ravens were known for their aerial acrobatics. Still curious as to why Zekiel had sought such heights, when this made no difference when using the ability to search a given region, Amparo nevertheless waited patiently.

"*I sense...I sense nothing. Nothing far and wide,*" Zekiel concluded telepathically after a short time, preferring not to shout. He then visually inspected the area with his keen eyes, using the height of the massive tree to survey the perimeter as far as he could see. Satisfied, Zekiel made his way back down, moving with no less precision and grace from branch to branch, a moment later once again at Amparo's side.

"Why the tall branch?" Amparo felt compelled to ask.

"I wanted to be sure. In case my eyes might see what the mind could not."

"Good," Amparo smiled, quite pleased. "Then I hope we will be safe enough tonight. I still do not understand how you were able to detect their presence whereas I could not. I fully intend on exploring the full extent of your powers, Zekiel, but for now, while we have a few moments, let us again discuss the Quest Blades."

"Ah," Zekiel said, quite eager. "I am most interested in hearing more about them. You have told me quite a bit about the blade you call 'Quest'. I would like to learn more about the other."

"The other is called Armageddon. And as I've told you before, this blade is far more dangerous," she cautioned, drawing the dagger from behind her back.

"This weapon is the 'objective blade' and even now, at every moment, works to complete my request. And that request...was to find the one who can and *will* kill Cain."

Zekiel's eyes went wide.

"You see, Zekiel...Quest is the blade that led me to you. It is Armageddon's job now to see the objective fulfilled. And the objective, as I have just said, is to kill Cain. *You* are the one, Zekiel. *You are the one who will do it.*"

"But Amparo," he pleaded. "How can this be? How is this even possible? How am I to do this? As you have said time and time again, I am but a mere fledging!"

"Ah, but you are a fledging already far more powerful than I. I know this to be true. Even in my weakened state...and such a thing should not be possible."

Zekiel stopped to consider her words, then turned to offer a serious look of his own. "Surely, I am not powerful enough to kill him. Nor the one responsible for the future of our entire race. I *felt* his power, Amparo. If only but from a distance, but I have no doubt. No doubts at all. He would *destroy me*," Zekiel concluded.

"Maybe now."

"What do you mean?"

"Think about it, Zekiel. The Quest Blades took centuries to even carry out the first objective...which was finding you. Perhaps in time, you *will* be strong enough."

"How much time?"

"Centuries, perhaps? Longer? Would that be a bad thing? To wait that long...with me?"

He thoughtfully considered her question but more importantly, the manner in which she had *asked*, paying close attention to that keyword:

Centuries.

It was hard to believe, but now that he was a vampire, and in practical terms, immortal, he hadn't really taken the time to properly digest what the word truly meant. How much *time* had actually been given to him.

The other observation worth noting was Amparo's direct suggestion that he remain with *her*. To think, that a woman, or in this case, a vampire could have that desire. To be with him.

But was that desire solely rooted in her commitment to see Cain destroyed? Or did Amparo truly have deeper feelings for him? Yes, they had made love, had even gone well beyond that when she had shared the deeper connection of her mind, along with yet another infusion of her blood. But how did Amparo really feel? Was she with him only because she needed him?

He didn't honestly believe that to be the case, but resolved to think about such complicated matters at a later time, tucking away these thoughts (among so many others), because what really mattered at present, was that he had agreed to help her, aid her in her quest, regardless of any personal feelings, as well as the potential consequences.

"Zekiel?" she questioned, noting the pensive look on his face.

"I'm sorry, Amparo. I was just thinking."

"I know. Your mind remains closed to me," she smiled. "This is a good development. But tell me, what is on your mind? Will you tell me? *Are* you willing to wait?"

And then a thought struck him. "Why don't we ask the Quest Blades?"

"I beg your pardon?"

"Why don't we ask the Quest Blades? If we are to wait together, you and I..."

Now Amparo understood and it hadn't occurred to her that she had not used the blades since the night her fledgling had been born.

"You said that it was the job of Quest to find me, which it has." Zekiel went on. "You also mentioned that Armageddon is the far more deadly of the two, which I am still very curious about. But what I would like to know first is..."

"What we are supposed to do next?" Amparo concluded for him.

"Aye." There was something about this one, Amparo couldn't help but acknowledge. He was sharp. Inquisitive. And when he focused, he thought only of completing the immediate objective. He had proven that on multiple occasions already. Not only was Zekiel strong of body, but was also proving at every turn that he was equally strong in mind.

"Can you ask them, Amparo? Right now?" he pursued, taking his own turn to interrupting her thoughts.

"I can," she said, drawing Quest to hold both daggers in her hands. "But we, *I*, must be cautious in their use. For this is where Armageddon has been known to be extremely deadly."

"How so?"

"We must choose our questions carefully, for whatever we ask and more importantly, the manner in which we ask, the way we shape our words, weighs heavily on the path the blade might take. And thus, we also must take care not to interfere with what I have already put into motion."

"I don't understand."

"For you see, Zekiel, Armageddon will see any objective carried out to completion...*if* it is possible...but also at great personal risk with no regard for the welfare of its current owner. We must be very mindful of what we say."

"But I thought you already asked Armageddon to complete our objective. You asked the blade to provide a path to kill Cain."

"True," she agreed. "But what we have not asked Armageddon is what we are to do next. Where we are to go. Leastways in the past, Armageddon has told me what to do when it sees fit. Whenever there is a need."

"Then ask. For are we not in great need? Is that not a simple enough question? Should it not be trying to guide us? Even now?" Amparo pondered Zekiel's argument very carefully and recalled her history with the daggers. They had led her true, had always instructed her on what to do next, but ever since the night of Zekiel's transformation, she now realized that the blades had not communicated at all. In fact, they had done nothing, had remained silent, even when they surely could have used their assistance with gaining more distance from their enemies.

Would they have guided the pair had Amparo chosen a dangerous path? A path that did not coincide with their mission or that would have put the quest at risk? Would they have intervened? Would they have warned Amparo if Cain had drawn too near? She even recalled that when they had instructed her to sleep, they had at least directly given her the command to do so. So why were they silent now?

"Amparo?" Zekiel questioned her after a prolonged silence.

"I'm sorry, Zekiel. I was pondering why the blades have gone silent. In the past, and even a few months ago when I found you almost dead on the battlefield, they had always guided me at every turn. Why they have gone silent now…disturbs me."

"Is it possible they are even now, plotting our course?"

"I…"

Suddenly, both Armageddon and Quest began to pulse, as if almost responding to their very thoughts. "They are becoming active again!" Amparo cried. "But why now? Why the delay?"

"At any given moment, if there is nothing for us to do, what would they do then?" Zekiel questioned.

"Nothing…I suppose. But typically, they would at least speak. Command me to wait. Offer a word or two."

"Are they speaking to you now?"

"I…"

Follow. Quest distinctly said.

Now. Armageddon added with a sense of urgency.

"We must go," Amparo said, quite shaken. "Never before have they commanded me to do something with so much urgency."

"What did they say? Where are we to go?"

The hand that was holding Quest, almost as if in response verily pulled Amparo's arm to the East.

"East?" Zekiel asked, knowing full well Amparo had not moved her hand on her own. The gesture had been too irregular.

"East." Amparo confirmed and sped off, her fledging right behind.

Chapter Fifty-Five

WILL FELT THE NEXT punch drive deep into his gut and knew he was finished. He struggled to get up, sprawled out on the ground, but Jack was already there, threatening to strike him again. Will then had the notion to stab him, using the long knife he kept at his side, but fortunately a strong mental caution put that sudden impulse to rest. Jack was in charge here, all of the men under his command, and to challenge Jack in any manner would trigger the fury of all. They were all Jack's men, loyal to a fault, and unless he had some other means to assume leadership, there was no way to defeat Jack...and still remain alive.

"Enough! I yield!" Will shouted, and it had been just in time, for Jack was more than eager to continue the fight. He had taken his share of blows, of course, but it was clear that Jack held the advantage here. Both physically and through strength of arms.

"Apologize!" Jack commanded, wiping the red from his lips. Despite the new bruises on his face, he stood easily, comfortable, and more than willing to trade more blows should his colleague be stupid enough to push the issue.

"Apologize to my wife," Jack added.

Val, who had been unable to leave, hoping the distraction might have offered her some means of escape, found herself held tight during the entire exchange, arms pinned to her side by one of Jack's men. She had been grabbed immediately, as soon as the fight had started, and she lamented that her strategy failed to provide any opportunity to flee.

"*Apologize!*" Jack screamed.

"I..." Will stammered. "I am sorry, Jack. I apologize," Will said carefully, doing his best to hide his gritted teeth.

"Go on." Go on? Will wondered how elaborate the apology was supposed to be. But when Jack nodded at his "so-called bride", Will finally understood.

"I beg your pardon, Miss Val. I did not mean to insult you."

"Better." Jack smiled. "That will do. Now remove yourself from my presence." Will walked away then, not even bothering to look at Lucy, who was similarly held from behind. Perhaps he would call for her in time. Perhaps not. Will was not exactly feeling his best and his stomach, along with his bruised face ached. But perhaps, it was more so his pride.

Jack turned his attention back to Val, whose attempt to sow discord among the group had ultimately failed and at best, had merely caused a minor delay.

"You will accompany me to my tent," he demanded, and Val fought the urge to vomit.

She was roughly dragged then, still tightly held by one of Jack's men, toward a crudely assembled shelter.

"Leave her," he instructed his associate and her captor immediately released his hold. "Bring hot water. A towel," Jack ordered, and with a short bow, his obedient servant set off on the appointed task.

"You will wash my face..." he began. "And then...I think you know what comes next. I've missed you, my dear," he said, inching close enough to trace a finger down her cheek. "Oh, how I have missed you." He smiled for only a moment before his expression changed to one Val had desperately tried to forget.

"Get in the fucking tent."

Chapter Fifty-Six

"Have you found them?" Melchiah's voice asked the pair. Both Morluun and Jeremiah halted their run, dawn still a few hours away.

"No, Master Melchiah. We have not," Morluun responded telepathically. "We were following the fledgling's trail but it has since disappeared, forcing us to..."

"Silence!" Melchiah silently shouted, his voice echoing painfully within their minds. "Lord Cain is not interested in excuses. You were given but one task...which is to find Amparo and a mere fledgling!"

"But Master!" Jeremiah pleaded. "He has learned to conceal himself! Amparo has instructed him well."

"And what of her?" Melchiah questioned, caring not who he spoke with. "Have you managed to find her?"

"The fledgling is with her, Master. If we cannot find him, how are we to find her?" Jeremiah reasoned.

"Enough!" Melchiah commanded a second time. "I've told both of you already that Lord Cain is not interested in your excuses. Know that if you fail me in this task, you fail our Master as well."

"Yes, Melchiah," they both said at once.

"The fledgling is young. He is likely to make a mistake. You will wait for this mistake. And until that time, you will hunt them down relentlessly. They must be found."

"But how do we hunt them when they mask their very presence, Master?" Jeremiah foolishly asked. Even through the telepathic connection, Morluun could feel Melchiah's impatience.

"Have you not heard a single word I have said? Ask me again, young Jeremiah," Melchiah hissed. *"I beg you to try my patience."*

"Quiet, you fool!" Morluun said out loud. Melchiah laughed, for Morluun's words had not been concealed from him.

"See that you listen to your brother," Melchiah added and with that, his voice was gone.

"Fool!" Morluun said, scolding his younger companion. "Have you any idea what Melchiah would do? Nay, what *Lord Cain* will do if we fail?"

"Tell me," Jeremiah asked, ignoring the threat. "Why does Lord Cain not find these two himself? Wouldn't that be simpler? Could he not do this? Would this task not be easy enough?"

"It is not our place to question the Lord Cain. Not in any capacity. We do as he commands. You would be wise to learn that, Jeremiah."

"But why not send Melchiah? Someone far more skilled? Someone far more powerful?"

"Who's to say that Melchiah is *not* doing this? Searching for them now, as we do?"

"Bah. I don't believe it. What I do not understand is why *we* are charged with this quest."

"What matters is that it is Cain's will, Jeremiah. Nothing more. Now come, we have work to do. For while we linger here, we accomplish nothing." Jeremiah conceded with a nod and the vampires started off again. They moved as one, blurs in the night, but after a short time, Jeremiah once again came to a stop.

"What is it?" Morluun quickly asked, for he sensed nothing to warrant the pause. Jeremiah meanwhile had his neck raised and stretched and gave a great sniff with his nose. A small smile found its way to his elongated face.

"Jeremiah..." Morluun warned, not at all appreciating the silence.

"Humans," Jeremiah said, speaking at once. "Do you not detect them, brother? Long has it been since we have had something proper to...eat."

Morluun, who had been strictly using his preternatural senses to search for Amparo and her fledgling, focused his far more powerful net to confirm Jerimiah's discovery.

"Hmm..." Morluun muttered.

"Brother?"

"Forget them, Jeremiah. We have work to do," Morluun decided, already fighting his instinct to engage the nearby humans.

"But Morluun," Jeremiah attempted to counter. "When was the last time you fed? Tasted the sweetness of human blood? Feasted upon an exquisite morsel? The voyage in which we took to reach this wretched land was long indeed. Far too long for my taste and appetite."

Despite Melchiah's recent warning, what Jeremiah said was true. He had not fed in some time, though Morluun, due to his age, could go for extended periods of time between the need for human blood. But, he mused to himself, these humans *were* very close...

"And besides, dear brother," Jeremiah went on, clearly trying to persuade his companion. "The blood of these fickle humans will only aid us in our search. Sharpen our senses. Surely even Melchiah could not argue against that logic. I sense at least ten such creatures this very moment. Ten! A feast for us both. Certainly, we could...briefly pause in our search, for such nourishment will only aid us, of course."

Morluun could sense the humans easily and Jeremiah made a compelling argument. And the more he thought about it, the more he found himself licking his lips. Yes, human blood always heightened their senses, always briefly increased their powers.

Fresh blood would make them sharp, focused, and most importantly, sated. At least for a time. And with dawn so near, they could rise the following evening, fed and ready, far more ready to resume their important work.

"We must be quick about it, Jeremiah," Morluun said, at last giving in. "And we must not linger. Dawn is still some time away and I mean to continue our search."

"Yes, yes, of course, Master Morluun. Surely our feast will be a minor delay, no more. But think of it. Five for me, five for you. Agreed?"

"Six for me," Morluun corrected. "I will graciously give you four...if you do not test me further."

"Of course, of course, Master Morluun. However you say."

"Then let us feast, little brother and let us be done with this. Yes...let us feast at once."

Chapter Fifty-Seven

Val soaked the rag and then gingerly brought the cloth to Jack's bruised face. She was trapped now, full and complete, and all thoughts of escape felt hopeless.

So this was it, she thought to herself. This is how her life would end. Not physically of course, for Jack had no intention to kill neither her or Lucy, but her life, as she viewed it, had essentially come to an end.

And Zekiel was gone.

She wondered then if her search had been in vain, in even thinking there had been a chance of finding Zekiel either on the road or in Scarborough...but now that she had been captured by the same men she had once escaped, did it even matter? And even if Zekiel had returned, returned to Henry's while she and Lucy had been away, however tragic that would be, knowing she *could* have waited, the question was still the same-did it even matter?

Zekiel would not find her here.

And even if he had managed to return to Henry's and even if he miraculously followed the same trail that she and Lucy had taken, Jack's band would kill him on sight. And if that wasn't enough to discourage her, she knew bandits rarely remained in any one place for long. Certainly not long enough for Zekiel to find her.

No. Zekiel would not find her here.

Zekiel was gone.

She felt a very deep and profound sadness as she cleaned Jack's face, knowing that her life, the life she had fought so hard to change, her life with Zekiel, which had only just begun, had suddenly come to an abrupt and unforgiving end. With Zekiel, her life had finally begun to have meaning, real purpose. With Zekiel by her side, she felt like a real person, had known love. With Zekiel...

No, she told herself. Zekiel was gone.

In time, he would become nothing more than a faded memory, and Jack, who would no doubt have his way with her time and time again, that memory would become even more distant. Distant to the point she feared the most: that her memories, those special, precious memories, those moments she had shared with Zekiel...would simply cease to exist.

"Why the long face, Val?" Jack inquired, destroying her contemplation, and soiling the memory she was attempting to hold on to for dear life. "Are you not pleased to see me?"

Val had no answer.

"Speak!" he demanded, always with that same volatile temper.

"I..."

"I understand, Val," Jack said in a tone that was somehow both venomous and yet calm. "I understand we haven't seen each other for some time, but it hasn't been *that* long. In time," he went on, reaching for her wrist, his sudden movement causing her to drop the rag. "I am certain we shall come to know each other again. Perhaps even more intimately than ever before." He pulled her wrist to his face in a mocking tenderness. "Oh yes..." he went on, smiling wide with anticipation. "*Far* more intimately than before." Val was revolted. Wanting nothing more than to rip his hand off her face and render it useless. "Understand, Val..." he continued, letting her wrist go. "I sorely, sorely missed you. And you hurt me, Val. You hurt me deep."

"What...and what if I refuse?" she dared to ask, knowing full well Jack understood her meaning.

"Refuse? No..." He laughed. "You won't refuse, Val. You won't. You can't. And would you like to know why?" His smile, having disappeared, was one now of absolute conviction.

"If you refuse, I will kill her, Val. I will. You know I will..." He paused simply for effect. Letting the words sink in.

"Now. Take off your clothes," he ordered. "Slowly."

Chapter Fifty-Eight

MORLUUN ENTERED THE CAMP silently, having played this game countless of times. Jeremiah, however, was not nearly so discrete. He burst into the first tent, intent on getting his fair share, and tore into the first human, who never had the chance to even scream. His victim, a pitiful human by the name of Gregory, was instantly torn to shreds, the artery in his neck ripped apart.

Unlike Morluun, Jeremiah was sloppy, spilling blood all over the place, wasting a good part of his meal. He latched onto the human greedily, making short work of him, his breaths coming in quick gasps.

Meanwhile, Morluun, seemingly forced into action for fear that Jeremiah would take far more than agreed upon, entered a second tent and took his first victim there with far more stealth.

When he finally emerged from the tent he had chosen, the fresh blood swelling within his veins, and having taken far more time with his own kill, he saw that Jeremiah was already fast at work on his second, and making far too much noise.

This human he had snatched out in the open, one who had been tending to the camp's small fire. But due to Jeremiah's sheer carelessness, the man managed to scream, which promptly alerted the others.

Morluun sighed. While he preferred to be silent, moving through his victims like a silent shadow, Jerimiah was nowhere near as reserved.

Those who had been asleep were awake now and came rushing out of their tents in a panic, three men in all, all of them brandishing swords. Jeremiah paid them no notice, instead sucking the life out of the man he cradled, eyes closed, refusing to be interrupted. Morluun could only shrug...especially when the men suddenly came to realize exactly what Jeremiah was in the act of doing.

"*Demons!*" One man screamed, and the very use of the word seemed to incite a rising panic within the group.

"Will?" The second man asked the third. "*Will!* What should we do? Where is Jack?" A fourth human then appeared. A woman. She screamed.

"Jeremiah, Jeremiah." Morluun scolded and Jeremiah finally looked up from his business. The human in his grasp, quite dead, was flung to the side like a weightless piece of dried-out rotted-wood.

Jack had been watching Val slowly undress, his eyes wide with anticipation. Hunger. Oh, this one was a beauty. A rare beauty indeed, he thought. How wonderful to have her in his company again. How so very fortunate.

Val had just removed her tunic, exposing her voluptuous breasts, and wore a look of sadness, of utter hopelessness on her face.

"Please, Jack." she begged. "Please don't make me do this."

Jack laughed. In the past Val had been cooperative, participating in any lewd action that Jack demanded of her. But now? All she felt was shame. Despair. Contempt. Fear. Loathing. A myriad of varying dark emotions. The thought of coupling with this man was simply too much to bear. Especially after she had finally found someone worthy of her love who also loved her just as deeply in return. Someone who could help her forget her troubled past.

But that one was gone. He was never coming back. And if he did come back, she was certain she would never be found.

And then, of course, there was Lucy. Poor, helpful Lucy who had given so much to help Val in her quest. And now Lucy, her dear Lucy whom she had come to know as a friend, would share the same fate.

Then came the screams. Screams, Val wondered? Was someone screaming? Did it even really matter at this point?

Jack took off his trousers.

Zekiel was doing his best to keep up, but Amparo was moving so incredibly fast. He had been able to keep pace with her before, easily in fact, but she was now moving with a determination that was difficult to match.

He bore down then, determined not to fall behind, but as he did not have the blades in which to guide him, to where he was being led, he was constantly having to adjust his stride to hers, weaving this way and that, altering his course on the fly.

Where were the blades leading them? What was the objective? And why such urgency?

Amparo, at last, began to slow and gradually came to a stop. "We are close," she sensed, concentrating on the daggers. "We are very, very close."

"Close to what?" Zekiel wondered aloud.

"Whatever it is we are to find. I..." Amparo paused and quickly crouched to the ground. Zekiel followed, sensing the presence too.

"Vampires," he whispered. "The very ones who have been tracking us! How? But we covered so much distance!"

Amparo was similarly confused. What was going on? "Have you been paying close attention to our whereabouts, Zekiel? Are you familiar at all with where we are?"

Zekiel took a careful look at their surroundings, but all he could see was the dense forest they were currently in. Nothing seemed out of place.

"I fear we have been traveling in circles," Amparo worried, voicing a deep concern. "Though why we are being led so near to our enemies, I cannot say. The blades are supposed to keep us safe."

"No." Zekiel argued, confusing Amparo further. "No."

"I beg your pardon?"

"Armageddon is at work here," he stated. "Do you forget your own tale?"

"I don't understand," she responded.

"Think about it," he reasoned. "You said yourself that Armageddon has a will of its own. More to the point, you *yourself* had stated that Armageddon oftentimes leads its owner into danger. *If* the danger coincides...or is connected to the objective."

"But what *is* our objective?" Amparo wondered out loud, still very much confused.

Will rushed Morluun, holding a sharp blade aloft and came at the vampire with all the speed he could manage. But with one lazy slap, the pitiful human was hurled away. The next two men came on as one, attempting to attack Morluun from either side, but the vampire merely laughed.

Both humans, hearing that laughter, that non-human laughter, surely felt their blood turn cold. "Drop your weapons,"

Morluun commanded, and both humans readily complied, already under the vampire's complete control. Spellbound.

"Damn you, brother!" Jeremiah called out, not at all pleased. "Let the humans fight!" he pleaded. "I enjoy so very much the look of fear in their eyes."

"Jeremiah," Morluun warned. "We are not here for play. Take your victims and be done with it."

Jeremiah growled.

Jack was ready. So very ready for this. She was his again. Finally. His for all time. This is what he continued to tell himself as he began to kiss Val all over her body. *Yes*, his mind screamed as he roamed his hands freely upon her. Yes! He was trying to savor every bit of this experience. Oh, how he loved to savor it.

He had yet to initiate the act but that would come soon. So, so very soon. She was placid, yes, showing no sign of emotion, but that did not bother Jack one bit. That, he knew, would surely come again in time...and there were ways. Especially with Lucy's life at risk. But at that moment, what mattered more than anything else? She was his.

For now, he was simply delirious, delirious is this moment, seeing her naked once more, knowing that in moments, for he was on the verge of losing all restraint, that this ecstasy would once again be his.

But just as he made his move, moving to get on top of her, Morluun boldly strode into the tent.

Chapter Fifty-Nine

I RAN A MENTAL scan, closing my eyes to focus, trying to discern anything in the area beyond the two vampires I could sense with ease.

Humans. Humans were also near. But what did this mean?

A scream broke out a second later and the twin blades that Amparo held flared to life. Armageddon went red, impossibly crimson red while Quest shone a bright, almost blinding blue.

"Never have they done this!" Amparo exclaimed, in a near panic. "*Never* have I witnessed them glowing like this before! Zekiel?"

"Do they say anything? Are they speaking to you now?"

KILL. A voice suddenly emerged within my mind. A voice that was neither vampiric, nor clearly Amparo herself.

We both had heard it, of that there could be no doubt, and one look toward Amparo, as well as my reaction, clearly stated as much. And I knew, just as Amparo did, that the direction had come from Armageddon itself. Even I knew it to be thus.

"Amparo, has it ever…?"

"No. This is new. And never has their voice been heard by another. Not to my knowledge."

KILL!!! Armageddon verily screamed.

The command we had both heard again was even more desperate, and delivered with such force that neither of us hesitated, even if it meant charging straight unto our doom.

We sped off at once, in the very direction of the humans I had sensed...and I realized but a moment later, that the vampires that had been tracking us, the immortals that we knew to be near...were there too.

"*What the fuck?*" Jack roared, both startled and angry over this intrusion, while Val instinctively sought to cover herself.

Morluun only smiled, a smear of fresh blood on his face. "Who the fuck are you?" Jack demanded, trying to sort everything out.

From beyond the tent came a scream. Then another. But if Jack cared in the slightest, he gave no indication, clearly far more concerned with being interrupted in what should have been his moment of glory. He was already on his feet, pulling up his breeches, but Morluun paid him no attention. It was as if Jack was not there at all.

Instead, the vampire was fixated on Val. Just hypnotized by her obvious attributes and incredible beauty. Morluun stood absolutely still, his mind already at work, considering the possibilities.

That's when Jack swung his fist.

Jeremiah did not see him coming, so lost was he in the blood, the deliciousness of the blood, that pumping luscious human blood. As he stood upright, having fully drained his fifth victim, and thus breaking the agreement he had made, he knew Morluun would be angry, perhaps even furious. But Jeremiah, giving in to his predatory instincts, simply did not care.

And then he was kicked in the face.

KILL!!!

I heard Armageddon say this, the word loud and clear in my mind, and spun as quickly as I could, looking to land another kick before I lost the element of surprise.

But what did it mean, kill? Kill who? This vampire I had engaged myself with? And if so, why was this vampire our objective? What would his death mean? What if I failed? What if I could not kill him? What if this foe was beyond me? And what of the second vampire, for I was certain that there were two. What of him? Were we supposed to kill him too? Could we even do these things? But now was not the time to contemplate these riddles.

The vampire I had struck was fully fixated on me now and easily blocked my incoming right leg while drawing a sharp blade from his hip. Shit, I berated myself, for I had no weapon of my own.

He swung at me then, viciously and with contempt, and I turned my torso sideways, narrowly avoiding the slash, briefly catching sight of Amparo in the process, and knew she was already seeking out the other.

Hard-pressed, I knew I could spare no further glances or distractions, for the vampire I faced was now coming on fiercely, the scent of his recent human kill pungent in my face. I knew not how many humans had been killed or why we had been summoned here, but without a suitable weapon and without a way to safely block his sharp blade, none of that really mattered.

Jack's aim had been true, his fist connecting hard against the vampire's jaw, only it was Jack who howled out in pain, the bones in his right hand completely broken.

Morluun glanced his way then, clearly irritated, and without the slightest effort, flung the human from the tent, the sheer force taking and uprooting the entire structure along with him, leaving Morluun alone with Val, under the open and cold night sky.

"Please…" was all Val managed to say, confronted with this new danger.

Morluun laughed. "Don't hurt you?" he purred, easily reading her thoughts. "No dear woman, I will not hurt you. But I am afraid you will have to come with me."

Val panicked, nearly fainting from the shock of it all, and it was only her bravery, that same bravery she had called upon when she had been surrounded by wolves, that had kept her from blacking out, though she secretly wished she had. She instead remained frozen in place, not yet daring to move other than to cover her bare chest with her arms. Not after what she had just witnessed.

Morluun, meanwhile, was still looking her up and down, inspecting her closely. "Long has my Master been searching for a woman of your beauty," Morluun said. "Long indeed."

Knowing he now meant to take her with him, Val tried to scoot back a few paces while keeping herself on the ground, but found herself almost too terrified to move.

She knew that while outwardly he appeared to be a man, at least in appearance, she somehow knew, after what she had seen him do to Jack, that no human could possess such strength. If he even was a man at all, Val deliberated. But if not a man, then what exactly was he? Who was he? And who was this Master of his?

"I hope he was not important to you…" Morluun commented, again reading her thoughts but finding himself unable to finish his sentence. Her beauty was simply uncanny. And what reward indeed might be his upon bringing this one back to his Master, he thought.

A sharp blade then pierced his back.

Thomas didn't know what to do. He was too paralyzed with fear. Several of Jack's band lay dead while those lucky few who were still alive were fleeing in multiple directions. Every man for himself.

"Tom!" a voice cried out. A voice he immediately identified as Jack's. "Thomas!" he called again. "Help me up, you fool." Ignoring him, Thomas took a look around, trying to make sense of what was happening. Details were difficult to make out, but he noticed what appeared to be a short man in a dark cloak, heavily engaged in combat with another he did not recognize. The one who had killed Gregory.

But what Thomas couldn't fathom was how the combatants *moved*. They seemed to disappear in the blink of an eye, only to instantaneously reappear in a completely different location, sometimes many feet away. It wasn't possible. His mind told him that what he was witnessing, was simply not possible.

"*Thomas!!*" Jack screamed again and Thomas, desperately searching for some much-needed clarity, finally found the strength to move. Jack lay sprawled out on the turf, still trying to get up and Thomas quickly hurried to get to his side.

"God damn bastard broke my arm, along with my hand," Jack cursed.

"Gregory. A few of the others..." Thomas tried to explain.

"Nevermind them. We've got to look after ourselves, Thomas." Jack dismissed, putting an arm around him to stand. "Good old, reliable Thomas. Help me to my feet. Quickly now."

The vampire I was currently entangled with was strong. Stronger than Jin. Faster too.

I was doing my best to dodge, trying to anticipate his movements, but he had caught me once already. A deep slash across my arm. And while that wound had nearly instantly healed, nor did I feel any lasting pain aside from the moment it had happened, I was not at all happy about the damage done to my cloak. That couldn't be as easily repaired.

I still did not possess a weapon of my own, and while I knew this foe was dangerous, a strange calm was even then starting to come over me, similar to what I had experienced before. I was starting to enjoy the fight. The challenge of it. The excitement.

Amazing how not so long ago, my instincts had been to avoid a fight at any cost. I used to do everything in my power to prevent them. But as I dodged his next attack, trying to find a rhythm to the battle, the thrill of this encounter was only building. I think I even smiled.

Morluun screamed in rage, more so than in actual pain, and scolded himself for letting Amparo get so close, for surely this was who he faced, recognizing the vampire at once.

He spun around quickly, her blade doing minimal damage, but he had clearly felt that sting and again reprimanded himself for being so unbelievably careless.

He should have detected her presence, should have felt her coming, but that one human, yes, that impossibly beautiful woman, had managed to cause a significant enough distraction. No matter, he decided.

Morluun quickly brought his own weapon to bear then, a fine and glaringly sharp one-handed axe. And then he drew another. Amparo, undaunted, stood her ground, poised and ready.

"Amparo, I presume," Morluun greeted her, leering at her closely. "At long last we finally meet."

But Amparo was in no mood for words. In response, she came at Morluun quickly, attacking with her fine daggers and only a swift reaction with a last-second parry on his part had saved him from another gash. Their weapons clashed and interlocked.

"Foolish bitch!" Morluun growled, their faces inches apart. "Falling right into our hands. You saved us much time, Amparo. And you know why we have come."

Amparo refused to speak. Instead, she twisted and spun, freeing their weapons and lunged again at her enemy, one dagger aimed high, the other low. Morluun dodged them both.

"If you have no words...then indeed we can play. But I warn you, Amparo...I do not wish to hurt you."

Amparo spat in his face. She had heard it all before. Cain wanted her alive, that much she knew for certain...and she had every intention to use that to her advantage.

Val, finding the strange man or whatever he was now occupied, found herself able to finally move and she wasn't about the waste the opportunity. Fear or no fear.

Scrambling out in the open now, not yet on her feet, Val hadn't the slightest idea of what was happening around her and she honestly did not care. For the moment, no one was paying her any attention and she fully intended to use that to her every advantage. "Get up, Val. Get up!" she cried to herself, desperately trying to give herself some much-needed encouragement.

She was on her feet a moment later, running to where the tent had been cast, and quickly rummaged through the wreckage to find her discarded clothes. She dressed as quickly as possible, saw a canteen she knew to be filled with water and took this also. Ready now to make her escape, she quickly scanned the area, trying to get a general sense of where she was.

And then someone took her hand.

Jeremiah kept attacking, swinging away with his sword, but the fledgling was impossibly fast. How was he so damn fast??

Jeremiah had managed one good slash, right at the onset, but had scored no attacks since then, and as with all injured vampires, this one had surely healed. Thus, no advantage had been gained.

"So," Jeremiah addressed him, thinking to try a different approach, speaking for the first time. "You are the fledgling we seek. The offspring of that bitch, Amparo. Is that right?" It was not a wise thing to say.

Jeremiah was suddenly struck twice in rapid succession and while the blows certainly stung, putting him slightly off-balance, his bigger concern was that he had no idea how he had even been hit. He hadn't even seen the fledgling move. Was it his hands? Had it been his feet?

The fledgling was somehow moving even faster then, faster and faster, further increasing the tempo.

His confidence slightly shaken, Jeremiah's next attack came in the way of a lunge made in desperation, a thrust that would have skewered any lesser vampire, but the fledgling surprised him once again. He rolled back with the blow, avoiding the thrust entirely, and threw himself upon the ground in a backward summersault, rolling himself near one of the fallen humans. But before Jeremiah could begin to track the motion to attack once more, the fledgling deftly moved and was already rolling again, this time in the direction of a second victim, and so when Jeremiah at last found himself facing him once more, the resourceful fledgling was back on his feet and now held two long swords in his hands. Weapons discarded by the dead.

And then he attacked. He came at Jeremiah in a flurry of attacks, both blades spinning over in his hands, and managed to score a solid slash on Jeremiah's free hand, drawing a thick stream of blood. It certainly had not been a fatal blow, nor even crippling, for Jeremiah was already a second later healing from the wound, but one thing had become perfectly clear.

This strange fledgling could hold his own.

Amparo did not show any outward signs of fear but her private concerns were pressing in upon her, mounting beyond measure. Morluun was a worthy opponent, dangerous in every sense of the word, and just like her battle with Jin, Amparo could not help but wonder if she had enough stamina to somehow win out here.

Her thrusts were getting slower, less measured, less accurate, but whether or not Morluun had picked up on this, he provided no indication. Unlike Amparo, Morluun surely had not begun to tire and perhaps was even biding his time.

The battle tone then shifted. What had started out as a game of cat and mouse, with both combatants measuring each other's prowess and ability, had quickly become far more lethal. Morluun's pace increased, along with the complexity of his attack combinations, and Amparo was forced back several steps, with no choice but to remain solely defensive during the next exchange.

Morluun knowingly smiled and proceeded to press her further, putting his axes through another deadly routine, looking to land a decisive blow...

And then Amparo was hit.

Thomas made a second grab for her one free hand but Val, now over her initial shock, instinctively fought back.

"Grab her, Thomas! Hold her steady!" Jack instructed, moving to lend the man a hand while Val continued to thrash, seeking any means to escape.

"Release me!" Val shouted, but Thomas, now with a solid grip on both of her hands and refusing to budge, even managed to pin her arms at her sides, holding her fast.

"If you want to live, you will follow me," Jack addressed her, getting right in her face. "You hear me, Val? I won't hesitate to put a blade to your throat."

"You will do no such thing!" she snarled at him through clenched teeth, refusing to fall for such an empty threat. To accentuate her point, she even spat in his face.

"Oh, you will pay for that. Indeed, you will pay," Jack promised, wiping his face as he spoke. "But this is neither the time...nor the place and for the moment, you will do as I say."

What could she do? Who would come to her aid? Would she have been better off had she been taken captive by that...that strange man? Whatever manner of creature he was?

"Now *move!*" Jack commanded and the trio fled into the deeper woods, away from the camp.

Her voice cried out, like an alarm in my mind, and I knew at once that Amparo was in immediate danger.

"*Zekiel!!!*" she cried again.

I scolded myself. I hadn't been taking my opponent seriously, too eager to once again test my powers, too eager to simply fight, and by doing so, was also potentially putting Amparo at risk. I had been enjoying myself with wanton disregard for her safety. Selfishly. Knowing full well I hadn't been giving this my all, thus foolishly ignoring our mission and the importance of what we had come here to do.

I had to remind myself that this was not a game. Lives were at stake here, including my own.

I had to get to Amparo. I charged at my opponent, no longer weaponless or helpless, and I tried to find my rage, tried to find my center, looking now to end this battle with all speed.

He parried once, then twice, my two blades against his one. I struck again and again, trying to work even faster, but I was beginning to get sloppy, even careless, my coordination suffering from a lack of concentration. Amparo's voice still lingered in my ears.

"Zekiel!!! I need you!" Amparo shouted, this time out loud and startling me in the process. Her voice was desperate...and hurt?

Desperate myself to reach her, I found myself moving faster than I had thought possible, hands now moving in a blur, and I managed to draw blood more than once, albeit nothing fatal.

I did not relent. I stabbed, I lunged, frantic now to reach Amparo. But at this rate, if all I could score were minor cuts, there was no telling how long this encounter would last.

Seeking to use a tactic I had used before, I slashed high and wide with my right blade on purpose, attempting to lure him in close. My opponent, unable to resist such an opening, came in fast, knowing I had left myself wide open, and knowing too I would not be able to block in time with my second blade. As predicted, he took aim and lunged, fully committed, seeking to skewer my exposed right side.

I let myself collapse upon the ground, much to his surprise, and rolling back fast on my shoulders, I rolled right back into a standing position and launched my own attack at his exposed back.

I drove my right blade in deep, through his back and out his stomach, and the vampire howled in pain, dropping his gleaming sword in the process.

Thinking myself victorious and seeking to take his head with my left, it was my turn to be surprised as he deftly went into a roll of his own, freeing himself of my blade in the process, and narrowly avoiding what surely would have been the killing blow.

"Shit," I cursed out loud.

Amparo's right arm had been nearly torn to shreds, the force of Morluun's blow dislocating the arm in the process. Despite the pain, and having nearly lost her arm, she still maintained a hold on both Quest and Armageddon, but that fact brought her little comfort. She knew with absolute certainty that she would not prevail here. Not without aid. Her right arm, now nearly useless.

Morluun realized this as well and took her sudden pause in battle as a sign of her unconditional defeat and surrender.

"*Melchiah,*" He called out far and wide, seeking an audience from afar. He made no attempt to conceal this communication from her, in fact, did this openly, knowing her to be completely helpless.

The reply came only seconds later.

"*Have you found them? Speak, Morluun,*" Melchiah replied, a voice Amparo recognized from the past. It was a voice she hadn't heard in some time, centuries in fact, but there could be no mistaking the speaker's identity. And this one, Amparo knew, was even more dangerous.

"*Yes. I have found them, Master Melchiah. Amparo and the fledgling. What orders, my Master?*" Morluun asked.

"*Make haste, Morluun, for dawn draws near. Bring them both to me at once.*"

"*Yes, my Master. It shall be as thou command,*" he purred, ending the connection.

Amparo, with but one arm, attacked again.

Val took a glance behind her even as she was being ushered forward through the darkness. Was it possible her ears had deceived her? Had...had she heard a woman's voice call out the name: *"Zekiel?"* She struggled to make sense of this even as she craned her head around, back towards the camp.

She witnessed what she thought were two figures, locked in combat, but the figures were constantly moving in a blur, faster than what should have been possible.

They would both disappear and then reappear, completely and often, but nothing in these bizarre moments had made much sense. No sense at all.

And then the combatants had suddenly stopped, just stopped, at an apparent stand-off, seemingly to take measure of one another. Val tried to gather what details she could.

Even from this distance, both appeared to be clad in black, one much shorter than the other, but beyond this and due to the dim lighting of the nearby campfire, there was little else to really see.

"Keep moving." Jack turned to warn her, and in response Thomas prodded her forward once more, serving as the rear guard. But as she was forced along, she couldn't help but take another look behind her and saw that the shorter of the two combatants had shifted, giving her a better look at his profile, whereas before his back had been facing her. And there, even against the dark of night, with the campfire not far from where he stood, she saw that this figure had long hair. No, she corrected herself. Not long hair. Those were bangs.

"Zekiel?" She dared to whisper.

"I told you to keep fucking moving!" Jack snarled, angry that Val had stopped again.

On instinct alone, and no longer being held by Thomas, Val bolted.

Or tried to. She had scarcely moved a few steps before Jack had grabbed her from behind with a bear hug, unable to effectively use his right hand, but now Val was hysterical and Jack may as well been holding a wild animal.

"Zekiel!!!" Val screamed. "*Zekiel!!!*"

"Help me, damn it! Help me hold her still!" Jack yelled at Thomas. Thomas rushed over and took hold of the thrashing women, allowing Jack the use of his left arm again.

The last thing Val would remember was a fist speeding toward her face.

Chapter Sixty

Zekiel, even without his preternatural hearing, even as he continued to press the stubborn vampire, had not missed that scream. That frantic scream that had no doubt called his own name. But where or when had he heard that voice before?

It had not come from Amparo, of that he was sure, although she had certainly been calling for him as well.

Amparo! He still had to get to Amparo.

But where had he heard this newest voice? He was certain he had heard it before. What bothered him now, even more than the source, was how desperate that call had been. But Zekiel, distracted as he was, had already lingered on these thoughts for far too long and could no longer afford to lose his focus.

His opponent had already managed to regain his fallen blade, capitalizing on these multiple distractions, and Zekiel could only scold himself for his continued mistakes, for losing concentration. And to make matters worse, he had given his opponent ample time in which to heal.

Amparo called out to him again.

Amparo stubbornly continued to fight, despite the use of her right arm, which hung limp at her side. She refused to let go of Armageddon, no matter what, and in fact, was still imploring the blade, asking it to guide her attacks, begging them to see her through this.

If only she had enough time to heal! But Morluun was not about to give her that chance. On Amparo's next pass, coming in the form of a rather lazy left thrust, Morluun easily batted away the attack with one axe while striking at her legs with the other, severing one of her hamstrings.

Crying out more from frustration than the actual pain of the brutal cut, she readied herself once more, determined to fight on. He circled her then, knowing she could barely support her weight on her one remaining good leg and watched her limp just to keep him in front of her.

With a sigh, for he had hoped for a greater challenge, Morluun struck again. And then again…until Amparo found herself on her knees. But even then, she desperately tried to stand. "Don't make me kill you!" Morluun screamed at her, knowing that his instructions had been clear and that Amparo was to be taken alive. "Just yield, damn you."

But Amparo would not give up. "*Never!*" she cried. And then somehow, she hurled herself at him, blindingly fast with her left arm leading, and managed to drive Quest deep within Morluun's right shoulder. He cursed. Like Amparo, Morluun was far more upset with himself for dropping his guard versus any pain he felt from the attack itself. He angrily responded in turn, cleaving her right arm clean off with a vicious swing of his axe.

Amparo, looking at her missing appendage and watching her precious blood empty out onto the turf, fell back to her knees, defeated.

With dawn now quickly approaching, Zekiel knew he was running out of time. Amparo was no longer calling out to him, a fact that disturbed him greatly. And as he started to consider the possibilities, along with the countless errors he had made, and caught up in his thoughts instead of focusing on the battle at hand, Jeremiah meanwhile, sensed his opportunity.

He started to press Zekiel even harder then, noting that the fledgling was defending far more than attacking now, and managed to score a vicious slash to Zekiel's left shoulder. Then again to Zekiel's right. Zekiel cried out, nearly losing the grip on his weapons, and only split-second timing had stopped a third strike, his swords crisscrossing in an X, trapping Jeremiah's blade a mere inch from his face.

Zekiel attempted to push off, to gain some separation, his two swords against Jeremiah's one, but the stubborn vampire stood his ground, refusing to budge. Again Zekiel attempted to separate them, growling as he did, but this time Jeremiah allowed it, even baited the fledgling into doing so, only this time, offering no resistance. And as Zekiel came forward, his swords now high and wide, Jeremiah ducked, quickly stepped in and slashed horizontally, drawing a bright red line across Zekiel's midsection.

But instead of crying out in pain, Zekiel screamed, now absolutely furious, and then something from within him…broke.

He was all over Jeremiah then, gritting his teeth in rage, weaving his blades at a speed that was difficult for even Jeremiah to track, throwing endless combinations his way.

But the older vampire, ever-adapting to the constant changes in their battle, somehow met the charge and the combatants found their blades interlocked once again, their faces only inches apart.

"Give up!" Jeremiah screamed, no desire left to fight this newly enraged creature, wishing only to end the conflict. Zekiel growled in response and set his blades into motion again, spinning in a tight circle to first separate their blades, then thrusting them out again, seeking to impale Jeremiah's head.

But Jeremiah had been ready, turning his own circle in the opposite direction, and met Zekiel's blades with incredible force, shattering both swords in the process. The swords had been forged by humans, and so had been weak, brittle, and it was surprising that they had fared for as long as they had. But Zekiel was hardly finished, nor did he hesitate. He spun another circuit, dropping his broken swords in an instant, refusing to relent in his attack. He kicked out as he done before, purely on instinct and with an extended left foot, rapidly struck Jeremiah in the face once, twice, and then finally a third time, breaking his neck in the process.

His eyes rolling back in their sockets, Jeremiah dropped his sword, his body going completely limp. Unable to stand, Zekiel caught him easily, bringing his fangs in close.

"I'm coming, Amparo. I'm coming," Zekiel whispered, and then he began to feed.

Morluun replaced his twin axes to the dual loops sewn onto the belt he wore, and bent low to retrieve Amparo's weapons, carefully closing his hands around each. "Lord Cain will reward me quite handsomely for this. I thank you. I thank you so very much," he said sincerely, hardly believing his fortune.

Amparo lay motionless, the pain now too much to bear, and kept staring at her decapitated arm that lay nearby. But at that point, even she had to wonder- did it even matter? At that moment, all seemed lost, her mind unable to focus.

"How do they work?" Morluun questioned her, holding the blades aloft. "Tell me. Tell me at once. Tell me how they are used," he demanded.

Amparo slowly turned her face toward him.

"*Tell me!*" he said furiously, bending low to slap her in the face, having set Armageddon down in order to do so.

When Amparo refused to speak, instead staring at her dagger intently, Morluun bent low once more.

"Listen and hear me well, Amparo. I have orders to keep you alive and that, I will surely do. But do not think for a second that I have to bring you back in one piece. Oh, I know I need not remind you of what miracles our kind can perform, nor how much I can take apart...nor how very close I can bring you to the brink of death, for that matter. I do so hope it does not have to come to that, but if it does? You *will beg* me to die. I promise you that. This is to be your last warning, Amparo. Do not try my patience."

When Amparo refused to speak, he slapped her again. Harder. And then again. And then Amparo did something he did not expect. She launched herself at Morluun's leg, much like a vicious animal and found purchase there with her fangs.

"Bitch!" Morluun screamed, striking down upon her head with the hilt of Quest. "Fucking bitch!" He struck again and again, over and over, but if Amparo was suffering from his blows, she refused to give any sign, her focus solely upon his leg.

Morluun continued to strike, harder and harder, enraged that she had sought to feed upon him. So be it. He would continue to strike until she disengaged, her face quickly already becoming a bloody mess.

Zekiel continued to feed upon Jeremiah until he became nothing more than an empty husk. It was grotesque in a sense, watching as the deceased vampire was finally reduced to smoldering ash, but Zekiel felt no remorse, not even a little.

He let go then, having no form in which to hold, the blood already rushing through his veins. He felt new vitality in his toes, legs, his arms, hands, fingers, and throughout his entire being.

He felt stronger, faster, and teeming with new energy, and he took a few deep breaths in which to steady himself. Not to breathe oxygen of course, but to once again find his center, his balance, and to focus on the battle, he knew to be ahead.

Chapter Sixty-One

I CREPT TOWARDS where I knew Amparo to be, easily sensing her presence. I knew that she was still in danger, but I also knew it would be unwise to simply rush to her rescue. I wanted to examine this newest enemy first.

Jeremiah had not been an easy victory and I considered myself quite fortunate. Especially since I had clearly underestimated him. I knew that I had been faster, but perhaps not stronger, and owed my victory to sheer desperation, a little luck, and finally catching the vampire unawares at a crucial moment.

The honest to God truth was that I had no idea *how* I had actually done it. For the fatal blows I had delivered had not been something I had planned or had even been conscious of doing. I had simply...reacted. My swords at that critical moment had been broken and so I had simply acted upon instinct. Jeremiah had not. And now, Jeremiah was dead.

And yet, it felt like there was more to it than that. Almost as if my rage, or this predatory instinct I am still coming to know (for they are difficult to differentiate), I felt as if I had not been in full control. Almost as if had tapped into something *primal*. Was this simply a part of my nature? As a vampire? No, I realized. Because there was a time in which I had done that before. On that battlefield.

When I had lost all reason and had simply wanted to kill everyone. Was that what had happened?

Did my concern for Amparo, fearing her death, cause that feeling to stir within me? Much like I had been thinking of Simon before I truly lost it? I wasn't sure. But I also couldn't afford to spend another moment thinking about it.

Amparo was still very much in danger.

I continued to cautiously draw closer and closer, crawling like a snake on the ground and approaching what sounded like a battle yet still in progress. But when I finally came upon the two, I was not at all prepared for what I beheld.

Amparo was being beaten, beaten beyond recognition, and I felt my body tense, felt that uncontrollable anger welling up inside of me again, more than prepared to die at her side. More than ready to do whatever I could to rip this bastard apart.

Her right arm was gone, simply gone, and only a quick glance revealed to me where the missing appendage had ended up.

Could her arm be fixed? Could Amparo heal such a wound? And if so, what then were our limits? Amparo surely knew, but if there was any hope at all of repairing her arm, we had to escape first.

But caution and focus were needed here, not brazen stupidity or even bravery, and it took all of my self-control at that moment to remain still.

I could sense too that this vampire was powerful. Very powerful indeed...but with Jeremiah's fresh blood, rushing even now through my veins, I very much wanted to see what I could do against such a worthy opponent.

But I had to get even closer. Closer still...and so I silently crept forward to get a better angle. From my new vantage point, where I blended into the many shadows, I saw that Amparo was firmly latched on to his leg, and despite the beating she was taking, I could not help but smile at the crafty maneuver.

She had to be weakening him, possibly even gaining some strength, but perhaps her healing was compromised, as he continued to batter the bloody mess that had once been her beautiful face.

I am coming, Amparo...and I am here, and ready to pay this one back in full. A low growl escaped my lips. I crouched and made ready to spring.

Morluun should have been paying more attention, should have sensed the fledgling's stealthy approach. But so heavily preoccupied with Amparo, he did not.

The next thing he knew, Amparo was somehow free of his leg and the one dagger he held had been jarred from his hand. And in Amparo's place was this newest challenger who had even somehow brought him to the ground.

He struggled to turn over, as he had been immediately pinned face down, and Amparo's fledgling (for who else could it possibly be, Morluun gathered), was raining blow after blow, unrelenting in his attack. But what Morluun could not begin to understand was how *hard* he was being hit. By a mere fledgling? He decided it did not matter.

"*Enough!*" Morluun roared, and using his considerable strength, managed in one powerful motion to rise, shaking his attacker loose. But if the fledging was put off by this, for surely this was the offspring of Amparo, the fledging did not appear the least bit surprised and hurled himself at Morluun once again.

But this time, Morluun was ready. He sidestepped the aerial assault but was surprised to find that the fledgling had been ready too, had even expected as much, for he immediately pivoted on his landing leg and propelled himself right back, this time delivering an uncontested punch to Morluun's face.

CRAAACCKK!!!

He had felt the sting, that much was certain, for Morluun's face with his newly bloodied lip revealed a look of shock, amazed by the power behind the blow. But when the fledgling tried to follow with another, this time swinging with his left, Morluun easily ducked and countered with a well-placed punch to the fledgling's gut, dropping him where he stood.

"Too easy," Morluun lamented, thinking the fledgling finished, for he had hit the poor creature with no small portion of his power. But then, much to Morluun's continued surprise, the strange young vampire slowly looked up from his prone position wearing an almost sinister smile.

Without warning, the fledgling suddenly leaped backwards, executing a powerful fully extended backflip in the process, then another, before landing some distance away. He stood easily, wearing the same smile, and even paused as if to show his respect.

"Impressive," Morluun complimented him, taking a moment to address his opponent during the brief respite. "I take it that you have come here to save your beloved Maker? Then allow me to properly introduce myself," he said quite cordially. "You may call me Morluun...and you are more than welcome to try."

"Who said anything about *trying*?" the challenger responded confidently, his long bangs blowing in the gentle breeze. "No, Morluun. I am here to *kill* you."

Morluun's eyes grew wide, and for just a brief but passing moment, had almost seemed put off by the fledgling's bold statement. Surprised that one so young would dare to possess such a cavalier attitude...but Morluun ultimately laughed it off.

"I see," he mocked openly. "As I stated, you are more than welcome to..." But he never finished his sentence. The fledgling was in his face in a flash, attacking as though possessed, moving with a velocity that had Morluun briefly overwhelmed...that is, until Morluun doubled his own speed.

He blocked the fledgling once, twice, then a third time, a fourth, even a fifth. Growing annoyed, Morluun retaliated with an attack of his own, a devastating front kick to the fledgling's face.

The force of Morluun's kick had stopped all of my momentum and I was rocked back on my heels, feeling dazed and unbalanced. And when he kicked me a second time, clearly with more force than the last, I knew I was clearly out of my league here.

I was struggling to even stand, had even nearly lost consciousness, and feared that one more hit like that would end it. Even now, even with my considerable rapid healing ability, my stomach still ached from that very first punch to my gut.

Morluun then raised his leg to kick me yet again, only it happened in the blink of an eye, that movement. Forced to go on the defensive, I struggled to escape his reach and could only lean back, his foot snapping just short of my chin.

I desperately needed a moment. Even just a second to find proper footing, but Morluun knew I was off balance and the bastard came on, now drawing two one-handed axes in the process only to immediately put them into motion.

I was once again without a suitable weapon, a fact that hadn't escaped me, and I verily had to dive sideways, for I hadn't the footing to do anything else, just to stay clear of his reach. I resolved at that moment that I sorely needed to carry weapons of my own, provided I could escape with my life.

I scrambled to get to my feet, had to create some distance, but Morluun was there, somehow already there, forcing me to roll instead. He tried to stomp me then, and again I was forced to roll, only this time, as my left hand made contact with the grassy turf, I pushed off hard, launching myself back on my feet, knowing already that Morluun was tracking my every move.

He *wanted* me off balance, wanted to keep me on the defensive, but that also meant he was predictable. Thus the second my feet touched down, I knew he would be there, trusted he would be there, and I immediately vaulted into a forward somersault where

I predicted he would be. Sure enough, Morluun was there, and I passed right over him, over his very head only to land directly behind him.

"*Zekiel!*" Amparo called, communicating directly with my mind and I risked a glance her way to see that she once again had Quest and Armageddon in her possession. She threw them to me at once, one right after the other with her one working arm...but they would not reach me in time. Not in time to block what was coming, for Morluun had turned around to face me in an instant, an angry expression on his face.

With the axe in his left hand, Morluun managed a backhand slash to draw a thin gash across my chest, tearing easily through both cloak and tunic, but this had been a necessary sacrifice and I had taken the cut intentionally. Thankfully, I managed to avoid the worst of it, for the wound was rather shallow. Keeping my focus, while having refused to move, I reached for the two daggers which had been thrown perfectly and found myself armed a moment later, having snatched them from the air.

Morluun paused, even gave me a look of understanding, for I think we both knew I could have avoided his last strike...and he was now staring intently at the daggers. He started to circle me then, a newfound respect and caution in his eyes, but then unexpectedly stopped, and stood to face me once more.

Unsure as to what he was planning, I tightened my grip, thinking perhaps he meant to try and take them from me. Instead, he suddenly lunged, taking me by surprise, and his speed, my God the speed. I barely registered the movement and brought my daggers to bear, but once again, Morluun had been the quicker. I managed to deflect one blow at the last possible moment, aimed at my face no less, but his second axe caught me on my right hand and I nearly lost my grip on that weapon.

Luckily all my fingers remained, but had he been more accurate, or had I not accepted most of the hit within the small hilt of the dagger, those digits, if not my hand itself, would have surely been lost. He continued to press, his axes swinging in so many different directions that my eyes struggled to track these attacks, and I found myself dodging as much as deflecting.

I couldn't keep this up. I couldn't even attack. And though every wound had already healed, happening almost instantly, even that didn't truly make me immortal. I struggled to formulate a plan, while my hands fought a desperate battle to make each and every parry, but even I knew it was only a matter of time, perhaps even seconds, before I would surely be slashed to pieces.

And then we both felt it. Dawn. Dawn was swiftly approaching...and both of us, lest we perish where we stood, would have no choice but to soon seek shelter. Surely, I felt this more keenly than he?

We both paused. But then suddenly, Morluun cringed and bent low with his guard down. Was he already feeling the effects of the not yet risen sun? Before I? Was this a trick?

Regardless, I didn't hesitate. I swung at Morluun with both blades, seeking his head or neck, but at the last possible moment, he somehow sensed my movement and moved his head harmlessly aside.

But I wasn't finished. I let my momentum carry my blades up and over, so while my first attack had been horizontal, I swung a half circle and was seemingly coming right back for his head, but this time vertically, much how a blacksmith would hit an anvil.

Again, Morluun moved his head harmlessly to the side...but that had not been what I had truly been aiming for. And by the time Morluun realized my true intent, he had been much too slow. I split his left arm in two different places, one cut upon his shoulder, separating his arm, and a second on his elbow, the daggers slicing through as easy as if through butter. I watched the two pieces drop to the ground.

"*Treachery!*" Morluun screamed, attempting to stop the gouts of blood flowing freely from his shoulder. He struggled to maintain his balance.

"Treachery?" I questioned him, wondering if I somehow had a chance to finish him right then and there. "I see no treachery here.

Only a foolish vampire who is meddling where he should not. Consider us even, Morluun."

"Even?" he questioned, backing up several steps.

"I took from you only what you took from *her*." Pointing a blade in Amparo's direction, where she remained on the ground, practically motionless. "Now be gone from this place. Leave before I take your life," I finished, trying to sound a lot more threatening than I felt, reminding myself that I had been strangely fortunate in the encounter.

But the other side of me, filled with that anger I felt when I looked at Amparo, wanted to rush him. Wanted to end it. But I reminded myself that it was still too risky. True, Morluun had but one arm but the sun was steadily rising…and I still had Amparo to worry about.

I think he may have hissed. I wasn't quite sure, but I watched him very closely as he picked up the remains of his arm, quite defeated. Once the pieces were collected, he made ready to leave but turned to address me one last time.

"We will meet again," he promised. "And when we do, we will finish what we started here. Oh, be sure of that. We will."

I had no words and simply watched him go. In truth, I wanted no business with that one ever again.

Chapter Sixty-Two

With Morluun gone and the sun steadily rising, I turned my attention to Amparo. I had to get us out of here. She was weak, needed much healing, and her face was still swollen and heavily bruised.

"Come," I tried to comfort her, gathering her into my arms, picking her up easily.

"My...my arm, Zekiel. My arm," she whispered. She was struggling even to speak.

"Right. Be still. I'm going to get us to safety."

And so I took the arm as well. With Amparo secured and cradled against my chest, and with but minutes to spare, I bolted from the place, running with all speed, away from the rising sun.

I ran as far as I could, deeper into the woods, and started looking for a suitable location in which to dig. I did not have time to scout the area as much as I would have liked, but we were far enough away from where we had fought Morluun, which I gathered to be the most important thing.

I set Amparo and her arm gently upon the ground and immediately started to dig. And dig, and dig, and dig.

I think I was starting to panic. I did not, as of yet, have the proper experience to sense exactly how much time I actually had remaining before the rising sun would render me unconscious, but for Amparo's sake, as well as my own, I worked with all speed. But as did so, I could not help but to recall and wonder about what had just taken place.

How and why did Morluun feel the rising sun more keenly than I? How was that possible? He was older, stronger, and it just didn't make logical sense.

I did not know how much these things had contributed to his apparent lack of tolerance for the rising sun, that surely should have affected me far more, but it wasn't just that. Morluun clearly knew how to fight, was far more experienced, and by default should have been far more aware of his limitations, whereas I had been operating thus far solely on instinct alone.

Looking back on our brief battle, I had been lucky. That much was clear. And had it not been for the rising sun, I wouldn't even be alive. That much I took for fact. So why? Why had the sun affected him sooner? What was the difference between Morluun and me?

Had it been the blood of that other I had killed? So recently before my fight with Morluun? Had that infusion of blood affected my tolerance for such things? My powers, which I was still trying to understand? My limitations? I would have to ask Amparo...but had no time to do that now.

My hole was now sufficiently deep enough for us both, and I brought Amparo down and tried to make her as comfortable as possible.

"Zekiel?" Amparo stirred, her eyes still closed.

"We are safe, Amparo. The sun rises," I told her.

"My arm, Zekiel. You have to re-attach my arm. Please," she implored, speaking in a whisper.

"Tell me what to do."

Without explaining a thing, her eyes flared open suddenly and she clawed her wound open, right where the arm had been detached.

"Attach it now, Zekiel! Now!"

"Shit, Amparo!" For I had been caught by surprise.

"Now, Zekiel, now!' She commanded. "Before it starts to heal again."

I did as I was told, affixing the arm as best I could, but she wasn't healing quickly enough, not fast enough for the arm to hold on its own. If the sun rises…

"Blood, Zekiel. Spare me but a small amount of your blood," she begged, noting my confusion. "Pour a few drops on the wound. Quickly. Please."

I gashed my right wrist with my fangs, not giving it a second thought, letting the blow flow freely onto her ruined shoulder. Within seconds, my wrist was already healing and I made ready to do it again.

"It is enough, Zekiel. Enough. Your blood is already quite potent. I thank you." And with that, without so much as another word, she closed her eyes.

I inspected the arm then, not daring to touch it of course, but it indeed seemed attached, but as yet not nearly healed.

I stood up then, feeling the coming paralysis that overcomes all vampires at dawn…and quickly brought the dirt down upon us.

PART FIVE

THE BOOK OF VAL

Chapter Sixty-Three

Val woke up late the next morning feeling cold, sore, tired and hungry...and worst of all, found herself next to Jack. Had she been carried for awhile? Yes. But that had been earlier. While she had been unconscious.

It all then started to come back to her. After she had fully regained consciousness, Jack had insisted they cover as many miles as possible last night and had continued to push them forward, the trio stumbling along with no discernable direction.

"Where are we going?" Val had asked several times but never got a response from either of the two men.

The truth was, Jack did not know. He only knew that he had likely suffered a broken arm, having been hurled out of his own tent, and without medical attention, without setting the bones back in place, would not be using the arm anytime soon, much less his hand which was similarly injured. Val was well aware of that fact and perhaps, at the very least, it might buy her some time in avoiding Jack's crude advances. As for Thomas, she had nothing to fear there. It had been Jack, she knew, who had knocked her unconscious.

Thomas, for the most part, was a quiet man. Young, naïve, and a follower who basically did as he was told, thus Thomas posed no real threat to her. Perhaps at some point, especially with Jack having the use of only one arm, she had to hope that she still might find the means in which to escape.

Her biggest problem, that she could fathom, was the weather itself, as Spring was still several months away and she was without any supplies.

The group, having marched far longer than Val would have liked, had finally been forced to spend the remainder of the night under the open sky, without a tent or shelter of any kind. Clearly a dangerous situation to begin with, as Val very well knew, but fortunately, Thomas had been resourceful enough to start a fire.

But the night, or what was left of it, was still miserable, her sleep; miserable, as she had been forced to sleep between both men, simply for their warmth, as well as to keep an eye on her. But at least they had survived to see the light of day, as well as slightly higher temperatures.

Sitting up now, having refreshed her memory, she turned her thoughts to a very different time, and vainly recalled some of the many nights she had shared with Zekiel. Particularly that freezing night when they had been forced to share warmth in such naked intimacy within the shallow cave. Yes, they had been cold, soaked, and yes, the conditions had not been great, but she had been with *him*. And at this moment, she would have done anything to find herself in that cave once again.

But that thought, in turn, forced her to once again re-examine even more recent strange events, those of last night, which were as of yet, still fresh in her mind. Especially concerning the stranger that she had seen from afar.

The stranger with the long hair. Or...had they been bangs? As in bangs that could have only belonged to one person she knew of...But Val had trouble finishing that thought. She simply couldn't dare to hope.

But what had exactly happened? Who or what had raided Jack's camp? And what was she supposed to make out of what she swore she had heard? Had she really heard a woman's voice call out the name: 'Zekiel'? Or had she simply imagined that?

"Val!" Jack barked, startling her from her contemplations. "Thomas!" He continued to rant, "What food do we have? Wake up, damn you, and make yourself useful." Thomas finally stirred, got up, and went to work on the task appointed to him, which apparently meant preparing Jack's breakfast.

Thomas, not for the first time, privately wondered if setting off with Jack had been the best option, and could not help but wonder if he would have been better off on his own. It was one thing to work for Jack, sharing amongst their band what gains they managed to acquire, but why work for the man alone when he clearly had nothing to offer in compensation?

He knew their band was separated, knew that some men had even lost their lives. There was no doubt about that. He had witnessed what happened to Gregory. Poor Gregory.

And now this. Forced to be with this man who no longer had anything to offer. Jack had no supplies or resources from their old camp that Thomas was aware of, nor did Jack have a band anymore to lead. What gain could Thomas possibly achieve here?

"I said..." Jack warned.

"I heard you, Jack. I heard you. I'm looking." Thomas needn't have bothered. For when he searched through their belongings, he couldn't find a thing. Not food, not water, no supplies of any kind.

"We have nothing, Jack. We ate what little we had yesterday," Thomas finally replied. "Nothing left at all. When we fled our camp last night..."

"I know what happened, Thomas. I was there," Jack retorted, casting an angry look upon the man. "We walk then," Jack concluded after a time. "But first we need to determine where we are. We need to find a town. Food. Supplies. Perhaps some of the other men."

"Most of your men are dead, Jack," Thomas dared to comment. "Or worse, lost in these woods, same as we. With no food or water..."

"We must walk," Val put in, drawing the attention of both men. "What Jack says is true. We cannot stay here without any food and we cannot risk another night in the cold with no shelter. I don't think we have a choice."

"You see, Thomas?" Jack smiled, mistaking Val's agreement as a sign of affection. "It is as my wife says. We walk. We need to find resources. Shelter. And besides, my arm is fucking killing me." Val was about to comment, about to insist that she was not Jack's wife, but for the moment, fully understanding their predicament, wisely decided to hold her tongue.

They set off at once, after packing what very little they had, having no other option. Jack insisted they travel west, back in the direction of their old camp, as there remained a chance to salvage anything that had been left behind. Perhaps too, they might learn the fate of their other companions, or better still, regroup with any that may yet still be alive. But because they had fled blindly most of the night, covering many miles, there was no guarantee (and not knowing exactly where they even were), that they could even find the camp again. And passing through such dense forest, where keeping one's direction was a constant challenge, there was a good chance of missing the old campsite by feet or miles simply by sheer accident.

What they needed was a road. That would at least give them a general idea of where they were. And in Jack's line of work, most roads were known to him, even the most remote pathways. But with no road in sight thus far, they continued to walk, mostly keeping their silence, continuing to journey well past mid-day before taking a short rest. By mid-afternoon, they were all tired and hungry, especially Jack, whose complaints about his arm had become relentless.

"You will need to set the bone, Jack," Val finally advised, tired of listening to the man talk of nothing but the pain.

"Val is right," Thomas agreed. "The arm will only get worse."

"And I suppose you know how?" Jack irritably asked, knowing full well Thomas had no medical knowledge whatsoever.

"I know how," Val said. "I've actually done it once before."

"Ha!" Jack laughed. "I know you too well, Val," His expression then turning to one of anger. "You would seek to cripple me. Or at least try to make me suffer even more. No. I will have none of your help. Not the kind I know *you* will offer. I prefer to take my chances," he scoffed.

Val made no further attempt to convince him. She *had* thought to injure him further, that *had* been her intent, for such pain could render him unconscious. But certainly, Jack could prove no such thing. No matter, she thought. Let him suffer then. Let him walk in constant pain. Perhaps, should his arm get worse, Jack would have no choice but to trust her.

The group moved on with no further discussion on the matter, the day slowly giving way to night. They were dragging their feet now, starting to stumble in the dark, on the verge of giving up and making camp, when luck was at last upon them.

A small campfire burned nearby.

Chapter Sixty-Four

MORLUUN AWOKE THE following evening, still in horrible pain, and cursing the fledgling who had somehow bested him in battle. His right arm was still in two pieces, for he hadn't had the time to properly attach the appendages and clearly, was not happy about it. Not happy at all. Morluun struggled to reach the surface.

Just as Zekiel had done, Morluun too had dug himself into the ground. It never bothered him to do this, taking rest in the Earth, but he was becoming quite irritated with it now, as he awkwardly clawed his way to the surface with only one good working arm. While it did not take him much longer than usual to finally break free of his resting place, it had still been a nuisance if nothing else.

Now to see to his arm. The wound where his arm had been separated had completely healed, but he hesitated to re-injure himself without first ingesting a small amount of blood to aid in the procedure.

Normally, re-attaching a lost limb would be no issue, with nothing more needed than his own powerful blood, but Morluun had lost no small amount, thanks in part to the cunning Amparo.

And unfortunately, this was no longer his only problem.

He had also lost Jeremiah. But Jeremiah, truth be told, meant nothing to Morluun. He was simply someone he had been assigned to work with. But the loss was still Morluun's loss, and while Cain would certainly not be bothered at all by Jeremiah's recent death, he would however be furious that Morluun had ultimately failed...at what he had been tasked to do.

Worse yet, Morluun felt certain that Cain already *knew*. Somehow the old vampire always knew when one of their kind was created, or when a vampire met their demise in combat, by murder, the light of dawn, or possibly some freak accident. Somehow, Cain knew all.

He had known when Amparo had surfaced again after being hidden for centuries with the Quest Blades, had known precisely when she had sired the rogue fledgling. And so most certainly, Cain knew what had happened to Jeremiah. But did Cain know how Jeremiah had died? Did Cain have that ability? Could he know that one as old as Jeremiah had been killed by a fledgling only a few days old?

Granted, Jeremiah was not considered very powerful when compared to most of their kind, but a fledgling, especially one as young as this, and regardless of the Maker save Cain himself, should not have had the strength to defeat him.

Morluun looked at his missing arm and again recalled his battle with the fledgling. He knew himself to be the better fighter. Seasoned, experienced and he certainly knew himself to be stronger, even much faster. But even Morluun could not deny how well the fledgling had held his own and how utterly composed he had been.

Morluun knew he had the young vampire even beaten, knew he should have prevailed...had it not been for the rising sun. But that, in turn, begged the question: How had the fledgling outlasted him in that regard? Morluun knew each vampire was different. Each could possess different powers, strengths or even weaknesses...but *the sun*? Surely, his centuries as a vampire should have given him far more resistance, but it had not been so.

Perhaps, Morluun wondered, seeking to answer the riddle, was that he had been far too confident during the battle, failing to place enough importance on what Amparo had done just prior. Specifically, how much blood she had taken from him.

But as Morluun stretched his limbs, knowing there would not be any lasting drain on his blood or strength, even after what Amparo had taken, even he was forced to admit this should not have made a considerable difference, nor should it have played a significant factor.

No, he concluded, this fledgling was somehow different. He had adapted too quickly, fought too well. Almost as if he had been a vampire far longer than the day-old creature Morluun knew him to be. And when the opportunity had presented itself, recalling again that pivotal moment, the fledgling had not hesitated...and removed Morluun's arm to accentuate the point.

So be it. Morluun had vowed he would face him again and greatly anticipated that battle very much. So much in fact, that instead of immediately reporting to Cain, as he surely should have done, Morluun hesitated, instead carefully considering his next move.

His first order of business was restoring his arm. It would be pointless to seek out the fledgling before tending and healing his wounds and perhaps, he considered, a night of hunting would be best to gather his strength. Yes, surely that would aid him, restore him, and give him the means to also heal quickly. Yes, seeking out a proper meal sounded just about right.

His battle with the fledgling...and Cain, could wait.

Chapter Sixty-Five

I AWOKE THE following evening feeling refreshed, even well-rested, and immediately turned my attention to Amparo. And I marveled at how even in the dark, beneath mounds and mounds of dirt, I could see her clear as day. She was still resting peacefully, though would soon awaken, and so I made the conscious decision to let her be, though I was unsure if it were even possible to rouse her in the first place.

One thing I understood, or was at least beginning to understand, was that each of us, as a vampire, was unique in his or her own way. It remained a mystery as to why I continued to awaken each night before she did, for I thought that our age played a part in this regard, but Amparo had stressed numerous times that this was not always the case. Not the case at all.

I looked at her closely, focusing on her beauty, the peacefulness of her sleep. Her face was now fully healed of course, a marvelous trick in itself, but I really wanted to inspect her arm. I refrained for fear of waking her, but even my keen vision failed to detect the slightest flaw, and it appeared as whole as ever, as if the arm had never come to harm. There was not even the slightest indication that she had suffered an injury only the night before.

What of Morluun then? I wondered. Had he similarly healed from his wound? Where was this vampire now?

Feeling quite restless, I wanted to reach the surface then and so wasted no more time, climbing out of my resting place easily. The night was cold with a light snowfall in the air, and I found myself amazed at how none of these things affected my comfort in the slightest. I had my heavy cloak, of course, but hardly needed the warmth. The winter had no hold upon me whatsoever. I took a deep breath then, purely out of habit, and focused my memory on recent events.

Much of what happened last night had left me puzzled and I hadn't sufficient time to explore these many mysteries. Foremost, why had the Quest Blades ordered us into that battle? Were we not trying to avoid these creatures? Had Amparo and I failed the blades by not destroying Morluun? What had been the point of that encounter? Why had we been sent there and *why* with so much urgency? I could not make sense of it. I tried to replay all those specific events in my mind, carefully reviewing what had happened moment to moment. And then I remembered something else. Something I had nearly forgotten. Something that was odd above all else that had taken place.

Someone had called out my name.

I tried very hard to recall that moment, struggling to determine if I had, in fact, heard my name or if it had been Amparo.

No. I remembered even then making that distinction. The voice had not come from Amparo.

So, the question was, as I stood there pondering, who had called my name and *had* my name been spoken in the first place? I immediately concluded that I had indeed heard it, for the reason became perfectly clear.

I was a vampire. My hearing was not flawed. Even considering my brief time in this new form, I knew my hearing to be far beyond that of a human. Immeasurably beyond. It would be one thing to have vaguely heard something, perhaps if I had been some distance away, but the words had been clear. I had to trust my senses.

And so my task now was to try and remember the voice. Specifically, where I had heard it before, for surely there was a familiarity to it, but I simply couldn't recall when or where. Clearly the voice had been female, that much was certain, but for some reason, I couldn't place it. At the time, I had been heavily distracted...but one impression that rang out in my mind, was that this person had called out to me in great distress.

I looked back at where Amparo slept. And though she would rise soon enough, I was already entertaining other ideas. I wanted to return to the scene of that last battle. Perhaps there I might find a clue to both riddles. But did I dare? Dare leave her like this when we both might well be better served by traveling together? With caution? Of course. And yet...I felt a strong insistent pull, unlike anything I had felt before to seek out these answers alone.

I knew Morluun was still out there, one arm or two. But at this given moment in time, I didn't much care. Was I losing my mind? Did I have an instinctual thirst for danger? Ah yes, the thirst. This was yet another issue I wanted to address. But at present, even this could wait. At least for a time.

I stood a moment longer, mentally plotting my course while running a quick scan of my immediate area. There were no other immortals about that I could detect, but I had to ensure that Amparo would remain safe during my brief absence. Fortunately, I knew she would awaken soon, and would no doubt attempt to track me down, and I suspected that I would see her soon enough.

That was fine. Let her come. Let her follow.

I think I just wanted a head start.

Chapter Sixty-Six

Val, Thomas, and Jack approached the campfire with caution, uncertain of their safety and still unsure of where they were. Still, a fire promised heat and all of them were miserably cold. Thomas was ordered to go first and he did so, leaving Jack and Val behind in the thick brush. He counted at least two individuals and when he drew near, breathed a sigh of relief.

"David!" He called out, happily recognizing the men from Jack's band. "Richard!"

"Well met!" David returned, rushing up to greet Thomas, enthusiastically clasping his hand in friendship.

"Jack! Val!" Thomas called back to his companions. "All is well. We've found David and Richard!"

Great, Val thought to herself, wishing they had found anyone else instead. She had nothing against David or Richard personally, but any friend of Jack, much less members of his band, were no friends of hers.

"Excellent," Jack sneered, smiling wide at his good fortune, taking Val by the hand. "Glad we are to have found you," he added, greeting each man in turn. "Do you know what has happened to the others?"

"No," Richard said. "I think we are all that remain. Gregory is dead, John also. Will was left behind, but certainly not by choice," he tried to explain.

"How so?" Thomas asked.

"You were there," David said, and involuntarily shivered as he recalled the gruesome scene. "Did you not witness what we all saw with our own eyes?"

"I don't know what I saw, to be honest," Thomas confessed. "Not that I didn't see anything. Only that what I saw I can't rightfully explain."

"I do not know what manner of *men* they were. Or if they even *were* men. And yes, I know how crazy that sounds," David added. "But surely every man in our camp who was…still capable, ran for their lives. But alas, Will was not among us. There was little time to organize a retreat. After what had happened to Gregory and John."

"What exactly did happen to Gregory and John?" Jack asked, for he had not witnessed what had happened.

"They were murdered," Richard spat. "Killed by men that were not men, I tell you. And then two others came, I think. One of them had an unusual look about him. I mean, given the circumstances. It was his hair. I ain't ever seen a man with hair like that. A woman was there also. They could have already been there for all I know. But at some point, these…*things* started fighting amongst each other."

Val, who had been listening with more than passing interest could not remain silent. "Who was this man?" she demanded. "The one with the unusual hair? What exactly did he look like?"

"What's it to you?" Jack turned to flare at her. "Who gives a shit who he was? Gregory and John are dead. As Richard said. Possibly Will too, by my reckoning."

"What of Lucy then?" she asked Richard, ignoring Jack. "Did anyone see what happened to Lucy?"

"Perhaps, if she was lucky, she managed to escape like the rest of us."

Jack didn't like this. Did not like this one bit. Many of his men were killed or had fled. Were they safe here? Even now, he had to wonder.

"Come," David offered, breaking the uncomfortable silence that lingered. "Let us get you something to eat. We do not have much, but I'm thinking we need to stick together. That is, of course..." He paused, deferring to Jack who had always been the one in command. "If that is all right with you, Jack."

"Lead the way." Jack responded, quite pleased to know that he was once again in charge.

Chapter Sixty-Seven

When Amparo awoke a short time later, she instinctively knew that Zekiel was gone. She quickly freed herself from the hole he had dug and carefully inspected her arm. It was fully attached, good as new it appeared, albeit a bit weak. She regained the motion of those fingers and went on to test her control of them by drawing forth the Quest Blades. She still held them easily, comfortably, and even put them through a few mock attacks. Everything seemed to be in order...except...Zekiel.

Why had Zekiel left without the daggers? Out of respect? For her own safety? Where exactly had he gone? To feed? Would he show up suddenly, his disappearance all but a simple misunderstanding?

Somehow, Amparo did not believe that to be the case. So, where had her fledgling gone? And why? For what purpose? Why would he venture out alone without her? Was he upset with her in any way? No. That was foolish, but it still left her with considerable unease. Zekiel could be vulnerable, at only several days old, and surely should not have set out on his own.

Had he been taken? But this thought did not seem very likely either. There was no sign of a struggle and there was nothing else to indicate otherwise. Amparo scanned the area. Nothing. Not so much as a trace. She reached out further with her mind, but if Zekiel had heard her call, he was not responding. In fact, she could not detect his presence at all which could only mean one thing. Zekiel was quickly learning how to effectively close his mind to her. And if he could do this now, shut out his own Maker, surely he could guard his thoughts from others as well.

The Quest Blades suddenly flared to life.

Morluun. Morluun. They cryptically said, repeating the name several times. *Morluun.*

"What about him?" Amparo wondered aloud. What about Morluun? What did killing Cain have to do with Morluun?

Locate. The Quest Blades replied, leaving her clearly unsettled. *Follow.*

Amparo had no desire to see Morluun again. Not so soon. And certainly not after she had just recovered. Was still even now, recovering.

But perhaps, she wondered, perhaps Morluun would lead her to Zekiel...or maybe Zekiel himself was in danger. Was that why he hadn't answered her call?

It didn't matter, she decided. She had been given her objective and she would obey without question; and no more answers were to be found by simply doing nothing.

She took off with all speed then, moving as fast as she could manage, needing no further prompting.

Chapter Sixty-Eight

"Morluun!" The distinct voice of Melchiah shouted in his mind.

"*What is thy bidding, Master?*" Morluun coolly replied.

"*Where are you?*" Melchiah demanded. "*You were to return to my side last night.*"

"*There was no time, Master. The dreaded sun was rising. I was forced to seek shelter.*"

"*Excuses!*" Melchiah shrieked. "*Our Lord Cain is not pleased.*"

"*Indeed.*"

"*You will mind your tone, Morluun,*" Melchiah warned. "*We know what fate has befallen your companion, Jeremiah.*"

Hmm, Morluun wondered. So they did know. But how much? Did they know that he had lost both Amparo and the fledgling? "*My apologies, Melchiah.*"

"*You will address me as Master!*" Melchiah screamed.

"*Of course, of course, Master Melchiah. My apologies.*"

"*What of Amparo?*"

Morluun knew then he was stuck. "*She...she eluded me at the last possible moment, Master. The fledgling intervened on her behalf. He was formidable.*"

"He is but a mere fledgling!" Melchiah screamed again. *"I am not interested in your excuses! Nor is Lord Cain!"*

"Again, my sincerest apologies."

"We are not interested in your apologies. Only results."

"Yes, Master Melchiah."

A pause. *"Do you know where she is now?"*

"Of course," he lied. *"I am on my way to capture her now."*

"See that you are."

"But Master," Morluun dared to remark. *"I am only one whereas they are two. Without Jeremiah..."*

"Jeremiah was weak. Expendable. Understand, Morluun...failure in this matter is not an option. Do not tell me you cannot handle a mere fledgling."

"No, Master Melchiah. Of course not."

"Good. Amparo herself should not give you much trouble. After creating her fledgling, she is bound to be weak."

"I had her defeated, Master. She was *defeated. If only the fledgling hadn't..."*

"I grow tired of hearing about this fledgling who is seemingly causing you great distress."

"He is no match for me, I assure you, Master. Had it not been for the rising sun..."

"This conversation is over, Morluun. You have your orders."

Melchiah promptly destroyed the connection.

I reached the destroyed camp from the night before, having picked up the trail quite easily, the smell of blood damn near assaulting my senses, even from afar.

I knew at once that several humans were present here, some injured, some dead. I reminded myself that I was not here to feed, though I was very much thirsting for blood, but instead managed to inspect the bodies one by one, searching for any clues as to why Morluun had been here, why Amparo and I had been *sent* here, despite what could have been plentiful feeding, of course.

As I was deep in thought, going over the events in my mind, but still not finding anything out of the ordinary, I hardly registered the fact that I had been seen. Was verily being watched.

I didn't really much care. I was not attempting to move about in secret nor had any reason to fear any human. Not anymore.

"You there," a man called out to me.

I turned to look in his direction, a bit annoyed at this intrusion and saw that this man had his back up against a tree, sitting quite still, clearly injured. I recognized the man at once.

It was Will.

Morluun contemplated his next move. He knew he had to locate both Amparo and the fledgling, but he was not sure where to begin his search, nor did he know how much time Melchiah had given him. He had already attempted to locate both with his mind, stretching his considerable net as far as he was able, but discovered not the slightest hint of another vampiric presence.

He did, however, note that there were humans nearby. Possibly survivors from the night before. Six miles to the East. And East was precisely where he meant to travel, since it was unlikely that the fledgling had gone West, as Morluun had done. That still left North and South, but at this point, any direction was as good as another.

Morluun reasoned that East was the general direction of where his battle had taken place with Amparo and the fledgling and logically, they could not have gone far. Not with dawn approaching so quickly. Because just as he had done, they would have had to seek shelter and were likely still nearby.

Perhaps if he drew closer, it was possible that his mental net would yield more results. Perhaps. But perhaps not. Certainly not if both were cloaking themselves. At this point, nothing was certain.

One thing that Morluun did know is that he certainly had no intention of engaging either Amparo or the fledgling with a missing arm.

So be it. He would travel East... and learn what he may.

I casually approached Will and where he still rested against a tree, but because my hood was drawn over my face, I was quite certain he had not recognized me. Not yet, anyway. And so I came to stand before him, dropping my hood in the process.

"Z...Zekiel?"

I laughed. This was too good to be true. "Hello, Will," I said with mock politeness. "It's been a while, hasn't it? Do what do I owe the pleasure of your...fine company this evening?"

"Ah, so it is you," he wheezed, taking labored breaths as he spoke. "The polite coward. You here for the girl? Travel far, did you?"

"What girl?" I asked, suddenly more interested in conversing with the man. Did he mean the woman who had called my name?

"What girl indeed," he sneered.

In no mood for games and wanting to establish who he was really dealing with here, I roughly grabbed him by the neck, lifting his entire body in the process, using just one hand.

"Jesus!" he cried, looking below to see his legs dangling. "Holy...what the fuck!!!"

"I'm only going to ask you one more time, Will. I beg you not to test my patience."

"H-how?" He struggled to understand. "How is this possible?"

I flung him. Tired of his babbling, or perhaps to prove a point, I flung the fool. He landed in a heap, quite unable to stand, and judging by his heavily labored breathing, I assumed that several of his ribs were already broken, and perhaps I had broken a few more. I didn't really care.

"Like I said, Will." Coming to stand over him again. "I'm only going to ask you once more…and it would be wise to listen closely. What girl do you speak of?"

I started to reach for his neck again and think that sobered him up.

"Your wife, Zekiel! Your wife, of course!" he blurted, quite panicked by now.

"My wife?" I asked, thoroughly confused. "Perhaps you have me mistaken with someone else. No doubt due to the injuries you have sustained."

"So…the girl. Val. She wasn't your wife after all? After all that fuss at Henry's place?" He tried to laugh, but it clearly pained him to do so. "Ha!" he coughed. "I see your needs are not so different from my own. Sounds like you just really wanted her all to yourself."

"I suggest you explain. And quickly," I warned him, wondering where this was leading, not knowing what the hell he was talking about. "What do you know of my former companion?"

Will coughed a few more times before speaking. "I don't get you, Zekiel. Zekiel the coward. I don't understand you at all."

"What's to understand? And if you *ever* refer to me as a coward, if I so much as hear that word whispered from your lips, I promise to convince you otherwise. Perhaps I might in any case. Would you like that, Will? Would you like to *see* how much of a coward I can be?"

I don't know what came over me, but I bent low, bringing us face to face and deliberately showed him my fangs. "You like to prey upon the weak. Don't you?" I whispered, leaning in closer. "So, let me ask you…how does it feel to be the one preyed upon? Do I have your attention now, Will? Or do you need further assistance with this?

He backed away sharply, horrified and afraid. *"What are you?"* he barely whispered.

"What you should be concerned about is whether or not I allow you to live. And you stand a better chance of that, if you answer my questions."

"Zekiel?" a voice called from behind me. I turned away from Will to face this newest voice, which I recognized at once.

"Lucy?" She seemed to crawl out of the very darkness, crying as she did so, and it became clear this was indeed, Lucy. But why was Lucy here? She appeared weak and malnourished, as if she had not eaten in days.

"Oh, Zekiel, it *is* you!" she cried and flung herself into my arms.

I pushed her at arm's length as gently as I could and tried to hold her still.

"Lucy, are you all right?" I asked her. "What are you even doing out here?"

"Everyone is dead, Zekiel! Dead! Dead or run away!"

"Slow down, Lucy. Slow down. I am here now," I attempted to console her. "Please, I beg. Start from the beginning. What are you doing out here in the dead of winter? With these men no less?"

"To find you, Zekiel! To find you!" Lucy said, as if the answer were obvious.

"Me?" I responded, quite confused. "Lucy, are you sure you are all right?

"I'm cold, hungry, but otherwise fine. Zekiel, you have to listen to me."

"All right, Lucy. I will. But first, let me get a fire going. Without one, you will likely to freeze to death. Both of you," I said, turning an eye upon Will. I quickly gathered what branches I could find but most of what I found was wet with snow.

It was difficult moving around Lucy for I had to really keep my powers in check and my instinct was to move about as I knew I could. I wanted to get this done in a short amount of time and certainly could have worked a lot faster had she not fastened her eyes upon me, watching my every move.

"Will," I called over to the man.

"What...what do you want?" he asked, clearly still uneasy with me around.

"Can you stand?"

"I...I don't know. My legs...my legs are cold."

I nodded. "Lucy, I need you to fetch a few more branches while I try to get a fire going. Can you do that for me?" The woman nodded and did as I asked. Now, for the fire.

I knew how to start a fire of course, but did not have a flint or a sharp rock to serve as one, nor any way of drying wood fast enough. Though there was a different method, one that involved rubbing two sticks together and thus creating enough friction, I figured I could handle that easily enough.

I got to work at once, hands moving too fast to be seen, and noticed Will was watching me closely, mouth wide open in disbelief.

I smiled at him openly, as if further confirming who was in charge here, but berated myself a moment later for causing him undue stress. As much as I disliked the man, there was no need to be overly cruel, my point having already been made.

I went back to focusing on the task at hand. Sure enough, I was creating quite a bit of smoke but the branches were simply too wet. I just couldn't get a spark. I tried again and again and was quickly becoming frustrated. I even had to start over several times, having broken several branches already. I didn't really have time for this.

"Light, damn you, *light!*" I cursed, perhaps a bit too loudly, for Will had to cover his ears, but then something quite unusual happened.

A fire suddenly sprung to life. I had no idea how it happened but the fire was now burning, burning brightly, though it had definitely not originated from the friction of the fagots.

No. Somehow, the fire had come from *me*.

Chapter Sixty-Nine

VAL STARED AT THE bowl of gruel she was given and while the contents were hot, the mixture smelt awful. She ate her food in silence, too hungry to be picky about what the foul substance tasted like, and wondered at the disaster her life had become. She was cold, still hungry, even as she finished the bowl, but worst of all, found herself once again with Jack, as if there were no escape from her past.

She thought about Zekiel often, nearly every moment in fact, and wondered where he was, whether or not he was even still alive. Once again, her thoughts returned to the night when she was nearly certain she had heard his name and perhaps had even seen him. But how could that be? Even if Zekiel *had* been there, surely he too would have been slain by whatever *things* had attacked their camp, perhaps even the same one that had so easily broken Jack's arm.

And what about Lucy? Had she suffered the same fate as everyone else they had left behind? Likely now dead? Val could not help but feel responsible, and as if she didn't have enough to worry about, now deeply regretted that she had ever allowed Lucy to accompany her.

Yes, Lucy was likely dead and Val now had to wonder if she would be better off sharing the same fate. Did she really want to live the rest of her days as Jack's imprisoned mistress, forced to do his bidding until old age rendered her undesirable?

Thankfully, Jack was showing no interest in her at present, but once his arm healed, at least to the point where he could resume his disgusting demands, she would soon find herself exactly where she had started.

As if on cue, he sat down beside her. Perfect, she thought.

"I'm happy to have you here, Val," Jack said in a gentle voice. "Very happy indeed."

She knew that voice. And had not heard him use that tone in a long, long time. This was the voice Jack had used when they first met. At first, she had thought him kind, even generous, and despite the nature of her work, most of the time even respectful.

But all of it had been a façade. As time went on, his requests had become increasingly lewd, oftentimes asking her to do sexual things beyond the typical paying customer. Far beyond providing a man simple gratification. No. The things Jack had asked her to do, paid her to do, had been disgusting. Demeaning. And as their 'relationship' progressed, it had only gotten worse.

And when Jack finally refused to pay when his 'business' had started to dry up? That's when Jack got angry. Very angry. The physical abuse only escalated at that point. Far beyond the imagination his requests had taken.

"I'm talking to you, Val," Jack interrupted her thoughts, annoyed that he had yet to get a reply. But Val continued to remain silent. Instead, she just stared ahead, eyes vacant, trying to mentally distance herself from the man.

"Val!" He growled and this time roughly grabbed her arm with his remaining good hand. "When I call your name...you fucking answer me, bitch."

No. There was no getting away from this. No getting away at all.

Amparo continued to move with all speed, trusting the blades to guide her course precisely. She still had no clue as to how or why Morluun was connected to all of this, or her plot to kill Cain, but had learned to trust the blades without question.

The Quest Blades never made mistakes. She repeated this fact to herself over and over, often times thinking about how they had led her to Zekiel in the first place.

And when they had first met, leastways when he had come of age, and had found her that night in the forest near his home, the blades had wisely guided her away, letting her know in no uncertain terms that that particular meeting had not yet been the right time. Nor later, even on the battlefield, when he had been so close to death.

So where did Morluun fit into all of this? And then a thought occurred to her. What if the Quest Blades were leading her and Zekiel on a path of destruction? Not a path without purpose or meaning, but what if Zekiel, or herself for that matter, were being led to destroy Cain's ranks one by one so that in time they could possibly overpower Cain himself? Was that a possibility?

Zekiel had already slain two vampires single-handedly, and had no doubt grown stronger because of it. He had fed off those vampires, and together they had shared a third, the vampire Jin. And as for herself, she had slain the vampire Kabaal, a vampire of considerable age and power, just before Zekiel's transformation. That encounter had been a blessing she now realized, for having drained the blood of Kabaal *immediately* before she started the process, had surely both strengthened her and enhanced Zekiel's transformation.

To think, he already carried the blood of Cain, her own untainted and undiluted blood, as well as the powerful contributions of old Kabaal, Victor, Jin, and most recently, the vampire Jeremiah. All within the span of a few days, no less. And that history was of vital importance as well. She also knew that those first few nights were crucial when it came to a newly created vampire reaching their full potential.

Obviously, the transformation itself was momentous in nature and undeniably crucial. But on a smaller, barely detectable scale, cumulative changes...even very small ones which were in those first nights still occurring, solidified the process, rendering each vampire unique and complete.

Without a doubt, any mortal once given the blood, naturally became, and was henceforth, a vampire. But Amparo also knew, after her centuries in the blood and having witnessed countless transformations, that the blood continued to make changes for at least a few days, similar to a cold or infection that would get increasingly worse before it got better. And that's exactly what a vampire's blood was to a mortal body. An infection. And one that took at least a few days to fully manifest.

But if one were to introduce additional vampiric blood during what Amparo determined to be about a three-night window, in which the changes became complete, any new blood would mingle again, affecting the initial and final transformation.

Determining the three-day window as a viable theory had been no small fact to discover. But it seemed that on the third day, the thirst of a vampire seemed to increase dramatically- as if the blood had at last run its full course of transformation. Afterwards, the vampire also seemed to have better control of their faculties and inherent powers.

Naturally, this timeline was easily overlooked as it was assumed that a fledgling was simply adapting day by day, similar to how any creature becomes better at something with practice.

Thus, none of this was easily detected, as each and every fledgling needed time to adjust, which is how this knowledge seemed to go unnoticed. She wasn't sure if Cain himself knew, but time and time again, having witnessed countless transformations, that third day following transformation had been when the new vampire truly ceased to be human.

Again, she knew a vampire was of the race the second the transformation happened. But what many vampires did not realize, was that there existed a small opportunity for even *more* change. A time in which a fledgling vampire could become even stronger.

It had taken Amparo several centuries to become acutely aware of this, but after witnessing those transformations, she had slowly pieced the theory together. Amparo could even recall when she had made the discovery.

A long time ago, when a vampire by the name of Kalib had been brought over by Cain, Kalib had gotten into a dispute with a vampire named Jeb. Jeb had been cocky, sired a few centuries prior by none other than Azuul himself, Cain's second-born, and the argument had quickly escalated into an all-out battle to the death. But Jeb had been sloppy. Overconfident. In the end, Kalib had slain him quite by accident, but upon absorbing Jeb's blood, Kalib somehow became nearly as strong as Melchiah. No small thing.

It was true that a vampire's strength increased exponentially by consuming the blood of a vampire far older, and the effects had always been dramatic. That in itself was common knowledge.

But to absorb so much blood, so much ancient blood during a fledgling's first few nights was a far more potent combination. Because for Kalib to have become as powerful as he did? No. Kalib had been Cain's eighth born, and what had happened far exceeded what a vampire *beyond* that three-night window should have gained.

In time, all vampires gained strength and every vampire began his life at what Amparo would simply coin as their point of creation. But if a vampire began their life already considerably powerful, what effects would centuries have then?

Never in Amparo's long history had she known of a vampire who had been created under similar circumstances surrounding Zekiel's transformation. She had yet to test Zekiel's strength, but already knew him to be faster than she was, albeit briefly. She had a feeling he was stronger too. And no amount of blood should have made that possible. Especially since she had been his Maker, and none of the vampires he had already killed had been stronger than Amparo herself. At least not prior to Zekiel's transformation, for that left any vampire weak long afterwards.

But even beyond Amparo's theories, Zekiel had already shown considerable fortitude in learning the difficult art of keeping one's mind closed, as well as fighting and defeating foes far stronger and more experienced than himself. And Zekiel had done something she had never seen any vampire do before. He was boldly experimenting with his powers, making use of them in ways she had never seen. No, even beyond the blood and her three-night window theory, there was just something about Zekiel that she could not explain.

It wasn't that he had done anything extraordinary, well...even that wasn't true because he *had,* but it was simply the way he adapted to a given situation. Being a vampire was seemingly natural to him.

She thought about his acrobatics, the way he seemed to know no limit or fear. He simply did these things as if this were common to all vampires when in fact, it could not be further from the truth. Amparo was well aware of his antics as a youth, having looked upon him from time to time. She knew he practiced tumbling, and that during his mortal life had even practiced with his make-shift weapons.

But even then he had lacked any real skill or training, and what Zekiel was doing now was not at all due to those routines he had put himself through. No. This was something far beyond. Almost as if Zekiel's only limitation was his own imagination.

Sure, Amparo had witnessed great warriors before. Excellent tacticians. Cain was certainly one of these, but for someone so old, seemingly older than time could remember, that much should be expected. But what Zekiel had done, what she had witnessed, in only days, was truly something unique. She firmly believed that. She could only wonder then, what strengths of his she would discover next.

She smiled briefly then, still at a full run, trusting the Quest Blades to lead her true. It was comforting to think of him, of her dashing and daring fledgling, and as she reflected on these thoughts, once again on the road to certain but unknown dangers, Amparo couldn't help but wonder about all the possibilities still yet to come.

Chapter Seventy

Morluun found the humans easily and wasted no time entering the small camp that had been made that very evening. They noticed him immediately, getting up at once from the meal they were sharing, albeit with fearful eyes, and Morluun recognized that these humans were the very survivors from only the night before.

"At arms!" Jack suddenly commanded his remaining men. They got up and surrounded Morluun at once, hoping to take him by sheer force of numbers, leveling their crude weapons his way. He stifled a small laugh.

"Kill him! Kill him!" Jack screamed, holding a sword with his remaining good arm and behind him, a woman rose to her feet and fled, not bothering to take a second look behind.

Morluun recognized her of course, much to his delight, but knowing full well how many humans were present, and this much-needed opportunity to feed, he could ill afford her more attention at the moment.

The humans were pathetically weak, scared, and certainly he had no reason to fear them. Even with only one arm. But at the same time, he had no desire to be skewered either. Not when he needed all his blood and more to repair his obvious injuries.

And besides, he could catch up to that woman, that incredibly beautiful woman, in no time at all. But first things first. Using his single working arm, Morluun struck two of the four men with blinding speed, disarming both in a flash. He turned then, facing the two others, who hadn't even registered his prior movements and similarly disarmed them as well. All in the span of a second.

Jack, blinked several times before realizing he was no longer holding his blade, then turned and fled, coward that he was. The others, drawing the same conclusion, and wisely fearing this dangerous foe, followed Jack in close pursuit, each and every one fleeing in terror.

Morluun stood still for a few seconds, just to savor that fear, before going into motion, needing but a moment to reach for the closest man.

"How did you do that?" Will asked me, attempting to stand but clearly having a hard time. "I saw you. How did you do that?"

"How did I do what?" I asked him.

"The fire. I saw you, Zekiel. How did you do that? How did you light the fire?"

I didn't really care that he had seen me, but the truth was I did not know *how* I did it, nor did I know exactly what I had actually *done*. I knew the fire had come from me, yes, but beyond that, had no idea how it had transpired. It felt...it felt like it had come from deep inside, buried very, very deep and I wondered in those next few moments if I could do it again.

"Zekiel?" Will said, addressing me again.

"What?"

"The fire, Zekiel. How did you..."

"It's not important, Will. Nothing you should concern yourself with."

"But..."

"*Enough!*" I shouted without meaning to. After that, Will went silent and I knew once again that I frightened him. Just then, Lucy entered the camp again, carrying an ample supply of wood. Like the rest, it was wet but could still be used in time.

"Oh, Zekiel!" she cried. "You managed to start a fire!" She dropped her pile and came to join me where the fire was now burning in earnest.

"Come. Sit, Lucy. Warm yourself," I invited her, but she already had her arms outstretched and was already rubbing her fingers together, soaking up the fire's warmth.

"Will," I addressed the man shivering from cold and fright. "Come. You are welcome to join us. Even I have no desire to see you freeze to death."

I could see that he wanted to, desperately wanted to warm himself, but he was either hesitant to move or lacked the strength to do so. Perhaps too it was fear. It didn't really matter and I sighed. I stood up then and walked over to him slowly and bent low to pick him up.

"Do not be afraid," I told him but his eyes said otherwise and he was already starting to panic.

"I'm...I'm sorry, Zekiel. I am sorry I called you a coward. Please, I beg. Don't hurt me. Don't kill me."

"Zekiel would never hurt anyone!" Lucy scolded from behind us, but the look in Will's eyes clearly told me he wasn't buying it. Good. That's how I wanted it. I wanted him to hold on to that fear for I was already formulating a plan.

"What Lucy says is true," I whispered, so that only he could hear me. "However"—and here his eyes went wide—"do not test my kindness, Will. Nor my patience...for I very much desire to kill you here and now. I'm inclined however, for Lucy's sake, to give you a second chance. I pray you won't take this opportunity for granted. Can you manage to do that for me?" I showed him my fangs once again and Will's head nodded back and forth as if he had too much ale.

"I am glad that we are in agreement, yes?" I said with a smile and easily picked him up. I deliberately did this quickly, demonstrating to him that his weight meant nothing. Indeed, his taller and much heavier frame would have been impossible for me to manage before, but obviously was no burden to me now. Again, his eyes went wide and he even glanced towards the ground as if I had picked him up by some other means.

I carried him to the fire, gently put him down and took a seat between him and Lucy. It felt strange now to be around humans. Strange to be around what any other vampire would consider a meal. I instinctively took another glance at Will and unconsciously licked my lips. As much as I would surely enjoy draining that one, I was resolved to keep my focus.

"Now, Lucy," I said turning to her, trying to focus on other things. "What is it you need to tell me?" Lucy did not answer for many moments and she stared into the fire for what felt like a long time.

"Lucy?" I asked her again.

"Oh! Zekiel!" she said, coming out of what I could only guess was some deep contemplation. "I'm sorry. I was...I guess I'm still in a state of shock from what happened last night."

"Will said something about Val. My old companion. Were you traveling togeth...?" I stopped mid-sentence for I suddenly felt his presence.

Morluun. Morluun was close.

"Zekiel?" Lucy asked, but now it was my turn to barely register her voice. I had already closed my eyes, scanning for his exact location, while also searching for other vampires in the area.

He was alone. No. Not alone. He was in the company of humans. Four? No...a fifth I was sensing also...and I knew too that all of them were on the run.

I had to go. I had to go now. I could not and would not let Morluun escape. It was true I had no real desire to face him. Not at all. But at that moment, keenly aware of his presence, and knowing him to be nearby, some other emotion was coming over me. An emotion that was quickly overcoming my fear of him.

Was it my lust for battle? The challenge? Or was there something else tied to all of this for me to discover? But what that 'something' potentially was, as well as why this strange and sudden pull was coming over me, I surely did not know.

Call it instinct, call it a hunch. Perhaps I was unconsciously following whatever it was that the Quest Blades wanted me to do. It was a feeling unlike any other, one I had never experienced before and yet somehow, I knew. Knew without a shadow of a doubt, that finding Morluun, despite my fear of doing battle with him again, was the road I was destined to take. Dare I call it destiny?

"Lucy, Will," I said, quickly standing up...and far too quickly I might add, for Will was once again looking at me in disbelief. I didn't have time for this.

"Zekiel?" Lucy asked, quickly standing and wearing a look of alarm. "Are we in danger?"

"No, no, Lucy. You are in no danger," I said, taking her hands in my own, for I knew then I had startled her. "But you need to listen to me. You too, Will."

"Zekiel?" Lucy asked, very much confused.

"I'm sorry, Lucy but I'm afraid I have to leave you now. I need to leave this very moment." I turned away from her to quickly scan the area, knowing time was short, looking for any discarded weapons. I found a single rusty sword and sheath and quickly fastened it to my hip.

"But why, Zekiel, why? Why?" Lucy responded, rushing to keep up with me, on the verge of panic.

"Lucy..." I said, stopping to stare deep into her eyes. "I need you to listen very closely." She obeyed at once, going completely silent, and I paused, curious as to how easy it had been to calm her. Another power perhaps? It didn't matter. I had to stay focused.

"Do you know how to get home from here? Back to Henry's?" I asked.

"I...I think so."

"Will," I said, similarly addressing him. "Do you remember the way?"

"Yes. Yes, I know the way."

"You are certain?"

"I am."

"I need you to try and stand. Your legs should be warm now. Yes?" I asked, letting go of Lucy and offering him a hand. This time he obeyed without question and even took my offered hand. Good. I had to finish here quickly. He managed to stand with a little assistance but soon was able to stand on his own. I just hoped his strength would last.

"I need you to do something else for me. Can you do that?"

Will nodded.

"I need you to get Lucy home. Safe. Can you manage? Just the two of you?" Again he nodded, not the slightest bit of hesitation.

"Good. Swear to me no harm will come to her." He nodded again.

"Not good enough, Will. I need you to swear. If I could get Lucy home myself or by any other means I would do so. I certainly do not enjoy having to ask this of you. I don't think I need to explain why."

"No," he answered without malice.

"Then swear."

"Zekiel, you have to listen to me," Lucy interrupted.

"Swear it, Will," I repeated, ignoring her.

"I swear. No harm will come to her as long as I live."

"Good. You are to both leave at once. Even if you must travel all night. Take whatever you can salvage and take a brand as well. Both of you. Do not rest until you are free of the forest. Take rest only if you must or during the light of day, but I implore you to make all speed. This forest is no longer safe. Not anymore."

I turned to leave at once, eager to conclude these mortal affairs, but Lucy made a grab for my arm. "Lucy. I am sorry. You don't know how sorry I am to have to leave you like this. Please forgive me."

"It's not that...and I honestly trust that Will can get me home safely. I'm worried about Val."

"What about her?"

"What about her?" Lucy shot back, clearly irritated. "We were traveling to find you, Zekiel! Val left Henry's with me to find you!"

"Val is out here? Now? In this cold?"

"He doesn't seem to remember," Will interjected.

"Remember? Remember what? Speak clearly," I said, growing annoyed again.

"You have to find her, Zekiel! She's with Jack! Or worse, somewhere out there alone! You have to find her! You have to..."

"Jack?" I asked, recalling the name from what seemed so long ago, cutting Lucy off. "The Jack she used to work for? Jack was here?" Lucy nodded and the situation suddenly became far more complicated.

"Look, both of you," I addressed them and taking a deep breath to think. "I admit I don't quite understand what is going on here, but I no longer have time to discuss these things. I have to leave at once."

"But Val!"

"Rest assured I will find her," I promised. "Perhaps she can explain what this is all about but I have to leave you now. Do you understand?" Will nodded and took Lucy gently by the hand; I was relieved that he seemed to be taking control of the situation.

"I will take care of Lucy. As I promised." Will said with confidence.

"Thank you. Don't think I won't return to confirm her safety," I gently warned.

"I'm...I'm truly sorry, Zekiel. For everything."

Was this an honest change I was sensing in him? Or was he simply afraid of what I might do? Or perhaps it was the change that surely comes over a man when faced with his own mortality. In that, I could at least relate. More importantly, he sounded sincere.

"I'm sorry I called you a coward...and I'm sorry too for the altercation we had," Will added. Ah, yes. The altercation. I recalled that Will had nearly broken my nose, but struggled to remember why we fought in the first place. I fumbled through my memory. I knew it had something to do with Val, but could not seem to remember those details clearly. Had he insulted her in some way? Yes. Yes, that had to be it. But why the memory loss? Was I under that much stress at the moment? I was already lingering here far too long.

And Lucy," Will continued, turning to her. "I am sorry too. I hope in time you can forgive me for..."

"I'm sorry too," I interrupted, happy the man was apologizing but at the end of my patience. "But I have to go. Now."

I promptly vanished from sight.

Val was running as fast as she possibly could, faster than she had ever run before in her life. As quickly as one could run in the snow, at least.

She had enough sense to grab several items before she actually fled the camp and now possessed a discarded sword, a worn but serviceable cloak and several small pieces of soggy bread. She almost left the camp without these items that could potentially save her life, and silently applauded herself for thinking on her feet as she rummaged through her foul companion's belongings. Meanwhile, the strange creature (the very same one from last night), who looked like an ordinary man but clearly wasn't, faced off against Jack's men.

During that eternal moment, she had felt painfully slow, knowing that every second was crucial, but in looking back as she ran, not knowing what untold dangers lay ahead, she was confident that her diligence had been well worth the risk.

Val exerted herself to exhaustion, plodding through the thick snow cover that hindered her way, feeling the cold air blasting into her lungs. She felt so tired, as if she was steadily losing breath, but Val could only run on, anxious to put as much distance as she possibly could behind her.

She didn't have any clue as to where she was headed and the cloak she had taken was already starting to feel heavy. She gritted her teeth, ignored her rising fatigue and tried to find a rhythm to her pace, a pace she feared she could not long sustain. What then? When all of her energy was spent? What would she do? Sleep in the snow? Attempt to find some sort of shelter from the cold?

At the moment she was warm, almost painfully so, and she continued to perspire heavily, her hands and body already wet with sweat. On instinct, she scooped up a handful of snow as she ran (nearly tripping in the process), and rubbed it over her hands and then as an afterthought, smeared in on her face.

The snow felt refreshing, stinging her wide awake and she continued to place one foot before the other, never pausing once in her desperate pace.

By the time Amparo arrived at the camp, Morluun was already gone. The Quest Blades were still pulsating, indicating she was not to linger and that the dangerous vampire was still nearby. She paused only a moment, to view the carnage, and counted three bodies, all human, each not more than a dozen feet apart.

So Morluun had fed, that much was clear, and Amparo had to wonder if it was wise to do the same. She had yet to fully recover and while her right arm was firmly attached and in working condition, her grip with that hand remained weak. Hardly suitable for battle. But dare she wait when the blades were imploring her in no uncertain terms to pursue the fiend? After all, wasn't Morluun similarly impaired?

Surely, the resourceful vampire had used the fresh blood he had taken from the humans to accelerate his healing, for Amparo had no doubt that Morluun's first priority would have been reattaching his severed arm. However, Amparo noticed one significant error. The bodies were too close together which revealed that Morluun had consumed the humans one after the other in obvious haste.

What Morluun should have done was consume the first victim, or even the first two, before killing the third in succession. Had he spared the last, even for a few minutes, he could have accelerated his healing by draining that human *after* he completed the reattachment of his limb. But instead, Morluun had taken them all at once and then likely seen to his arm.

It was a minor thing overall, yes, but perhaps that small error could give her a slight advantage. His arm was bound to be weak, perhaps even weaker than her own. For while she had reattached her own arm with the aid of Zekiel's blood, Morluun had clearly used his own.

Yes, he had consumed a fair amount of human blood, was likely whole once more. But once the blood from his victims had been absorbed into his being, much of the healing he could have gained from absorbing the third human *after* his impromptu surgery had been lost. Wasted.

As Amparo made ready to leave, she contemplated one other important fact she needed to keep in mind. Likely, Morluun had not found the opportunity to heal his arm last night. At least, that is what she was led to believe. And if that were true, she had already gained precious time to heal her arm, while his own healing process had just begun. Perhaps she could use that to further advantage?

Just then, she heard a whimpering nearby. She instinctively tensed for a moment, more so on instinct before realizing there was a fourth human she had missed, hiding in the deep brush, and silently reprimanded herself for not initially picking up his scent earlier.

She had been getting careless of late, falling subject to her contemplations and vowed not to be caught so unaware again. She could not afford to make any more mistakes.

For that matter, questioning herself, why *was* she making so many mistakes lately? Was it the loss of blood she had given over to Zekiel? Were her senses compromised? She made a mental note to explore the issue further.

Thankfully, in this case the mistake was a mere human, and perhaps amidst the excessive smells of blood and gore, she could excuse herself for the slight error. Yet it angered Amparo that her senses had once again betrayed her. Failed when it was well within her power to discern the unmistakable presence.

"Come out...Jack," Amparo said smoothly, easily discerning the human's name from his mind, getting back to the task at hand. But upon hearing his name, and despite the fact that her voice was distinctly female, Jack bolted.

Amparo sighed. Moving too fast to be seen, she placed herself directly in his path, startling the cowardly man in the process. He tripped, stumbling a few times before falling face down in the snow. When he finally found the strength to rise, using his one good arm, he found a beautiful woman standing before him.

"Why do you run from a woman?"

"I...who are you? What do you want?" he mumbled, trying to make sense of this. He had seen many strange things over the course of the past two nights and Amparo's presence here was surely no exception. He attempted to regain his bravado, though surely remained on guard.

"What do I want?" Amparo asked. "That depends. What do you have to offer?"

"Look, woman," Jack began, and at that crude reference, Amparo nearly laughed, but allowed the man to continue. "I don't know who you are, or what you are doing here, but I've seen some weird shit as of late and you are no exception," he said, sharing his thoughts.

"And what exactly did you witness? Tonight, for example."

"I don't have to tell you shit."

"Oh? Is that so?" Amparo whispered, moving closer. Jack's taller, lankier frame stood well above her short stature; yet he still took a few steps back, quite against his nature. Still advancing on him, Jack continued to retreat, clearly intimidated until be backed himself up against the trunk of a very large tree.

"You will tell me all that I desire to know," Amparo stated. Suddenly, she was in his mind, tearing through his thoughts, searching for the details of events that had occurred only minutes ago, when Morluun made his most recent kills. Jack remained still, quite unable to move, locked in Amparo's powerful trance, arms going limp at his sides.

She wasn't able to discern much unfortunately, and most of what she did learn were details she had already pieced together. Amparo was not even sure what she hoped to discover from this pitiful human, but just as she was about to relinquish her grip upon his mind and to simply kill the man where he stood, she stumbled upon the face of another human. A face he had plastered in the forefront of his mind.

Amparo gasped. She knew that face. Amparo knew the face well. And that fact disturbed her greatly...far more than the images of Morluun himself.

Chapter Seventy-One

AMPARO STRUGGLED TO make sense of this latest discovery and continued to shake her head in disbelief. How was this possible? How could such a thing be? She asked herself repeatedly. The odds of this startling development were too disturbing to ignore and nothing seemed to make logical sense.

She let Jack go then and the pathetic human slumped to the ground, still under her complete control. She debated killing him right then and there, but a second startling thought came to mind.

Morluun had left this human alive. Why? Was he in such haste as to let the human escape? Was there some other reason she had yet to discover?

She attempted to contact Zekiel then, wondering where her fledgling was, and why he had still refused to answer her call. Where was he? And why did he seek to be alone at such a critical time?

She let Jack go then, releasing him from her mental hold, convinced the human had no more information to offer. He started to babble incoherently, still dazed from the mental intrusion, speaking utter nonsense.

And then it hit her. The reason why Jack had been kept alive. And knowing full well that she had played directly into Morluun's hands.

Val, while in mid-run, stumbled hard and watched the ground rush up to meet her. She landed painfully on her side, though she tried to break the fall and immediately tried to get back up. But she could not. Exhausted and unable to find any strength, she remained where she was for some time, her head still spinning, her body completely spent.

And then Morluun was there.

I knew Amparo had awakened, but had not yet answered her call. I didn't want to. She called to me periodically, begging a response, but at the moment, all I could think about was Val.

Val was out here in the wilderness. Alone or worse, with the old company she used to keep. And as her former companion, I felt an obligation to help her. How could I not?

What was beginning to bother me more than anything else was something Will had said. He had referred to Val as my wife. But why? Why would Will say such a thing? And no less important, why would Val seek me out? I struggled to keep my thoughts organized, with so much going on, and reminded myself that Amparo was very much alone too.

I knew where she was, of course, having sensed her presence easily, despite her attempt to cloak herself. I knew she was near, very near in fact, perhaps at the campsite where we fought Morluun the night before if I was not mistaken. How I could so easily *sense* her, I could not begin to comprehend, nor did I have time to solve yet another riddle regarding these strange powers I now possessed.

I simply *knew* where she was. What continued to astonish me, though I had had very little time to reflect on much of anything as of late, was how doing these things, such as discerning her whereabouts, took but a mere flicker of my concentration. It was effortless to detect her...which also begged the question: Was it then possible that Morluun also knew where she was?

I took a deep breath. On one hand, I knew I was the one responsible as to why Val was out here, and thus an onus was placed upon me to go to the aid of my former companion. But on the other, felt an equal need to seek out Amparo so that together, we could attempt to rid ourselves of this vampire who was still on the loose. When it came to Morluun, I wanted our next confrontation to be on our terms and not his.

Upon realizing these things, I was starting to regret my decision to leave Amparo. I had been impatient, impudent, and altogether foolish. When I abandoned her at dusk, still sleeping peacefully in the earth, had I really been prepared to face Morluun alone had our paths crossed?

And then Lucy and Will had further complicated things. But had that encounter hindered me as much as I thought? Perhaps that unanticipated meeting had allowed me to come to my senses. See things in a proper perspective. Perhaps it even saved my life. Facing Morluun alone, even taking the risk that this could happen, had been poor judgment on my part. Or maybe, what it all boiled down to was that I had wanted to be on my own for a bit. Just some time to myself.

I had to think. Had to make a decision.

If Amparo were in danger, I was fairly certain I would know. But if I charged off to find Val, and Amparo were to engage Morluun alone or if he, in turn, found her, could I reach her in time? To come to her aid? I didn't know what to do.

Just then, even as I was mentally scanning for any human in the area, but Val in particular, a woman's scream pierced the cold silent night, impossible to miss with my preternatural hearing. No more than a few miles away.

So be it.

Morluun gazed intently upon the woman, once again taking in her beauty. He had his assignment, yes, but certainly Cain would not be opposed for a pause in his quest for this, this gorgeous specimen of a mortal woman. No doubt Cain would reward him handsomely...as well as provide additional resources for tracking down the rogues.

It was well known that Cain had not taken another bride since Amparo's disappearance, and Morluun was quite certain that this fetching woman would fancy his eye. This human was Amparo's equal at the very least, no less striking and perhaps even more so. More than a worthy replacement. Her hair was raven black, quite the opposite of Amparo's, tangled and wet with snow, but even the harsh winter conditions did little to diminish her appearance.

And as for Amparo, Morluun could not help but utter a small chuckle. He was certain that she, along with her fledgling, had by now realized why he had kept the mortal 'Jack' alive, but their discovery came too late. Because from the moment that Amparo made herself known to the human, Morluun had been aware. He had also tracked the human's thoughts with his mind from afar. So when he sensed Jack's terror, he was prompted to read Jack's thoughts through his own connection, and was made aware of her exact location. More importantly, he knew that he was soon to be pursued, if not already.

He lamented that he could not use that information to go after Amparo now, which would have been his preference, but he was also keenly aware of his own weakened state. Better to return to face her and the fledgling after he recovered his strength. And with this additional prize before him, one of no small importance, he had no doubt that Cain would show him mercy for his prior failures.

Yes, he had lied to Melchiah about his progress for fear of what Cain might do, but this too, he knew would be forgiven. And thankfully, for his sake, this stunning human had come along to provide a way for him to avoid Cain's wrath.

"Please...don't hurt me," Val begged, convinced that her initial screams had gone unheard and that no help would come.

"Hurt you?" Morluun purred, brushing away his thoughts to give the human his full attention. "No, fair mortal. I will not hurt you. This, I wholly promise." He offered her a sly grin.

"What then?" Val dared to ask. "What do you want with me?"

"Ah, but it is not what *I* want," he coolly responded. "It is what my Master will want. But come now, no more questions. All will be revealed in time. Oh, yes. I promise you this as well."

"Make me no promises but one," Val boldly demanded, summoning the courage to rise to her feet. "Let me go." Morluun laughed again. How Cain would love this one! Feisty, determined, so much like Amparo.

"Let me go!" Val demanded.

"I'm sorry, dear woman. That I simply cannot do. Perhaps, and I dare say I hope I am wrong, but perhaps the Master will do as you ask. He is so dreadfully choosy, that one." Morluun paused to gather his thoughts. "But mind you," he elaborated. "I do expect that the Master will have plans for you. In this regard, and if the Master is pleased, you should feel fortunate indeed. You have no idea of what could possibly be in store for you. But come"—he politely offered her his hand—"you are to come with me and we are to leave at once."

"And if I refuse?"

Morluun threw his head back in laughter. "I think you know that refusal is not an option."

Val bolted, running with the speed of panic...only to find the strange man impossibly in front of her. She then fled in the opposite direction but to her mounting horror, found him before her again, seemingly everywhere at once.

"Come now. Certainly, you are smart enough to know that escape is not possible. I would have liked to walk by your side, properly escorting you as mortals do, but am afraid that I am pressed for time." He grabbed for her then and easily slung her over his shoulder, her struggles no more than a minor nuisance.

"It is far easier to travel if you do not resist," he advised. "I would not want to accidentally harm you in any way." Val, realizing that her efforts were useless, held tightly by his impossible strength, felt her body go limp. Defeated.

"Good," Morluun commented. "I thank you for your cooperation. Now brace yourself, my lady. We will be moving quickly and you humans are such delicate creatures."

"Pardon the interruption," a familiar voice suddenly called out from behind him. "But I'm going to need you to set the young lady down. *Now*."

Chapter Seventy-Two

Morluun whirled around only to see the hated rogue fledging standing before him. "You!" he hissed, roughly dropping his prisoner to the ground. Val looked up from her prone position, recognizing the newcomer at once.

"Oh my God, oh my God, oh my God..." she started rambling, tears already forming in her eyes.

"Well met yet again, Val. It's been awhile," Zekiel addressed her casually, trying to speak as calmly as possible. "Everything is going to be all right now."

"Zekiel! Oh my God, Zekiel! I thought I would never see you again!" She cried.

She wanted to rush him, bury herself in his arms, wanting nothing but to be near him again, but a stern gaze from Morluun warned her otherwise.

"You two know each other?" Morluun asked, curious about this new development.

"He is my husband, you cock sucking piece of shit!" Val screamed at Morluun, unable to contain herself. Zekiel suddenly wore a quizzical expression but sobered almost immediately, giving Morluun his full attention.

"Husband? Zekiel?" Morluun questioned. "So that is your name. I wish I could say well met for a second time...Zekiel. But you'll forgive me if I am not at all pleased to see you."

"Likewise," Zekiel responded indifferently. "So, let me say this once. Let the girl go and no harm will come to you. I give you my word."

Morluun actually considered the offer. On the one hand, he had no desire to engage the unpredictable fledgling in combat. Not now. Now when his arm was weak. By the same token, dawn was still many hours away and Morluun quickly reminded himself that it had been the rising sun which caused him to lose the encounter. Less so the resourceful fledgling himself. There was also Cain to consider, who would not accept further failures without significant reason.

If Morluun were to surrender the human now, he would have no choice but to return empty-handed and with nothing to show for his efforts. His choice becoming clear, he knew what he had to do then and swallowed hard. Surrender was not an option.

"You are in no position to make any deals," Morluun carefully said at length. He mentally bolstered his confidence, remembering how powerful he truly was and scolded himself for even considering the fledgling's ridiculous offer. How old was he after all? A few nights? At the most? How dare this young upstart demand anything!

Morluun then assumed a defensive posture and for Zekiel, that was indication enough of his answer. "I assume we are through with words?" Zekiel responded, assuming a similar stance.

"Ah, but there is one question I would ask," Morluun said, beginning to circle Zekiel. "Where is your Maker? Where is Amparo?" But the fledgling gave no answer. Not to Morluun anyway.

"Val," he whispered, chancing a glance in her direction. "Give us some room. And keep your distance." Val nodded immediately, hanging on his every word and started to back away, step by step, trusting Zekiel implicitly.

"But do not go too far..." Morluun added, who had no doubt heard, turning his head in Val's direction.

"Speak to her but once more and I will take your tongue," Zekiel promised, overcome by a sudden wave of rising anger.

He felt obligated to help Val. Of course he did. But something else was starting to permeate from within. A certain protectiveness over her that he could not deny. He risked another glance in her direction where she held his eyes with her own. And in her eyes was such intensity, a depth he could not begin to fathom. Why was she looking at him like that? He knew she was frightened by Morluun, but there was something else. Something behind those eyes he could not read. He almost dared to read her thoughts then but knew he could not. He had to remain calm and committed, focused solely on the battle soon to take place.

"You were there last night. Weren't you?" Val could not help but ask, even as she continued to move further away. It was obvious she had no intention of leaving him, and though she feared for her life, as well as his own, she was not about to let Zekiel out of her sight.

"Yes," he answered, watching Morluun closely now. "I was there. Do not fear for me, I beg. I've dealt with this one before." Even as he finished his sentence, he wished he felt as confident as he made himself out to be. Last night he had been fortunate...but now with dawn still hours away, even with his reattached arm, which Zekiel had noticed from the onset, Morluun was to be taken seriously.

"Why not tell her the truth, Zekiel?" Morluun countered. "Come now, let us all be honest."

"What truth do you speak of?"

"You got lucky. Both of us know it," he spat. "The rising sun will not save you this time."

"That depends on how long you talk," Zekiel dared to quip.

Morluun's body tensed with a growl and Zekiel instinctively braced himself by lowering his stance and centering his weight. In a mere instant, Morluun was in his face, impossibly already in his face, and launched a right fist with blazing speed, making it near impossible for Zekiel to block. The punch struck him hard, a solid shot to the jaw, and Zekiel felt his legs buckle. Morluun did not slow. He threw a second heavy punch directly into Zekiel's gut with his left and finished with a right uppercut, knocking Zekiel clear off his feet and sending the fledgling hard to the ground.

Morluun surely felt the strain on his newly attached left arm, but the strike had been worth it, and showed no signs of any lasting discomfort.

"Get up," Morluun called, pausing in his attack, but Zekiel did not hear him. His head was spinning, his mouth full of blood, and he struggled to even remain conscious.

Three punches. Three punches were all it had taken. Three punches had defeated him, and he found himself unable to stand. His insides felt like they were on fire, as if his very organs had been ruptured, the blow to his stomach surprisingly having done the most damage. Now he wondered through clouded thoughts why he hadn't even had time to draw his sword.

"Get up!" Morluun demanded again and this time, Zekiel heard him. He also heard Val scream. Screaming for him to get up as well.

If only he could. Never had he been hit with such force, such devastating power, and that had only been the beginning.

Morluun had been smart. Cunning. He had come at Zekiel with everything he had and struck as fast as he possibly could. It had been a gamble, yes, risking so much power as well as the use of his arm, but the fledgling had not seen it coming. By giving Zekiel no time to defend himself, a strategy he had also used last night, this time, Morluun had risked all for a sudden decisive victory.

Refusing to let Zekiel even begin to recover, Morluun started kicking him there on the ground, punishing him repeatedly in the arms, his chest, his face, his back. Anywhere Morluun could find a target.

Zekiel knew he had to stand up, lest he be beaten to death. Somehow, he had to find a way. But all he could manage was to curl himself into a ball.

And Morluun was relentless, taking no chances this time, giving Zekiel no time to move, no time to even *think*. All Zekiel felt was wracking pain. Torturous pain. Constant and ever-increasing, unlike anything he had felt since taking the dark blood.

Meanwhile, Val kept screaming. Screaming at the top of her lungs for Morluun to stop. Pleading for Zekiel's life. Finally, after what felt like an eternity, far too long in her eyes, Morluun paused.

Zekiel, who somehow was still conscious, took this opportunity to spit out the contents of his mouth, creating a thick pool of blood in the snow.

"Like I said," Morluun taunted. "You were lucky the night before. And with Jeremiah's fresh blood no longer on your lips, any momentum you had has been lost. Fool!" Morluun continued. "Did you actually think that you, a mere fledgling, could stand up to the likes of one as old as I? Did your foolish Maker, that traitorous bitch Amparo, tell you *nothing*? Nothing at all? Nothing of the dangers of facing one centuries older than yourself? Tell me, where is your beloved Amparo now?"

Zekiel remained silent, only because he couldn't answer, unable to do anything but clutch at his body in such agonizing pain.

"Zekiel!" Val cried out, unable to stop herself, rushing to his side. "Zekiel?" But even for her there came no response, at least not with any words, for all he could do was softly moan.

"Step away from him, my dear," Morluun ordered, drawing his twin axes as he spoke. But Val, all fear gone, instead threw herself at Morluun in a flurry of fists and curses at which Morluun simply laughed.

"I promised I would not hurt you, and to this I hold," he said, weapons at his side and accepting her hits. "But I'm afraid I do not have time for your anger to play itself out. Cease this moment and stay your distance," he commanded. Incredibly, Val's arms went limp and she nodded in accord, moving out of the way. She walked trance-like, a good twenty paces away, before turning around and standing completely still.

The Quest Blades were now pulsating with an urgency Amparo had never felt before and she pushed herself to the limit, fearing the absolute worst. They throbbed in her hands, seemingly desperate, escalating her worst possible fears.

She never ran faster in her long life, knowing she was being led toward almost certain danger and she called out to her fledgling repeatedly. Receiving no answer, and fearing that Zekiel had indeed found Morluun, Amparo could only pray that she would somehow arrive in time.

"So now, where were we?" Morluun said to Zekiel, walking a tight circle around him.

"If you harm her...in any way..." Zekiel somehow managed to whisper, still tightly clinging to his sides.

"You will do nothing!" Morluun concluded. "And to think," he went on. "I actually considered enlisting more aid in your capture...but I see now, my concerns were...misplaced," he laughed. "I do not understand how you managed to defeat Jeremiah, but I can assure you, your short immortal life ends here. Here and now."

And then Morluun stalked in, kicking Zekiel one more time for good measure, eliciting another moan before coming to a standstill before him.

"Is there anything else you wish to say before I cut you to pieces?"

But Zekiel said nothing.

"I am disappointed. I would have loved to hear you beg for your life. In any case, be thankful I am merciful and thus will kill you swiftly. I do wish I had the time to see you properly suffer...for *this*."

He indicated his arm. "But as it stands, I am pressed for time. Maybe..." he reconsidered. "Yes. How inconsiderate of me. How could I not make time enough to sever your arm before I take your head? Yes, I do believe that would make us even. Worth even the slight delay. Surely my Master can wait for that. Wouldn't you agree?"

Zekiel strained to locate Val, unwilling to let his last image be of his killer. "I'm sorry," Zekiel whispered, wondering why Val stood so lifeless. Stiff, as if she were a statue. She was simply staring straight ahead, with the most vacant expression on her face.

Morluun raised one axe to strike...

Chapter Seventy-Three

"*Z*EKIEL!" AMPARO'S VOICE rang out from high above Morluun. "*I am here!!!*"

Surprised, Morluun looked up, barely halting his killing stroke only to see the airborne vampire descending upon him, her blades glowing through the darkness. Morluun snarled in defiance, attempting to bring his axes to bear, but Amparo was quicker, drawing two deep gashes on Morluun's right shoulder before coming to land before him.

"Bitch!" he roared, throwing himself into a backward ground somersault, seeking to create some distance between them. Amparo pursued immediately, glancing at Zekiel as she passed, hoping he hadn't sustained any lasting injury. Her brief glance had not told her much, but he was still very much alive and for that, she breathed a sigh of relief.

But so too came her anger. Zekiel looked as if he had been nearly beaten to death, and while she knew he could recover completely, this did little to cool the blood boiling in her veins. Morluun would pay dearly for this.

Amparo, rarely failing to take in every detail, also detected a mortal nearby. A female, she surmised, but could not spare a glance, needing her utmost concentration. Never slowing in her stride, she met Morluun head on in a fury, barely giving him a chance to get his feet underneath him. His hands came up in a flash, faster than Amparo anticipated, and he somehow met her next attack with a perfectly timed parry.

"I was beginning to wonder when you would show!" he growled, their faces only inches apart. Amparo, never one to exchange words in combat, rotated a full circuit to separate their weapons and lunged low, both blades leading, seeking to slash his knees. But Morluun intercepted both, with a single axe no less, and countered with the other, aiming to take her head.

She had seen the attack coming of course, had even anticipated it, no novice in combat herself, and reversed her own momentum, rolling harmlessly aside. She was back on her feet an instant later, ready for Morluun's next attack, but found the vampire instead standing still.

"I do not wish to destroy you," Morluun said calmly, keeping his weapons ready.

"Then it appears we have a problem," Came Amparo's cool reply. "For I very much desire to see you dead!" She crouched, ready to leap for him anew.

"Wait. Stay your hand," he said with an appraised hand. "Perhaps we can deal."

Amparo spat. "Speak," she demanded, on guard for any foul play.

"Return with me, offering no less than your unconditional surrender, and I promise that no harm will come to you or your fledgling. Leastways, not by my hand. In fact, I will even let him go free."

Amparo laughed. "Return with you? Return to Cain, you mean. To be at his mercy. And as for Zekiel, I do not doubt you would let him walk away, but you must think me a fool...for Cain's minions will simply track him down at a later time."

"That is my deal." Amparo just laughed again. "Perhaps you are not thinking clearly," Morluun tried to advise. "Your fledgling has proven to be resourceful. Clearly so. And you yourself have escaped the Master's hand for centuries. If you have instructed your fledgling well, and I gather you have, perhaps he too will find the means to…"

"You have orders not to destroy me. Same as the others. And thus I gain nothing by accepting your so-called deal," Amparo interrupted.

"You presume to know much," Morluun warned. "And…accidents happen all of the time. You get to keep your life, as well as that of your fledgling. At least for a time," he admitted.

"I don't think Cain would be pleased to know that I was killed by accident, do you?"

Morluun shrugged and motioned with his eyes to the human standing nearby. Amparo followed his line of vision and risked a glance herself.

It was *her*.

"Oh my God," Amparo whispered, drawing a confused expression from Morluun.

It was *her!*

But how could it be?!

How was she here?

Why was she here?

Amparo started to panic.

"So, I see you recognize your replacement," Morluun surmised, incorrectly reading Amparo's horrified expression. "Your concern over the human is touching. She is beautiful, is she not?"

"I care not for this mortal," Amparo growled.

"Is that so?" Morluun asked, confused. "You will forgive me if I do not believe your words."

"Then kill her," Amparo said in all seriousness. "See for yourself."

"Truly? Ah, but that I simply cannot do. For if you are unwilling to agree to the terms I offer, then I will not return to the Lord Cain empty-handed. Even if that means I must destroy you."

Amparo laughed again. "Cain will kill you if any harm comes to me."

"Ah, but if not for this mortal, who surely is beautiful, I would be inclined to agree. But to receive such a prize in your stead, Cain would forgive me, I'm sure."

"Well...then let us find out," Amparo challenged. "Come then, Morluun. I believe you are out of excuses."

Morluun nodded his accord. He was back in Amparo's face a second later, swinging his deadly axes, but Amparo was more than ready this time. She parried his attacks time and again utilizing her own series of counters and offensive strikes. It soon became clear that the skills of both combatants were proving to be on very even ground, much to Morluun's dismay.

"You are a far more worthy opponent tonight...but surely, you have yet to recover from creating your fledgling filth. Tell me, what has changed?" Morluun asked between exchanges, but Amparo refused to answer.

That answer, quite unknown to Morluun, was simply Val's presence itself.

Amparo was infuriated that she was here, *here* of all places, and her unbridled hatred and jealousy of the human effectively fueled her furious pace. She could not help but wonder if Val was the reason that Zekiel was here and so enraged was she with this thought, that Amparo actually increased her tempo. Amparo forced Morluun for the first time to go solely on the defensive, and the veteran vampire, confident of his advantage here, soon found himself hard-pressed.

By this time Zekiel was beginning to stir, rolling over to witness the battle before him. He still felt painfully sore, pathetically weak, and he lamented that he felt quite powerless to aid his companion. He needed more time to recover.

"Amparo," Zekiel tried to whisper, still struggling to remain conscious. "Amparo...please be careful." Amparo heard him of course, and even took some comfort in the fact that he was at least speaking, but he fell silent a moment later, knowing that Amparo could ill afford any distractions.

As an afterthought, Amparo again took a quick glance at Val, only to deliberately increase her fury. She started to press Morluun even harder, working the Quest Blades to deadly effect, and it took all of his considerable skill just to keep her at bay.

Morluun was still holding his own, but had accepted many nicks and other insubstantial wounds in order to avoid a potentially lethal strike. Though by now, even Morluun recognized that it was only a matter of time before a thrust or slash penetrated even his fine defense. Against these formidable blades, his own weapons, while finely crafted, could not match them. Not in durability. And if it were not his skill that ultimately failed, then surely his weapons would do so in time. As it stood, Amparo had already come dangerously close to skewering him several times.

He began to wonder how long they could maintain this frantic pace, and if Zekiel himself would once again enter the fray.

He didn't fear the fledgling overall, not now, but to face them both at the same time was something Morluun could ill afford. He needed to end this battle now with a decisive victory. Just as he had with the fledgling. If only Amparo would give him a chance...some small window of opportunity.

After many more minutes of frenzied fighting, the moment he hoped for finally arrived.

Amparo was beginning to tire. She was expending far too much energy by constantly staying on the offensive while he had largely defended, conserving much of his strength.

When her next attack came, a vicious stab aimed at his heart, Morluun, on impulse, accepted the hit on a dangerous gamble.

The dagger missed his heart, thankfully, but instead plunged deep into his ribs. He hissed in protest, even as he allowed the dagger to penetrate deeper, bringing Amparo in close.

Growling against the sudden explosion of pain and gritting his teeth in rage, he parried her second dagger, meant to take his head, and brought his other axe across in a deadly horizontal slash. His aim proved true and Amparo reeled back in shock, clutching at the blood gushing from the long red gash that had been drawn across her entire stomach.

The wound was deep and this fight would be long over before the healing could even begin. While she knew it was hardly fatal, Amparo lacked the time to recover, and her overall blood loss would be greater than his.

Amparo stared directly into his eyes then, despite their being mortal enemies, and couldn't help but silently congratulate Morluun for such a cunning maneuver. Having willingly exchanged one blow for another, Morluun's own wound now looked minor in comparison to the deep cut across her midsection.

Amparo, now needed both hands to stem the flow of blood and was forced to dislodge her own blade. Morluun wasted no time, aiming his deadly ax for her shoulder, once again trying to remove her weakened arm, but Amparo refused to be caught a second time so easily.

She managed to dodge the brunt of the attack, but his cruel axe still connected, biting deep into her flesh.

While Morluun's latest attack inflicted less damage than he would have hoped, he raised his bloodied axe again, only to realize that his last strike had been enough.

Amparo dropped both blades in surrender. No. Not just surrender. She simply had no more fight. No energy. Her resources and blood, still spilling out before her, utterly spent.

Chapter Seventy-Four

"You are wise, as you are beautiful," Morluun remarked, cautiously making his way towards her. He was still on guard for any treachery, a trait all too common when dealing with this vampire in particular, so Morluun, on impulse, lunged in quickly to club her in the face with the butt of his axe. As he expected, Amparo had no defense to speak of, and was hit with the full force of the axe's handle across her face, laying her already kneeling body down low.

He came at her again, seeking nothing but complete victory, and this time struck out with his foot. She attempted to block with a lazy hand but the foot still connected, thrusting her head back violently. Amparo's body went very still.

"You are still quite far from death, I assure you," he beamed, confident now that the battle had been won. "But alas, because of your unwillingness to deal, your fledgling will not be as fortunate. For while you will recover in no time at all, for Cain will see to that himself, I'm sure...I do however, have explicit orders to kill that which you have made. And so, he shall now be *unmade*."

"Zekiel..." she barely whispered.

"Yes, Amparo," Morluun replied, turning an eye on the incapacitated fledgling.

Morluun suddenly moved with blinding speed, quite aware that Zekiel was even now deceptively trying to stand up and promptly struck him multiple times, with devastating kicks to the face. And then Morluun kicked him once more for good measure.

"Your fledgling's ability to recover is truly commendable. Impressive even," he admitted, speaking to Amparo but remaining next to Zekiel's still form. "And I must honestly congratulate you on your fine work with this one. A pity you did not ask for the Master's permission before you so…foolishly set off on your own. This one could have been useful to us and in time, indeed quite powerful. But alas, I have my orders and I strive to never leave our Master disappointed. You must understand," he said almost mockingly.

"Bastard," Amparo swore.

"I don't blame you for hating me. And perhaps, I would be wise to watch my back in the future. I will deliver you to Cain, of course, and he will do with you as he wills. Oh, I don't suppose he will ever trust you again, nor do I expect that he will let you out of his sight…for a time. It is a fate far better than most," he reasoned. "But come now, we have much to do and a considerable distance to travel and I dare not keep my Master waiting any longer than is necessary. Understand, dear Amparo, you will not enjoy what comes next."

An evil smile crossed his face and he kicked Zekiel repeatedly again, but if Zekiel felt anything, he showed no sign. Morluun shrugged then, as if it did not matter, and made his way back to Amparo, bending so low that they were face to face.

"I will drain you almost to the point of death," he whispered, wanting to see her reaction. "And oh, how I will enjoy the taste. The taste of you on my lips, that powerful blood on my lips."

Amparo's eyes went wide.

"Come now, Amparo. Did you actually think we could travel as you are? No, no, no. That we simply will not do. I will have you as weak as a kitten.

Oh, and just between you and me? I cannot deny I will surely enjoy this."

He lunged for her neck then and Amparo futilely attempted to avoid his snapping maw to no avail, her blood flowing into him at once.

He drank but for a moment, simply to revel in the taste of her, and with uncanny discipline slowly pulled back, seemingly in utter bliss.

"Aaahhh," he moaned, savoring the few mouthfuls he had taken. "Long have I waited for this day, and longer still have I desired you for my own. Be assured, my little drinks will be many...and more moments like this we will share along our road. But first, I must conclude my business with your fledgling. I promise you I won't be long."

But Amparo could no longer hear him, her blood loss too great. Morluun rose to his feet then, reminding himself of his orders, and slowly walked to stand before Zekiel once more. "Amparo will trouble us no longer, but I am afraid our own road has also come to an end."

"If you have brought...any harm to her..." Zekiel managed to whisper, at the moment curled into a ball.

"You will do nothing!" he snapped, grabbing Zekiel roughly by the hair.

"I will deliver your precious Maker to the one I serve, along with the mortal you strived so hard to protect. So, go on now," he scoffed, lifting Zekiel's head and roughly jerking it from side to side so that he could view both Amparo and the still-comatose Val. "Take one final look at what your pathetic existence has wrought."

Morluun laughed.

Zekiel stared long and hard at both women until his eyes settled solely on Val. She continued to stand in thrall, seemingly unaware and perfectly still, and Zekiel unconsciously found tears in his eyes. She didn't deserve this, nor did Amparo, and he felt overcome with grief. He strained to look back at Amparo to see how she fared, but his eyes continued to betray him, focusing instead on Val. He began to feel a swell of foreign emotions.

"Pray tell me, I beg," Morluun began once again, unable to resist his curiosity. "Since the two of you obviously know each other so well...does the human know what you are? What we are?"

"I don't see... I don't see how that is relevant, nor does it really matter. Not now," Zekiel whispered roughly.

"No, no you are correct. It doesn't matter. But let me ask you this before I destroy you. Do you know what I intend to do with the human? Once I've finished with you?"

Zekiel did not respond, but was suddenly very anxious to hear Morluun's answer. He was even unconsciously tightening his fists.

"We will make her one of us, of course, and she too will serve the Lord Cain...in ways you cannot possibly imagine. Oh, the things he will do to her. Such a delightful name too. Val."

Something inside Zekiel snapped.

Chapter Seventy-Five

ZEKIEL RAVEN WAS not even conscious of his next actions, nor did he register the primal scream of his own voice. Morluun was powerfully hurled backwards, having not even seen the fledgling move, his mind scrambling to understand what was happening. Morluun hit the ground hard, scattering snow and debris in the air but the old vampire was quick, standing up in an instant. But in that instant, he was immediately assaulted again, the fledgling all over him, and Morluun was brought back to the ground with devastating force. He tried to fight back, tried to stand once more, any way to remove this crazed creature, but Zekiel's body had him pinned fast, his strength unreal.

And then came a rain of blows. Morluun sought to protect his face, to get the seemingly possessed vampire off him, but Zekiel was unrelenting, striking him again and again, fist after fist, his fists landing like a weighted sledgehammer.

"*Enough!!*" Morluun screamed, attempting to summon his full strength, somehow managing to take hold of Zekiel's arms, still in a blur of motion. He attempted to throw Zekiel clear, pushing with all his might, yet the stubborn vampire refused to yield, responding in turn with a perfectly aimed head-butt.

Morluun felt his nose crush under the blow, his own blood filling his mouth. Zekiel struck yet again, and then again, stubbornly using his head as a bludgeon until Morluun had no choice but to release the fledgling's arms. And then the devastating blows came once more.

He was clearly being beaten to death, and Morluun's broken jaw had now gone slack. He didn't understand what was happening here, didn't know how it was possible. *Where* was the fledgling getting his strength? How and where did he get such raw power? How could he have regained any strength at all? Zekiel had been completely and thoroughly beaten, his mind screamed over and over. *He had been beaten!!*

Morluun growled again, his left eye now swollen shut, and refusing his own defeat, pushed once more with everything he had, finally dislodging his attacker. Morluun stumbled once but managed to steady himself, all the while gasping with shock and searching with his one remaining eye for Zekiel. But the fledgling was nowhere to be seen.

Morluun looked left, then right, wondering when the next attack would come and quickly readied his weapons.

He needn't have bothered. He sensed the air literally shift around him, but for Morluun it was already too late. Down came Zekiel from above like an angel of retribution, leading with his left foot, and plastered it across Morluun's face. Both of his weapons were suddenly dislodged from the sheer force of the blow and Morluun's face went numb, the fledgling now directly before him.

And that's when Morluun briefly caught a glimpse of the fledgling's eyes. Zekiel's pupils were simply gone and in their place was a glowing haze of brilliant yellow light. And emitting from these eyes came thin smoky yellow tendrils, curling about as if alive.

"*Your eyes...*" Morluun murmured, unable to fathom what was happening, thinking his one working eye had deceived him. But then he saw the fledgling slowly, deliberately, cock back his fist to strike.

"*Plea—*" Morluun tried to beg for mercy but was instead struck so impossibly hard that he heard and felt his neck bones snapping and breaking and knew that it was over.

Never in his entire life, never before had Morluun been hit so hard, or known any other vampire to move so fast. In fact, he hadn't even seen the fledgling's hand move. He staggered on his feet then, simply welcoming oblivion and wondered what was taking so long for him to fall to the ground. Oh, he realized. The fledging was holding him up.

Zekiel let go then, an emotionless expression on his face, and let Morluun slump to the ground. Whatever consciousness Morluun still clung to, fear and panic now dominated and in that fleeting moment, Morluun realized his doom. So it came as no surprise either when he felt the dual punctures entering his neck only a moment later.

"How...just tell me how..." Morluun whispered, knowing he had but moments, that his immortal life was at an end.

And while Zekiel had indeed heard the question, he didn't himself know the answer.

Chapter Seventy-Six

I LET GO OF MORLUUN'S deceased form and watched as the drained body became a husk of dark ash. I then scattered the remains with a slight brush of my hands, hands that were even now still trembling.

I felt his warm blood permeate my being, healing my prior wounds and felt a sudden surge of newfound strength. Nearly losing my balance, so potent was Morluun's blood, that I stumbled, taking several long breaths to steady myself.

After several minutes, I once again felt calm enough to survey my current surroundings and was simply thankful to still be alive, but very much uncertain as to how I had managed to defeat him, as well as what had come over me.

"Ze...Zekiel?" I heard Amparo say and I didn't hesitate to rush to her side.

"I'm here, Amparo. I am here," I said, cradling her small form.

"Morluun..." she whispered, her eyes still closed. "Where—?"

"Dead."

"Dead? How? How did you..."

"Rest, Amparo, rest."

I started to roll up the sleeve of my cloak.

"Drink," I instructed her, bringing my wrist to her lips and Amparo paused for only a moment to consider before I felt her own sharp fangs penetrating my flesh.

The blood began to flow.

I let her drink from me then, letting her feed for several long seconds before I began to feel a bit of a strain, the sudden blood loss making me slightly dizzy. I then eased her off my wrist as gently as could be managed, knowing I still needed my strength to get us as far away as possible.

I paid close attention to Amparo then, watching as my blood worked through her, healing her recent wounds with remarkable speed. Within a short time, she appeared as good as new, leastways in appearance alone.

I pulled her close.

I could tell she was still relatively weak, needed much rest, much blood and no doubt she would need to feed again soon, but for that moment, I was simply happy to have her in my arms once again. Relieved that we were once again safe.

And then I remembered...

"Val!" I said out loud before I could stop myself. I felt Amparo stiffen and pull back.

"I'm sorry, Amparo," I said, taking her hands in mine. "I did not mean to shout. But the mortal that is here...she was a dear companion of mine. The one I once spoke of. And somehow..." I paused then, remembering my manners. "Are you..."

"I am fine," Amparo stated somewhat bluntly. "Go see to the mortal. Ensure that no harm has come to her."

I nodded my accord and turned to face Val, but found she was already staring intently at us both, the enchantment Morluun had apparently placed upon her, broken.

"Zekiel?" She whispered with a look of dread on her face. I had no idea how long she had been watching us, nor did I know exactly what she had seen.

I stood up at once, very much concerned, but not wanting to frighten her further, not knowing at all what she had been through. Naturally, I could have easily read her mind, had I the desire to do so, but that just didn't seem right. I simply had too much respect for her.

We stared at each other for many heartbeats and I fumbled through my mind on what I might even say.

"Are you...are you all right?" I tentatively asked, wanting nothing more but to end the silence between us. Beside me, Amparo was now also getting to her feet.

"Who...who is *she*?" came Val's eventual reply, but the tone she had used left me confused. Her voice was cold, accusatory.

"I am," Amparo began, answering in my place. "That is, *we* are lovers, of course...and dear companions for some time."

Did Amparo just use the same phrase I had used to describe Val and I? Did it matter? Did I honestly care? Amparo then deliberately took my hand in hers.

"L-l-lovers?" Val asked, eyes wide. "Companions?"

Amparo was now wearing a wicked smile, while Val's own face appeared to break. Even worse, tears were quickly forming in her eyes. But why? What was the meaning of this? I unconsciously let go of Amparo's hand and slowly took a step forward, feeling compelled to close the distance between us.

"Stay back!" Val shouted before she could stop herself. Her tears were now streaming down her face.

"But why? Why my old friend? It's me. Zekiel. And I promise you I mean no harm."

"*Friend*?" Val mocked with obvious anger. "That is how you would refer to me? As a *friend*?"

"I don't understand," I replied sincerely.

Val took a small step closer, then another. Staring at my face intensely. I remained perfectly still.

What did she see? I wondered. Could my old companion recognize that I was no longer mortal? Had I even seen my own reflection as of late? Since I had been turned? I don't think I had.

Val had come to stand before me and she tentatively reached out with her hand to touch my face.

I allowed this of course, curious myself as to her reaction, but when her fingers finally made contact, touching my smooth face, she retracted that hand in an instant. As if her hand had been burned.

"Zekiel?" she questioned, growing visibly nervous, her hand now trembling. "Are you, in fact, the...the man I know? *Still* the man I know? Your face...everything about you is...is different," she finished, looking me up and down. "Even your posture is different...even your hair slightly...but how? How can this be? And where," she continued, eyes searching our immediate area. "Where is that strange awful man? I don't...I don't understand what is happening."

And then Val started to back away.

"Val, wait. Please," I started again. "Let me try to explain."

"Explain?" Amparo questioned, turning an eye to me curiously. "Be mindful of the words you choose, Zekiel," she warned.

"And what should he be mindful of?" Val suddenly snapped defensively, stopping in her tracks. Neither Amparo nor I answered her question and surprising us both, Val slowly came to stand before me once more. All fear for the moment, gone.

"Question?" she asked me directly, staring deep into my eyes. But there was something different about her tone. I'd never before seen her so serious.

"Answer," I responded without any hesitation.

"Zekiel!" she breathed, eyes going wide and she suddenly and quite forcefully flung herself into my arms. She held me then with no indication of ever letting go and I looked to Amparo confused, eyes begging her for any advice. But Amparo said nothing, simply watching me intently.

After a few moments, I managed to pull Val free to arm's length but she was once again touching my face, surely noting that my skin was different. Felt different. And for whatever reason, perhaps it was my continued curiosity, I found myself lacking the willpower to stop her. Amparo was clearly uneasy and I'm not sure what she was making of all this.

"What...what happened to you?" Val questioned, similarly now inspecting my hands. "When you left for Scarborough, all those months ago...what happened? Did you find Simon? Why did you not return to me? I...I couldn't wait any longer, Zekiel. I had to find you...you don't know how worried I was...I..."

"Easy, Val. Easy," I said, doing my best to calm her. "I'll answer all of your questions."

"You will?" Amparo rudely interrupted.

I'm not sure what had come over her, or why Amparo was being so rude and overly cautious. I took her tone to mean that she feared I would say too much, reveal my true nature perhaps, and so I quickly shot her a response from my mind, emphasizing that I had no intention of telling Val what we were. What I had become.

Amparo, no response forthcoming, simply continued to watch me closely. I was seeing a very different side of her then, and I did not much care for this behavior. Not at all. Not when we had absolutely nothing to fear from Val.

"Zekiel?" Val asked again, impatient for any answer. "What's happened to you? Where have you been all of this time?"

"I did make it to Scarborough," I began, for the first time recalling those painful memories.

"And?"

"And..." I started to choke on my words.

"And?"

"I...I learned that Simon was dead."

The memory of that horrible day, how I felt that day, how I still felt...it was all being recalled. I visibly started shaking.

Simon. My dear, Simon. How long has it been since I had thought about Simon?

"Zekiel," Val said, with genuine concern. "Zekiel, I am so sorry. So very, very sorry. I know how much he meant to you."

"It...it's all in the past now," I said solemnly.

"But...but then, why didn't you return? You promised me you would return?"

"I did?" I asked, having a hard time remembering any such promise.

"You...you don't remember?" she questioned me, looking very confused.

"He has had a...difficult road," Amparo put in, finally breaking her silence.

"Zekiel? Zekiel, who is this woman? And..."

"Her name is Amparo. She has been looking after me," I gestured, but

one quick glance at Amparo and I could tell that she was absolutely furious with me for having revealed her name. It wasn't something I had intended to do, I had simply blurted it out.

"Wha, what do you mean, she has been looking after you?" Val started to stutter, trying to grasp all of these details.

"After I learned of Simon's death," I went on to explain. "I found myself on the field of battle. It was foolish, wholly foolish, but after what had happened to Simon...I had left Scarborough in a rage."

Val was listening intently and so I decided to continue.

"Near Hastings, there was a battle. The war I just mentioned." I swallowed hard, remembering it all. "I was in it, Val."

"Oh my God," Val said with wide eyes. "We, Henry, Lucy and I had only heard rumors. We heard that the King had lost."

"Aye. I learned of that as well some time later. But during the battle, I was injured, wounded badly. And if not for...Amparo," I continued, seeing no harm in stating her name again. "I surely would have perished."

"What do you mean?" Val questioned, hanging on my every word.

"She found me that night, stabbed and wounded. There among the dead. And had she not found me...I would have died, Val. It was she who then cared for me, she who restored my health. And even had I wanted to, I was not fit to travel for many months. So many months indeed."

"Then I owe you my thanks. My deepest gratitude," Val said directly to Amparo, obviously trying to take this all in, but my impassive vampire companion merely nodded, uttering no verbal response at all.

"But tell me," I started again, anxious to change the subject. "What are you doing out here of all places? By sheer coincidence, Lucy and I found each other. Lucy of all people! This very night in fact, and..."

"*Lucy*? Is she all right?" Val asked.

"She is well," I assured her. "On her way back to Henry's place. This very moment...and with Will of all people."

"With Will?" Val asked shocked.

"Aye. The very same. But you need not concern yourself with that. He gave me his word that he would return Lucy, and safely I might add, back to Henry's place."

Amparo glared at me again as I had yet to inform her of that meeting, but I hadn't exactly had the chance. Why did it even matter?

Val merely nodded. I could tell she was sorting this all out by the pensive look on her face, but in a moment, it was gone. And then there was something else. Some other look she gave me. Trust, perhaps? The details weren't important to her, that much I knew, and yet somehow, I just got this sense that she trusted me implicitly.

"Lucy said you were looking for me," I started again, ignoring Amparo's continued disapproving looks. "But why?"

"W...why?" Val stuttered, in seeming disbelief, as if I had erred in some way. "*Why?*" she said in rising volume, starting to grow agitated.

"Are we not...that is, do you no longer...?"

"No longer what?" I interrupted, anxious to know where this was leading and wondering why she was clearly getting upset.

"Do you no longer...desire...what we had? What...what we once shared?" She was trembling now, verily trembling uncontrollably. I didn't know what she was getting at. I didn't at all understand her distress.

"Val...I...I don't understand," I said sincerely, very much confused. "But now that I think about it, Lucy had also said something strange. Will too, if I recall..."

"Enough of this!" Amparo snapped, starting to pace at once. "Zekiel, we do not have time for this. We don't belong here."

"What...what does she mean? Why don't you belong here? Is there somewhere else you need to be? Zekiel? Who is this woman to you? Why do you keep her compa...?" But then Val stopped talking, her eyes darting back and forth, as if in deep thought. As if she had realized something?

"Oh my God," Val said, covering her mouth in shock. "It...it's *her*. Isn't it? The woman you had set out to find! *This is her!*"

"What is she talking about?" Amparo asked, now very much interested. "You told this woman about me? About us?"

"What does she mean? About us?" Val fired back in a panic. "Oh my God," she cried.

"Zekiel," Amparo addressed me, this time with her usual composure. "Zekiel, we must go. *Now,*" she demanded, and by the tone of her voice, I wasn't to argue.

"But...we can't just leave her like this. Not out here in the cold."

Val fell to her knees then, starting to weep uncontrollably.

"What would you have us do?" Amparo asked, and I could see that she was very much trying to control her temper. I didn't know what had gotten into her, why the haste...and why the obvious hate towards Val, but Amparo practically reeked of it.

"I won't leave her out in the cold to die," I said as much as stated, my own temper rising.

"You would leave me?" Val asked between sobs, looking up at me.

My head was beginning to hurt. Something about all of this just felt wrong. Even out of place. And my head. Why was I starting to have what felt like a mortal headache? Was that normal? Was I simply tired and in need of rest? I tried to stay focused.

"No...no. I won't leave you out here. Absolutely not," I finally answered, for I had no intention whatsoever of leaving her out here just so she could freeze to death.

"That's not what I meant," Val tried to clarify.

She sobered then almost immediately and slowly rose again to her feet. She was staring at me again, staring at me with that same intensity as if I was failing to grasp something. Failing to understand...

"Am..." Val began.

"Amparo," I finished for her.

"Amparo. Yes. Something she said earlier. She said..."

"I'm right here," Amparo nearly spat.

If Val was the least bit intimidated, she certainly was not showing it and so she turned to face Amparo directly.

"Did you say that the two of you...that the two of you are..."

"Are lovers?" Amparo finished for her.

Val nodded.

Why was this so important to her?

Amparo smiled wickedly, that same wicked grin I saw before and Val started breathing hard.

"Question," she addressed me again, and even here, where I stood, I could *hear* her heartbeat, knew it was beating fast.

"A...Answer." I responded, not understanding at all why I had once again responded in such a manner.

Several moments of silence passed and I felt my knees go weak.

I felt...I felt as if...I felt as if I were strangely connected to her. Like we had shared something but I couldn't remember what. I even felt a wave of emotions, emotions I couldn't begin to understand, assaulting me all at once. Assaulting my senses...all from just looking at her.

What was it that I couldn't remember?

"Do you love me?" Val finally asked.

And there it was. This was the question she had most desperately wanted to ask. But...

"Why do you ask me this?" I asked, speaking my thoughts out loud.

"*Why?*" she responded, wearing a confused expression. "You ask me *why*? Can you not answer the question?"

"I..." But I didn't know what to say. I didn't know how to make this right.

"Did I not mean anything to you?" she went on. "Did our love mean nothing?"

What was she talking about? And why was she speaking of love? *Our love* she even said. I had no words in which to reply, my hands suddenly clutching my head, my thoughts spinning out of control.

But Val would not relent, taking my hands now in hers. I looked to Amparo whose own eyes had gone wide. "That night...that night we first made love," she continued, her eyes streaking wet with tears.

I think I audibly gasped.

Made love? Her and I? What was she saying? When did she think this happened?

Why was my head throbbing?

Why was my head suddenly throbbing???

"Did I mean *nothing* to you?" she continued to question. "Did I mean nothing to you at all? Are you no different at all than all the men I wish I hadn't fucked?" she screamed. "*Are you?*"

She started sobbing again, collapsing once again to the ground while Amparo stood by, continuing to smile. Why was she smiling? Why the hell was she smiling?

I couldn't worry about that now and resolved to confront Amparo about it later. In front of me, this woman's heart was damn near breaking.

"Val...Val, please listen to me," I said, trying to choose my words carefully, trying to sound as soothing as possible. She looked up at me then and I almost couldn't bear to speak. The pain on her face too great.

"You have to know you mean much to me. We were companions for quite some time...and I don't take our friendship lightly."

"You speak as if we had never shared anything at all!" she accused.

"But you speak to me of...of having shared a bed!" I said exasperated, attempting to defend myself. "I think you have me confused with someone else."

"Indeed?" she fired back. "Let me then recall what you deny to remember." She stood up yet again, so much back and forth with this woman, but I wisely kept my silence, waiting for her to speak. Amparo looked eerily uneasy.

"The first time was by the stream, in the glade, on the day you had caught us the fish. It began that night, when both of us were in the water. You carried me on to the grass, right before the fire. And it was on this night that we declared our love for one another. We made love more than once that night and then again, once more even in the dawn. We made love again at Henry's, in the room we shared, the night before you left..."

"I don't...I don't remember any of this," I interrupted, sincerely.

"But..." Val pleaded.

"I remember the night at the lake," I answered. "But...not at all in the manner you described. Nothing like that at all. I'm sorry. I remember...I remember catching the fish, I remember sleeping under the stars. I even remember sharing a room at Henry's, but..."

"But you don't remember...me? Us?"

"Of course, I remember you. It's just that..."

"It's just what?" she demanded.

"Just not in that way, Val. I mean...making love? You and I? Forgive me, Val. Please. And please understand I have no intention of upsetting you, *hurting* you, or even lying to you about this. But I just don't remember...that is to say, I remember those nights very differently. I..."

But my head was throbbing again. Why was my head throbbing so much? I clutched my head in pain.

"You really *don't* remember," Val stated, eyes wide, no longer in a tone that was accusing. She suddenly turned to Amparo and Val's face immediately flared with anger.

"*What did you do to him*?" she screamed, advancing on Amparo fast. "What did you do to him!" she repeated and then Val took a swing with her fist.

With a gentle, but firm wave of her hand, Amparo brushed Val's fist aside and roughly grabbed her arm in the process.

"Attempt to strike me again and I will make you wish you hadn't," Amparo advised her, on the very edge of her patience.

"Zekiel?" Val called out.

"Release her!" My voice boomed, far louder and more forceful than I had intended. I visibly started shaking.

What had come over me just now? Why had I lashed out like that? And why did I feel so very protective of her?

What I did know though, is that Amparo had released her at once.

Was that a look of fear on her face? For she was staring at me with wide eyes, and stood perfectly still.

Val rushed to me then, burying herself once more in my arms and I held her tightly on impulse, still uncertain as to what had come over me. Uncertain as to why I had gotten so angry.

After a long pause, Val pulled back, frantic now, hands once again touching the sides of my face. "I don't know what she did, my love. I don't know what she has done to you!" Val said, her voice breaking. "I don't even care that you are...that are different somehow. Zekiel, I don't care! I even believe you when you say you don't remember, but I swear on my life that all I have said is true. I swear it!! It happened!!! *All of it happened!!!*"

It must have been pure impulse, or perhaps my old companion had simply lost her mind...but suddenly, her lips had found my own.

At first, I did nothing. At first...I was simply paralyzed, shocked even...and then...and then quite uncontrollably, with a will that was not my own, I started to kiss her in return.

The moment felt frozen in time. I felt as if I were in another place...and I found myself pulling her in closer, as if I were in some long-forgotten dream.

And then my head started to throb once more. I pulled back from her due to the pain, my thoughts becoming almost clear at once, and almost immediately the pain, this sharp, stabbing pain in my head started to lessen.

Uncertain as to what had just happened, uncertain as to why I was holding Val so close, why I had kissed her, she suddenly started to go limp in my arms. "My husband..." she managed to whisper, and then her eyes had closed, fainting right there in my arms.

Chapter Seventy-Seven

"Val?" Zekiel asked the completely still woman he was holding. "Val?" he repeated with obvious concern. But Val would not respond, her body supported only by the strength of his arms.

"Amparo?" he called to his companion, becoming quite frantic. "Amparo, is she ok?"

Amparo approached him slowly and casually inspected her work. "She will be fine, I assure you," she answered. "Please understand, I did it for her own good."

"*You* did this?" Zekiel asked, appalled. "You caused her to faint like this? But why?" he demanded, his anger once again rising.

"She was rambling like a mad woman. And you said yourself that the grand tale she told was nothing at all as you recalled."

"Amparo..." Zekiel growled, setting Val's body down gently in the snow. "You had no right to do this. You...had...no...right!"

Zekiel then assumed a different pose. A pose Amparo took to mean one thing. He was crouching, readying himself to attack. But Amparo refused to be intimidated, instead, more than matched his anger, and fearlessly let loose with words.

"*I* had no right?" she screamed and her tone gave Zekiel pause. "I had no right?" she repeated with equal force. "You *kissed* this mortal right in front of me!" she hissed.

"She kissed me."

"And you kissed her back!" she flared. "Don't take me to be a fool."

He slowly straightened his stance then, no claim in which to deny her logic. "I..." he stammered, now taking an apologetic tone. "I...I don't know what came over me."

"Indeed," she replied almost mockingly.

"I'm sorry, Amparo. I just...I'm sorry."

Her angry visage started to soften then, slowly becoming the Amparo of old, and soon that compassion, the compassion he knew her to have, returned to her face. "Do you love me?" she asked softly after a pause. "The mortal asked you the same and now I seek to ask this as well. Do. You. Love me?"

Zekiel stood still for many moments. Trying to digest all that had taken place.

"Do you love me?" she repeated.

"There are things we would discuss."

"And we will discuss these things, I assure you. But at present, you are avoiding the question. Do you love me?" she asked a third time.

He hesitated only a moment longer, unable to deny the truth, unable to deny what he surely felt when he looked upon her. "You know that I do."

They both fell silent and simply stared at each other a long while, both lost in their own contemplations.

Zekiel could not deny that he loved her, would not deny it, and yet...looking at Val's body, lying there peacefully in the snow, found himself struggling with so many emotions. So many conflicting emotions.

He reminded himself of what he was. Who he was. The vampire he had recently become. It was foolish to think of himself as otherwise, and consorting with mortals was a mistake, he realized, and had brought nothing but harm.

Amparo, after giving him a moment, slowly approached him.

"I'm sorry for what I did...and I am sorry for how I reacted," she apologized, taking his hand in hers. "Forgive my jealousy, I beg," she pleaded. "Seeing her in your arms...understand this was difficult for me to see."

He looked deep into her eyes, becoming lost in their beauty, once again becoming lost in her. Lost in the beautiful vampire before him. "Do you doubt how I feel? About you?" he asked.

Amparo responded with a kiss of her own, fierce and full of passion, and started to slowly but deliberately bring them both down to the ground. The passion of the moment nearly took them both, but at length Amparo pulled back, giving Zekiel pause.

"The sun soon rises," she said.

Chapter Seventy-Eight

I BENT LOW TO COLLECT Val's delicate sleeping form and gently cradled her into my arms.

"The Quest Blades?" I asked my companion.

"Silent. It appears we are once again safe. Safe at least for a time."

I nodded my accord and stood up, Val in tow.

"How far to the mortal's town?" Amparo asked.

"Not far," I said after a quick scan of the area. "We can return her safely, surely before dawn. If we hurry. That is…if you are well enough to travel?"

Amparo nodded. The two of us set out at once and we quickly navigated the forest, moving with preternatural speed. We maintained a good pace, encountering no delays, nor any forthcoming warnings from the mysterious daggers that Amparo carried. Something of a relief to us both, I think.

Before long, we had reached the outskirts of the town, a town I was very familiar with, but a town I had not visited since that fateful day when I had decided to leave in order to journey back home. My once again distant home in Scarborough.

"It isn't far now," I informed my counterpart. Amparo nodded.

We descended upon the town as only creatures of the night could. Silent, unseen, moving as swift as the breeze. Henry's door was of course locked, but Amparo opened it with ease and I brought Val upstairs without so much as a sound, setting her down to rest upon her still empty bed.

A quick mental scan of the house told me that there was only one other occupant here this night, that person being Henry, the owner of the establishment himself.

Lucy and Will would no doubt reach these doors by tomorrow, midday at the latest if they encountered no delays, and I suddenly remembered that I had one other promise to keep this night. Searching quickly for some parchment and ink, I located what was needed near the bar downstairs at a small desk and I sat down to pen a letter.

"What are you doing?" Amparo whispered, not wanting to awaken the Master of the house.

"I made a promise to Lucy."

"You mentioned her before. Another mortal friend, I presume?" This time there was no scorn in her voice and I merely pleaded with my eyes for a moment more of her continued patience. Amparo merely nodded, and silently went to stand by the door, allowing me some space and privacy in which to work.

I quickly wrote and finished my letter with but mere moments to spare and immediately fled off with Amparo, hand in hand, to avoid the coming of the rising sun.

The Book of Ravens concludes

with Volume Two

Now available

where you purchased this book

Printed in the USA
CPSIA information can be obtained
at www.ICGtesting.com
CBHW021558081024
15571CB00026B/503/J

9 798991 194835